DRAGONARD BLOOD

DRAGONARD BLOOD

8th. Earl of Wycliffe
(WYCLIFFE HALL, NORFOLK, ENGLAND)

Peregrine Roland
(THE STAR PLANTATION, LOUISIANA)

Richard Abdee
(DRAGONARD PLANTATION, ST. KITTS, W.I.)

Albert Selby — Rachel Selby

Honore Jubiot

Ta-Ta

Lilly — Monk

Roland Selby

Lloy

Peter Abdee — Melissa Selby
(DRAGONARD HILL PLANTATION, LOUISIANA)

Imogen Abdee   Victoria Abdee   Veronica Abdee

Naomi, ST. KITTS
Kate Breslin, GREENLEAF
Barry Breslin
Duncan Webb
Royal

DRAGONARD BLOOD

RUPERT GILCHRIST

SOUVENIR PRESS

CONTENTS

Prologue

TWILIGHT

Petit Jour
New Orleans
1829

A struggle developed in a dimly-lit bedroom, a quarrel between a white man and two black prostitutes. It had grown from an argument about the rough way in which the negresses were abusing him.

The white man expected the prostitutes to treat him as if he were their body servant; such an arrangement was supposed to build slowly like a game, the white man not to feel unduly threatened by his temporary mistresses.

But their way was too quick. Too savage. Not childlike. Not an easy graduation of events that could spellbind him to these full-breasted negresses. He wanted hypnotic persuasion from them and, knowing that many respectable men came to this bordello for that very treatment – judges, bankers, leading politicians, rich planters—he had paid a steep price for his pleasure.

Rather than any form of love, though, a battle ensued.

The prostitutes were trying now to overpower the white man with brute force, their quick hands grasping for his arms, their long nails ripping at his skin. They were going far beyond the physical stimulation he desired – could endure.

The man was a young, sandy-haired gentleman of New Orleans, dressed in white breeches, riding boots, and a full-sleeved shirt. Although he had broad shoulders and strong arms, he was fighting hard to keep the two women from toppling him.

The negresses clung to the man like excited hounds, lean, fast, and powerful. They wore tightly-laced corsets with black web stockings covering their long legs, enabling them to kick at the white man, tripping him when he tried to escape. They obeyed no playful rules of love-making.

The tumbling course proceeded across the bedroom. A table overturned. An eggshell vase crashed to the floor. The crystal beads on a wall sconce jangled as the white man reared back to avoid their lunges. He next dodged behind a bulky four-poster bed.

The women followed, their dark eyes gleaming with the excitement of the chase, their chocolate-coloured breasts flooding the tops of their corsets with each heavy breath, their long fingers arched like black snakes with pink bellies.

A third negress stood silently in one corner of the bedroom. She had prune-black skin and was dressed also in a scanty corset and web stockings like the other two females. She gripped a riding crop in one hand, watching her two accomplices pursuing the white man.

Flailing his arms, the man shouted at the third negress, 'Call them off! Call your crazy bitches off me!'

She ignored the man's plea, holding her large red lips in a smirk of contempt.

The white man's panic increased. He kicked awkwardly at his attackers. He had come wilfully to this bedroom with all three women. He had paid his money happily to their mistress to enjoy some wild excitement. But the evening had started the wrong way. The prostitutes had ignored the way in which he wanted to be seduced from the moment they had entered the bedroom and now he frantically swung his arms, protesting, 'I don't want this! I don't want this *shit*!'

Temporarily free, he struck one black woman across the face and, as she tumbled against the other woman, he pulled open the door.

The gas lighting in the hallway was as faint as in the bedroom. A sweet smell of incense hit the man's nose. His eyes strained in the near darkness. A door was closing across the hall from him. He caught a momentary glimpse of a yellow-skinned girl binding leather thongs around the scrotum and penis of a white man with salt-and-pepper hair, who, in turn, had his mouth on the penis of a naked black giant. From the closed bedroom door on one side came guttural moans. The sound of strapping emanated from the other.

These noises, that sight, intensified the fleeing man's panic. He looked in confusion up and down the hallway. He felt lost, caught amidst the crude sounds on the upstairs floor of this bordello called *Petit Jour*.

Petit Jour offered the most bizarre physical entertainments in New Orleans, unmatched even in Charleston, Natchez, Savannah. The girls here were exotic. There were also male prostitutes in the stables of *Petit Jour* and the theatricals staged in the cellar surpassed any man's wildest sexual fantasy. The prices were high. But seldom was there a complaint. Except when a customer became too drunk. The girls either exceeded or neglected their duties. Or a man did not clarify how intense he wanted his own private fantasy to become. Then tempers flared, Problems arose.

Now, as the frightened white man got his bearings in the hallway, he heard the three prostitutes behind him. He quickly ran for the stairs and, taking three steps at a time, he soon crossed the thick Turkish carpet in the foyer, running for the carved oak door of the office.

A burly negro guard with a shaved head sat in a fanback chair in front of the office door. He sprung to his feet when he saw the white man coming toward him.

The man pushed past the guard and began to beat on the door with both fists, shouting for the owner to let him in, demanding protection from her whores, shouting general obscenities about black people.

The guard was powerful. He wrapped a dark arm around the white man's neck and bent him easily to the floor.

As the white man sank, he gripped the muscular arm that choked him and simultaneously kicked at the base of the carved door, ramming it harder and harder with the heel of his riding boot.

The three negresses from the upstairs bedroom had reached the foyer. They now stood watching the guard press the young customer into limp submission.

A key clicked in the lock on the other side of the carved door and, as the door slowly opened, the black guard eased his hold from the white man's neck.

* * *

All eyes studied the figure of the small woman standing in the open doorway of the office. A long black *crepe de chine* dress clung to her slim body. A black veil hung over her face, its rich lace pattern falling in folds around her slim shoulders. Wearing white kidskin gloves, she rested her hands on the silver knob of an ebony cane. She was Madame Naomi, the mistress of *Petit Jour*, the woman to whom the young white man had earlier paid his money.

The black people standing in the hallway – and the man crouched on the floor – all stared at the veiled woman.

Down the hall, the laughter of women and men drifted from a draped archway. Glasses clinked. A piano gaily tinkled. A woman's throaty voice sang *Matelot, O, Matelot* . . .

Remaining motionless in the doorway, Madame Naomi still did not speak.

The negress holding the riding crop stepped forward and, pointing it at the man on the floor, she said, 'He got shit scared of us, Mistress Naomi. I thinks his ideas maybe stronger than his ass!'

The two other girls nodded, still breathing heavily from the chase, their breasts rising and lowering at a rapid pace inside the reservoirs of their corsets.

Naomi did not move, her gloved hands continuing to rest on the silver knob of her cane.

The guard said, 'It's him kicking your door, too, Mistress Naomi.'

Kneeling on the floor, the white man gulped for air, trapped like a field rodent.

Laughter rose in the distance. The song stopped. Applause and whistling echoed. A gypsy violin now joined the piano.

Naomi remained impassive, aloof, cold.

Then, suddenly, the white man lunged at her, angrily ripping at her dress, jerking for the black lace veiling.

The guard grabbed to stop him. The three women dashed forward. Naomi pulled back. But it was too late. He had torn her bodice, yanked the veil from her face.

His eyes then—what he saw—checked any further aggression.

He sank back on his haunches. His hands fell limp to his sides. He stared at Naomi's face.

Madame Naomi of *Petit Jour* was a black woman. A slave long-ago freed. This was a known fact. She had come as a rich woman to the city of New Orleans from a West Indian island called St Kitts. She had bought expensive slaves in the markets here, the blacks who were called 'Fancies' and could be a credit to any master or mistress. Naomi had commissioned agents to send her furniture, wines, crystal from Europe. But throughout all the dealings and arrangements in New Orleans since her arrival from the Caribbean, Naomi had never shed the protection of a lace veil.

The white man on the floor now gaped at that guarded face, at the naked features which remained immobile – and savage – like an African tribal mask carved from wood and covering a human face.

Naomi had the same basic blue-black colouring of the negress who held the riding crop. But Naomi was a much older woman. And the texture of her skin was not smooth, not continuous in its colouring, and it had been roughened by more than wrinkles. Naomi's face was severely marred by burns, the facial and neck wounds healed into stretched patches of variously hued and seared skin; some light, some dark, Naomi's flesh was mottled and it pulled at her eyes and dislocated her nostrils. And her facial distortions were starkly framed by a white frizz of hair – white, wiry, very short hair spreading back into patches over her skull.

The black guard held his arm around the man's neck again and the three negresses grasped his hands. But the shock of seeing Naomi's burnt face had sapped all his resistance, had obliterated his previous fears and hysterics.

Naomi did not rush to cover her face. She began to speak to the white man. Her voice was coarse and hateful. She said, 'You fool. You stupid fool.'

The man began to quake, to appear very young. He cried, 'I didn't mean it. I paid my money and . . .' He finally became an obsequious slave. To a black woman.

'Paid!' Naomi screamed, suddenly raising her ebony cane and bringing it down against his head with a thud. The guard backed away. The prostitute let go. Naomi hit the man a second and third time, screaming, 'Paid! *Paid*! You paid to be beaten! And, by God, you'll get it! You'll get it!" Repeating the words over and over, Naomi followed each blow of the cane with a harder one.

The man tried to protect his head by raising his hands. But Naomi continued to smite him, breaking his knuckles, cracking his fingers, beating him on the wrists and the arms and – when his bleeding hands fell away – she continued to cane his skull.

Finally stopping, Naomi bared her teeth, large white teeth which glistened against the marred discolouration of her face. Her breasts heaved with anger under her ripped bodice. Her gloved hands quivered as she gripped the silver knob of the cane. She stared down at the white man lying in a bloody heap on the floor in front of her and she whispered, 'How dare you! How dare you touch me!'

The white man could not answer. He was unconscious. His face and neck and hands were matted with blood, hair, pieces of battered flesh. He could have even been dead. Naomi did not care.

The guard stood dumbly behind the limp body. Looking down at it, he asked, 'What I do with him, Mistress Naomi?'

She did not answer. She was now reaching to her shoulders for the lace veil and began re-covering her face, draping her head.

The negress with the riding crop fell to her knees and, sticking the crop under her arm, she began to pat the man's chest and stomach. Shortly, she withdrew a wallet from inside his shirt.

16

Before she stood, though, she looked at the crotch of his tight breeches. His penis formed a firm rod on the inside of the fabric. And a large blotch spread at the head of his penis. It was damp like the blood smears on his shirt but, instead of being red, it was white. The negress reached toward the dampness and, touching it, she brought her fingers to her nose. Laughing, she said, 'Shit! He shot his load! You made the son-of-a-bitch shoot his load!'

Naomi grunted disinterestedly. She said, 'They never know what they want.' She motioned her gloved hand for the wallet.

Standing, the prostitute handed it to her as the other two girls and the guard inspected the sperm blotch on the dead man's breeches.

Flipping through the wallet to count the bank notes, Naomi said to the guard, 'Dump him in a swamp . . . Miller's Swamp this time.'

The guard obediently lifted the body from the floor.

Pointing the tip of her cane at the blood smears on the carpet, Naomi ordered the three negresses, 'Get them wiped away quick, you sluts.'

The prostitutes hurried to fetch cloths and spirits.

Naomi shrilled after them, 'Then come back and tell me what went wrong this time! You know they're no good to us dead, you stupid bitches!'

Turning, Naomi angrily swept into her office, locking the carved door behind her, shutting out the sights and noises of *Petit Jour*, the bordello in New Orleans whose French name translated to 'twilight'.

Petit Jour. Twilight. The name aptly fit the shadowy escapes sought by many white people who flocked to New Orleans these days. Their pockets were filled with newly-earned money. Their bodies ached for fresh pleasures. They searched for fantasies to release the pressures of running their plantations, remote kingdoms which were making them rich, powerful, but, often, demented and miserable lords of the American South.

Madame Naomi waited for such men at *Petit Jour*.

17

Book One

THE ANCIENT STAR

Chapter One

THE STRIPPING

The deep Louisiana countryside was fastly ripening into a hot summer. The elm and oak trees were heavy with leaves and the pine woodlands lay thick with underbrush, lush ferns and wild raspberry branches fanning across the dirt path along which young Imogen Abdee now hurried.

The morning air was fresh, sharply scented by the pines. But Imogen did not dawdle to breathe in the smells as she would have liked to have done. Instead, she had to rush to the springhouse to fetch some butter for the kitchen of the big house.

The big house! House chores! Supervising the cooking! Although Imogen Abdee was only twenty years old, she would have preferred to be working in the fields rather than running herd on 'kitchen niggers'. She loathed the domestic obligations of a female and wished that her mother were still alive if for no other reason than to supervise the home.

This land was called Dragonard Hill. It belonged to Imogen's father, Peter Abdee. This plantation hewn into the Louisiana wilderness now boasted more than three thousand acres of green-seed cotton land and Imogen would have loved to be riding a stallion in those fields, keeping a watchful eye on the rows of workers. She felt part of the earth. She was not intimidated by the black slaves who hoed and planted and picked there, the labourers of Dragonard Hill. She knew she could handle them. All she needed was a bullwhip coiled around her saddle horn and, perhaps, a pistol tucked into a leather belt.

Unfortunately, Imogen's father would not consider the idea of allowing her, his eldest daughter, to pursue the life of a man. An overseer. Not even a planter acted as his own overseer. A white man was hired for the job. Or, as in the case of Dragonard Hill, a dependable slave was entrusted with the responsibility of overseeing the work on a Southern plantation. But never a woman. Especially not a planter's own daughter.

Imogen's only consolation was that she had not been sent North to boarding-school like her two younger sisters, the twins, Veronica and Victoria. An arrangement such as that would have killed Imogen Abdee. She hated schooling. Detested everything that went with it – frilly gowns, tea dances, insipid young men who did not know a plough from an anvil. Imogen hated male companionship. Especially town boys. And Northern town boys were the worst.

Suddenly, Imogen stopped on the wooded path. She heard a noise near her in the bushes. Listening, she caught the sound of soft laughter. Private laughter. Giggling.

Holding her breath, Imogen's bright blue eyes moved quickly over the brush on both sides of the dirt path.

Momentarily, she heard the tinkle of the nearby creek, the gentle sway of the tall pine trees, only the natural sounds of this dark woodland behind the big house.

But then the voices continued. She heard a man's soft words and – then – the giggling of a female. She could tell by the tones that the voices belonged to two negroes. A pair of slaves. Dragonard Hill's black people. But what were they doing here? And at this time of the morning?

Seeing the leaves move on an elderberry bush, Imogen realized that the two blacks were lying in some brush near the path. They were probably only a few feet to the right of the spot where she now stood. Remaining motionless, Imogen strained her ears to catch more of the muted exchange.

As the whispering and giggling continued, Imogen cautiously moved off the path, slowly passing through the brush in its direction, carefully placing one booted foot in front of the other so as not to crackle even a twig.

Her heart quickened as she imagined what she might discover. She began to compose a diatribe that she would deliver

22

to the blacks who had sneaked away from their morning duties. She was not frightened by chastising even the most brawny black buck. She handled the fully grown women like children. Imogen Abdee seized every opportunity to govern, to exert power, the little with which she was entrusted.

But then Imogen's mind went blank. She froze as she saw two black people lying together on the ground. Their naked bodies lay intertwined on a soft patch of clover. They were a wench and a buck. Indeed, they were! Imogen saw a coffee-coloured male lying on top of the woman, his sinewy body wedged in between the wench's spread legs and holding her breasts in his hands.

Imogen studied the spectacle with amazement. She saw how finely the negro's back was muscled. She watched his firm buttocks squeeze slowly together as he pushed his groin forward into the negress and the way that it split like a ripe peach when he pulled back. Imogen also noted the manner in which the female raised her breasts toward the male to hold and kneed like unbaked loaves, tossing back her head and moving her hips to match his steady drives.

Having been raised on a plantation, Imogen knew about sexual practices between male and female slaves. But she was still a virgin herself. And she had never before seen a coupling. Not among slaves. Only animals. Sex did not intrigue Imogen. Not even the prospect of satisfying a husband. It had always been another cold fact of the life ahead of her.

But, now, a lump formed in her throat and, still keeping her silence, Imogen watched the negro slide his hands around the woman's slim brown waist and, rising to his knees, he pulled the woman with him. The couple still maintained their rhythm, the wench resting the pink soles of her feet on the man's brown calves, dropping her arms limply to her side, allowing him to use her as he wanted.

A curious anger then slowly began to build in Imogen Abdee. The excitement of finding these lovers had passed. She now hated the man. She loathed – even envied – the power which he wielded over the lithe female. The buck looked so powerful. So masterly. Sleek and subtle and strong. If places were to be changed, Imogen would have chosen his. It was not the act that excited her. It was his role. She silently cursed him.

The words of the diatribe which Imogen had originally formulated suddenly returned to her mind, the reprimand to the slaves for abandoning their morning duties. And quickly snatching a branch from a bush, Imogen rushed forward in a frenzy to punish the naked negro buck.

Beating him across his bare back, she shrilled, " Stop it. Stop it. Leave her alone."

The naked couple abruptly stopped, raising their heads to look at Imogen.

Imogen continued to beat wildly at the man, her slim face becoming red with anger and long strands of her straight black hair tumbling from the knot on top of her head.

The negro by now had extricated himself from the woman and, as he stumbled to his feet, he held his hands awkwardly in front of his moist, bobbing phallus. The negress lay help-lessly on the ground, her hands criss-crossed over her breasts and her bare legs squeezed together to cover the furry patch of her vagina.

Imogen was shaking with anger. She faced the black man's naked body. She could smell his raw, musty odour. She knew that – regardless of his stature – he was frightened of her. She was his mistress. An undisputed power on the plantation. A white person.

Keeping her eyes on his broad face, Imogen demanded,

'Why aren't you working? What are you doing back here?' She ignored the female, concentrating her anger on him.

The man stuttered, nervously blinking his eyes.

'What's your name?' she screamed.

'Hopper,' he said, quickly adding the proper address due to his young mistress, but pronouncing her name as did all the black people of Dragonard Hill. 'Me's Hopper, Miss *Eye*-mo-gen, Mam. Me's Hopper but me don't mean no harm, Miss *Eye*-mo-gen.'

His childlike innocence increased her fury. How could anyone be so powerful, control another person with such dexterity, and still act so . . . innocent?

Imogen wanted to punish him, too, for having that simple quality. She said coldly, 'Hopper, I want you to go to the stables. Right now! And I want you to wait there for my Father.'

Hopper blurted, 'Your Daddy's up building the new house, Miss Imogen, Mam.'

'I know where my "Daddy" is,' she snapped. 'But I also know where he's *going* to be when I tell him about you! In the stable! With a whip! And I'm going to tell Nero about this, too. And Lady Alice. I'm going to tell Lady Alice about you breaking her breeding schedule. And you're going to be whipped, Hopper. Whipped so hard that all the skin will be stripped from your back.'

The naked man gaped at her. The threat of a whipping stunned him. There was never a whipping on Dragonard Hill. Not by Master Peter. Not by his black overseer, Nero. Not by anybody. Especially not by Lady Alice, the kind old negress who was in charge of birthing on the plantation.

Imogen next lowered her eyes to the black girl still lying on the clover bed. She knew who she was. She recognized her as Clara, a wench from the Looming House. Imogen told her, 'Put your smock on, Clara, and go straight back to work. I'll deal with you later.'

'I don't want no whipping, Miss Imogen, Mam,' Clara wailed, sitting up now and still trying to hide her large breasts with crossed arms.

'Stop whining. You've disgraced yourself enough today. And just hope he didn't knock you up, Clara. Because if you do get knocked-up, I'll yank that baby right out of your belly. I'll yank out that baby with my own bare hands! Before it even gets born!'

The negress squealed at Imogen's threat. She knew that her mistress was capable of doing anything. Imogen Abdee was not gentle and soft like her younger sisters. Not like white ladies were supposed to be.

Turning back to Hopper, Imogen said, 'It's him who's going to get stripped. The flesh all stripped off his big tough back. I'll see to that myself if I have to. I'll whip him myself!'

Glaring at the nakedness of Hopper's bulging chest, the muscle strength which she could not match, Imogen's small hand tightened on the switch and, in a flash, she felt a resurgence of anger and frustration. Beginning to beat him impetulantly across the chest, she repeated, 'I'll whip you. And whip you. And whip you.'

Then, throwing the switch down to the ground, Imogen stormed back to the path.

But instead of hurrying now to the springhouse, Imogen headed toward the building site of the new house. She could not understand why her father was wasting his time building a new home for Dragonard Hill when he did not even have his own slaves under a firm hand.

In anger, Imogen Abdee lost control of her usual sly self. She became a mad woman, a china doll with unkempt black hair and blazing blue eyes – wishing she were a man.

*   *   *

Peter Abdee could be found no other place these days than on the building site of the new house. He had patiently waited to build a home and, as this was the first one that he had ever provided for his family, he wanted it to be worthy of them and a credit to the development of Louisiana.

But he was sorry that his wife was not still alive to see how far their young dreams had come. Melissa, he felt, would be very pleased. Melly would love the new house. Never dreamed that it was possible. Even a little aghast at its promised magnificence.

The site on the plantation that Peter had chosen set back in the hills from the old manor house, commanding the land high from a timbered rise. The new house could be seen from the public road, beyond the fields of green-seed cotton that was making Dragonard Hill rich, even richer than this plantation had been in ancient days when the land here had been called 'The Star'.

The new house was now passing into its most exciting phase for Peter. The outside walls were raised, the high rafters fully beamed, the floors divided, rooms sectioned, and the stone walkways already leading from the main quarters to the kitchen and the summer rooms. Dragonard Hill would be a true manor house, comprising three floors, eight main bedrooms, and two columned breezeways which connected the outer quarters. Those pillars were smaller replicas of the four Doric columns which graced the front porch and the upper gallery of the house. The New Orleans architect, Reginald Turner, had designed it in the new, popular Classical Revival style, one of the first in this backwoods district of Louisiana.

Peter Abdee was proud of his accomplishment; many Southern planters were haughty and arrogant over the riches they were taking from the land. But Peter Abdee's pride was simple. Arguing that he was no better than a farmer – and quick to ridicule the aristocratic pretensions that the planters were cultivating – he attributed his good fortunes to this plantation's rich soil.

Likewise, Peter recognized the good luck of having had green-seed cotton growing on this land at the time when Eli Whitney invented his cotton gin. The older variety of black cotton became outmoded when green cotton could finally be cleaned in an efficient manner. The Northern and European mills took all the cotton that Dragonard Hill could produce.

Peter Abdee gave credit, too, to his people, the black slaves of Dragonard Hill. Peter Abdee had known no other labour system but slavery. He had been raised to accept it. But, unlike his slave-keeping peers, Peter Abdee's natural generosity made him treat the black people more like hired workers than bonded slaves.

He had bought his one and only parcel of slaves when he was twelve years old. Included in it was Nero, the negro who

27

was now his overseer. The slaves of Dragonard Hill reproduced themselves.

On this early summer morning, Peter Abdee was showing the progress of the new house to a neighbour woman. She was Kate Breslin, a young widow who lived nearby at Greenleaf, a smaller plantation than Dragonard Hill, but efficiently run by the energetic red-haired woman, who had no help except from her honest overseer, a small stable of devoted slaves, and occasionally from her twenty-two-year-old nephew, Barry Breslin.

Dressed today in green and yellow gingham, Kate Breslin lifted her full skirts as she stepped over timber piled on the unfinished floors. Although she was a Southern lady who owned land, Kate Breslin still had the vigour of her ancestors who had come from County Donegal, Ireland.

Peter guided Kate into what would soon be the reception room, pausing now in front of the framework which would encase the tall French doors overlooking the front driveway.

He was not demonstrative, but often shy, a man who had failed to shed all his boyishness. That trait became most apparent when he felt proud but refrained from boasting. Then his generous mouth turned into a grin, the dimple deepening in his strong, square chin.

He now stood tall and silent beside Kate, his hands tucked into his trousers, secretly pleased to be in a room that he and his people were building.

Kate immediately envisioned the final result of the room, imagining decorations and furnishings and, putting her hand on Peter's bare forearm, she said, 'You are doing the right thing for your girls, Peter. They need a home like this. I'm so excited for them.'

Patting her small hand, he said, 'I have to have someplace, too.' That was the extent of his bragging, the modest demands for his own life.

Peter Abdee was in the dawn of his forties. His body was slim and hard from manual work. The sun had tanned his olive skin to a rich bronze. His shiny black hair was only touched with grey at the temples. He wore mostly rough work clothes – nankeen breeches, a shirt with sleeves rolled up to the elbows, tall riding boots.

Many families in the neighbourhood pushed their marriageable daughters in the way of Peter Abdee, girls who were even younger than his own daughters. But he had once had a wife, and now that Melissa was dead, he was dedicating his life to raising his girls – Imogen, Veronica, and Victoria.

Not marrying, though, did not keep Peter Abdee from making love. He was a very physical male. A sexual drive showed in his cornflower blue eyes. A sexuality alive and romantic.

But Peter never chose a female from the slave quarters to be his bed wench. He had learned many lessons from his late father-in-law, a rough code of gentlemanly conduct from the man who had once owned The Star and then heired it to Peter Abdee as 'Dragonard Hill'. Albert Selby had raised Peter as a son, had given him his daughter to marry, and in all those years, Peter had never known Albert Selby to bed wenches at home. He had gone away from the house for his pleasuring. And Peter found that a similar arrangement suited him, too.

Peter Abdee and his Irish neighbour, Kate Breslin, were lovers.

Standing together now in the framework of the French windows, Peter pulled Kate toward him, saying, 'I'm seeing you and me sitting together here, Katie. I'm picturing a cool November afternoon. A fire on the hearth. Nobody's around. Just us. We have –'

Pulling away from him, Kate warned, 'We have workmen all around us now, that's what we have! Now don't get so excited.' She knew how his words could easily progress into actions, seductive advances which she found difficult to resist. She had a mature appetite for sex, too.

'Don't worry. I'm not going to do anything.' His large fingers squeezed under her shawl at the neatness of her waist.

'I should hope not,' Kate said, looking around at the yellow rafters to see if they had been observed. She continued in a lower voice, 'You have to wait until tomorrow.'

'I'm still coming to you.' He looked overhead, as if studying the structure, while his hand gently patted her buttocks.

Kate stepped away. She whispered, 'I hope you are. I had a hard enough time getting Barry out of the house for a day. I don't know if I can use the same excuse twice. I swear, he's always so dense. Except when I want him to be.'

Fabricating excuses for Kate's nephew and Peter's daughters was only one of the many obstacles which they had to face in order to meet secretly. Peter knew that their relationship would become more difficult when the twins came home from Boston. But he would deal with that when the time came.

He said now, 'I'm predicting your harvest tomorrow, aren't I?' His hands were back on her body. He was pressing his body behind her. His words were not important.

Allowing herself a small taste of him being near to her, she said, 'If you say. While Jeb Conway comes from Troy to look at yours. But I think it's a pretty ridiculous story. If you say it makes sense, though, then . . .' Her words stopped when she felt both of his hands cupping her shoulders.

Almost touching her ear with his mouth, he said, 'Dragonard Hill is bigger than Greenleaf. Jeb Conway has to come here. To make arrangements for the gin himself.' His words – the fabricated conversation – were growing more faint. But his penis was expanding inside his breeches.

Kate was beginning to quiver. She felt silly discussing crops and the cotton gin when Peter's hands were exploring her body. She said, 'Jeb Conway. You trust him. I think he's conniving. And sneaking. And . . .

Peter now wrapped his arms around her from behind, encasing both her breasts in his hands. He said, 'Don't take everything so seriously, Katie. Conway's . . .'

Suddenly Kate pushed off Peter's arm. She stepped forward and whispered, 'Stop.' Then she pointed her parasol down the driveway at the spot where she had left her carriage. She saw Peter's eldest daughter, Imogen, walking quickly up the hill toward the building site.

30

Peter muttered, 'Shit.'

Kate said, 'Stop that!'

But now he was busily rearranging himself in his breeches, bending to pull his erect penis from his thigh and hoping somehow to get it all tucked between his legs.

* * *

Kate Breslin and her twenty-two-year-old nephew, Barry, were familiar faces at Dragonard Hill and, when Imogen saw Kate standing with her father in the tall window frames of the new house, she did not hesitate in going directly towards them.

Lifting her muslin skirt, Imogen jumped up onto the un-finished flooring and said, 'It's gone too far, Father. Too far this time.'

He was not listening. He was trying to recover from his closeness to Kate. But he could see that Imogen was angry. Something had happened to her.

Imogen's small face was tightly pinched with irritation. The strands of dishevelled black hair hung around her forehead. She did not even bother to greet Kate Breslin.

This annoyed Peter. He forgot about himself and began feeling anger at Imogen for her lack of manners and the untidy way she was dressed – scuffed boots, a rough skirt, an unfamiliar blouse that was open at the neck like a man's shirt. He could not understand how such a finely featured young girl could be so coarse, take so little pride in her appearance.

Pointing back toward the lush clump of trees which spread behind the roof of the old house, Imogen said, 'The niggers are taking over down there.'

Peter's face drained of the contentment that he had shared with Kate. He quickly shook his head, indicating to Imogen to watch how she was speaking. He did not like her calling black people 'niggers', and especially not in front of outsiders. Not even Kate.

But Imogen was angry. She said, 'Go ahead. Keep thinking

they're all your children.' She still had not acknowledged Kate's presence.

'Just a minute now,' Peter firmly said. He knew he had to get this situation into hand. The bliss had ended.

Imogen could not stop, though. She angrily explained, 'I just found Hopper. Found him with a wench. They were—' She faltered for the first time. 'They were rolling in some brush.'

Turning to Kate, Peter said, 'I think you better excuse us.'

Kate gaily waved them off with her parasol, saying, 'I can happily wander around by myself.' She made no attempt at greeting Imogen. She knew how single-minded the girl could be.

Peter beckoned Imogen to follow him out from the reception room, leading her into the hallway where a skeleton of the double staircase led to an upper balcony.

Alone with her father, Imogen quickly resumed, 'I found them like dogs!'

'I know exactly how you found them, Imogen. You've made that quite clear. You're talking like a – like a I don't know what.'

'Like a white man,' she snapped.

Peter said calmly, 'I always hoped you'd see yourself as a lady, Imogen. But if you want to act like a red-neck farmer then at least show some respect for other ladies.' He nodded toward Kate in the drawing-room.

'Kate Breslin? She knows the facts. And so do I! And I know that Hopper must be punished for breaking the breeding schedule. Father, you or Nero must punish him. Whip him. Right now. Today. This kind of thing cannot spread.' She gripped her small fists in anger.

'Imogen, do you know what you're saying?'

She glared at him. 'You refuse to whip a nigger, don't you? It's the same excuse. "Be good to the black people". "Don't beat the niggers".' She was taunting him.

'I told you never, ever to use that word, Imogen. Your mother didn't like it. I don't like it. It is not a word we use here.'

'What mother did or did not like has nothing to do with what I found this morning. Now, Father, are you going to have Nero whip that nigger I found this morning? Or are you going to do it yourself?'

Peter felt tempted to slap her across the face for being so insolent to him. But he had never struck any of his daughters and hoped that he would never have to do it.

He began calmly, 'Nero has not whipped anybody for ten years at least.'

'Nero hasn't done much of *anything* for ten years. It seems to me that you could find a lot better overseer than Nero.'

'Don't tell me you're going to start criticizing me, too, Imogen. Telling me I shouldn't have a black man for my overseer? You're getting to be more like a white trash sand-hiller every day, Imogen!'

Ignoring the accusation, she argued, 'At least I could do a better job running this place than Nero does. He is so—' She waved her small hands.

Peter was getting angry. He asked, 'Nero is getting so what, Imogen?'

She said plainly, 'Nero does not do his job. It's that simple. He preaches at church on Sunday. Sure. But that's about all. And there's more to running a place than preaching to a bunch of goochy-eyed niggers.'

Peter took a deep breath. He knew Imogen's hateful attitude had not come from her home surroundings. He feared they had to do with blood. Her grandmother's blood, Grandmother Selby. Or blood on his side. His father's blood. English tyranny.

He forced himself to be patient with her. But still frank. Mature. He asked, 'Imogen, tell me honestly. Why are you so upset? I've never seen you this way. Is it because you saw people making love?'

She turned away her head. 'I know about that. But they should have been working.'

Peter spoke plainly to her. He said, 'Fine, Imogen. They probably were doing wrong. They had left their work. But, Imogen, black people as well as white people have urges to

33

mate. To make love. I'm sorry, but I have to speak very plainly to you. This is a farm. A plantation. It's earthy. People are suddenly overwhelmed with these . . . urges. You cannot *whip* them for it.'

She ignored the rebuke. She said, 'They seem to get those urges more than the white people I've seen.'

He thought about himself and Kate. He said, 'Don't be sarcastic. And I won't have you talking about black people that way. In fact, while you and I are on this subject of mating, I think you should worry more about the halfcastes being born here lately. What about them? What about all those yellow babies suddenly being born? The fathers of those aren't black. The children wouldn't be so light-skinned, not coming from dark parents. Why don't you put yourself to work figuring out that one?'

'I'll just force the mothers to tell.'

'You know as well as I do how frightened they are.'

'Whip them!'

He threw up his hands. 'Imogen, everything is not solved by a whip.'

Imogen said, 'There aren't that many white men around here to point the finger at, is there?'

Peter knew what she meant now. She was accusing him of seducing the black women. He refused to dignify her accusation by defending himself.

Knowing that she had spoken too rashly to her father, Imogen returned to the matter that was important to her. She asked directly, 'So you're not going to do anything about Hopper?'

'No I am not. Not after you make all this commotion about it,' he said firmly.

'Very well,' she said, turning away from him.

'Imogen, where are you going? I have not finished talking to you.'

Walking briskly toward the front door sills, she said, 'I have work to do.'

'Come back here.'

'I have my own work to do. But I'm not going to the springhouse for butter for those silly niggers in the kitchen. And I'm not airing rooms and hanging out blankets for those two stuck-up brats coming home from school in . . . *Boston*!'

'Imogen, I won't have you complaining about your sisters again.'

But it was too late. She had already hopped down from the house and was walking angrily down the driveway, her muslin skirt sweeping the dust.

As Peter stood looking at the small figure of his eldest daughter disappearing down the dirt path that soon would be a driveway, he wondered if he should go after her. He had forgotten about her demands to whip Hopper. He was worrying instead about the twins coming home from school. They would be back in less than two weeks' time. He did not want to see his three daughters fighting. He did not need that kind of problem here on Dragonard Hill.

*   *   *

The name for the slave quarters on Dragonard Hill was 'Melissa's Town', named in honour of Peter Abdee's late wife, Melissa, who had always disliked its former name – Niggertown.

Since the quarters had been renamed, though, the black people had shortened it to something more pronounceable. They called it simply 'Town'.

Apart from the name, the buildings of the slave quarters had also changed. Peter Abdee's father-in-law, Albert Selby, had allowed the place to collapse, not fixing it up since the small cabins had been built many years ago by this land's original settler, Perigrine Roland.

Now, the original lines of cabins had been razed, the old logs burned, the land ploughed and replanted with cattle feed after a proper dormant period. Then the new slave quarters were built to the west of what had once been Niggertown.

Melissa's Town – or Town – was a neat community of homes, small cabins built on stilts to prevent dampness from creeping into the floors. The black people also believed that the long legs on which their houses stood protected them from snakes.

Peter Abdee would not allow more than six people to live in one cabin. This meant that new homes were built yearly, extending the line of tall houses further back into the pine forests.

But Peter still followed the custom of sending the newly-born infants away from their mothers. The children of Dragonard Hill – the saplings – lived in a converted warehouse called The Shed, growing-up under the care of the old negress, Lady Alice, who also supervised which wench would be sired by which buck, the arrangement known as the Birthing Schedule.

Peter Abdee often thought that a birthing schedule, and the removal of young infants from their mothers, was a heartless and cruel practice. But as he had accepted his land, he also had to accept the slave system which tilled it. It would have been impossible to work here with paid labour. There was not the money nor the men to work in the wilderness. And a family unit was anathema to the entire slave system. Peter Abdee must accept the basic rules of slavery, regardless of his frequent belief that the white planters themselves were often mastered by a system foisted upon them by circumstances and previous generations, a system that could soon prove to become dangerous, but a system hard to stop. He could not foresee any bloodless way out of it. He could not imagine who would fare the worse, black man or white?

By noontime today, four fieldhands had followed Imogen's orders and brought Hopper to the main stables in Town. Imogen was already waiting inside the stables and, although the lower half of Hopper's shiny brown body was covered by tow breeches, Imogen remembered his complete nakedness.

Holding a whip in her small hand, she called to the field-hands, 'Strip him.'

36

The fieldhands paused, their eyes quickly questioning Imogen's order.

Hating them for respecting her feminity, she repeated the order, '*Strip him!*'

Obediently, they reached for the rope tied around Hopper's tow breeches and, as Hopper hung his head to his bare chest, the rough weave pants fell to the dirt floor of the stables. Hopper made no gesture to cover his genitals with his hands now. His arms hung motionless at the sides of his muscled thighs. His penis arced over the protrusion of his scrotum, dangling limp and greasy, a sheath of dark skin now protecting the crown.

Imogen glanced fleetingly between Hopper's legs. His penis was still large, true, but the sight of its loss of strength gave Imogen the first hint of satisfaction and her hand tightened on the butt of the whip, anxious to proceed with the punishment.

Nearby, two of the fieldhands were driving wooden pegs into the dirt floor with a mallet; the other two men were binding Hopper's wrists and ankles with ropes to secure him to the floor pegs. A small group of black people were gathering outside the stable door. They were silent as Hopper was pressed face-down to the dirt, his wrists and ankles bound to the wooden pegs.

Imogen waited for the men to finish knotting Hopper into position. Then she quickly hitched her long skirt up to her belt and approached Hopper's spread-eagled body, facing his parted legs, the spread of his round buttocks, the wide target of his rippling back. She did not have the expertise, nor the experience to flail a long bull whip but a burning anger drove her to begin, to bring it down petulantly again and again, first striking too high, then hitting him on the buttocks.

The whip continued to crack. Hopper let out loud cries. He had energy to pull in terror, jerking his hands and feet, tugging at the wooden pegs driven into the hard dirt.

Imogen cursed at the antiquated method of holding a slave

in subservience. She thought fleetingly about the grandness of the new house for Dragonard Hill and became more angry about the ancient methods of torture left over from the days of The Star.

Quick to gain a rhythm for her lashes, she thought now of what she was doing. She thought of revenge. The revenge on Hopper for breaking a law. A revenge against her father for not heeding her words.

Imogen Abdee also was driven by the third reason, the third and most important reason for whipping this male slave. She sought revenge on Hopper for being so manly. Muscular. Powerful. Exerting masculinity over females. She wanted to bring him down to her size now. Even lower.

Punishment was an overseer's duty on the plantation. And as Imogen took longer pulls of the whip, learning how to aim its bite against Hopper's bare skin, she also wondered why she could not be the overseer herself. Not immediately. She knew that she was young. But even when she grew older, she could not foresee how she could ever have such a job.

Hopper's back soon became a coagulation of blood and loose skin. He had soiled himself during the first few strong lashes.

Imogen still did not stop, did not flinch at the sight nor hesitate at the smell. Nor did Hopper struggle now.

Behind Imogen stood Lady Alice, a grey-haired negress who nervously wrung her gnarled hands together, wondering when Imogen would stop. Lady Alice did not approve of this. She had threatened to tell Imogen's father. But Imogen had warned her that, if her father heard of this, she would also whip Clara, the girl who had been caught with Hopper.

So far, Lady Alice had counted thirty-seven strokes. This punishment was becoming more than unjust. It was unlike anything that had happened on Dragonard Hill. The worst punishment for a black person here was to be locked away from companionship for a week, confined to a small log gaol called The Prison. The black people accepted that. They feared The Prison because they hated to be away from their friends, their lovers. But they still received their food and drink there. They were not mistreated.

This whipping was cruel, though. And Lady Alice knew that many black people could rise against such treatment.

Finally, Imogen stopped. Like a general proud of a victory, she waited to see the defeated dragged away.

Two men stooped to untie and then lift Hopper's motionless body from the dirt floor. He was unconscious.

Finally, when they managed to move Hopper's arms around their necks, dragging him up from the floor, Imogen suddenly gasped. She saw that the whipping had firmed Hopper's maleness. Although Hopper was unconscious, his penis stuck out erect from his groin, the crown filled with blood and protruding strongly through the greasy black foreskin, as if in defiance to Imogen's frustrated womanhood.

*   *   *

Late that same night, a young negress sat in the corner of one of the small, stilted cabins in Town. She looked at Clara cradling Hopper's head on her lap.

Hopper lay motionless on his side now. Lady Alice had given him a root nostrum for sleep. The light from a fire on the iron brazier in the middle of the floor illuminated the welts on his neck, back, and buttocks. A layer of salve covered the markings, glistening in the soft light like thick yellow syrup.

The young girl in the corner looked from Hopper's wounds and studied Clara's sober face. She knew that Clara and Hopper were in love. She knew that Clara wanted to have a child by Hopper. It did not matter that they could not raise their child. They would see the child grow and be proud.

Also, the girl in the corner remembered the story that Clara had told her this afternoon in the Looming House. Miss Imogen had threatened Clara that she would rip a baby from Clara's stomach if she had one. Miss Imogen would rip out Clara's baby with her own bare hands.

The black girl in the corner was named Maybelle. Lady

Alice had felt her and told her that she already was carrying a baby in her own stomach. The father of Maybelle's unborn child was named Ham. He lived in this cabin, too. Ham was a wagon teamster who drove to the cotton gin in Troy when the harvesting was done. That time of year would begin soon.

At this moment, Ham was sitting out on the front ladder to the cabin. Maybelle wanted him in here with her. But Ham was worried tonight. He knew Maybelle had found out about a threat made to him.

The owner of the cotton gin was a white man called Master Jeb Conway. He had threatened that an accident would happen to Ham at the cotton gin if Maybelle did not pleasure him. Some black men got hurt at the cotton gin. They had accidents – lost arms, broke one or two legs, perhaps even got killed. But the black men whose women pleasured Jeb Conway never got hurt. Conway knew the black women would do anything to keep their man safe. He knew that a black man would sacrifice his arm – or his own life – to protect his woman, but that a woman would find some way to keep him from doing it if she heard the gossip. And Maybelle had heard it.

Tomorrow, Maybelle knew that Master Jeb Conway was coming to Dragonard Hill. That was why Ham was worried. Conway was coming to see Maybelle. She must let Jeb Conway take his pleasure with her tomorrow in a tool hut. And she would, regardless of what Ham did or said. She had nothing else in this world except the love of one man.

And, tonight, looking at Clara and Hopper in the low firelight, Maybelle felt both fear and hatred for the white people. White people could make blacks do anything. Master Peter was good to them but what did that really mean? Nothing. Any white person could whip them. Break their legs. Rape them. Rip out their babies. But there was nothing that a black man, a black woman could do to fight back against any white person.

Maybelle knew that she dare not talk about this to Nero. Nero was black but he also was a white man's overseer and

Jeb Conway would find out in the end that Maybelle had talked. Conway had threatened to maim or kill Ham even if Maybelle talked.

Standing up now, Maybelle pulled the smock down around her body which still showed no signs of the new life now growing inside her. She had to rise early tomorrow morning but she was not sleepy now. She wanted to be with Ham.

Going out through the strings hanging in the doorway which kept out the flies, she sat down behind Ham on the ladder. Putting her hands around his neck, she whispered, 'What you thinking about, Lover?'

He stared straight ahead. He answered, 'You, little Gal.'

'And your baby?'

Ham nodded his shaved head. And holding both of Maybelle's hands in his now, he said, 'I want you keeping away from all white men, Gal. Go near none of them. Whatever happens.'

'Shhh,' she said, rocking her body against him.

The black sky arced above them, twinkling over their long-legged home on this land called Dragonard Hill, the slave quarters named Town.

Chapter Two

DOG MAN

Since the day that Peter Abdee first decided to build a new home for Dragonard Hill, the house where he, the girls and servants lived was instantly referred to as 'the old house'. Then as the new house took on a shape, demanding more carpenters, bricklayers, lug men, the old house fell increasingly into disrepair. All skilled labourers – any man who was not a field-hand – was needed on the building site; even the yearly whitewashing had been neglected on the old house and it began to look more and more like its new name.

The old house sat at the end of a long drive, an avenue of double oaks which ran between it and the pole gate posts planted at the public road. No sign nor insignia announced that this land was Dragonard Hill. Peter Abdee had ordered two brass plaques from New Orleans to be embedded in the stone pillars being stacked and mortared farther up the road to Troy, the namegates for the driveway which would lead to the new house, a low climbing approach that cut through a long double line of young cypress trees.

But visitors to Dragonard Hill these days still passed under the pole gates and travelled over the rutty road, arriving at the old house, which looked like a ramshackle fortress, the boards turning grey, its front porch sagging, the bougainvillaea vines withering around the windows. Even the gardeners were needed now up on the hill.

The only bustle of activity in the old house these days was in the kitchen, a room built into the main living quarters, which made the house hot in summer, and the voices of the cooks, their clanking in the kitchen, carried freely into the dining-room. But this would all be remedied in the new house – like most Southern manor houses, the kitchen there would be detached, connected only by a covered breeze-way.

The head cook at Dragonard Hill was a negro male called Posey. Tall and willowy – with high cheekbones and short cropped hair that clung to his high-domed skull – Posey was in his early thirties. He had never worked in the fields with the other black men. He hated children and was frightened of animals. His only connection with the out-of-doors was his lifelong passion for flowers, the reason why he had received his name.

Posey was male in gender only. He had no attraction to females and he thought that male negroes were clumsy and oafish. He had been brought to the big house as a young boy by Storky, the black matriarch of Dragonard Hill, the imperious negress who had then been the head cook and had taught Posey her secrets for cooking delicious food for white masters and their families.

Confined to a rattan chair in the middle of the kitchen floor, Storky sat propped up by goose feather-filled pillows, a willow cane resting on the side of her chair. She still exerted her authority over the kitchen, although she did no cooking, made no preparations, except for supervising the distillations of fruit brandies in the autumn. In deference to Storky's long record of service, everyone – even Posey – addressed her as 'Miss Storky'.

Storky and Posey's helper in the kitchen was a sober, almond-eyed young negress named Belladonna. Both Storky and Posey ignored Belladonna until they needed her to fetch something. She sat on a three-legged stool in the corner, staring into the lap of her white smock and trying not to listen to the steady flow of chatter that passed between Storky and Posey.

This morning, Storky and Posey talked about what had happened in Town. They knew that Peter was not home today, that they could gossip freely. They were talking about Imogen whipping the slave, Hopper, yesterday in the work stables.

43

Sitting in her creaky rattan chair, Storky said to Posey, 'It's sad to see a young lady acting so trashy.'

Posey nodded with his usual animation, his hands flapping as he rushed about the kitchen, making a fresh batch of raisin bread today.

Storky continued, 'What this place needs is a woman. Not a man like Miss Imogen pretends she's being.'

'Her Daddy not even that ornery,' Posey called from a stack of crockery bowls. He chose one and rushed back across the kitchen, a long white apron rustling around the legs of his baggy white trousers. He looked as if he were wearing a skirt with starched pantaloons.

'Miss Imogen's Daddy is quality,' Storky said proudly. 'Master Peter's a real fine quality gentleman. Miss Imogen's Mama was quality, too. There was nobody as quality as Miss Melissa was. Fact is, Miss Melissa took after *her* Daddy. She had that Selby blood in her. Kind blood. Good blood. Quality folk. But Miss Imogen. No, she's feisty and mean like her old Granny Roland. She got that Roland blood boiling in her. Mean, hot, spiteful blood. Like too much red pepper.' She shook her head, letting her large lips flap in a shuddering sound.

Posey remembered the girls' grandmother – cantankerous Rachel Selby – all too well. He clanked some pans loudly rather than comment on her.

Storky said over the din, 'What that new hill house needs is a lady. A real fine white lady running it.'

'I ain't doing bad here,' Posey said.

'You a man, Posey. You a nigger-buck man, if you like it or not. Least, that's what you supposed to be. Regardless of that dinky little worm you got dangling between your two sissy legs.' Storky was always quick to remind Posey about the minute size of his penis. There were few facts on Dragonard Hill that Storky did not know. And, although she no longer made love with Samson the old blacksmith, sex was still an important part of her thoughts. She and Posey often discussed it.

44

Posey now threw his nose petulantly into the air at her gibe about his private parts.

But Storky was used to his feminine affectations. She even encouraged them. She fuelled his anger. She said now, 'My sick legs keep me from getting abouts all I likes to. This family needing me so much now and I can't helps them.' She shook her head, her short hair covered by a starched white kerchief which stuck out over the nape of her neck like a bird's beak turned the wrong way around.

Posey felt that Storky interfered too much in the kitchen. Sometimes, even hampered his work. To exert his own power now, he turned to Belladonna, ordering, 'Get me some sugar, wench.' He snapped his long brown fingers at her.

Belladonna quickly jumped to her bare feet.

Storky shouted to Posey, 'Mayhaps those twins will change things when they get back home. Mayhaps Miss Veronica and Miss Vicky learned to be right proper ladies up North.'

'Yankee ways,' Posey said disdainfully. He did not really know what 'Yankee' meant but he had heard Peter talk about them – Yankees.

Storky continued, 'Those two girls always ladies. Miss Veronica more ladylike than Miss Vicky. Course, then, Miss Veronica better behaved than Miss Vicky because Miss Vicky – poor tyke – she had that terrible trouble happen to her. The reason she had to go North to school in the first place.'

Posey shot Storky a quick look. She was not to talk about the trouble that Miss Victoria Abdee had had three years ago. Especially not to mention it in front of someone as lowly as Belladonna. No other black people on Dragonard Hill knew what had happened to young Vicky, except for Posey and Storky. They had found her crying in the bushes and they had told Master Peter. And he had ordered them to forget about the ugly incident. He did not want it to mar poor Miss Vicky's life.

To change the subject, Posey said, 'I just don't like hearing you talking about them girls coming home, Miss Storky. They

45

be here before you can shake a stick. Two weeks fly mighty fast. And I got too much work to do between now and then.'

Storky pounced upon this opportunity to belittle Posey again. She said, 'The work you have to do, you can do with one hand tied behind your back. You never saw the work *I* had to do here in the old days. Cooking from morning to night, I did.'

'It's not only the cooking,' Posey smugly said. 'I copes with the cooking easy. It's moving. It's managing. It's just doing everything. Everything! If I depended on you remembering, Miss Storky, I'd plumb forget about that Mister Conway coming here today, for instance. I got to have a bite for Mister Conway to eat, too, today.'

'Mister Conway? Jeb Conway? He coming here today from the cotton gin?' Storky asked.

Posey raised his head triumphantly. 'See! You done plumb forget about him coming here. Mister Conway coming from Troy to look over the crops. Master Peter likes us to have little snacks for Mister Conway when he visits.'

Storky snorted. 'Master Peter don't like that Conway man one bit. Maybe that's why I forget about him coming. Master Peter not stayed here to see him, did he? No! Master Peter gone to Greenleaf to get away from him. Yes, I forgot about him coming because Master Peter thinks him trash.'

Posey argued, 'Master Peter not here because he's helping Matty Kate.' He used the name for Kate Breslin – Matty Kate – that the house servants at Greenleaf called her. It was an abbreviation for 'Madame' and Posey felt privileged to know such facts from another plantation.

Storky likewise used that name for the owner of Greenleaf, if for no other reason than to let Posey know that she knew whom he meant. She said, 'Master Peter going to help Matty Kate just to gets away from that Conway man. Master Peter hates Jeb Conway. Calls him the "dog man". Says he keeps so many dogs at his shack near the cotton gin in Troy it's like a dog farm down there. Stinks worse than a field nigger's shack.' Apart from using a pretentious way of referring to certain white people, Storky also was the worst offender of a house servant exerting superiority over fieldhands. But Posey was fastly becoming her equal.

He said now, 'I hope that Conway man don't bring no dogs with him here today. Cooking for white trash man bad enough. But I puts my foot down cooking for . . . dogs!'

'Trouble with you, Posey, you worry too much about ifs. Ifs don't always happens. No, you just pay mind to facts, Posey! That's the only way you might get this kitchen going again.' Shaking her head, Storky said, 'My, my, my, how this kitchen was hot when I was on my feet.'

'This kitchen is old and no good,' Posey said, throwing more wood into the stove. 'In the new house, everything will be fine and wonderful. Just like I wants it to be. My new kitchen ain't going to be built into the house, neither. Not like this old kitchen of yours. In the new house, my kitchen will be set apart. That makes the house real cool.' Posey fanned himself with a pie tin and smiled.

'What you putting airs on for, nigger pansy? You ain't going to be in no cool big house fanning yourself. You'll be in the kitchen slaving with that Belladonna wench.'

Posey returned to his work. 'I know that. I was just thinking about white ladies enjoying cool shade.'

'You just remembers you a black man working.'

Again, Posey petulantly sniffed.

Storky still had the upper hand in the kitchen and, to force it, she said, 'And as far as *you* planning that new kitchen, that's a lie, too. Master Peter tells *me* to do that.'

Posey was caught. He knew Storky was right. Even in her infirmity, she was still head cook in Master Peter's eyes, if not in practice in the kitchen.

He said, 'I sure thinks it too bad Master Peter won't have that new house done by the time the twins gets back home.'

Storky was in an argumentative mood now. She grumbled, 'Those twins can just help their Daddy finish the house.'

'Pooh! No fine white ladies can help with no building. Not

47

after all that fancy Yankee schooling they been getting day and night for three long years.'

Belladonna spoke up for the first time,' Miss Imogen can helps her Daddy. Miss Imogen works hard.'

'You never mind about Miss Imogen, nigger slut,' Posey called to Belladonna.

'Nothing wrong with working,' Belladonna mumbled. 'That's what Miss Imogen says.'

'Good for a nigger gal like you!' Posey said, standing with his hands on his hips. 'Now shut up your big mouth and stop making so much talk. You scare the flies with your mouth blabbering all the time. The flies buzz all around me then and I could . . . scream!' He raised his fists to his ears and shook them.

Belladonna fell silent again. She knew that she could not win an argument with either Posey or Miss Storky.

But, sitting quietly in the corner on her three-legged stool, Belladonna still had her own opinions. She believed that Miss Imogen was the best white person in the whole world. She admired Miss Imogen. She hoped that someday that she could tell her so, too. In the meantime, though, Belladonna had to contend herself by just daydreaming about Miss Imogen. And listening to Posey and Miss Storky talking derisively about the field workers, insulting one another, and occasionally asking Belladonna, 'Why don't you pester with no bucks, Belladonna wench? What's the matter? You scared of getting knocked-up?' Those were the day-to-day topics in the kitchen – their superiority over field niggers, rivalry for power in the old house, and sex.

*   *   *

There was one black woman living in the old house who obeyed no one.

Storky's – and Posey's – authority extended outside the kitchen, ruling the slaves who cleaned and served in the old house. There was a small daily staff of two black women who came from Town to dust, mop, sweep in the old house. Apart from Storky, Posey, and Belladonna, there were also two additional black women, Eulalia and Ori, who slept there, acting as parlour maids to Peter and Imogen – the twins had taken a third parlour maid, Brownie, with them when they had gone to school in Boston. Like many boarding-schools in the North which attracted young Southern ladies, there were provisions at Pemberton's for personal servants.

Boxo, the groom at the old house stables, and a young negro, Royal, were also attached to the manor house at Dragonard Hill. Royal waited on table and, three mornings a week, he helped Peter Abdee with the ledgers. Unlike many white masters who feared their slaves would learn about freedom, rebellion, facts about the outside world from books, Peter always encouraged those black people on Dragonard Hill who showed an aptitude for reading and numbers.

Peter's and Imogen's bedrooms were on the middle floor of the old house. Veronica and Vicky had bedrooms there, too. Since Storky's infirmity, she now slept in a small cabin behind the old kitchen, and was helped there each night by two house servants. Posey had assumed Storky's old bed, a pallet behind the stove in the kitchen.

The rest of the servants slept on the top floor or in cabins near the back. But there was a room on the top floor of the old house that was occupied by a negress who had no part in the housework. Her name was Ta-Ta. She was left alone, allowed the privacy of a retired nursemaid. The new black servants believed that Ta-Ta had indeed been a nursemaid, had taken care of Master Peter in his childhood on The Star.

Ta-Ta's role in Peter's childhood was more complicated than the others imagined. The story of her part in Peter's background was told by crude pictures drawn on the board floors, walls, sloping ceiling of her small attic room.

Never coming out of her room, Ta-Ta sat in a rocking-chair by the dormer window and looked at her primitive murals, or gazed down at the domain of Dragonard Hill.

But often Ta-Ta's fading eyes did not see a Louisiana cotton plantation. She saw visions of the West Indies. She saw the sugar plantation where she had lived on St Kitts. The island home of the French lady whose crude portrait was now chalked on her wall – among pictures of palm trees, outlines of little men with sharp teeth, blood gashes on the crotches of pirates' breeches, whips whose tips were splayed like a mythical dragon's fangs, maps which meant nothing to anyone except Ta-Ta herself. And, among her wall-paintings, was a stick drawing of a small baby named Pierre. Near Pierre on the wall was another child. It was a black boy. A long brown tail had been drawn between his legs, a monkey's tail. And a long gun had been sketched over his head. All cryptic signs – and memories – that made sense to Ta-Ta.

Food was brought twice daily to Ta-Ta's door, left on covered trays. Her chamber pots were dutifully collected. Bottles of brandy left on schedule for her. Ta-Ta had not received a visitor in her attic room since the twins had gone North to school. Veronica always trudged the winding stairs to visit Ta-Ta at the top of the old house.

Vicky and her older sister, Imogen, dismissed Ta-Ta as a crazy, skinny, withered old witch. Posey and Storky – the latter not being able to climb stairs, anyway – had reasons to believe that Ta-Ta might poke a long gun at them if they came snooping in her room.

Nobody bothered Ta-Ta. Nobody tried to boss her. Every-one left her alone. Even Peter Abdee, the man she had raised as Pierre. He knew that she wanted to sit in privacy with her pictures, a richly-coloured past which gave Ta-Ta a truer picture of her life than what she saw out of the attic window of the old house on Dragonard Hill.

*　　　*　　　*

Kate Breslin kept the conversation light during lunch that afternoon at Greenleaf, as whimsical and capricious as the food which she had ordered her cook to prepare.

Cold whitefish mayonaise. Lettuce hearts sprinkled with

capers and dill. Green beans and lemon. And a bottle of white wine left to chill in the creek under the springhouse for so long that the French label had washed away. The luncheon was to be finished with a silver tray of iced mints and a pot of coffee. The maid left the tray on a sideboard in the dining-room and asked her mistress, Matty Kate, if she wanted anything else. Kate shook her head, thanked the black girl, and told her that she could leave now for an afternoon to be spent with a friend.

From the moment that Peter Abdee had sat down at the round draped table in the yellow-and-white dining-room at Greenleaf, he responded to Kate's joyful suggestions, questions, conversation. She asked him about his first horse. She urged him to tell her about New Orleans before Thomas Jefferson had purchased Louisiana from Napoleon. She asked only questions about Peter's childhood at The Star, skipping the misery of losing his wife, and staying clear from present day complications. Kate Breslin did not once mention Peter's three daughters. Nor referred to the yellow babies being born on Dragonard Hill.

Peter knew that Kate was manipulating him today. Her efforts pleased him, though. He was flattered that she would take this trouble to make him happy. Home life at Dragonard Hill had been hectic. Last night at supper, Imogen had barely spoken to him. She had not mentioned the matter of having Nero whip the slave, Hopper, nor did she press Peter to replace Nero with another overseer. Peter hoped that she had forgotten both of her earlier demands. Also, she had not mentioned her sisters.

Last night, though, the faces of the black people in the old house told Peter that something had happened on Dragonard Hill that he did not know. He suspected it had to do with Imogen. All the blacks shied away from her. Peter had planned to ask Nero about it this morning but, in his preparations to come here to Greenleaf, he had forgotten. He would try to remember when he returned home late this afternoon.

But these moments today belonged to him and Kate, who

now had Peter laughing, telling her stories that even he was surprised to remember.

The main object of the afternoon, though, was not to meet for a light-hearted lunch. The true purpose waited upstairs. And as soon as Peter had folded his white napkin and set it beside his plate, Kate rose from the table, moving to take the coffee tray from the sideboard.

Following her from the dining-room, Peter said, 'You organize well, Katie.'

She was climbing the stairway to her bedroom. She said, 'Don't make me seem so eager.'

He laughed. 'I mean the food. It was filling. But I still feel – what? Capable!' He put both hands on her hips, letting her lead him up the stairs.

'I don't want you falling asleep. These afternoons are too difficult to arrange.'

Stepping in front of her at the top of the stairs, Peter opened the door to her bedroom and, as the drapes were already drawn, he took the tray from her hands; Kate moved quickly to the tall windows to let in a narrow shaft of afternoon light.

Peter now was unbuttoning his shirt, sniffing the bedroom's sweet aroma as his fingers moved down his chest. 'Hmmm. Violets?'

Kate nodded. 'And probably a whiff of cloves from the pomanders.' She sank into a blue velvet chair, beginning to pour coffee into two gold china cups.

Going toward her, Peter held her head in his hands and, after she set down the pot, he gently pressed her face to the thigh of his twill breeches. He toyed with her dark-red ringlets and murmured, 'No nice smells like that on me.'

Kate drank Peter's masculine aroma, his freshly laundered clothes, still mixed with the dust of the road and a hint of his clean perspiration. She did not answer him. Her enjoyment was silent, nudging his thigh like a cat.

Soon, Peter had pulled Kate up into his arms and their mouths pressed tightly together, his tongue licking the sweet-

52

ness from her lips, the remnants of a mint. He then plunged deeper, exploring the sides and top of her tongue.

The test of Peter's and Kate's attraction for one another was that, after five years of love-making, they still hurriedly dropped their clothes on the floor. They both had an insatiable desire to join one another in bed as quickly as possible. Kate's body was trim from horseback riding; her skin, soft and sweetly scented, as was everything in her life.

She found the touch of Peter's naked body firm, lithe, reassuring. Their mutual lack of immodesty in bed made them believe that their actions were rational, that they were not sneaking to meet like this – although they had to be surreptitious for the sake of less broad-minded people. And nephews and daughters.

The only thing that had altered in this five-year relationship was, now, that the newness had passed, they could happily sustain themselves, letting their excitement build and build and build until . . .

Kate screamed when she felt herself finally bursting. And that was why she had to send the servants far away from the main house on these occasions. She could not have them hearing their 'Matty Kate' scream out – again and again – in such an abandoned fashion.

Now, as Kate lay tossing her head side-to-side on the pillows, crying with the ecstasy exploding inside her, Peter propped his arms on each side of her shoulders, driving deeper into her, feeling himself grow thicker, watching this one milky-skinned woman literally becoming delirious as he touched farther into her, thrusting even deeper as he himself burst, and then pushed into the liquid warmth that they made together.

Then, still together, Peter and Kate lay with their hearts pounding, realizing that the trouble of all their plans to meet was worth it. They languished now in their spent fervour.

*   *   *

On that same afternoon, a one-mule wagon moved slowly down the public road from the small town of Troy, the shoulders of the lone driver stooped forward and a blade of sweet grass hanging from the corner of his purple lips. It was Jeb Conway on his way to Dragonard Hill.

The public road was dirt. The wagon rattled as the wooden wheels now slid into a deep rut and then stopped. Jeb Conway snapped the leather reins with his withered hands and the patchy brown mule resumed its lazy pull.

The sun was high in a clear blue sky. The poplar trees lining the country road were filled with sparrows. An occasional crow cawed. A brown rabbit hopped across the road. A black-and-white dog ran barking from a log farmhouse near the road. But neither Jeb Conway nor his mule paid any heed to the noisy animal. The wagon continued slowly jogging through the leafy countryside, Jeb Conway looking in no particular hurry to reach his destination.

Jeb Conway was an enigmatic man. He had inherited the cotton gin at Troy from his father, the local banker who had married late in life. Jeb Conway's mother was a comely but uneducated mountain girl, one of fourteen children and considered by the citizens of Troy to be a poor match for a respectable gentleman like Banker Conway. When Jeb's father died, his mother ran away from Troy with a river man. Not even a captain or a gambler. She had chosen a wood-stoker as her true love. The town's sceptics felt reassured by this action. Bad blood always showed in the end, they said. And Jeb Conway was further proof of what they felt to be white trash. But, as owner of the cotton gin, he was more powerful in the community than many of his social betters.

All the planters in the vicinity used Jeb Conway's cotton gin. He received a percentage of the sales to the cloth agents and was satisfied with that. Jeb Conway was not a greedy man. Not for wealth. He and his wife, Noreen, lived in a tumbled-down shack next to the gin. Noreen Conway looked even more shabby than her husband. She was a sickly woman but she could be found working every season at the gin, even on days when Jeb was roaming the countryside. The Conways had no children.

54

Jeb Conway's only extravagance was his dogs. He kept a penful of black mastiffs in the rear of his shack. The dogs belonged to Jeb. His pale wife only fed and watered the animals when Jeb made his journeys in the neighbourhood.

The dogs never accompanied Jeb on his trips. He felt that the animals were too valuable to travel. He worried that they might come to some harm. And neither did Noreen Conway go with Jeb in the wagon. She had to stay home to feed the dogs. Or so said Jeb Conway.

Passing the negro masons working on the new stone entrance to Dragonard Hill, Jeb Conway did not return their friendly waves. He had no use for negroes. Especially not the black people of Dragonard Hill. He felt that they were too pampered. And holding his eyes to the road, Jeb Conway continued rattling toward the old pole posts through which he would pass to enter Dragonard Hill.

Jeb Conway did not stop in front of the old house at the end of the oak drive. Posey called frantically to him from the porch steps, holding a covered tray in his hands. But Jeb snapped the reins and the scrawny mule kept going. Jeb knew where he was headed. What he wanted today. And it was not on the food tray that Posey was holding in his hands. Jeb Conway hated Posey the worst of all the black people here. But there was no way in which he could harm Posey.

Finally stopping in front of a tool hut which stood near the site of the old slave quarters, Jeb pulled the reins and threw the handbrake on the work wagon. He looked around but saw no one. The working fields were through a clump of poplars. The new house was being built about a furlong in the other direction.

Jeb saw that the hut's door hung open on its leather hinges. He had expected that. It was according to the instructions he had given to the teamster named Ham.

Stepping down from the wagon, Jeb uncricked his left leg and walked slowly toward the hut. Stopping outside the half-open door, he reached toward his belt and pulled out a pistol. Jeb Conway was also a cautious man.

Standing in front of the half-open door, he called into the blackness, 'Maybelle? You there?'

He heard a shuffle.

'Maybelle?' he repeated louder.

A timid voice answered, 'I here, Master Conway, sir.'

'You alone, girl?'

'I alone, Master Sir.'

'I got me a pistol here, Maybelle. If you or that Ham man of yours is thinking of trying any smart stuff with me, I'll let you both have it in the gut.' He clicked the pistol's hammer.

'Ham ain't here, Master Conway, Sir. I come in secret.'

Grunting, Conway uncocked the pistol and put it into the pocket of his jacket. He had dealt with enough slaves to know when they were telling the truth. He knew when niggers were frightened enough to obey. Maybelle was one frightened nigger, he thought. She would not attack him.

Standing inside the doorway of the hut now, Jeb could see Maybelle cowering in the far corner. The mere sight of her being so frightened already excited him. Her panic was arousing the bone in his droopy trousers.

He called in a thick voice, 'You a real smart gal, Maybelle. You a real smart nigger gal protecting your man, this way. If you didn't come here like this today, I know damn well that something terrible might happened to Ham at the gin. Yes, it sure is smart of you taking out this insurance on your man. Jeb laughed, fidgeting harder at the bone which now poked forward under the rough trousers.

Walking slowly toward the black girl, he said, 'Peel off that shift you're wearing, Maybelle. I want to see your big titties.'

Maybelle nervously obeyed. It was as she had expected.

'Ahhh,' he said, looking at her breasts and digging at his crotch, 'those are some titties you got there, ain't they? Yeah!'

Maybelle did not know whether to stand or sit or kneel. All she could think about was this terrible man hurting her Ham.

Jeb said, 'Now sit back and spread open those knees. I want

56

to see how pretty you are 'tween your legs, Gal.'

She hesitated.

Jeb's craggy face began to tighten. He did not like people to disobey him. But the only people that he could force to follow his orders were the ones whom he trapped and threatened. The negro slaves.

He sneered, 'It seems right foolish to me that Ham might bleed, Maybelle. Bleed plumb to death just 'cause his woman ain't showing me her sweet hairy hole.'

Maybelle's slim legs slowly opened.

Looking at her fur patch, Jeb Conway now unbuttoned the fly on his trousers, fumbling with his hand and watching the young girl crouched on the floor. His penis was near hardness when he pulled it from his trousers. He worked his hand back and forth on it, a penis that was narrow and pointed like a carrot.

When he was erect, Jeb moved his hand and shoved his penis into Maybelle's face, forcing her to look at it.

He asked, leering at her, 'That scare you, Girlie?'

She did not answer. She was trembling.

'What's the matter? You think it's ugly? The sight of it put you off? Make you want to puke? Run and cover your eyes?'

Maybelle was too smart to say no. But her repulsion was too great for her to say yes, that she wanted him. She could only think of her own man.

Cradling his penis in his hands, Jeb whispered, 'Suck me . . . I like being sucked, Maybelle . . . I want your big lips on me sucking, Gal. . . .'

The hut was small; the smell from Jeb Conways unwashed penis was strong. And now the close air was filled his odour, both sweet and sickeningly rancid. The odour was all his.

He goaded her. 'Go on, suck some.'

Slowly, Maybelle moved her quivering mouth forward, forcing herself to open her lips, trying not to smell the unwashed parts. She thought of Ham, who worked hard all day and was always cleaner than this. Ham smelled like flowers and honey when he held her in his arms at night. Ham and Maybelle often took one another in their mouths. But his taste – her taste – was good. Sweet. Clean.

Jeb Conway's excitement was not as prolonged as his bravado and after Maybelle worked him with her mouth for only a brief time, he quickly yanked himself out of her mouth and drenched the palm of his hand with saliva from his own mouth. He smeared the saliva over his penis and, roughly kicking open her bare legs with his boot, he rammed down toward her.

One, two, then on his third attempt, Jeb Conway drilled his red point into her firm patch. But it was suddenly over for him. His excitement passed quickly. He shuddered. Drove into her a few more times and, when he pulled away, his penis was soft, limp, shrivelled.

He rose to his feet without another word or gesture.

Maybelle fell forward on her knees, pleading now with Jeb Conway to promise that Ham would be safe. That Conway would not cause harm to him at the gin.

But Jeb Conway was out the door of the hut and already climbing back into his wagon. His moment of supremacy had passed. He had forgotten about Maybelle. To him, she was just one more black person to scorn now.

Snapping the reins, he hunched over the mule, returning once again to being sullen Jeb Conway, the cotton gin owner from Troy, who was known behind his back as the 'Dog Man'.

*   *   *

A gentle evening breeze blew the long strings hanging in the doorway of Maybelle and Ham's, Clara and Hopper's house in Town. Although Hopper had not been able to go weeding in the field today, his back still being raw from the whipping yesterday, Clara had taken him outside when she had come back from work in the Looming House, walking and exercising him on a woodland path.

Maybelle and Ham now had the long-legged house to themselves; Maybelle lay curled into a ball in one corner of the house, her slim arms wrapped around her knees, her head thrust forward in the position of a child still living inside its mother's womb.

Ham stood above her, dressed in baggy tow work pants, not having washed yet in the wooden trough at the far end of their row of houses. He stared down at Maybelle's curled body on the floor and asked, 'You crying?'

Maybelle's answer was faint. 'No.'

'You done something.'

'Done nothing.'

Falling to his knees beside her, he said, 'Woman, you saw that Conway man today. That Conway came here and you saw him.' There was anger in Ham's deep voice.

She sniffed, saying bravely but weakly, 'I ain't scared of no Conway man.'

Grabbing Maybelle by the shoulders, he pulled her onto her back and, as her arms fell to her side and her legs spread flat, he looked down at her pretty face and demanded, 'Woman, why you go trying to do things for me you don't understand?'

Maybelle's voice became hard as she stared up at his brilliant brown eyes, perspiration dripping over them from his strong forehead. She asked, 'What for you go working every morning? You understand that? What for you a slave? You understand that? What for when a white man say "shit, nigger!" you shit? You understand that?'

'You my woman! *Mine*!'

A smile creased her large eyes and, wrapping her long arms around his neck, she asked him more softly, 'You telling me lies?'

Still angry, Ham moved to stand. He knew he could not argue with a woman like Maybelle. She made him go weak when she smiled at him and, when she talked, her tongue made his ears spin. He grumbled, 'I stink. Let me go wash.'

Pulling him down to her on the floor, Maybelle wrapped both arms and legs around Ham's dusty body, desperately

59

whispering now, 'Let me smell you, Man. Let me smell you and hold you and have you, Big Bragging Man.'

But Ham's mind was still filled with Jeb Conway's threats and Maybelle's decision that she had to save him. And the fact that she had obviously done it this afternoon both sickened and angered him.

Feeling Ham's strong body resist her, knowing his masculine pride, she murmured, 'We'll get them, Honey. We'll get them whities some way. Even just a little way. But we'll get them.'

He could not agree to this sudden threat. To him, it was only a surrender at the moment. And, worst of all, he felt that there was not much that they could do. They were slaves and that only meant work. They had no way to fight against white people.

The desolation of that thought made Ham forget about going to the trough to wash now and he fell upon Maybelle's waiting body.

Enveloping him with both legs, she whispered, 'Come in me. Come in me, Big Bragging Man.'

She used words of play, calling him 'Big Bragging Man', but Ham knew that she was desperate. He felt her body clenching him, her breasts pressed tightly against his perspiration-soaked chest. Her breath tickled his ear as she whispered her words to him, and then holding his ear in her mouth, she tongued it, kissing him, locking him tighter in her legs, begging more forlornly, 'Come in me. Come inside me . . . inside me . . . inside me.'

Ham's penis was firm and, as he clasped Maybelle in his arms, he felt her lithe body working to grip him and provide his entry into her vagina.

Eagerly, she continued in whispers, 'Make our baby black, Man. Make sure our baby's black, Man.' She had finally seized the head of his penis in the lips of her moist vagina and, lifting herself higher to catch its position, she began to work herself slowly down onto him. She gasped, 'Black him with your juice, Man. Black him with your juice.'

Maybelle's pleas unleashed a power inside Ham, making

him drive deep and hard into her now and, as he locked her tightly in his arms, he answered, 'Your baby's going to be mine, Woman. Going to be mine. Going to be mine.'

The passion of their love-making obliterated all memory of Jeb Conway from their minds; their dark bodies were interlocked, their mouths joined in desperate kisses, their arms straining around one another, and their midsections twisting, pressing, joining deeper and deeper to ensure that they would give only a black child to Dragonard Hill.

Chapter Three

UP NORTH

Veronica Abdee missed Dragonard Hill. She disliked the noises of Boston, the constant clattering of carriages on brick streets, the shrill of voices in the malls, the bells clanging in the port. She had lived in this din for three hateful years and she wanted to go home.

Her twin sister, Vicky, loved city life. She had teased Veronica mercilessly for packing her trunks so early. Vicky called Veronica a country mouse. A homesick bumpkin. A fastidious old maid for putting everything in order two weeks before they were due to depart for Louisiana.

Those two weeks had now dwindled down to only twelve hours before they were to leave. Vicky still had not packed and Veronica finally had done it for her.

But what bothered Veronica more than having to pack for her carefree sister was that, now, the night before they were to leave Boston, Vicky was not back at the school. It was almost midnight. The school was empty. Other girls had left long ago on their voyages home. Only the Abdee girls remained. And at this late hour, the Pemberton sisters who ran this school were fast asleep in their quarters at the top of the house. Even the matron, Mrs O'Higgins, had gone to Philadelphia to be with her mother.

Sitting in her room, Veronica stared sober-faced at Brownie, the negro maid who had come with Veronica and Vicky from Dragonard Hill. Brownie was dressed in a dark blue smock with white collar and cuffs. She also was rigid with excitement about leaving for home. She hated the dampness and the grey days of Boston. Also, as there were very few black people in the North, the white people here stared at Brownie and she was constantly frightened. But it had been worse before

Veronica had bought Brownie the navy blue uniform. Many white men here thought that all black females were prostitutes. Many times, Brownie had come crying back to the school.

Breaking the silence now, Brownie asked from her chair in the corner, 'What if Miss Vicky don't come back no more, Miss Ronny?'

'Of course she'll come back.' Veronica was not usually so irritable with Brownie. But tonight her nerves were frayed. She had tried to do needlework but she did not have the patience. *Midsummer Night's Dream* did not hold her interest. She did not care now that she would miss seeing the play here on the stage.

Brownie insisted, 'But what if not, Miss Ronny? Say what if Miss Vicky don't come back? Do we leave without her?'

'Brownie, how could you even think such a thing? Of course, we can't go home without Vicky. What would Father say?' Veronica's heart sank at the idea of staying here in Boston, though, another minute to wait for Vicky. But she thought that it would be typical of Vicky to torture her in such a malicious manner.

Brownie lowered her frizzy head. She could not argue with Miss Ronny. But she would not mind leaving without Miss Vicky. She thought that Miss Vicky was nothing but trouble. Brownie had been with Vicky one afternoon when two white men had mistaken Brownie for a prostitute and Vicky had teased, 'Go on! See if you can get some money! Maybe you'll get enough to buy me a new bonnet!' Brownie thought that Vicky had no decency.

Vicky was with Duncan Webb tonight. Veronica knew that. Vicky had been with him every night this last month.

Shuddering, Veronica wondered how far her sister's relationship went on these long evenings spent with Duncan Webb. She strongly disliked him. He was handsome, in a dark way, with his thin moustache and macassar oil on his hair. He had an athletic body and fine skin. But Veronica thought that he was the kind of man to take advantage of a young girl. She also felt that Duncan Webb was an example of manhood whom her sister could have only met in a Northern city. She longed to get Vicky back to the South where she could meet a nice, polite country gentleman.

Over the last three years, Vicky had been in trouble many times with the Pemberton sisters. Abigail Pemberton had written a letter to Peter Abdee, complaining about Vicky's deportment. But when Veronica had heard that Miss Abigail Pemberton was writing a sharp letter, she had pleaded with her not to send it. She did not want her sister to be expelled. She hated the idea of disappointing their father. Veronica had reminded Miss Abigail how clever Vicky was with her languages. How she had won praise for the school with her fine singing voice. That Vicky could be a model young lady when she applied herself. But sometimes the devil seemed to get a hold of Vicky, Veronica had argued, and she went hopelessly astray. To expel her would be to put her in worse danger.

Looking now at the gold watch pinned to her fawn linen dress, Veronica seriously began to worry that this was another one of those very occasions. A danger. It was *past* midnight now.

Looking at Brownie, Veronica asked, 'What do you think we should do? She knew it was senseless to ask Brownie such a question but she had to talk to somebody.

Brownie's eyes widened. 'You think we should leave without her?'

Veronica sighed at the black girl's response. She should have known better than to expect any other answer from Brownie.

Finally, Veronica said, 'We can not leave now even if we wanted to. The coach leaves at noon.'

'The coach? Brownie asked. 'I thought we going by boat, Miss Ronny.

'We are. But not on the Atlantic boat like we came North. We're going home on rivers! And to get to them we have to travel by coach, silly!

Brownie was not listening. She had an idea of her own.

She said, 'Maybe you and me, Miss Ronny, might catch an early coach. Are there coaches tonight?'

'Go tonight? And leave Vicky?'

'Miss Vicky will find us. She's clever, Miss Ronny. And I sure want to see Miss Storky and Posey and Eulalia and . . .'

Veronica understood how homesick the black girl was for Dragonard Hill. She felt the same way. Standing now, she began to pace the pink-and-yellow papered room. She knew she worried too much. But that was her nature. Vicky chided her, too, for being so serious, for behaving like some old black woman. She called Veronica her 'nigger mammy'.

Also, Vicky continuously reminded Veronica that she was not very attractive, that she should try to fix up herself more. To use cosmetics. Have more elaborate dresses made for herself. Show more bosom. Have Brownie lace her tighter into her corsets. Pin switches into her hair instead of wearing it so plain and, as Vicky called it, 'frumpy'.

Veronica's hair was sandy-coloured. Her father had told her it was the same shade as her mother's hair had been. He had said that Veronica reminded him a lot of her mother. Vicky's hair was much lighter than Veronica's, her eyes bluer. She had a creamier complexion and, although their busts and waists were the same size, Vicky had implemented ways to make her figure more voluptuous. Veronica would not be surprised some day to see Vicky actually rouging her cheeks, putting kohl on her eyes like an actress or a dancehall girl. Vicky had often threatened to do it, complaining about how drab the Boston weather made her skin.

The idea of painting her own face repelled Veronica. She knew that she was not very attractive to men, not like her twin sister. Men whistled at Vicky on the street. Veronica would be mortified if that happened to her. But Vicky seemed to want that kind of attention. She thrived on it. Veronica wondered what Vicky would do without all the male adulation she got in Boston when she returned home to the Louisiana wilderness.

Thinking of home now, Veronica began to fidget about

what questions that her father would ask them. Would he have somehow found out that Vicky had run wild in Boston? Would he blame Veronica for not reporting such news to him? Also, their older sister, Imogen, would certainly have something to say about Vicky. Veronica knew that they were enemies. She knew that Imogen had a sharp tongue – sharper than Vicky's – and that she would not stand for any silly city nonsense. But Vicky would fight back at Imogen. And then there would be an argument. And, thinking about such a thing happening, Veronica worried about her father becoming upset.

Veronica loved her father. And one thing that Vicky said to Veronica never bothered her. That Veronica – Little Ronny – was her father's pet, Veronica was proud of that fact.

Thinking now how her father would want her to act in an occasion such as this, Veronica said to Brownie, 'Go get Vicky. Find her and bring her here. Right now.'

'I don't know where Miss Vicky is,' Brownie protested

'Of course you do. She's at Duncan Webb's.'

'What's that?' Brownie blinked her round eyes.

'Stop playing stupid. You know where he lives. Back Bay. Go there right now and get Vicky or I'll . . . I'll . . . I'll *pinch* you.' Veronica crooked her thumb and forefinger at the black girl.

The threat of a pinch always prompted Brownie into action. Veronica never laid a finger on her. But she had discovered that two crooked fingers were very effective, moving toward Brownie like the pinchers on a sand crab.

Hurrying for her cape, Brownie listened to the orders which Veronica gave her for bringing Vicky back to the school. She gave Brownie the brass key for the front door and money for travelling both ways in a carriage. She knew that her sister never had any money left after a visit to Duncan Webb's. She always gave her money to him.

The Lord only know what he does to earn the money, Veronica thought now as she stood behind the closed door, nervously biting her lower lip, listening to Brownie's feet descending the outside stairs.

Then, alone in the room, the same old question returned to Veronica, a thought that had haunted her since she had come here three years ago.

Why don't I have any boyfriends? Why don't I like any of the beaux who are attracted to me? What's the matter? Am I really going to be an old maid? Or do I have to choose one of those pale-skinned, freckled-faced, bumbling. . . .

The idea of marrying any of the men she had met here was too depressing to contemplate. She could not give her love to a young man she did not admire physically. But was that wrong? To like how somebody looked? Were she and her sister from the same mould? Two young ladies who – without the advantages of money and a conscientious father – would be no better than common whores? Wanting men for physical attributes?

*　　*　　*

Laughing, standing in front of a cheval mirror, Vicky giggled at the reflection of herself and Duncan Webb undressing together.

Then she saw Duncan hold a long finger to his mouth . . . *Shhh! He heard something.*

Vicky thought that he was joking. Talking about his phallus. Sometimes they pretended that it was a stranger who came and visited them. Vicky always had to welcome the stranger. Her laughing grew louder at the idea.

Duncan Webb was moving away from the mirror. Vicky then saw only herself. She thought that he was going to take off the stranger's coat. Bring him to her. And, waiting, she focused on her oval face in the mirror. She raised her head, tucking the loose blonde ringlets which had tumbled down from the hair piled onto her head. She had tousled her hair when she had frantically pulled off her dress. It lay in a yellow heap on the floor with her petticoat. Her yellow calf slippers lay nearby.

Vicky and Duncan had had this race earlier to see who could get off their clothes faster. They had been drinking champagne. Their spirits were merry. But now she must make herself pretty to welcome the stranger that Duncan was bringing to her. The stranger must like her.

Suddenly, Vicky saw another reflection in the large oval mirror. It was not the stranger. It was not Duncan's undressed phallus waiting for her welcome, to entertain and make happy. She instead saw the blurred reflection of a woman standing behind her in the room. A woman almost as brown as the room's oak panelling. A young woman in a blue cloak. A girl. Vicky froze. It was no stranger. Vicky knew her.

Without turning, Vicky angrily demanded, 'What are you doing here, Brownie?'

Brownie's voice cracked with fear. 'Miss Ronny sends me, Miss Vicky, Mam.'

'Go back and tell her to suck eggs.'

Brownie said, 'Miss Ronny's worried about you –'

Vicky screamed, 'That mealy-mouth is always worried about me.' Turning, Vicky reached for her tulip-shaped glass of champagne and demanded, 'Duncan, tell this whiney nigger bitch to leave your room or I'll leave!'

Duncan said, calmly, 'Why can't you both stay?' His brown eyes glistened, the thin moustache turned up at each end as he smiled.

Vicky slowly nodded, saying, 'Yes. Why can't we both stay?' She did not like the idea but would consent to it if Duncan wanted Brownie here.

Backing toward the door, Brownie nervously protested, 'Miss Vicky, Mam. We must go back to school. Miss Ronny, she says . . .'

'Shit on Miss Ronny! Shit, shit, shit on Miss Ronny Pet!'

Brownie lowered her frizzy head. She did not like to hear Vicky use such foul words. But she did use them. Frequently.

'And shit on you, too, Brownie, for being such a pest. Duncan and me were just beginning to have fun.' She looked lovingly at him. 'Weren't we, Duncan?'

Duncan Webb did not answer. He was studying Brownie's trim body between the opening of her cape. He was forming an idea for another nocturnal amusement. He ran one hand through his long black hair and began to nod his head.

Vicky knew his thoughts by the way in which he appraised Brownie. She said, 'You wouldn't dare?' It was a new game. She stifled a giggle. A hiccup.

'She *is* pretty,' he said.

'Of course, she's pretty,' Vicky said, moving toward Brownie. 'We only have pretty niggers on Dragonard Hill, don't we, Brownie? And you let them all screw you silly back home, Brownie, don't you? You're a real old . . . whore!' Vicky laughed at the idea, laughter interrupted by another loud hiccup.

Brownie nervously reached for the white collar on her uniform.

Duncan moved closer to Brownie, saying, 'I never tried a black woman before.

Vicky cocked her head. 'And you want her now? Right now?' She was thinking about herself and the stranger whom Duncan would introduce to her.

'Why not? She's your maid.' He bowed, flourishing his arm.

Vicky had consumed more than a half bottle of champagne. She dropped her glass to the floor and, lunging for Brownie, she shrieked, 'Then take her! Take her if that's what you want. See if I care.' Vicky's voice was suddenly hard and brittle.

Brownie struggled, waving her small hands in fear of Vicky's temper. But Duncan saw how he could stop Brownie's struggling. It was simple. He hit her across the face. Brownie fell to the floor.

Standing over the sobbing girl, Vicky murmured to Duncan, 'You play rough, you bastard.'

'Of course,' he said, knowing that Vicky would like him to be even rougher with her at times. But he was the master of his own evilness.

'Do you want to take her here? On the carpet?' she demanded.

'Are you jealous?' he asked, mockery in his voice.

'I'll show you how jealous I am,' Vicky said, bending to lift the skirt of Brownie's blue uniform.

'That won't be necessary,' Duncan said, intervening to lift Brownie and carry her to a chaise lounge which set in an alcove.

Brownie was too frightened now to fight. And as Duncan laid her down on the plush chaise, unhooked the clasp on her cape and tore open her smock, Brownie squeezed her eyes shut, begging for him to stop.

Duncan clamped a hand firmly over her mouth, saying, 'If you bite me, I'll bite you right back.'

Then, the action was quick, a rough movement to pull down Brownie's drawers. Next, Duncan shed the remainder of his own clothes and, as he held Brownie in control with one hand, he mounted her struggling body.

Vicky stood a few yards away, quietly surveying the scene, watching her lover lying astride her maid. Vicky's small face was set with both anger and determination. She was rising to Duncan's taunt. She did love him. It was a passion. She adulated his body. And rather than to admit jealousy, she went along with this, yet one more of their games.

To add to Duncan's amusement, Vicky picked up his champagne glass from a book shelf and walked to the chaise. Standing over the couple, she trickled champagne from the glass onto Brownie's small breasts.

Licking it from between Brownie's cleavage, Duncan shouted, 'More . . .'

Emptying the glass on Brownie, Vicky then stood back to watch them, looking less at Brownie than she did at Duncan. She admired the way in which he handled the black girl. His strength, the manner in which he seduced women excited Vicky.

She now imagined that Duncan was licking the bubbly wine from her breasts, nibbling her nipples, dragging his erect phallus down between her legs and up her locked thighs. Vicky was imagining that she was Brownie. Protesting against Duncan. Frightened of being raped. Of course, that was not possible. Duncan would not ever let Vicky play that game with him. He knew better. He knew Vicky was too ripe, far too eager to play virgin. Duncan always told Vicky what he wanted and she would obey. She would do anything for Duncan Webb. And she planned to keep doing so. She would not be leaving him in Boston tomorrow. She would not do what her sister intended her to do. Vicky had her own plans for the future. Her life would be much different than it had been in the past. Even with Duncan. She already envisioned how he would mistreat her more harshly in their love-making.

*   *   *

Vicky was fifteen years old the spring that Carter Birgadot came to Dragonard Hill. Birgadot was a trunk pedlar, a travelling salesman who trudged through the Louisiana wilderness with his wares in a large wooden trunk.

The trunk pedlars usually visited the Southern plantations in early springtime, appearing in the driveways, riding their scrawny mules or swaying-back horses, even carrying the trunks on their back like Carter Birgadot. Trunk pedlars brought bits of news from other parts of the world, carried gossip from plantation to plantation, words about the crops, marriages, and lynchings.

It was the custom for trunk pedlars to go around to the back door of a manor house, to be invited into the kitchen or chased away with a broom by the black cook.

But Carter Birgadot traipsed bravely up the front steps of the big house at Dragonard Hill and, dropping his trunk down onto the porch, he began beating the dust from his faded clothes with his grimy felt hat.

Nearby, Vicky sat motionless on a porch swing. She had been brushing her hair, watching the pedlar walk down the driveway. He had not been able to see her. She had been protected all the while by a leafy trellis of bougainvillaea.

Now she was in full view. The brush lay on her lap.

She called to the pedlar, 'You selling something pretty?'

Although he had not acknowledged Vicky's presence on the porch, the pedlar was not startled by the sound of her voice. He continued to beat away the dust from his trousers, answering casually, 'I got a few nice things. Is your mama abouts?'

'I don't have a mother.'

'Oh,' he said, then asking, 'Your pappy?'

She said, 'My father is in the fields.'

Stopping, estimating the size of the house, he said, 'Then your mammy must be hereabouts.' He knew all rich southern girls had a black woman who took care of them, guarding white children like a hen, would most likely be inside the doorway at this very moment.

Vicky said, 'I only got Imogen. She's my big sister. But she's with Veronica. She's my other sister. They're having a picnic in the meadow.'

'Don't tell me you're all alone. No mammy? No cook?'

'We got Storky and Posey Boy. But they're probably scrapping with each other out back.'

He nodded.

She asked, 'And why shouldn't I be alone?'

He shook his head. 'No reason.'

'What you got to sell me?'

'Don't have much for little girls. Just special things for wives. And for young ladies big enough to be betrothed.'

'I have plenty of beaux asking for my hand,' she lied.

The pedlar looked cautiously around him. The house looked deserted. He heard no noise. He saw no black servants in the yard. No buggies. He heard no voices or singing from the fields. And the young blonde girl appeared to be very sure of herself. Mature in many ways.

Looking down at the rough porch flooring, he said, 'These boards look mighty far apart. Valuable objects could fall through these cracks. Then I'd lose them. Gold trinkets.

72

Jewelled earbobs. Pearl necklaces. Shell combs for your hair.'

'You got all that?' she asked eagerly.

He shrugged, setting the hat back on his head. He was a lean, swarthy man with bright hazel eyes. He was not old but his quick eyes told that he had seen a lot of the world, a world outside Dragonard Hill that Vicky longed to know. Also, there was something familiar about his face, reminding Vicky of someone whom she could not place.

Standing quickly up from the swing, Vicky said, 'Bring your trunk inside with me.'

He looked around him, seeing a small gardenia clump in front of the steps. The house might be empty but he did not trust houses. He said, 'Nice grounds you have here.'

Cocking her head, Vicky said, 'You'd rather stay outside, wouldn't you?'

'Always partial to outdoors.'

Vicky led the pedlar down the steps, toward the gardenia bush. She sat down on the ground and, spreading her blue-checked calico skirt around her, she ordered, 'Now show me what you've got in the trunk.'

Squinting one eye, the pedlar glared up at the sky. 'The sun's hotter than it looks today, ain't it?'

Vicky understood. And taking a deep breath, she irritably moved under the branch of an oak, a spot that was shady. But this new location was also behind the gardenia clump, out of view from both the big house and the driveway. They could not be seen here.

The pedlar was at last satisfied. He set down his trunk on the grass and began to unbuckle the brown belts around it. Next, he took a key on a dirty white cord from around his neck and turned it in both locks.

Vicky was very excited now to see what he had. This was the first time that a pedlar had shown his wares solely to her. Imogen and Storky and Posey were not crowding to get a look. Vicky enjoyed the importance of the situation. It made her feel adult, independent from the rest of her family. That was what she wanted.

But, as soon as the pedlar opened the wooden trunk, he quickly shut the lid again.

Vicky looked quizzically at him. She asked, 'Why'd you do that?'

'I'm a trader.'

Her face was blank.

Sitting down beside her on the grass, he explained, 'I trade you something. You trade me something.'

'I don't have nothing to trade.' She reached for her gold locket. 'Except this. Do you want this?'

He shook his head. 'Shiny. Pretty. But no good to me.'

'I don't have any money. I'd have to get that from Father.'

'You don't always need money, you know.' His voice had lowered.

Their eyes met.

The silence between them added to Vicky's feeling of being adult. She knew that this was no school game she was playing. Neither was it a typical barter.

The pedlar held his eyes on Vicky, studying her long blonde hair, how soft the skin was on her bare neck, the way in which the cotton dress rounded over her breasts. He nodded his head.

Vicky did not jump when he felt his hand on her leg. Nor did she budge when she felt the hand work under her skirt.

She said, 'You are very bold.' Her voice was touched with a precocious flirtation.

He kept nodding his head, saying, 'I think you want me to be bold.'

'What's that supposed to mean?' There was a slight catch to her words now.

The pedlar smiled, working his hands under her skirt, up her smooth leg.

Vicky liked the feeling of a man's hand. It was light and ticklish, very exciting for her, much better than having a picnic in the meadow with her sisters. She felt very grown-up.

The pedlar ordered, 'Look at me.'

She obediently raised her eyes to his face.

He asked, 'Why are you breathing so hard? See. You're all excited.' He nodded at her two fully matured breasts.

Vicky lowered her head to look down at her breasts, too.

'Ummm.' The pedlar continued, 'You're nice and warm here.' He wiggled his fingers between her thighs.

'Don't,' she whispered, trying to brush away his hand now.'

'No need to get worried,' he assured her.

Vicky felt her heart beating wildly.

The pedlar whispered, 'Feel *me* now.'

She did not understand.

He repeated, 'Feel me.' He nodded to his crotch.

Vicky did not move. She did not want him to see her hand shaking. She did not want him to know she was really only a child. Had not done anything like this before.

Gently taking her hand, the pedlar put it on his trousers and, lying on the ground, he pulled Vicky beside him. He had lifted her skirts as he moved, prodding his hand deeper into her thighs for a touch of warm moisture. He found it.

Vicky's hand lay motionless on his crotch. She felt his pants moving, something throbbing against her hand. She knew what it was. But she did not move her fingers, even when he urged her. She only began to follow his urgings when he toyed with her underclothing, probed the lips of her vagina through the thin cotton.

The pedlar's movements then became stronger, pulling Vicky closer to him on the ground. Soon, he was free from his cumbersome trouser and Vicky's skirt was around her waist. She freed her own legs from her underclothes.

She did not fight him. She waited, lying on her back and trying to glance down at the man's phallus. She did not want to stare but she wanted to see it. To see more of it. She saw a large purplish head and cords that made it look strong. She thought of a horse and became more excited. She liked the feeling of a horse between her legs.

Soon, he had rolled over on top of Vicky and she felt him

75

pressing between her thighs. She opened for him. But he was as excited as she was. He was quivering. He still was not in her. She liked the touch of skin against her legs. He smelled of old perspiration, but it was not offensive to her. The smell excited her, too.

Then, suddenly, she felt a warm explosion against her upper thigh and it spilled over her brown patch.

The pedlar cursed under his breath. He froze. Then he rolled back onto the ground beside Vicky.

She still lay on her back, her legs opened; her breathing, very heavy. She was still waiting for something to happen to her.

But the man was sitting now, mopping himself with a red rag he had taken from his pocket, looking quickly around him.

Vicky finally looked down at herself and saw a thick, white puddle on her leg and her brown patch. She realized that this was all that was going to happen. The man was going to give her no more than the thick white puddle. Something had gone wrong. She suddenly hated him. He had cheated her. She felt betrayed.

Smoothing his hair, the pedlar scooted toward the trunk, reaching for the brown leather straps. He had lost his calm manner.

It was then that Vicky began to scream, putting her hands across her eyes, shouting for help.

The pedlar became frightened, trying to calm Vicky, assuring her that she had not been raped.

But Vicky would not stop calling for help; finally, the pedlar jumped to his feet and ran through the gardenia bush toward the road.

Storky was the first to find Vicky. Then Posey. Vicky was still lying on the ground. She did not explain to them what had happened. When they saw her lying there, screaming, they quickly guessed the worst.

Nor did Vicky correct their supposition. She let them think that the worst had happened to her. Storky sent Posey to bring Peter Abdee from the fields. And when he came, he saw the wooden trunk with the name 'Carter Birgadot' carved onto the top.

Peter Abdee took his daughter to Doctor Babcock in Troy. He also contacted the sheriff in town. A road block was set up for a trunk pedlar named Carter Birgadot. But he was never caught.

After examining Vicky, Doctor Babcock said that there was no sign of rape. The hymen was still intact. The doctor assured Peter that the trunk pedlar had been frightened away in the nick of time by young Vicky's screaming.

Vicky soberly nodded, agreeing that – yes – she had frightened him away, had screamed before the familiar-looking stranger had had a chance to do something bad to her. She did not say that she screamed in hatred for the man, detesting the stranger for not carrying out his advances, wanting the stranger to stay with her until she learned about a woman's excitement, for the true badness to begin.

*   *   *

Vicky felt that same empty feeling now.

Tonight, riding in a carriage back to the Pemberton School, Brownie sobbed beside Vicky in the carriage whilst Vicky leaned in depression against the window shade. Duncan had mounted Brownie but Vicky had come away without anything, and that same empty, untouched feeling which she had first known three years ago now returned to her.

The trunk pedlar had not raped Vicky. He had exploded before he had penetrated her. Since then, she had learned to call those white puddles by many names. Duncan had taught them to her in the games they played about the stranger coming to see her and other secrets they shared.

But, tonight, Duncan had not seduced Vicky. He had taken Brownie. Duncan Webb satisfied Vicky frequently but, on occasions like tonight, when he did not make love to Vicky, she felt the same hungry feeling that had ripped through her body on that afternoon when she had been left waiting on the ground at Dragonard Hill.

And that was why Vicky was not leaving Boston without Duncan Webb. She had developed an appetite for what Duncan could do to her and make her do to him. She would not exist without those times spent together. Not here. Not at home. She was taking him with her to the South. Duncan understood Vicky more than anyone else. He sometimes told her that she was bad and she enjoyed those words and taunts as much as she enjoyed their games. But she waited until even he could know her better and learn how much she really needed from a stranger.

Chapter Four

A STRAW PHARAOH

Church services on Dragonard Hill were held every Sunday in Town; a small board chapel stood at the intersection of the two long rows of stilted houses. The chapel – unlike the houses – sat on the earth, its dirt floor covered with fresh cedar boughs every Sunday, filling the high-peaked room with a rich scent and also making an appropriate setting for the slave's favourite hymn, *There Will Be A Green Hill Tomorrow*.

The overseer, Nero, stood behind a small pine table this Sunday morning, leading the black people in the song. Nero often explained to his congregation that the words of the hymn referred to a Heavenly reward. But the old negroes, the slaves who had been brought across the sea in shackles from Africa, or those men and women who had heard stories about their distant place of origin, still believed that the hymn referred to the lush, rolling hills of Africa and that there was hope of them returning home some day as free people.

More like a kind pastor to the black people of Dragonard Hill than an overseer, Nero was patient with them. His handsome face had matured kindly over the years, his hair was shaved short, beginning to form grey-and-black peppercorns on his strong skull. For Sunday services, Nero wore a loosely cut black tunic over his natural-coloured cotton shirt and baggy trousers. With his head thrown back now in song, the muscles of his neck stood out from his shiny brown skin, his arms waving to the people, urging them to sing louder and be rejoiceful on this day of rest.

Nero had found contentment on Dragonard Hill. He personally remembered the injustices done to his people by the Atlantic slave traders. He had been chained in a slaver himself. Had lived through the subterranean atrocities of a

Brazilian mine. Had endured the depravities inflicted upon a male 'Fancy' in a bordello when he was a handsome young man. Also, Nero had emerged alive from a slave insurrection on the West Indian island of St Kitts. He had seen the worst of slavery. But he also had seen the best. He knew that the enslaved black men and women of Dragonard Hill were lucky to have Peter Abdee for a master. There were far worse white men, some in this very neighbourhood, and slaves who lived in more cruel and inhumane conditions than Dragonard Hill. Nero often preached about the futility of insurrection. He had seen too many deaths, too many severed heads planted on stakes along the road, too many black people's stomachs ripped open with a machete and their intestines spilling out onto the ground. Too many black people thrown alive onto roaring fires.

This morning after the first singing of *Green Hill*, Nero delivered a sermon about false prophets, men who were not what people believed them to be. Basing his almost childlike story on Biblical tales, Nero again dressed up the facts to make it more interesting – more understandable – for his congregation.

Nero spoke this Sunday morning about a straw pharaoh, a weak man put on the throne of ancient Egypt and used like a doll by the cruel men who actually ruled the land. Nero first paced along one side of the chapel as he spoke, then went to the wide doorway and the open windows along both sides – the louvers propped high for the services – and he called out to the majority of black people who crowded the dirt yard to hear his sermon. These were the fieldhands, the labourers, the workers from the many plantation industries who had no rank in the slave hierarchy which warranted a seat on the wooden benches inside the chapel.

Peter Abdee, Imogen, Posey, and Lady Alice sat on the first bench in the chapel. There were two empty places for the twins, Veronica and Vicky. Behind them sat Belladonna; the maids, Eulalia and Ori; Boxo, the groom, and the houseboy who helped Peter with the ledgers, Royal. And one place was reserved there for Brownie. Next came the black men and women who were the foremen and matrons of the Looming House, the Barns, the dairy, the work stables, the blacksmithy, the leather works. The women wore bright kerchiefs around their heads, or straw hats decorated with flowers picked especially for the services. The men were dressed in clean white broadweave shirts, many wearing chains of long and tightly-plaited grass around their necks, a treasured shell or a pine cone pendant dangling over their chests.

The point that Nero was trying to make in his sermon this morning was for the slaves not to listen to trouble-makers. Abolitionists were coming down from the North, spreading tales of freedom. Nero warned the black people that there was more to freedom than a promise. He told them that free people had to have jobs to buy food, to provide shelter, to have pride. He reminded them of the pride they enjoyed here. He told them to think of the misery and shame of many white people who lived around Dragonard Hill in the mountains. They were free. But they were trash who never washed their clothes, did not have the energy to cultivate a garden, could not even go to church on Sundays. The black people looked down upon the poor whites, compared them to their rich white masters and found them despicable. The black people associated themselves with their white masters and felt proud. They even assumed their owners' names, or the name of the plantation, as their surnames.

Peter Abdee sat on the front bench with his head lowered, listening to Nero's dramatic rhetoric, surprised as usual to hear the quiet-mannered man become so animated when addressing his people. Nero always discussed the words of the sermon with Peter before he delivered it on Sunday. And listening now to him, Peter thought back to earlier words that Nero had spoken. Stories that Nero had told Peter shortly after he had bought him in a New Orleans slave market.

Peter knew that Nero still suffered from the past. He had been in love long ago with a young black girl when he had lived in the West Indies. But after seeing her killed in a slave uprising there, he could not love anyone again. Nero was not the kind of man who could make love indiscriminately.

Since his youth in the West Indies, too, Nero had hoped for a day when white and black people could live side-by-side. And Peter wondered now as he sat in the chapel, listening to Nero's sermon, if his overseer truly believed that life here at Dragonard Hill was coming close to that goal. Peter could not accept that. There were still many changes yet to come for the black people who had been taken away in chains from their homeland. Peter Abdee was no fool. How could he call a black person his friend and still think that he was content living the life as a slave?

But Peter felt some reassurance that the words of Nero's sermon were true. Sundays here on Dragonard Hill allowed the black people more free time for themselves than enjoyed by the poor whites. A work week here was not drudgery and, on Sundays, they cleaned their houses after church, visited with their neighbours, talked together in the communal garden where they grew their own vegetables, or they went fishing, planted rabbit snares, sewed and embroidered on a set of good clothes. Also, on Sunday night, the black people had a barbecue in Town, roasting the pigs that Peter sent to them from the plantation swineyard. Slavery was nothing to rejoice about but Peter Abdee tried to give his people as many opportunities as possible for some cheer, however small. He did not know what else to do. Nor how to do it. Peter Abdee was no politician, no doctor of social wrongs.

The black people formed a huge circle around the entrance of the chapel every Sunday after the services, waiting to greet Peter when he emerged with Imogen on his arm. Sundays were the one occasion on which Peter wore a glistening white suit. He knew the people like to see him finely dressed. It reflected their own importance.

Imogen Abdee, however, always received a cooler reception than her father. The black people nodded dutifully to Miss Imogen. But no one groped for her hand, nor greeted her with wide and happy smiles.

She cared little, though, about what the black people thought about her. She wanted a different respect from the slaves than her father. Although Peter Abdee still had not heard about the whipping in the stable, the black people all knew about it and they pulled away from Imogen this morning as she haughtily preceeded her father through the crowd. Showing them that she was not frightened by their great numbers, that her attitudes toward discipline were still the same, Imogen slapped the fringes of her shawl against her arm as she passed through them, whipping the shawl and staring at the black people with narrow, hateful eyes. The black people understood.

Imogen continued to walk away from the chapel alone; Peter lingered to speak to a group of men.

Posey prodded Belladonna at the edge of the path to the old house, telling her not to gape at Miss Imogen. Then they continued toward the old house, taking news of the Sunday service back to Storky, repeating the content of Nero's service, telling her who had sat where this Sunday. Storky's infirmity prevented her from attending the chapel these days.

Now catching up with Imogen, Peter asked, 'Why are you in such a bad mood?' He was happy. He always liked seeing the people together, looking healthy, showing affection toward him.

Imogen grumbled, '*He* should talk about straw pharaohs.'

'Nero?' Peter asked. 'Don't be so critical. Not on Sunday at least.'

'Who's he to talk about people made of straw? Men not doing their job?'

'You're still not complaining about Nero being overseer, are you?'

'Why not?'

Peter shook his head. 'You're always so glum, Imogen. Try to think of some good things for a change.' He did not want to defend himself this morning of all mornings.

'Like what?'

Peter thought. 'Your sisters.' He had to broach the subject, anyway. They would be home in a few days.

Imogen did not answer.

Peter asked, 'How would you like to have a party for them? A welcome home party? Get something exciting going?'

She made a face. 'We won't be moved into the new house yet.'

'But what's the matter with the old house? We'll have a party there!' He liked the idea. He had not had friends around for – how long? – years.

'A waste of time, parties.'

'They are, are they? Well, what about tonight? Do you call tonight a waste of time?'

She kept walking. 'Kate Breslin?' she asked, remembering that Kate and her nephew had been invited for Sunday supper.

Peter was thinking now. He suddenly said, 'You know Barry Breslin is quite interested in you, Imogen.' He had now decided to tease Imogen, to see if that would brighten her mood. At least change it.

She wrinkled her lips. 'What does that have to do with what I'm talking about?'

'Fine. Nag and complain about your sisters. Moan and whine over Nero. But tell me this. What actually are you doing about any of those problems?'

She looked at him. 'What do you mean?'

'You get married, girl, and then your husband can have a say in the plantation. How about that?'

'My . . . *husband?*'

Peter's eyes were dancing. He thought that the only way to deal with his sour daughter – without fighting with her – was to tease her. He resumed walking, saying, 'But then you don't like Barry Breslin, do you? Although, I've heard from a very good source that he's quite sweet on you.' He knew that Kate would not mind if he lied on her behalf. She, in fact, would be relieved to get Barry out of the house, although Peter could not imagine the dull bog going courting. He did nothing but sleep.

Imogen ignored the report of Barry Breslin's affections

toward her. She asked instead, 'You mean you'd let *him* help run Dragonard Hill? That wet fish?'

'He'd be your husband. He might even inherit it . . . as your husband. Like I did from your Grandad.'

'You'd let a ninny like Barry Breslin have a say *here*?' She looked around her at the flowering trees, the climbing fields, the lush woodlands.

'You'd have to help him if he's such a "ninny", wouldn't you?' Peter was enjoying this.

But Imogen thought. She pondered very seriously what her father was saying. She knew he was saying it flippantly. But it was the germ of an idea. A start. And she liked the idea very much. She would not let her father easily forget it. Tonight was the first social supper which she had ever anticipated.

* * *

So if she married Barry Breslin she would inherit Dragonard Hill! Be jointly responsible for the management! Imogen thought about the idea all afternoon and, during supper that night, she ignored her father's and Kate's chatter and kept thinking about herself and Barry. But she tried not to stare across the table at him. She did not want to frighten him. Anyway, not quite yet.

Overseer? It was not a noble job, she knew. Most white people looked down on it. So-called 'aristocratic' white people. Nevertheless, Imogen held it in esteem. So did her father. An overseer was in a direct line of power under the planter himself. Sometimes an overseer often knew more about a plantation than did a planter.

Power. Knowledge. Direct contact with the work. That was what Imogen wanted. And that was what Peter Abdee was willing to give his future son-in-law. There would be talk in the neighbourhood, of course, about Peter Abdee giving a job that he had once bestowed upon Nero – a nigger! – to his own white son-in-law. But Peter Abdee had no concern for gossip. And for that trait of her father's, Imogen was grateful. In ways, they were very much alike.

The twins coming home from Boston. The harvest. Progress on the new house. Those were the three topics of conversation at supper. Pretending to listen, even straining herself to show interest, Imogen stole glances across the table to look at Barry Breslin, whenever she knew that he would not notice her.

Barry had a pleasant but long face. He was certainly not handsome. Tall and sandy-haired, he had soft brown eyes but – as Imogen quickly studied him – she saw how his eyebrows grew in a continuous line across his forehead. Also, his ears were very large. But physical imperfection mattered little to her.

As usual, Barry Breslin was nervous and self-conscious in company. Imogen waited for him to knock over his tumbler of milk when Peter discussed the crops at Greenleaf with him.

Kate Breslin, too, took part in the trivial exchange of plantation talk. Imogen did not mind that. Kate Breslin impressed her more than most females but she felt that Kate spent too much time worrying about feminine things. Clothes. Furniture. China. Recipes. Kate Breslin had lost her husband seven years ago and Imogen guessed that that was how she now filled her days – fussing over dress patterns and puddings.

But Kate was not Imogen's concern tonight. Silently, she sat imagining what Barry would be like as a husband. Imogen had never considered marriage before. Like cotillions, matrimony seemed to be an institution for other girls. But if marrying a man meant that she could have a more active voice in running Dragonard Hill, she would certainly do it. Why had she not thought of it before?

Imogen knew that she could handle Barry. He would not be a difficult husband. She noticed how he always looked to his aunt for any help with questions. Kate kept nodding her head at Barry, urging him to say exactly what he felt. Imogen saw herself in Kate's place. She stifled a grin. The ninny, she thought. It was the first time that she felt like smiling in weeks.

Again, she reflected about particulars.

The institution of marriage meant joint ownership of property. There were further implications for husband and wife, such as love-making and raising a family. But Imogen preferred to concentrate now on the legality of such a union. What it would do for her status as a female. As a daughter. Only a son could inherit Dragonard Hill. Be a true heir. So, there was only one choice open to her. Marriage. To bring a son-in-law into the Abdee family. And it was obvious that her father did not detest this boy, that he would oppose this match. Did not he suggest it?

Also, Imogen did not have that much time. The twins were coming home from school soon. And what if one or even both of them were to marry? What if Veronica or Vicky presented Peter with a son-in-law, a husband of their own? Imogen realized that she would be left without a say about anything.

When supper was completed, Peter asked Kate if she cared for a stroll before coffee. A silly custom, Imogen thought.

Barry bashfully followed suit, asking Imogen to walk alongside him behind Kate and Peter. The words were barely out of his mouth when Kate declined Peter's offer, saying that she had walked too much today.

They are both in on this together, Imogen thought. They want to get Barry and me alone but silly Barry does not suspect a thing.

Before Barry had time to recall his invitation, Imogen quickly accepted the offer for a stroll. Barry's toe-shaped head turned scarlet, more red than his aunt's home-curled hair, Imogen thought.

*   *   *

Imogen played the game, the grown-up's pastime of chit-chatting about current events. But she waited until she and Barry had reached the bottom of the front steps of the old house, deep into the cool evening, and then she suddenly began discussing the building of the new house. She said that she thought too much fuss was being made about one home. She asked Barry to tell her about Greenleaf. Even his childhood in Charleston.

Once Barry began talking, he quickly went from one subject to another. Imogen realized that, obviously, no one had ever asked him about himself before. He talked and talked. About how his parents had both died of influenza in '19. How he had come to live with his aunt and uncle here. How then his uncle had died.

Listening to him, Imogen sensed that he was very nervous about being alone with a female. That he talked so rapidly – so matter-of-factly – to keep her distracted. He was frightened that she might attack him.

How right you are, she thought.

They had reached the public road at the end of the driveway and, now, by the pole gates, they turned to stroll back to the old house, the lights flickering in the distance. Imogen insisted on walking on soft grass beyond the oak trees. Barry was explaining cities to her.

Stopping, Imogen turned to him and asked abruptly, 'Barry, are you attracted to me?'

She could see that the question hit him like a skillet on top of the head. He stared at her.

Imogen narrowed her eyes, asking slyly, 'Or do you already have a sweetheart?' She had taken special pains with her dressing, tonight. She had even tied a white ribbon around her slim neck. And had made certain that all the dirt was gone from her fingernails.

Barry shook his head. He barely looked sixteen, a gangly youth who would rather be having a midnight swim in a fish pond. Imogen would certainly never guess that he was twenty-two.

Continuing her brazenness, she asked, 'Do you *want* a sweetheart?' It was so easy with Barry Breslin. He was pliable like pitch gum left in the hot sun.

His eyes widened.

Now Imogen could not stop. She asked, 'Do you have a bed wench at Greenleaf?'

Barry stiffly shook his head, obviously horrified that a white female should ask him such a question. Imogen suspected that his pockets were filled with bits of string, marbles, and probably even a frog. That he would expect her to ask him about lead soldiers rather than bed wenches.

She persisted, 'Do you like Dragonard Hill?'

He began to speak, opening his mouth.

But Imogen would not let him answer her. She wanted to make her position perfectly clear. She said, 'You know, Barry, I have no brothers.'

Bewilderment.

'Also, Father is very, very fond of you, you know.' She reached for his hand, which was large and rough like the paw of a big dog. She knew that her father had lied to her this morning. Barry had not shown an interest in her. Not at all. But two could play the game.

Barry was beginning to quake at her advances.

A sudden repulsion over his weakness seized Imogen. But it also strengthened her suspicions. She *could* control this jelly-baby. She *could* make him marry her. He had no resistance to a strong character like hers.

Marriage. Man and wife. A union. Yes. She had to show this numbskull that such an arrangement between them was possible. But she had so little time. The twins would be coming home soon. She had to act tonight.

She said firmly, 'Kiss me, Barry.'

Staring down at her, he lowered his watery eyes to study her lips. And, as Imogen brought her small face up to his, he extended his mouth to hers – but with his eyes still wide open, looking at her like a barn owl.

Imogen had never kissed anyone before, not a male, not on the lips. She felt the oral contact with Barry Breslin to be cold and wet. It was not what she had considered romance to be like at all. But who was looking for romance? Imogen

Abdee? Hell, no! she thought. I want land. Property. My own say.

Pressing her body closer to his, she flung her arms wildly around his waist. She knew to what goal she was working, too. She knew the equipment of a man. He would not be much different from an animal. Or a nigger. And, pressing against him, she finally felt a hardness forming in his breeches, goudging against her stomach.

Her mind suddenly fluttered with the image of Hopper mounted upon Clara. The idea of being subservient to Barry in such a way repulsed her. But she was willing to sacrifice even that to convince this fool that they were a good match. That they could be married. That compatability was no question.

His kisses soon warmed. He kept kissing her. The kisses became more passionate. He reminded her of a dog lapping water. But his mouth tasted of milk. And his face smelled of lye soap.

Finally, Imogen thought that the kissing had gone far enough. It was time for her to lead him to the next stage.

Pulling away from his arms, she looked around them in the night. They were well beyond the avenue of oaks. She whispered, 'We're safe here.' She quickly began to unbutton the top of her dress.

Again, Barry was shocked.

Looking at him, she asked, 'What's the matter?' He certainly knew what followed, she hoped.

Shrugging his large shoulders, Barry faintly smiled, a nervous smile.

Nodding at his breeches, she bossed, 'Drop them.'

'Imogen?' Barry finally said. 'Miss Imogen?'

She was having difficulty unbuttoning the small pearls on her bodice. She did not answer.

He spoke again. 'Are you sure this is right, Miss Imogen?'

Without raising her head, she said, 'Pull down your pants.' Her voice was firm.

Reluctantly, Barry reached for the brass button on his waistband.

But then his hands dropped, his arms hung awkwardly at his sides. He said, 'Imogen, I don't think we should do this. Not here.' His voice was deep but soft and unsure of its own timbre.

Quickly reaching for the waistband herself, Imogen forced the breeches down to his thighs and said, 'There! Now do the rest yourself.' She was not going to have him ruin this. She had to show him that nothing was impossible. They would be married.

'I can't,' he stuttered.

'What do you mean, "you can't"?' She looked at him with frustration. She could see that his penis was already as firm as a broomstick in his underpants. Did he not know that half of the work was already done?

He stood motionless in front of her, his hands at his side, his underpants bulging with undeniable excitement. But he seemed unaware of its presence.

So, quickly grabbing him by the hand and dragging him down to the grass, Imogen lifted her skirts and moved closely to him.

His body became tense.

'What's the matter?' she repeated.

Lowering his head, he said, 'There's something I have to tell you, Imogen. But I can't. You being a lady . . .'

'I won't be shocked. Come on. Tell me what's troubling you, Barry.' She was trying to show some concern.

Hesitantly, Barry began, 'Do you know what . . . Do you know what . . .' The confidence was difficult to share. He began again. 'Do you know what testicles are, Imogen?'

She nodded.

'You do?' he asked.

'What about them?'

'Well, a man. Most men. They have two.'

'You don't have none?'

His face showed its first sign of indignation. 'Course I do! Hell, what do you think I am? Some kind of Cleopatra's eunuch?'

'Shhh. I'm sorry,' she said. 'I didn't mean to offend you."

He sniffed. 'I only have one. That's why I never been with no girl before. Not even no black wench.'

'Because you couldn't? Or because you're scared to? Ashamed to show yourself?' As always, Imogen had to know the specifics of the situation in order to solve it. And, as always, she had no time for talk. The bulge in his pants seemed to be sufficient to her.

'I'm scared, I guess,' he confessed. Nodding down to himself, he said, 'I get hard, you know. Get hard and able. But I guess I'm ashamed. Both. Scared and ashamed and ، . .'

'Well, there's nothing to be embarrassed *or* ashamed about. Not as long as you're . . . able, Barry. And a man don't screw with his balls, anyway. Why, I bet you're probably better than most men with two. And like you say, Barry, you're . . .'

Before Imogen could finish her words, Barry had thrown his arms around her, clutching her to his chest. She did not know if he was sobbing or preparing to rape her.

Bracing herself, Imogen soon realized that Barry Breslin just wanted to be held, to be assured that he was normal, to feel wanted.

She could assimilate all that. For the moment.

Comforting Barry on her shoulder, she began to speak softly to him, reassuring him that his deficiency did not matter to her, that they could be happy together whatever afflicted him. And all the time that she was consoling him, she toyed with his crotch, working his penis back into hardness, squeezing it through the cloth of his underpants and slowly easing the head of the penis through the vent.

Barry happily allowed her to proceed working on him with her hand, even being relieved that the loss of his virginity was being taken care of by somebody for him.

The bulk of Imogen's skirt proved difficult for her mobility, and she had to pull momentarily away from Barry to lower her drawers, and, then, after she yanked down his pants, pull him forward to her again.

Throughout the whole concern which she had for Barry's

92

performance, Imogen forgot about herself, not considering the loss of her own virginity. Chastity had little value to her.

The juices of excitement already dripped from Barry's taut penis, allowing him a natural lubrication. But when Imogen eased its blunt head toward the lips of her vagina – and Barry suddenly seized a new life, his penis suddenly ramming deep into the warmth he sensed – she felt a sharp pain cut through her body. She tensed herself now.

But Barry was lost in this new discovery. He became wild for the sensation for him. He did not notice Imogen's sudden agony. He lunged frantically in and out of her. And, gritting her teeth, digging her nails into his back, Imogen accepted his excited drives, suffering the wet kisses which covered her cheeks and neck and shoulders, waiting in anguish for the moment when he would burst his seed. She knew that that had to happen. Her common sense told her that she could gauge it by his gasping. Then she would stop him. Would push him quickly away from her.

Imogen Abdee did not want Barry Breslin's baby. She only wanted him, to give him to her father, saying 'Here he is. Here's my husband. Your son-in-law. Heir. Overseer. Straw Pharaoh. Now, Dragonard Hill can start to be mine!'

*   *   *

Dragonard Hill was the earth. Peter Abdee had urged his eldest daughter, Imogen, not to chastise the black people for having the urges to mate. This was the earth, he had told her. The people of Dragonard Hill worked that earth, being part of it.

The white people worked this land along with the blacks. The land was rich. It gave life. And on this warm Sunday night, the moon lit the fields and outlined the hills of this rich land that wasted little.

Near the old pole gates by the public road tonight, Barry Breslin soon exploded his seed onto the earth, a thick fountain that spurted in strong shots, not a waste but a baptism – Imogen believed – for her hold on this land.

The old house stood awkwardly at the far end of the drive. Peter Abdee and Kate waited in the front parlour for the sound of Imogen's and Barry's footsteps on the front porch. The longer they waited and heard nothing, the more they thought about their own lives. They often lived in this frustrated anticipation. The black slaves sleeping intertwined together in the tall-legged houses of Town enjoyed more freedom tonight than Peter and Kate. The upstairs bedroom was close to them yet Peter knew that he could not take Kate there, not now on this Sunday night as the old house sat idle in the midnight hush, the sickly vines trailing across the neglected trellis on the empty front porch.

Peter stood in front of Kate, obstructing her from the view of the parlour doors. She sat on the edge of a chair, anxiously working Peter's firm penis in her mouth, working him quickly, pulling for the sperm that would give no life to her nor prosterity for this land. But it would keep alive the understanding between them. He was the master of Dragonard Hill. She owned Greenleaf. They were responsible for other lives than their own.

But this was no subservient act of Kate to Peter. She knew it was reciprocal. She often saw him kneeling between her legs. He would later tonight if there were no footsteps to warn them. Now, he stroked her neck, caressed her shoulders, rubbed her breasts and fondled her nipples into tenseness. She swallowed him deeper into her throat as he prepared her for his excitement, so this would not be a lonely and selfish act. They were a union. An understanding. But both were alive again tonight with frustrations.

Beyond the old house, over the patch of pine trees, and beyond the green cotton fields, sat a small shed in a potato field.

Seven black people squatted against the wall in the small shed, watching a field hand pumping relentlessly into a male body beneath him.

94

The fieldhand's name was Ben, a brawny black man whose muscle was made hard from chopping cotton.

The young man was a servant from the big house. He was Royal, the boy who helped his Master Peter on the ledgers. He did not have Ben's brawniness but neither was he effete.

The onlookers watched as Ben's thighs slapped louder against the round buttocks of the nineteen-year-old boy. Both cheeks of the boy's buttocks were diagonally lined with a single razor cut, now healed into a wound like an African tribal mark. These were the cuts that had originally forced Royal into this group, the slashes which were made when the men had first seized him months ago near the old house. Royal was threatened with more, even lethal slashes if he told his master of this group of perverse men.

The naked audience in the hut held their maleness in their hands, fondling themselves, as they watched Ben trying to drive deeper into Royal's squeezed buttocks. They discussed in low voices how the new recruit to their group could become better, debating whether he could ever grow to enjoy this act.

Ben held back Royal's legs to his shoulders now, holding the boy on his back, kneeling higher onto his own knees, taking deeper plunges into the boy's anus, using cooking grease on his fat phallus. He did not want to rip a fine boy like Royal. But the passage was still very tight. And the boy muffled his screams.

The onlookers all coaxed Royal to relax his legs, urging him to enjoy this, to provide them with an erotic exhibition. These spectators were fieldhands themselves, like Ben; this was a gathering of negro men who met to beget no children. They had originated these meetings out of their own frustrations. The plantation birthing schedule harmed their normal appetites. Their taste for buggery had grown and became a regular outlet for them, a way to unleash their energies. They were not allowed to mate with the female slaves for fear of siring more children on Dragonard Hill and now they did not want a female.

Also, these particular men's tastes were not for boys who

looked for such encounters; instead, they chose muscular young men who wanted to be with females. This added to the older men's pleasure, and they threatened them into their ranks and kept them there with sharply honed blades, becoming masters themselves over these other true males.

The houseboy, Royal, stifled his screams, blocking out of his mind the thoughts that he would have tomorrow. Remembering how he was a slave's slave. A male used as a female by a fieldhand. But hoping that he would not come to enjoy this like his black masters.

And ten miles from Dragonard Hill was the small, quiet town of Troy. There, near the cotton gin, stood the shack of Jeb Conway.

Conway was asleep in his single bed. He and his wife had slept apart now for over ten years.

Unlike the houseboy, Royal, Noreen Conway was a female. But she had no male to give her pleasure. She had her husband but he haunted the plantations in the district, threatening the black women who loved their own men.

Tonight, Noreen Conway was not in her bed. It sat empty across the low-ceilinged room for her husband.

Outside in a shaft of moonlight, the frail body of Noreen Conway crouched in the corner of a lean-to built adjacent to the pens. The pens held Jeb Conway's dogs. He loved them more than he gave love to his wife.

Recently, one of the black dogs had whelped. As Noreen fed the dogs, so also did she raise the litters.

And, tonight, Noreen Conway sat in the dark corner of the lean-to, the shaft of moonlight illuminating her as she squeezed a small black pup between her bare legs, throwing her head back in both pleasure and shame as the animal's wet tongue anxiously licked at the warmth between her thighs, going deeper into her as she spread the lips of her vagina with her calloused fingers for the dog to nuzzle deeper. The animal's nose was damp, pushing into her, the movement of his tongue grew quicker and created a feeling in Noreen Conway that she could not get from her husband. A female release. But she felt the shame of it. The loss of any beauty from her face, her slim body was the least of her recent deprivations. The loss of her pride was the most painful.

The time was past midnight now. A blackness still hung over the Louisiana wilderness before a new day began. This was a backwoods country – spotted with ostentatious signs of civilization – but a country struggling for a decent life. The rich earth. The lives of its white and black people. The rich and the poor.

Chapter Five

'LOUISVILLE PRIDE'

The 'Louiseville Pride' churned in Northern waters, a white, red, and gold steamboat paddling down the Ohio River, passing now through the state of Ohio. She was destined for Cairo, Illinois, with stops at any landing with a flag out, to load on cord wood more than passengers; the 'Louisville Pride' was voracious, eating its way almost half-way across the country, leaving nothing behind but billows of white smoke, turbulent silver waters, and wide-eyed people standing among the willow trees on the bank, longing to join the jolly travellers on their way west, to sun and adventure, possibly even to join the Mississippi River at Cairo and head south for New Orleans.

The 'Louiseville Pride' was a small wheeler but looked as big as 'The Ohio' or 'The Cincinnati Lady'. Its bright decorations fooled the eye; she held very little cargo and was not overly capacious for travellers.

There was only one parlour for the holders of prime class tickets. The other passengers sat on wooden benches under a scalloped canopy in the stern. There were less than two dozen private sleeping rooms, one dining-room, and – of course – the games room, the reason that the 'Louisville Pride' was the most popular paddle-wheeler on the Ohio with sporting gentlemen, and those women who followed the gamblers, painted ladies who were not unlike the scavenger fowl who flapped their wings in the boat's wake, squawking and grappling with one another for survival.

Apart from Veronica and Brownie, the parlour was nearly deserted again this second afternoon. An old lady in a black poke bonnet sat with a crippled girl by a small table draped with maroon plush. Near them, an attractive young white lady conversed with a well-dressed black man with whom she was travelling.

Veronica guessed that the young lady was travelling with her husband's, or father's, manservant. She also noticed that, unlike yesterday, luggage sat at the couple's feet, light calfskin cases which they had not entrusted with the roustabouts. Veronica supposed that the young lady must be getting off here in Ohio, would not be joining the Mississippi boat that would take them to New Orleans.

But Veronica had more concern for Brownie than the other few passengers she saw in the parlour. This long trip was proving to be more exhausting for her than Veronica. She had not left Veronica's side since she had come back to the school with Vicky in Boston.

Brownie had been trembling that night, her round face more puffy than usual, with definite bruise marks on her tobacco-coloured skin. After Veronica had forced her to speak, she had broken down, telling everything that had happened at Duncan Webb's rooms, Vicky's taunts, the whole sordid seduction.

The story sickened Veronica. She was even too repelled by it to confront her sister that night. She could only leave the matter for the long journey home.

But then something more horrid transpired. The next morning, Duncan Webb appeared at the school when Veronica, Vicky and Brownie were leaving. Vicky announced that he was travelling with them. She had invited him. Veronica was not able to create a scene with Vicky in front of the Pemberton sisters, still fearing that it was not too late for the spinsters to write a letter to their father.

Peter Abdee had made preparations months ago for his daughters to come home by a different route than they had travelled North three years ago. He had wanted them to see the countryside, at least just a fleeting glance at places like Springfield, Scranton, Pittsburgh on their way to the headwaters of the Ohio. He had thought that their company would

99

keep the coach journey from being too arduous, to be very enjoyable for the young girls.

Duncan Webb had ruined that. He and Vicky had laughed gaily, drinking from a silver brandy flask that they refilled at each posthouse, ignoring Veronica's and Brownie's presence. When they passed through Pittsburgh, he said that he knew a very interesting lady who lived there. He did not elaborate. But Veronica did not care. She just wanted to know how far he was going with them. If Vicky was inviting him home to Dragonard Hill. But she doubted that. She could not imagine Vicky having that much gall.

Now on the 'Louisville Pride', Vicky and Duncan were in the games room, Vicky spending the second day beside Duncan at the faro table. Veronica could hear the voices of whores, gamblers, thieves – and her sister, probably covering the losses of Duncan Webb.

Veronica sat in the parlour of the smoothly gliding boat, turning the pages of her book. She stopped occasionally to ask Brownie how she felt, if she would like some mint tea. She knew the girl was still in shock. There was nothing she could do about that except fume with silent outrage.

Also, Veronica was angry at herself for not having had Brownie examined by a doctor in Boston. There had not been time, though. She wondered if Brownie was in extreme pain. Or worse, was she pregnant? Veronica promised herself that she would take Brownie to see Lady Alice as soon as they arrived at Dragonard Hill.

Then, remembering Lady Alice, Veronica was sorry that it took such a long time to reach the South. She thought about everything waiting for her at the end of the next river – or, very near the end of the Mississippi. She, Vicky, and Brownie would be disembarking at Singer's Landing, in Louisiana, where they would catch a coach to meet their father in Carterville. She still did not know where Duncan was going. Except, that is, to eventual damnation.

*   *   *

Veronica and Brownie returned to the parlour from supper, after eating alone again tonight, and they found the gas lamps already lit and the maroon curtains drawn.

Coming in through the gold tassles hanging in the archway, Veronica was surprised to see the young white lady sitting in the parlour and holding the hand of the black man with whom she was travelling. The young lady did not know she was being observed. Leaning forward, she kissed the negro on, first, one eye and, then, the other.

Veronica gasped.

The couple turned at the sound.

Pushing Brownie back out through the archway, Veronica awkwardly called, 'I'm terribly sorry.' She turned to leave.

But the woman smiled.

The negro rose, saying, 'We're very rude. We've been travelling with you and haven't introduced ourselves.' He spoke like no negro whom Veronica had ever met. He was well educated, expensively dressed and impeccably mannered. Veronica could not help noting, either, that he was very handsome, with a strong forehead, widely placed eyes, a straight nose, and square chin. His sideburns were neatly trimmed and his teeth sparkling white.

He continued, 'I'm Solomon Wendell. This is Mrs. Wendell . . . my wife.'

Veronica could not control the surprised expression on her face.

Seeing her reaction, Solomon Wendell asked, 'You're a Southerner, right?'

Veronica nodded, fumbling with her gloves. She said, 'I'm just going home. I've been at school. In Boston. With my sister.'

Brownie had sneaked back into the parlour, also eager to see this strangely matched couple. She had momentarily forgotten about her shock and sore limbs.

Solomon Wendell stared at Brownie with the same astonishment that Veronica had at his announcement that he was married to the white lady.

Immediately, Veronica realized that he thought that Brownie was the sister with whom she had been at school and she said, 'Oh, no! This is just Brownie! She's only my . . .'

Then, hearing what she was saying, recognizing how rude it must sound to a black person – and to the white lady who was married to him – Veronica's voice trailed off, she blushed, lowered her head, and began to fidget with her gloves.

'She's your maid,' the lady offered, continuing, 'But how nice you are to her. We've noticed that. Every day you're fussing over her, taking care of her as if she *were* your sister. You must be a very nice person.'

Veronica dipped her head. She confessed, 'Sometimes I don't know what I'd do without Brownie. We are close.'

'Where are you from?' the lady asked.

Veronica's hands flew to her mouth. 'Oh, I'm sorry! I didn't introduce myself. I'm Veronica Abdee. As you already know, this is Brownie. And my sister's name is Vicky. She's my twin sister. But if you haven't been in there –' She nodded toward the games room. 'You probably wouldn't have seen Vicky.' Veronica shrugged and tried to smile. She liked the couple.

'I don't gamble,' Solomon Wendell said in his husky voice, but with a touch of mockery to it.

'Anyway, not on a steamer with so many Southerners,' added his wife, smiling.

Veronica meekly nodded her head. She understood the reason. And, then, suddenly, there were a thousand questions she wanted to ask them. She had warmed instantly to them both. It was the first time that she had ever heard a black man speak so well, and the first time that she had seen a black man not only accompanying but also married to a white woman. And not some white trashy woman. But a beautiful young lady. A girl hardly older than herself. Veronica noticed her subdued blue sateen dress. The white European slippers she wore. The small straw bonnet and its modest veil. And a long strand of very expensive pearls with a diamond-and-pearl broach.

Veronica said, 'I feel it's my fault we haven't spoken before now. I must learn to be more forward.'

The blast of a horn shook the boat. Voices began to shout outside the parlour. The boat was slowing, veering, jerking.

Solomon Wendell stooped for the bags.

Rising, Mrs Maxwell said to Veronica, 'Don't blame yourself, Miss Abdee.' Then, extending her hand to her, she confided, 'I am sorry, too. I could tell by overhearing your voice that you were Southern. That stopped us from approaching you. You can understand, I'm sure.'

Veronica nodded her head quickly. She felt like such an immature girl compared to her. Then gripping her hand, she said, 'Mrs Wendell, *do* believe me when I say how happy I am to have met you. I don't know why, but –' She hesitated, for fear of saying too much.

Looking at her husband, Mrs Wendell said lightly, 'See! There is hope, Solomon.'

Taking his wife's arm, he said, 'But we better get off in Ohio for the time being. I don't want to chance my luck of being spirited onto a steamer headed South – not for a few years, anyway!'

They both shook hands with Veronica and Brownie, laughing, and then they were gone, leaving the 'Louisville Pride' for the lights flickering on the Ohio shore.

Veronica sank spellbound into a chair.

It was the first time on the entire journey that Brownie forgot about herself. She asked, 'Miss Ronny, you all right? You've come over all flushed, Miss Ronny.'

She had. Veronica knew that she had become flushed. The meeting had stunned her. Here, she had been thinking that the black man was the woman's father's, or her husband's, man servant. But, in actual fact, he was her husband.

That black man, that very handsome black man is that lady's . . . husband!

And I talked to them! Veronica thought. *I talked to them as if such a thing were . . . normal!*

Somehow, someway, for some reason, Veronica thought that

the encounter had made her mind suddenly a little bit larger. A small bit more, yes, knowledgeable.

Was that feeling wrong? Had she acted badly to have spoken to them? To give their relationship the stamp of her approval.

But that was absurd! Stuffy! They had both been perfectly charming to her, more charming than many white people. Why should she have not spoken to them? Stamp of approval! Rubbish!

Veronica suddenly reeled, then, with another thought. She realized that, if they were married, they – the pretty white lady, who was barely older than Veronica herself, and that handsome black man, who was one of the best looking men whom Veronica had ever seen – went to bed together. They made love. Those two bodies, that milky white girl and that rich-brown man lay together naked in the privacy of their home, probably wrapped together on silk sheets, kissing . . .

Not knowing why, Veronica's heart quickened and she felt frightened. She thought of the pale, awkward Northern boys who had tried to court her. She thought of her past anguish of believing that she might have to choose one of them for her husband. But, then, when she thought about that negro – what was his name? Solomon Wendell? – she became literally weak in the knees. Yes, she felt quite unable to stand up on her feet.

*   *   *

The yellow wooden spokes of the open carriage turned quickly, revolving like glittery pinwheels, the carriage cutting at a neat pace through the forest of water oaks dripping with moss. It was returning home to Dragonard Hill.

Peter Abdee held the reins to the pair of high-stepping white horses as he talked to Veronica, sitting beside him on the green tufted leather seat. She held an open white parasol over her shoulder and a straw bonnet hung around the back of her neck by its pink ribbon. She had unclasped her hair and the wind now blew it behind her like a silky mantle.

Brownie sat in the rear seat, looking excitedly to her left and right as the carriage travelled farther away from Carterville where it had met them.

Beside Brownie, Imogen turned in the seat to see if the work wagon was still following them. She and her father had driven to Carterville in the carriage this morning to meet Veronica and Vicky, bringing a wagon to transport the girls' three years' accumulation of luggage.

Imogen could no longer see the wagon behind them on the road. The carriage was too fast for the plodding draft horse, and it would probably not reach Dragonard Hill until much later tonight. Peter had foreseen that, though, and had written a pass for the driver, Boxo, for travelling alone on the public road after dark.

Smiling to herself, Imogen knew that, even if the trunks never arrived, they would have more serious problems at Dragonard Hill. If her father had admitted it or not to himself, the trouble had started less than an hour ago at the stage house at Carterville.

The stage had pulled into Carterville with a clatter of hooves and, when the dust settled, only one of the twins stepped down from the stage. Veronica. She was followed by Brownie. Vicky did not appear. Only Veronica had come home from Boston.

Now, riding in the rear seat of the open carriage, trying to piece together the real story, Imogen reviewed the facts that Veronica had babbled to them. Imogen knew her younger sister well enough to know that she was lying. Her story did not hold water. Why would Vicky go to New Orleans with an old school friend? Imogen knew that Vicky hated other females. Yes, the school friend was certainly a male. That made sense, Imogen thought, because she remembered Vicky as being no saint! She recalled the trouble with the trunk pedlar, a story she could not truly believe – Vicky being raped? Never. Not even at fifteen.

And why was Brownie so scarred and bruised? Neither could Imogen accept that story which Veronica had told them.

That Brownie had fallen down the stairs at school in excitement to come home. Nonsense! Girls – even black wenches – did not act in such a shocked state after a mere tumble down some dumb stairs. Imogen had noticed that Brownie was most decidedly jumpy. Nervous. She had nearly broken into tears when Veronica had mentioned Vicky's name. Imogen had even seen Veronica threaten to pinch Brownie, secretly posing her fingers at Brownie when she was near tears.

No, Imogen knew that Veronica was lying for some reason and she suspected that she was trying to cover-up for a man. A boy friend of Vicky's. Veronica was trying to spare her father some agony. Imogen remembered that Veronica had always been overly considerate of their father, dutifully obeying him, always being his pet.

But something else intrigued Imogen, too. Why was Veronica suddenly so interested in black people? Almost immediately after they had all become settled in the carriage, Veronica began asking her father about the black people on Dragonard Hill. She asked about niggers! Imogen wondered when that concern had started. Had three years in the North made her an Abolitionist!

Imogen could not tell yet if her father suspected anything about the Vicky situation. He allowed Veronica to babble on, obviously enjoying the hugs and little kisses which she flourished on him. But, at the same time, he had that slightly suspicious look on his face. Imogen knew that her father was nobody's fool.

But Imogen had to admit to herself that Veronica did seem genuinely excited to be going home. Veronica had not picked up any of the annoying Northern affectations that Imogen had suspected she would have. In fact, Veronica was not as simpering as Imogen had remembered her to be.

But then she had not remembered her younger sister to be a liar, either.

Imogen knew that she herself had changed, too, and not only in the last three years. The last mere week had seen a change in Imogen Abdee. She had discovered a way to gain

106

power at Dragonard Hill. She also had lost her virginity. But, more important, Imogen felt that she finally had lost her innocence. She finally knew exactly what she wanted and she knew how she was going to get it. The only problem now was to keep Barry Breslin away from Dragonard Hill for a while. He was anxious to announce their betrothal. But Imogen would not even let him approach her father or speak about it to his aunt. She had to get her bearings before she did anything drastic. And she wanted to know now more about Vicky. What if she did have a man? A serious relationship? A possible rival for control of Dragonard Hill?

The carriage turned now under the pole gates at the public road and entered the driveway. Imogen braced herself. She knew Veronica was about to begin on an onslaught of high emotions about returning home.

It was nearly dark now and, at the far end of the oak-lined avenue, figures dressed in white stood on the porch of the old house. They were the house servants waiting for the twins.

Soon it all started and Imogen tried to obliterate what she heard and saw. Veronica hugged Storky and Posey. Storky sat on the porch in her rattan chair, tears streaming down her withered brown cheeks. Veronica repeated the same stories to them about Vicky and Brownie that she had told her father. And, then, squeezing everybody again, she darted inside the double doors, disappearing upstairs to the top of the house to say hello to her old friend, Ta-Ta.

Quietly, everybody on the porch repeated amongst themselves how lady-like Veronica was looking, and purposely avoiding any talk about Vicky not coming home, nor drawing attention to Brownie's dark bruises.

Imogen began to lift the small pieces of hand baggage, bandboxes, and parcels, from the carriage. That much had not changed at Dragonard Hill. Somebody still had to do the work. The niggers weren't doing it, she noticed. So why not her?

*　　*　　*

New Orleans. And the carved doors to the bridal suite in the Hotel LaSalle sat open; the hotel manager moved from tall window to tall window, pulling apart the brocade draperies, letting the late afternoon sunlight flood onto the green carpet. At the same moment, an army of porters, dressed in green-and-yellow livery, carried luggage into the suite's sitting-room, on through the archway to the bedroom, and into the dressing-room which was fitted with tall ormolu mirrors and louvered wardrobes.

An orchestra played downstairs in the lobby, a syrupy waltz rising past the drooping fronds of the palm trees which fanned over the three balconies encircling the glass-domed court, and the music spilled through the open doors of the bridal suite.

Now, the hotel manager had finished opening the draperies. Three more negro servants arrived, bearing a silver bucket of champagne, a crystal vase with white roses, and blue Chinese bowl brimming with pears, oranges, grapes.

Bowing, handing the brass key to Duncan Webb, the hotel manager said that the champagne, the flowers and the fruit were gifts from the hotel to the newly-weds.

Clapping his hands sharply two times to call the porters from the dressing-room, the manager quickly surveyed the bridal suite one last time and, then, bowing again, he backed out through the double doors, closing them as he left, muffling the sound of the music playing below in the lobby.

Alone now with Duncan, Vicky threw her arms around him saying, 'Our honeymoon officially begins!' Then grabbing his hand, she led him towards the archway, standing in front of the wide bed swagged with white netting. The silver champagne tripod stood on one side of the bed, the roses rested on a tall table on the other.

Duncan was more concerned about the open windows, though. The temperature. He thought that the afternoon sun was still too strong to be pouring into the room. He also felt dusty. He looked for the bell cords which the manager had showed him, remembering which cord to pull for a bath. He went to the louvered doors of the wardrobes, anxious to see that the servants had unpacked the correct clothes. He called, 'I want a bath!'

Vicky still wore the yellow dress and feathered bonnet that she had worn at the brief marriage ceremony performed by the justice-of-the-peace. Pulling off the bonnet, she sank into a deep-cushioned chair and called 'Then we'll both have baths.'

Duncan ignored her. He came out from the dressing-room and passed through the voile panels to the veranda. He shouted, 'Do you think this hotel will be too noisy? Should we move?'

Vicky answered, 'Who cares if it's noisy!' She felt excited now. She was looking at the wedding ring on her finger. It was a plain gold band, not the elaborate diamond and emerald ring that she had wanted. But Duncan did not have any money at the moment and he refused to let her spend a fortune on her own wedding band. He said that he would buy her a suitable ring when he soon got some funds.

Caring little about the wedding ring, Vicky was fluttering with the adventure of getting married. Checking into the Hotel LaSalle as 'Mr and Mrs Duncan Webb, Boston'! Having this entire lavish suite to themselves! Vicky felt almost as if she had eloped.

Stopping, Vicky realized that she *had* eloped. No one knew that she was coming to New Orleans to marry Duncan. Veronica had not even suspected that. Her sister had thought that she and Darling Duncan were just coming to New Orleans to have more fun.

Well, we're going to have fun, Vicky thought, springing up from the chair to join her new husband out on the veranda.

Duncan was not on the veranda when Vicky looked for him there. Turning, coming back into the bedroom with a puzzled expression on her small face, Vicky found Duncan in the dressing-room, riffling through his clothes, digging for something fresh to wear.

He turned, dropped his black frock coat onto the floor, and slipped into a beige, lighter woollen coat. Turning back to the ormolu mirror, he asked, 'Is this too wrinkled?'

'No, Darling. But have it pressed anyway. While we're bathing.' She giggled at the kind of bath they would have — together. She would spill water, try to coax him to punish her.

Facing the mirror, Duncan shook his head at what he saw. Then shrugged. He bent to the floor and began to dig in a deep leather hat case. He mumbled to himself, 'Straw. Straw. I need something straw.' Taking a low-crowned, wide-brimmed felt hat from the case, he rose to his feet and studied himself in the mirror. He squared the hat on his forehead. He leaned forward to smooth his thin moustache. He turned his head sideways, eyeing his sideburns.

Darling Duncan looked handsome, of course, Vicky thought. But she was puzzled by his behaviour. He was ignoring her. This was their honeymoon. Their first time alone together as a married couple and he was acting as if his clothes were more important than she was.

He persisted in fussing about his appearance, digging now for silk squares, another pair of gloves, a different stud for his cravat. But, then, he always had been obsessed with incidentals. Accessories. The right touches.

Vicky finally could take no more, though. She forgot about his gentleman's philosophy for dressing. She demanded, 'What in hell are you doing this for? Now'?

'I'm going out.' His voice was clipped.

'Going out? Where?' She was beginning to see him now as he really was. Not as the dashing figure of a young groom. But how he sometimes could act. Selfish and conceited and spoiled.

Looking at her, Duncan said, 'I'm going out to see New Orleans. What else? I've never been here before.'

'Aren't you going to wait for me? What about our bath?'

Bending to kiss her lightly on the forehead, he said, 'You take your bath, Victoria. I'll have mine later.'

'Later? Victoria? Since when have you started calling me "Victoria"?'

He had walked from the dressing-room, crossing the bedroom, ignoring the wide, swagged bed.

Following him, Vicky asked, 'Duncan, what is the matter?' Her euphoria had passed.

Feeling the inside breast pocket of his coat, Duncan said, 'Money! I gave all mine to the judge.'

Vicky pointed to her velvet drawstring bag lying on the floor near the chair.

Digging into Vicky's small bag, Duncan withdrew a handful of bills. He stuffed them into his pocket and said, 'Don't worry. I won't get lost.'

'Lost? What about me? What do I do?'

'You're jealous, aren't you?' A smile crossed his lean, swarthy face.

'Why in hell should I be jealous? What are you going to do to make me jealous?'

He shrugged. 'Have time by myself. Not much else.' He smiled at her again. 'Unless something's offered to me.'

Vicky's face tightened. She realized now that he was going to use jealousy as a tool against her. His independence and her jealousy.

Shaking his head, Duncan said, 'Victoria, you must learn to check that jealousy. You're not a girl, any more. You're a married woman.'

He turned then, walking through the archway, crossed the sitting-room and opened the double doors. The orchestra's music momentarily filled the suite and then Duncan shut the doors behind him.

Vicky was alone.

She thought, Jealous? I'll show him who's jealous. The bastard!

*   *   *

Duncan Webb knew how to handle women. He had learned from the world's best possible teacher – his mother.

Miranda Cunningham had been the belle of Philadelphia, had had opportunities to marry the heirs of many Pennsylvania fortunes. But, in the end, Miranda Cunningham had chosen Duncan's father, Charles Webb, and her only hope to riches then existed through her son.

The frustrated woman had spoken frankly to her son, telling him often that her big mistake had been to let men take too many liberties with her. Such a thing was bad for a lady – but was always a gentleman's prerogative. Men were beasts, she said, and there was no reason why her son should not be the worst beast of all. He could seek revenge on her behalf.

Living now in near seclusion in Pittsburg, Miranda and Charles Webb seldom saw their son. They had no money to send him. Webb senior was a clerk for a shipping company and Miranda, a housewife who had little more than the memories of a bright youth that she has mismanaged, a brilliant future squandered by allowing high-born gentlemen seek pleasure with her too often. After she had been cast aside, Miranda married a hard-working and honest man. But he also was the dreariest person whom she had ever known. Charles Webb. Duncan's father. A man who overlooked his wife's tarnished past, so glad was he to have secured such a great beauty for his spouse.

Men are different, totally different from women in so many, many ways, Miranda kept reminding her son. Enjoying physical pleasure was only one small part of the chasm between them. Money was important, too, money for services rendered. If a woman accepted money from an admirer, she became a prostitute. But Miranda cited many examples she had known in Philadelphia where well-connected men accepted money, jewellery, stocks, valuable property from women because women often felt a need, a passion to lay down everything they possessed in front of a man. The right man.

To be a male was on the level of godliness, Duncan had learned at an early age from his mother, providing that the male enjoyed the necessary physical endowments and learned how to use them to his financial, and social, advantage. Then, he was a deity answerable to no one.

Marriage was of no consequence to a man. Making a marriage last. If a woman separated from her husband, she was suspect, a vagabond, a sinful divorcee, accused even of mental deficiencies.

But a man? Who had ever heard of a man being ostracized from society — interesting society, that is; boulevard society, not the stuffy parlour society of the Cabotts and the Lodges — because he dumped his wife? No, marriage was only one more trump card in a man's winning game of romance. Like good looks, potency, charm, marriage also was to be used against a female.

And Duncan Webb was now well on his way to achieving his mother's dream for him He had spotted Victoria Abdee soon after she had arrived in Boston. He could tell by the way that she moved her eyes that she was an inquisitive girl, that she wanted to learn more than what was offered at the stuffy school run by the Pemberton sisters.

Victoria Abdee was rich, too. Her father was a Southern planter who had sent his twin daughters North to an expensive school. Their pockets were brimming with letters of credit. And as Vicky was more free with her money than her twin sister, she easily got Veronica's share, too.

Tonight, Duncan had to be alone to consider his next step. He had finally married Vicky Abdee. He possessed legal documents to prove it. There was no way in which her family could disown him. And, slowly, he was lacing his new wife's mind with the drug that his mother had told him was the most effective way to secure total dedication from a female — the addictive drug of jealousy. He had begun doing that in Boston.

The place where Duncan Webb sat tonight, deliberating his next move, was a famous meeting spot in New Orleans, a bordello on Rampart Street, an exclusive salon where rich gentlemen came to drink, gossip, indulge in some licentiousness. Duncan had even heard of this bordello in Boston. It was called *Petit Jour*.

Although he had not come to *Petit Jour* with the intentions of having a wild fling, he gradually warmed to the idea as more brandy warmed his stomach.

As always, though, Duncan Webb waited for the opportune moment to make his move. He saw no reason why he should spend his own money on the girls here. There were many other gentlemen lounging around him in the richly-furnished parlour. He would let one of them pay his way.

Duncan Webb had also learned from his mother that men have an innate curiosity about how other men perform with a woman. It was a constant subject of discussion amongst males, Miranda had reported to her son. She had coached him how to cash in on that, too.

So, Duncan waited now, exhibiting his lean, finely-clothed body in the most attractive position, letting both the female prostitutes and the wealthy male customers see him and imagine what waited beneath the thin woollens, the monogrammed linen which he wore.

Also, by staying at the Hotel LaSalle, and having a pocketful of cash, Duncan knew he could not be easily recognized as the scoundrel that he was.

*   *   *

Vicky realized that she was lucky about one thing. No, she decided that she was lucky about two things. The first was that she had not unpacked all her trunks. Duncan's clothes hung in the dressing-room but she had allowed the maid to remove only a few of her things. She had sent most of her trunks home with Veronica, anyway. Veronica had neatly packed Vicky's belongings, listing the contents of each trunk on a sheet of paper and then pinned the paper inside the lid of the trunk. Thus, Vicky had been able to know what and what not to unpack.

The second bit of good luck which Vicky remembered at

this early morning hour was that she had not given all her money to Duncan. She still had some cash left, enough money to hire a private driver to take her home to Dragonard Hill. She would not have to suffer a public coach.

Vicky lay in bed, the man still sleeping beside her. She did not know his name, only remembering that the ginger-haired stranger had told her last night that he was from England – Yes, from Manchester – and that he was a cloth merchant visiting New Orleans. She had met him downstairs last night in the hotel lobby. He had bought her a bottle of champagne, and after their second bottle, they had come arm-in-arm upstairs to the room – Vicky's bridal suite.

Now, in the early hours of morning, Vicky knew why she had done this foolish thing. She had invited this ginger-haired man with a pot-belly to her room as an act of defiance against Duncan, to make Duncan jealous when he came back to the room. She wanted to tell him that she had a *real* stranger. Not one of their fantasies in which she pretended that Duncan's phallus was a stranger. But a real stranger in front of whom she had genuinely depraved herself. A stranger who was ugly. Yes, that would make Duncan seethe.

Duncan had not come back to the room. Not last night. Not this morning. The real stranger was still sleeping naked beside Vicky now. She saw the mound of his body silhouetted by the dawn breaking through the brocade draperies.

Cautiously stepping out of bed, careful not to awaken him, Vicky vaguely remembered how he had pawed at her last night, calling her 'my poppet' and 'sweet doxey'. The memory sickened her. He had been horrible in bed. He had not understood what she wanted from him, understood even less than Duncan. Compared to him, Duncan was the devil incarnate. But Vicky wanted the devil and hell, too! All its flames!

This morning, Vicky's head ached from champagne. Her mouth was dry. But she told herself that she must not become sick. She could not vomit or collapse back into bed. Nor could she get depressed. She must not admit defeat.

Telling herself that she must concentrate on only one thing,

Vicky began to fumble around the dark bedroom. She knew she had to leave here. Leave New Orleans. She must leave Duncan. If Duncan truly loved her, he would follow her. But she realized that if she stayed here, she would become defeated by him.

Ha! If he wanted a battle of wits, she would give him one. The idea of competing with him strengthened her.

And Vicky hurriedly dressed in the wrinkled yellow gown that she had worn at her wedding. She would have the driver stop the carriage on the road and she would change then into something more suitable for arriving at home. Also, she would take off her wedding band. Hide it. Not tell anyone at home about her marriage until the right moment.

As she hurried, she wondered if she should leave a note for Duncan, a small card saying that his wife had gone home. Perhaps even leave a little bit of money attached to the note. Money like bait for an animal. And say in the note that his wife had gone back home to Dragonard Hill. She knew that Duncan was impressed that her father owned a cotton plantation. All Northerners were. Smiling now, she imagined Duncan chasing behind her all the way to Dragonard Hill. That image of Duncan did not fit her idea of a true man, but he was the closest to come to it yet. She did not want to lose him.

*   *   *

By dawn, the narrow streets of New Orleans were becoming alive with the first signs of activity. Two barefoot negro men walked slowly over the cobblestones, carrying a pole between them from which hung a freshly-butchered calf. A fat woman waddled in the shadows, balancing a basketful of cackling hens on her head. Most of the painted jalousies along Rampart Street were still closed from the night before. But a maid in a crisp white turban was already scrubbing the marble steps of a narrow blue house. Across the street, an old Creole woman sat behind the iron fretwork of her balcony, smoking a cigar, carefully laying the cards of a Tarot pack – one by one – in front of her on a wicker table. The smell of chicory coffee filled the quarter, a fresh and sweet aroma drifted from the small shop marked 'Patisserie'. Two young dandies emerged, arm-in-arm, from a dim courtyard and looked up and down Rampart Street for a hire carriage. The concierge shut the grillwork gate behind them. A tall figure in a black djallabah moved past them, leading a monkey by its pink hand.

The pillars of the grillwork gate were unmarked. The courtyard within was dark and silent, a lush growth of ferns only becoming visible in the early morning light, the breaking of day which showed the figure of a stone cupid standing in the middle of a fountain. This was the only sign by which the bordello called *Petit Jour* was recognizable – the stone cupid in a fountain of ferns.

Inside *Petit Jour*, the mistress was still awake. She had not gone to sleep last night. Naomi always stayed awake when an unusual customer was on the premises. Last night, that customer had been a Yankee. A young man from the North who had intrigued Naomi enough for her to forego sleep.

Naomi was not fooled by the Yankee's well-tailored appearance. She had checked with the waiters to see who was paying for the champagne, the absinthe, the continuous flow of girls into the room called The Blue Grotto.

As Naomi had suspected, the big spender was not the young Yankee called Duncan Webb. It was the corpulent Hiram Hayward, a notorious pervert in New Orleans, a man disowned by his family in Natchez and living here on a generous remittance.

Now, as Naomi held up the veil from her burn-marked face, she looked through the curtains which separated the Blue Grotto from a stone passageway. And she saw exactly why Mister Hayward was paying for this party. The young Duncan Webb was giving old Hayward quite a show, Naomi saw. Hayward was kneeling on the floor, inspecting Webb's phallus as it drove into a prostitute. Hayward was giggling in his drunkenness, spreading his lips to catch the swing of

Webb's scrotum in his mouth, moving his head like a child bobbing for apples in water.

A messenger then brought the news to Naomi that young Mister Webb was registered at the Hotel LaSalle. But that his wife had checked out of the hotel a short time ago with her luggage, after making enquiries about hiring a coach to take her up-country.

Nodding, Naomi returned to look through the curtain which hung behind the couches arranged in a circle in the Blue Grotto.

Duncan Webb was still lying on the edge of a couch. But he had a young girl tonguing her way up his legs. He held his phallus in his hand for her goal but, when she approached it, Duncan Webb pulled it away, pushing her back down to the floor with his foot. And fat Hiram Hayward sat nearby on the floor, clapping his hands.

No, Duncan Webb's behaviour was not the usual conduct of white visitors at *Petit Jour*. The men who came here were more often like the host, Hiram Hayward. They acted in subservience. But Naomi was amused. Duncan Webb was performing better than many of her own people, slaves whom she had taught herself. Naomi often coached her black Fancies in ways which she had brought from her original bordello in the town of Basseterre on the island of St Kitts – the old West Indian whorehouse called *Chez Naomi*.

Now, watching Duncan Webb, Naomi thought about next Friday night. She remembered a certain party which had specifically booked a staged fantasy in the cellar. Naomi usually supplied such parties with at least one fine peacock of a male. Usually, he was one of her fancy black male slaves. Watching Duncan Webb perform, though, and remembering that his wife had left the Hotel LaSalle, Naomi wondered if, perhaps, this Friday's fantasy at *Petit Jour* might just feature a white stallion from the North.

Naomi would keep track of young Mister Webb's whereabouts in New Orleans during the next few days. And, if her suspicions proved correct, this young potent Northerner might very well accept the job she would offer him. She knew his sort. He was vain. He needed adulation. And, probably by next Friday – after a week of visiting the tailors and casinos in New Orleans – young Duncan Webb would also need money.

She watched Webb now as he looked toward Hayward kneeling on the floor across from him. He called to the fat man, 'It's worth the price of champagne to observe, isn't it, My Friend?'

Hayward anxiously nodded.

'What are you willing to do if you want to see more? At some other place? Like your home, for instance?'

Quickly shaking his round head, Hayward said, 'No worry, no worry, My Studship. Just concentrate on entertaining me now and we'll come to some arrangement. You'll be rewarded.'

Webb relaxed back onto the couch. A complacent smile settled over his face. He said, 'I am no gigolo to be rewarded with a pittance, Mister Hayward.

Hayward nodded, not paying heed to Webb's words. He was more intent on watching him perform now with the two quadroon girls.

Yes, I am right, Naomi thought. *The young stallion is out for money! And fat Hiram is interested! They are sniffing each other out. Young Webb will play hard-to-get next. He will probably end up taking fat Hiram for a big roll of money. But not immediately. A very good arrangement for everyone except* – she laughed – *for everyone except his poor wife!*

Chapter Six

BUGS, GNATS, PIGS OF THE EARTH

Summer began in Louisiana and, then, it abruptly ended and grey clouds obliterated the sun, bringing wind, cold, and entire days of hard-driving rain. Victoria Abdee arrived at Dragonard Hill at the head of the storm, laughing gaily that she had got home in the nick of time, twirling in a fresh white organza dress on the rickety front porch of the old house as the rain began the first stages of its deluge. The heavy drops fell onto the oleander bushes, bending the limbs, and she immediately began to distribute gifts which she had brought from New Orleans. She gave her father a bottle of French champagne. She had a blue-and-white China bowl for Storky. And a cut-glass vase for Posey. She saw no reason to tell them that these gifts had been presented to her and her husband by the management of the Hotel LaSalle in their bridal suite and that she had packed them in her suitcase at the last moment as a buffer against any ill-feeling she might receive at her home-coming. Neither did she see any reason yet to tell them that she was married, letting everyone believe that she had just come from staying with a girlfriend in New Orleans.

Kissing Veronica on the cheek, chucking Brownie under the chin, Vicky kept up gay patter. And when she saw her eldest sister, Imogen, standing glumly in the parlour archway, she hugged her warmly and confessed that she had seen the most handsome horse brasses for her in a New Orleans shop but, when she had left her girlfriend's home, the shop was closed.

Imogen slowly nodded her head.

Throwing up her hands, laughing, Vicky repeated how lucky she was to be home. She repeated, 'Aren't I the lucky girl! Oh, aren't I the lucky girl!'

The rain then began driving harder against the wavey-glass panes in the old house; the servants all hurried to make certain that every upstairs window was shut, rushing now in preparation for this storm that put an end to the first days of the Louisiana summer.

*   *   *

This was not the weather which Peter Abdee had expected at this time of year, nor was the reunion of his daughters on Dragonard Hill exactly as he had anticipated it.

Three years had passed since they all were together, though, and Peter told himself to be patient, to hope for the twins to settle slowly back into plantation life. But his hopes became more of a struggle as the first rainy days dragged by, the girls confined to the house.

These were not easy times for Peter in many respects; on the fifth day of the downpour a visitor beat on the front doors of the old house as he and his three daughters were finishing their midday meal. Vicky had chattered all through dinner, telling everyone about the times that she and Veronica had had at The Pemberton Academy, trying to amuse her sisters with imitations of Abigail Pemberton's voice, and telling how embarrassed she had been to accept the elocution trophy at a school banquet. Veronica kept her head lowered throughout all of Vicky's stories. Imogen showed even less interest.

Royal came to the dinner table and told Peter in a low voice that a man from Witcherley Plantation was at the door.

Surprised that someone from Witcherley would be calling at Dragonard Hill, Peter immediately left the table to see who the man was and what he wanted from him. The Witcherley family had feuded with the Rolands and the Selbys who had previously owned this land and had not been here in three generations.

The visitor on the porch was middle-aged, gaunt, and a full beard covered his weathered face. He refused to come into the house, using the excuse that his clothes were dripping with water. Peter had never seen this man before and, although he did not introduce himself to Peter by name, Peter still insisted that he accept the offer of a warm house and, perhaps, a glass of whiskey.

Again, the bearded envoy from Witcherley refused Peter's kindness, saying now that Mister Theobold Witcherley was waiting in a coach at the gates of Dragonard Hill. The man was anxious to explain that Mister Witcherley sent his regards to Peter Abdee and his family. He stressed that there were no ill-feelings between the Witcherleys and the Abdees. An oath sworn long-ago by Theobold Witcherley prevented him from stepping foot on this land, a hatred for the previous land-owners here, which had been fuelled by young Roland Selby eloping with Sarah Witcherley, an event that happened when Peter arrived here as a small child, a circumstance that had provided his opportunity to inherit The Star, making it Dragonard Hill.

Now, gripping his soaking hat in his hands, the envoy from Theobold Witcherley stated the reason of today's visit. A slave girl had escaped from Witcherley and he wanted to know if Peter had seen her here on Dragonard Hill. Her name was Rita. She was in her late teens, the man said, and not an unattractive wench, as far as nigger wenches were concerned. He then was quick to explain that there was a very urgent reason why she was wanted back at Witcherley.

Peter did not question the man for that reason but he assured him that he had not seen nor heard about a runaway black girl hiding on his plantation. He promised that he would ask his overseer and make enquiries in the slave quarters, even assuring the man that Mister Theobold Witcherley was free to search the woodlands of Dragonard Hill that bordered their property. Peter Abdee wanted no friction with his neighbours, not even those who obeyed an ancient pledge of hatred for this land.

Saying that a search would not be possible, the Witcherley envoy thanked Peter Abdee for his help, adding his gratitude for Peter's offer of hospitality and, then, turning on the porch, he looked momentarily at the heavy downpour of rain before pulling his hat back over his ears and ran out to his horse. The man galloped down the muddy drive to make his report to the Witcherley coach waiting at the gates.

Standing on the front porch behind a curtain of raindrops strung across the sagging eaves, Peter could barely see the bulky shape of a dark coach setting beside the pole gate posts at the public road, the horse-and-rider standing next to the coach. The rider finally moved away and the four black horses began to pull the heavy coach down the road from the gate, disappearing into the storm.

Lingering on the porch, Peter Abdee felt a chill pass through his body, a coldness that had nothing to do with the damp weather. This was the first time in his life that a Witcherley had made an advance to his home. Instead of a token of neighbourliness, though, Peter took it as a dark omen. And it was more than the fact that the Witcherleys were looking for a runaway slave girl. He sensed a deeper feeling of foreboding. The freak rains falling for over a week now. The danger it was threatening on the green-seed cotton fields. The work suddenly stopping on the new house because of this bad weather. His inability to visit Kate at Greenleaf since the storm. The strange relationship between Imogen and Barry Breslin, the almost cruel way she treated him when he rode through the torrential downpour to come calling. He was concerned, too, about Vicky's sudden appearance at Dragonard, giving him no good reason why she had gone on to New Orleans instead of coming home with Veronica. And Veronica was acting strangely, too, changing the subject whenever he brought up Vicky's name and still hiding her eyes from him when she talked to him about Brownie.

Then, this visitation in the storm, the almost ghostly sight of the Witcherley couch hovering at the gates of Dragonard Hill.

Staring out into the rain, Peter found himself thinking about an old negress who used to live here. Her name had been Mama Gomorrah and she had pulled a whip behind her on the ground like a long snake. The old crone had used her whip to punish black people whom she found committing what she called 'the sin of Gomorrah'. But she also used to flail the whip for another purpose. Mama Gomorrah had frequently stood in the yard around the big house and whipped the earth, hitting it harder and harder with her black leather snake, beating the evil spirits into the ground, keeping them from escaping and grabbing a hold on people's lives. Mama Gomorrah was dead now, buried at her request behind The Shed, where her spirit could protect the young black children raised there. But Peter wished that she were still alive, here with him now, standing out in the mud in front of the old house and furiously whipping the soggy earth with her leather snake, protecting him and his three daughters from whatever evils threatened them.

Peter Abdee was not a religious man, having never been baptized to his knowledge, nor taught Bible lessons in a church. But at this desolate moment on the front porch of the old house, he felt that he needed some supernatural help in his life. He knew that more than a storm was chilling the land and disturbing the people here, but the only religion he knew came from the ones whom he held in slavery. That irony made him unhappy, too.

*   *   *

Nobody had ever presented Storky with a gift unless they wanted something from her. She remembered when fieldhands used to bring her fish or a freshly skinned rabbit to the kitchen door and then awkwardly ask for advice to settle differences between them and their women. Wenches from the dairy or Looming House had come to Storky with an apronful of apples and, when she accepted them, they would fall to the floor, begging her to find them a hiding place for a day near the big house because some other black woman was looking for the wench with a stick for pestering with her man. Storky had received gifts from the white folks at Christmas time, a silver dollar, shoes, or a length of calico, but white people usually gave Storky presents out of generosity or as a token of gratitude for a year's good work.

Looking at the blue-and-white Chinese bowl that Vicky had brought her from New Orleans, Storky's suspicious mind wondered what was wanted from her now. This bowl was no repayment for services or token of gratitude. Storky felt that Vicky had bestowed the gifts on her and Posey like a child would make a loud racket to distract your eye from seeing something they had broken. Storky recognized children's tactics and she thought that Vicky was acting like a devious child now, probably trying to keep Storky from discovering that she had smashed something. Since Vicky's childhood, Storky had been a figure of authority in her life, being even maternal, and she knew that Vicky was still somewhat frightened of her. Storky wanted to keep her that way.

But Storky did not know what new badness that Vicky had done. She and Posey discussed their gifts, Posey having wrapped his crystal vase in a flour sack and was saving it for the kitchen in the new house. But Storky kept her bowl out on the work table in the kitchen and, sitting in her creaky rattan chair, she studied the bowl like a general looking at a campaign map, trying to decide the enemy's next move, or gazed at it like a gypsy fortune-teller with a crystal ball, searching for answers, waiting for some sudden illumination.

No answers came to Storky during Vicky's first week at Dragonard Hill. Vicky seldom came to the kitchen during the rainy week and the many times that her twin sister, Veronica, sat with her skirt tucked around her legs by the stove and chatted to Posey and Storky, she did not once mention Vicky's name. Storky suspected a tiff between the two girls.

Storky also noted how Veronica had been so protective of Brownie, hardly letting the black girl do any work. Veronica seemed to have forgotten that Brownie was her personal maid;

she was not exerting any authority over the black people and, since she had come back from school, Veronica had also visited very frequently with the houseboy, Royal.

Royal? He was acting sullen these days to Storky's eyes but she did not pay much concern to his sudden turn in behaviour, not trying to fathom his troubles. She did notice, though, that the only time that his wide-spaced eyes resumed their usual twinkle was when Veronica asked him to help her to arrange the dishes in the dining-room, or when he painstakingly explained details to her on the entries in Master Peter's ledger.

Royal was a good boy but his body was ripe under his clothes and Storky did not understand what sullen thoughts he was harbouring behind his handsome, brown face. Also, being an old negress and remembering the hard days of slavery here long ago, when black people slept under the moon and often had no clothes to protect their bodies from the sun, nothing but an iron collar around their neck and bands on their wrists and ankles, she did not trust a handsome young buck who had the fine manners and smooth language of a white man.

It was an outsider, finally, a white person who did not live at Dragonard Hill who made Storky break her week-long brooding silence. It was when Barry Breslin from Greenleaf rode through the rain to visit Imogen that Storky saw the first flicker of trouble. The china bowl had told her nothing about Vicky's past actions but, an increasing amount of gay laughter from the parlour warned Storky that there was trouble in the future – laughter between Vicky and Imogen's beau, Barry Breslin – when Imogen was not there.

Storky was quick to bring this to Posey's attention, asking him if he had noticed that Vicky was being troublesome, beginning to flirt with the young man whom Storky had pegged as Miss Imogen's suitor, although no official announcement had yet been made.

The kitchen was situated close to the parlour and Storky had to keep her voice low when she discussed this with Posey.

She said disdainfully, 'I thought Miss Imogen would never get her a beau. Never! And now that she catches one, shame! Miss Vicky comes back all fancy from school and tries to take him away from Miss Imogen.'

'She ain't taking Miss Imogen's beau,' Posey argued, still flattered that Vicky had honoured him with a present from New Orleans. It brought him up to Storky's level – a trusted house-servant.

'But Miss Vicky's trying to steal him,' Storky insisted, pounding the floor now with her cane. 'Miss Veronica, she knows it, too. That's why she's coming in here all the time and acting so nervous.'

'But what about Miss Imogen? It's her beau. What she saying about it?' Posey would not take Storky's words seriously. In his eyes, her mind was beginning to slip.

'Miss Imogen never says much. You know Miss Imogen. She's waiting. Miss Imogen's a sly one, she is. She don't miss a thing. She's just waiting to pounce.'

Posey did not understand. 'Waiting? What for Miss Imogen waiting?'

Although their conversation was muted, Belladonna had heard the mention of Imogen's name and, after straining her ears to hear what they were saying, she called from her stool in the corner, 'Miss Imogen waiting for something better to come along than that Master Barry Breslin.'

'Mind your business, wench,' Posey snapped at her. 'This is white folk talk.'

Belladonna sank back into her far corner of the kitchen, suspecting that she was right, believing that Miss Imogen was not truly interested in Barry Breslin. She let Posey and Storky continue with their argument, even hoping that Miss Vicky would get Barry Breslin for her beau and then they would get married and move away from here and go live at Greenleaf. Belladonna did not like Miss Vicky and she was glad that she had not brought her a present from New Orleans, too. That might mean that she would have to like her.

This was the first time that Belladonna sided – although secretly – with Storky. She believed, too, that Vicky was wicked and was hiding some dark secret.

The cotton pods were strong and had been spared by the torrential storms but the dirt roads, plantation driveways, and grassy traces were now deep in mire; the sunlight, cutting through the clouds on the tenth morning of the storm, found a countryside left soggy, the earth as soft as a tropical marsh.

The sun came hot and steam rose from the ground, a vapour often as thick as fog, bringing worms and earth slugs burrowing out from the brown slime.

The ground worms and molluscs were then joined by a soft-shelled bug, a type of centipede known in these parts as 'pigs-of-the-earth'. They covered the tree trunks, crawled over the wagons and buggies, and inched up the sides of the porch, being found around the old house these days in an abundance equivalent to the blight of worms. The black people walked stealthily in their bare feet, carefully trying not to step on one of the slugs, which would not bite nor sting them but they made an unpleasant feeling when trod upon by a naked foot, and felt slippery to the slide of a leather sole. The small bugs known as 'pigs-of-the-earth' rolled into a ball when they were threatened by pressure, remaining that way for many hours and formed a carpet of iridescent black pellets which made the yard look as if a herd of goats had passed through, leaving their manure.

Smudge pots were placed in the fields to protect the crops from insects. The boll weevil did not appear but mosquitoes were breeding in stagnant ponds of rainwater and gnats formed thick swarms in the many footpaths which divided and subdivided Dragonard Hill.

The Abdee twins seldom went from the old house on these days of plague that followed the long storm. Peter had resumed work on the new house, leaving early each morning to join in on a thorough sweeping of the building site, daily cleaning away the worms and pigs-of-the-earth that had crawled there during the night, using heavy-duty straw brooms made especially for the task by the black women in the Weaving House. He was determined to finish the house before the end of the year.

Imogen accepted these troubles as a test for her endurance, proving that she could meet any unexpected crisis on the plantation. She had worn a handkerchief tied around her face when she had helped place the smudgepots in the fields. She formulated an antidote made from paraffin to check the onslaught of vermin. She left her two sisters alone, even ignoring Barry Breslin when he rode from Greenleaf on afternoon visits. Imogen was developing an even more brittle veneer than she had had a few short months ago, working hard to get what she wanted, willing to use anything at her command.

Veronica had found an immediate place for herself in the work that was necessary to run the old house, often reminding Storky of how her mother, Melissa, had shown so much interest in domestic chores. These tasks were at a peak in the morning hours and, when afternoon arrived, Barry Breslin was usually in the parlour or swinging on the front porch, visiting with Vicky.

Then, this morning, word had come from Greenleaf that Barry had come down with an illness, a complaint that had been caused by the past dampness. The messenger arrived after breakfast to report that he would not be visiting this afternoon. Making a note of that information, Veronica had set the afternoon aside to talk to Vicky. The subject would be Brownie.

Veronica's worst fear about Brownie had come true. She had taken her to be inspected by Lady Alice and Brownie was pregnant. Before mentioning anything about this to her father and adding to his troubles, Veronica wanted to speak to Vicky alone. She would not let her escape this time.

But, then, as the bright sun had found the slugs, worms, and pigs-of-the-earth waiting in the mud after the storm clouds had cleared, so were Veronica's good intentions greeted by a type of pestilence.

Veronica went out to the porch in the afternoon to confront Vicky. And she found her standing at the top of the steps, waving a white lace handkerchief at a mud-splattered coach rumbling up the deep ruts of the driveway.

Jumping up and down on the porch with excitement, Vicky shouted, 'He's come! Duncan's come!'

Veronica froze in the doorway.

Imogen stood beyond the avenue of oaks, holding a pail of paraffin solution in one hand and staring at the coach slowing in front of the old house, the team of brown horses covered with foam from being driven too hard, their mouths sudsy with white drool.

Peter was walking around the corner of the house with three brooms over his shoulder. He also stared in bewilderment at the shabby conveyance and the surly driver crouched above the miserable animals.

Picking up the skirts of her pink organza dress, Vicky ran down the steps and through the mud toward the coach.

Peter looked at Veronica standing ashen-faced on the porch. He asked, 'Who's that?'

Veronica could not answer.

Looking down the driveway at Imogen, Peter called, 'Who is this?'

Neither did Imogen answer her father's question, staring coldly at Vicky running like a crazed woman to greet the visitor.

The coach then rumbled to a stop. The grey canvas curtain pulled open. A swarthy young man, with a thin moustache and long sideburns, leaned out his head and, looking at Vicky waving to him, and then at the shabby condition of the old house, he asked, 'Is *this* it?' Duncan Webb was not impressed with what he saw of Dragonard Hill.

Vicky did not notice his displeasure with her home. She pulled open the coach door and, flinging her arms around him, she said, 'Duncan! Oh, Duncan, I knew you'd come!'

Stepping down from the coach, kissing her lightly on the forehead, he flung the end of a forest-green cape over his shoulder with a great flourish and, pointing at the driver with a newly-acquired riding crop, he said, 'Unload my baggage, man.'

The driver spat over the side of the coach, snarling, 'What about some money, then?'

Duncan Webb looked at Vicky, shrugging.

Understanding the predicament, Vicky turned to Peter and called, 'Father, can you pay the driver?'

By now, the house-servants had gathered on the porch, staring at the elaborately-dressed stranger who had come through the mud to reach Dragonard Hill.

Peter answered, 'Who is your friend, Vicky? At least, introduce us?'

Looking from her father to Veronica, standing on the porch with her arm now around Brownie, to the rest of the servants, and then at Imogen standing down the driveway with a pail in her hands, Vicky took a deep breath and said, 'Why, this is my husband, everybody! This is Duncan! My darling, dear Duncan Webb!'

Quickly studying Peter Abdee's dirty clothes, the three soiled brooms he held over his shoulder, Duncan Webb tipped his hat to him and nodded, first, at Veronica and, next, at Imogen down the driveway. Tucking the riding crop under his arm, then, he turned to the carriage and lifted a grey fluffy cat from the seat by its two front legs and snuggled it in his arms.

Forgetting about her father and the money owing to the driver, Vicky grabbed for the cat and said, 'For me! For me! A present for me!'

Pulling the cat away from her grasping hands, Duncan said, 'Most certainly not! This is Jezebel. A gentleman friend of mine called Hiram Hayward gave me Jezzebel as a going-away present. Jezebel's mine, aren't you, puss?' he said, lowering his head to the cat, rubbing his fingers under the thick, grey hairs on the cat's chin.

Above him, the driver called again for his money.

*   *   *

Royal was sent to show Duncan Webb to an upstairs bedroom in the old house. The driver was paid and, only when he had received his money, did he allow the baggage to be unloaded from the top of the coach. Veronica shooed all the servants back into the house, leading Brownie by the hand, reassuring her that Duncan's presence here meant no threat to her. She saw now how wrong she had been, though, by not telling her father about Duncan Webb before this horrible occurrence had happened.

Events had gone too far now. And before Vicky was allowed to go upstairs and join the man whom she claimed was her husband, Peter called her into his study. Vicky now sat at one end of the cracked brown leather divan and Peter faced her from the swivel chair at his desk.

Vicky began to speak, hoping to get in her side of the matter first. She said, 'Father, don't judge Duncan until you get to know him. He might look like a . . . city boy. But how could you possibly, *possibly* think I'd marry some man who'd disappoint you?' She was trying to use all her guile on her father.

Peter's response was calm. 'It's not him I'm disappointed with, Vicky.'

She jerked her head. 'Me? You're disappointed with me?' She sniffed, looking across the room. She said in a lower voice, a hurt voice, 'You act like this and so there's no wonder why I didn't tell you.'

Peter kept his eyes fixed on her. She was nervously toying with the top tier of her full organza skirt. Mud was splattered on the hem. Her slippers were caked with filth. She was not an attractive sight. He said, 'So you are married.'

Vicky nodded, her eyes closed.

Peter said, 'You got married in New Orleans.'

Vicky nodded again, her mouth tightening.

He said, 'But you didn't meet him there.'

She shook her head. She said, 'Boston.'

'How long have you known him, Vicky?'

'Two years. No. Really three now.'

'Really three,' Peter repeated, nodding. 'And he was the friend you went to New Orleans with. Not a girl-friend from school.'

'I was too scared to tell you. Veronica knew. She should have told you.'

'Do not put the blame on Veronica. I can tell now that she has been trying to cover-up for you. For your lying. Your sneaky behaviour. Veronica knew how I'd feel.'

Vicky suddenly cried, 'Well, what about *me*?'

Peter looked at her. He asked in a low voice, 'Yes, what about you, Vicky?'

Her small pink mouth turned down at the corners, threatening to sob. She took a few deep breaths, faltered, and then asked, 'What do you mean?'

He kept his eyes on her, saying, 'I'll try not to be sentimental, Vicky. I'll try to be as practical about you as I can now. And, for a start, can your new husband support you?'

She held up her head now. She said, 'Duncan is very clever.'

'I'm sure he is. But that isn't what I asked you. Can he support you, Vicky? What's his trade? Does he have a job? Where's he from? Tell me, Vicky. Tell me all about this man who I've just met and found out he's your husband.'

Vicky had not expected her father to react in this calm manner. She had expected a harangue. A lecture. When she had first come into the library a few minutes ago, she had even envisioned herself and Duncan leaving Dragonard Hill together in a fury, saying that they never wanted to see this dreadful place again. She now wished that her father had taken a more angry tact. It would make things so much simpler for her.

Sitting now with her hands clasped demurely in her lap, she began, 'Well, Duncan is from Pennsylvania. Yes, he's from Pittsburgh. He's from a very, very, *very* good family there. He's a gentleman by birth. He's very cultured. And . . .'

'You still haven't told me what he does for a living, Vicky.'

She blinked. 'Why, nothing. Not yet.'

'He's just a gentleman – of leisure.' There was neither pride nor pain in Peter's voice. He was bland.

Vicky nodded.

'His parents are people of means?'

'Ummm.'

'You know this for a fact, Vicky. You've met them and you know. You've been to their home and met them.'

'I haven't exactly *met* them.' She lowered her eyes again, her hands moving nervously now.

And then Vicky got the rage that she had originally expected. Rising from his desk chair, Peter bellowed down at her, 'By God, girl, you said you've known him for three years. For three years you've known him and you haven't once met his parents. What in God's name have you been doing at school, whoring?'

Vicky's breasts heaved. Tears welled in her blue eyes. She realized how foolish and bad that the circumstances made her appear. But how could she explain Duncan to her father?

Sitting back down in the chair, Peter assumed a different tactic, a different way to reacquaint himself with Vicky who was now a sudden stranger to him.

He said, 'He seems to be a very handsome young man, your Mister – ' He paused.

'Duncan,' she said, sniffing. 'Duncan Webb.'

Shaking his head in disbelief, Peter said, 'Mrs Duncan Webb. And all the time I thought I had Vicky. Victoria Abdee back home.'

Sitting to the edge of the leather divan, Vicky suddenly pleaded, 'Oh, give him a chance, Father. You'll like him. I know you'll like him.

'I repeat, Vicky, it's not him I'm worried about. It's you. And as hard as I'm trying, I am not able to keep from feeling hurt. Very hurt that you lied to me. Deceived me. Did not tell me one word. One clue.'

Vicky was beginning to speak again, to implore forgiveness and understanding from her father when loud footsteps were heard running down the stairs, followed a few seconds later by a sharp rap on the door.

Peter called to enter.

It was Imogen, still dressed in her soiled work clothes, her black hair hanging down from the knot on top of her head.

Not looking at her father, Imogen fixed her cold blue eyes on Vicky, saying, 'You better go upstairs and calm down your husband.'

Vicky instantly vented her nervousness on Imogen, screaming, 'What did you say to him, Imogen? If you've done anything to Duncan, I'll . . . I'll.'

Imogen remained cold. 'Oh, don't worry. He's not hurt. It's Royal who's bleeding. Your husband just got through beating him.'

Vicky's eyes widened.

'Beating him?' Peter asked.

Imogen nodded, 'With that fancy riding crop of his. Royal accidentally dropped a suitcase on your husband's pussy. And your husband lost his temper.'

'Duncan?'

Peter rose from his chair. 'That man hit Royal?'

'Not just once, either,' Imogen said calmly. 'Royal's hurt pretty bad. Veronica's with him now.'

There was a shocked silence in the library and, as Imogen backed toward the hallway, she looked at Vicky sitting on the brown leather divan and she said to her in a flat voice, 'You know what I think, don't you, Vicky? I think he's a pussy himself. I think your husband is a pussy. Congratulations to the pair of you.'

She gently closed the library door, laughing.

*   *   *

Holding the full-skirt of her dress, Vicky ran anxiously up the stairs and found Duncan pacing the length of her bedroom.

Still wearing his green cape, Duncan swung the riding crop behind his back, shouting to Vicky before she had even closed the door. 'You call this a house? It's a barn! It's cold. The

135

floors slant. The walls are saturated with damp. There are bugs crawling over everything. Look! Look at the condition of this place. How do you expect me to live in a *hole* like this?' Pointing his riding crop at the grey long-haired cat sprawled in the middle of the draped bed, he said, 'Poor Jezebel. Even she's too frightened to walk on these floors, frightened of being bitten by a cockroach – or have some numbskull drop a trunk on her!'

Shutting the door, Vicky said, 'Oh, Duncan, what happened? Tell me what happened.' Her mind was spinning with her father's talk and the passionate feelings she had for Duncan.

His concern was the accommodations now. He waved his arm, the cape fluttering, and screamed, 'A barn! A pig sty!'

Vicky looked from Duncan to the grey cat to the room. It was warm and dry and still freshly decorated with chintz curtains and bedspread and the new mosquito netting hung between the four walnut posters of the bed. But she saw how rustic it all must look to Duncan's eyes and she became instantly apologetic, rushing toward him, saying, 'Don't worry, my darling. The new house will be finished soon.'

He brushed off her arm. 'Why isn't it finished now? Didn't you think I was coming?'

She watched him walk away from her. She was becoming angry at how cold he was treating her, especially after she had just finished defending him to her father. She said, 'No, Duncan, I did not think you were coming.'

'Did you expect me to desert you? We're married, aren't we?'

'You walked out on me, Duncan Webb!' Her voice was rising.

'You're probably talking about the Hotel LaSalle. I went to have a few hours by myself and, when I came back, I found my wife had left me.'

'A few hours? You were gone all night. Our wedding night, too! '

'Do you think it's easy for a man to get married? Do you

think it happens every day? There are changes he has to make. The least not being in his mind!'

'What about me? My mind? You nearly drove me crazy that night with worry.' She knew that she could play the wronged wife. He had obviously not found the ginger-haired Englishman in bed when he returned or he certainly would have mentioned it. He had obviously stayed out a very long time.

'Jealousy! That's the only thing that drives you crazy, Victoria. You are consumed with jealousy. And now that I've come to you, I'm suddenly trapped! Trapped in this cow barn. Oh, I'm beginning to wish I never went back to the hotel and found your note.'

'It certainly took you long enough to come to me, Duncan Webb.'

'See! There, you're doing it again. Imagining things. Letting your jealous imagination run wild. Go on. Tell me what you think I've been doing? Be unreasonable. Forget about the rain that's been flooding the countryside for the last two weeks. You should have seen the roads I've had to travel to get here. To come to you. The misery and torture and filth I've endured.'

Weakening again, Vicky said, 'Oh, Duncan. I know. I know how awful the trip must have been. Let's not be angry. At least, we're together now. That's all that matters.'

Pushing her away from him, he asked, 'How long before we can move into that new house? And when can I look at it? There might be some changes I'll want to make.'

She had not been prepared for this. She nervously answered, 'I don't know. You'll have to talk to Father.'

'Yes, what about your father? He's much younger than I expected but he certainly doesn't look like a gentleman planter. He's probably rather good-looking under all that grime. And his clothes. Does he always dress like such a . . . ruffian?'

'What did you expect, Duncan? A doddering old man in a glistening white suit?'

'I expected him to be a little more clean, that's what I expected.'

'Father works very hard.'

'What does he have all those niggers for?'

'Duncan, you might be sophisticated but you're very naïve when it comes to country life. You have a great deal to learn about Dragonard Hill.'

He said arrogantly, 'The little I want to know will not be difficult. It's not a gentleman's place to trouble himself about soil.'

'Father asked me what you did for a living, Duncan.'

'A living? A job?' He laughed at her. 'Your father sounds more and more like a common farmer. No gentleman planter would ever think of a question like that. What another gentleman does!'

'He's thinking like any other father – gentleman or otherwise – wondering how you're going to support his daughter. Your wife.'

Duncan looked at her with amusement. He said, 'But I do not have to support my wife, Victoria. That's the whole point. You've been telling me all along how rich you are. That you're the daughter of a very rich planter. You'll have to share your riches with me now, won't you . . . my wife? You'll have to teach your father how to treat a son-in-law who's a gentleman.'

'If you think like that, you might get more than a few surprises here, Duncan.'

He sank down onto the bed, reaching to pet the grey cat. He said, 'The surprises have already begun. Apart from finding this rundown house, I had no idea that niggers were so clumsy. I heard in New Orleans that niggers were stupid. But clumsy?' He shook his head, feeling the cat's paw, idly inspecting it for an injury.

'You should not have done that to Royal, Duncan. I must make two things very clear to you. Father does not strike his people, nor does he like them to be called "niggers".'

Laughing again, Duncan said, 'His people! Well, if someone is dumb and stupid – regardless of whose person they are, Victoria – then they must be disciplined, mustn't they?'

Vicky stood looking how handsome he was when he acted so arrogant, lounging on the edge of the bed, his strong legs sprawled over the side, the jacket clinging to his thin waist under the cape, his fawn-coloured breeches tight and revealing. She did not want to argue with him any more. Not now. She did not want to defend him to her father, nor to justify her father's way or the short-comings of Dragonard Hill to Duncan. Sinking down to the floor by the bed, Vicky wrapped her arms around his tall black leather boots and lowered her head to his thigh. She stayed on the floor in that position, then, one arm wrapped around his tall boot now, her other hand beginning to explore his breeches, waiting for Duncan to tell her how far she could go, when she must stop her hand and let him dole out himself to her – as he saw befitting. She secretly hoped that he would be very cruel with her, the most cruel that he had ever been. She longed for him to stop acting like a peacock and assume full superiority over her. To exert some real 'discipline' himself.

*　　*　　*

Storky and Posey were silent for the first time in the kitchen. Storky sat in her rattan chair staring at Royal slumped over the table, his head lying on his arms and Veronica standing behind him, carefully trying to remove the remnants of the fabric from his back, blood-soaked shreds of a thin summer shirt. Belladonna also stared wide-eyed at Royal from her three-legged stool in the corner of the kitchen.

Only a few minutes earlier, Posey and Belladonna had brought the news of Duncan Webb's arrival at Dragonard Hill to Storky in the kitchen, after Veronica had sent them into the house from the porch. His hands fluttering, Posey had excitedly explained to Storky that a young man had arrived in a coach, Miss Vicky said that he was her husband, and, then, as she asked her father to pay the driver, the man took an animal – a cat – from the seat of the coach. Belladonna had supplied Storky with the more intricate details of the event between Posey's breathless pauses – the cape was green and flowing, Miss Vicky had ruined her organza dress in the mud, Master Peter was looking very disturbed and took Miss Vicky with him into the library, and Miss Vicky's husband's cat had long silky grey hairs and he carried the sleepy-looking animal as if it were a baby!

Storky barely had had time to grasp the essential details – Miss Vicky was married without her father's knowledge of the matter and her husband had just arrived here from New Orleans with a cat – when Royal had come staggering into the kitchen, his back covered with blood, his face restraining both pain and indignation. Storky next learned that he had accidentally bumped the cat and Miss Vicky's husband had beat him.

Veronica had followed closely behind Royal and, now, studying his back, she said, 'Posey, get me a basin of water. Belladonna, can you quickly rip me some cloths. Storky, you must have some liniment or balm.'

Storky said, 'There's healing oil in a big stone bottle on the bottom shelf of the pantry. There's clean rags there with it.' She slowly was trying to make an assessment of the events. But one thing she had already decided was that a man who carried a cat like a baby could not be much of a man, especially if he whipped a black person for bumping the animal. Storky already knew she hated Vicky's husband and his long, silky-haired cat.

Belladonna found the stone bottle in the pantry, carrying the cloths over her arm now across the kitchen and using both hands to bring the oil to the table.

'Empty some oil in that . . . thing,' Storky said curtly, nodding to the blue-and-white Chinese bowl setting in the middle of the work table, the present that Vicky had brought her from New Orleans. 'I was just thinking of heaving it out on the trash dump. But might as well put it to some good use.' She was slowly beginning to realize, too, that Miss Vicky had betrayed both her father and Dragonard Hill.

140

Belladonna obeyed Storky's command and, soon, she had the bowl and the bandages laid out on a japanned tray, to which Posey now added a kettle of water. He was keeping silent for the moment.

Veronica asked, 'Storky, can I use your cabin? I can't very well do this here.'

Storky's eyes flashed only momentarily. But then she checked her shock at Veronica asking to be alone with a negro house-boy in her cabin. She knew from the sudden authority in Veronica's voice that she was intent on caring for Royal in the way – and place – she chose. Unlike her twin sister, Veronica was helping the household. Storky called, 'Posey, you give Royal some help to my cabin. Belladonna, carry that tray for Miss Ronny. And snap to it, wench. Quit gawking?'

Royal protested that he was quite able to walk by himself, insisting that he could go see Lady Alice in The Shed to tend to his back.

Veronica swiftly told him to put such ideas out of his head. She said that very shameful behaviour had just occurred here in more ways than one. She then told Belladonna that she could carry the tray herself, suggesting that Belladonna walk with Posey, guiding Royal down the back steps, across the backyard, and into the small log cabin which was now Storky's private sleeping-quarters.

There were no decorations in this backyard cabin, only a small white-washed room containing a single bed covered with a patchwork quilt and a small, scrubbed-pine table and chair. Veronica sat the tray on the table, telling Posey and Belladonna to lay Royal down on his stomach on the bed. She dismissed them when Royal was once settled, thanking them for helping her and advising Posey to boil his white smock to remove the bloodstains he had got on the shoulder from coming in contact with Royal's wounds. She also said that, if Brownie came into the kitchen, to fix her a cup of camomile tea and make her sit quietly. She did not explain why Duncan Webb's sudden appearance at Dragonard Hill might frighten the girl.

After they had gone, Veronica knelt on the floor beside the bed, studying the condition of Royal's back. She had completely peeled off the shirt in the kitchen and now she saw his bare skin with the blood drying in the deep welts. Hurriedly, she began to wash him gently with damp clothes, trying to clean away the blood before it completely dried. She talked softly to Royal as she worked, asking him to explain the figures on the accounts book which she had tried to understand yesterday, hoping to take his mind off the pain.

Royal lay face down on the bed, ignoring the sting of his wounds, answering Veronica's questions, even introducing new topics to divert the subject from the senseless incident with Duncan Webb's cat.

Since Veronica had come back to Dragonard Hill from Boston, Royal had seen life in a totally different way. Veronica actually talked to him as if he were a person. He was not just a slave to be used, some 'nigger' to run errands for a white girl, to fetch whatever she wanted. He had quickly seen her attention change toward him, too, to progress from the humane to one of friendship. She visited and laughed with him, never troubled by his station in the household. He often thought that Veronica's soft eyes flirted with him, but flirted only in the most ladylike manner. She was no white trash slut.

But imagining that Veronica was romantically interested in him was pushing it too far, he thought. More than for what he could hope. An absurd dream. He told himself that he did not care if their relationship did not go one step further than it was now. She was his friend. She was making him into a person, a man with intelligence, opinions, feelings, desires to talk about things other than the plantation. And the thought that Veronica might be attracted to him at least eased Royal's mind about the torment he suffered from the fieldhand, Ben, and his band of friends. Although Ben had not summoned Royal to the potato hut in the last few weeks, Royal still lay awake at night thinking that his time would come again soon.

Veronica was helping those fears, though. She was dispelling Royal's feelings about himself. He knew that he would never have to worry about his masculinity, be afraid that he would become like Ben and the small group of black men who forsaked the pleasure of women. Veronica aroused a definite physical desire in Royal. He knew that if he forgot his place in the world, he could easily be consumed with a passion for the white girl. But he was happy to bask in the luxury of their mental exchanges. Oh, she made him so very happy. He was even thankful for the accident with the cat. Yes, he had foppish Duncan Webb to thank for these few glowing moments with . . . Miss Veronica! *Feel! Listen! She is actually nursing me!*

Veronica knew that she would never be a good nurse, though, as she cautiously smoothed the oil over Royal's back. She could not help noticing what a fine body he had, the natural softness of his skin, how tightly it hugged his athletic frame. Even his manner was extraordinary. Royal was laughing now as they talked about Storky and Posey. Veronica had never noticed before what a deep, wonderful laugh that he had. And how he was not wincing when the oil stung him. He was strong both in body and disposition. And she felt a strong urge to bend down and kiss him on the nape of his neck, just on the spot where his closely-cropped black hair formed a V on his smooth brown skin, telling him that she very much liked taking care of him in this way.

Propriety kept Veronica from doing what she wanted, though. And she rued the day that she had seen the white lady and the free black man on the steamboat and realized that such a relationship was possible in some parts of the world. But those places were far away from this land in the Louisiana wilderness, where the only male who interested Veronica was one of her father's slaves.

*   *   *

A vote was taken that night in the long-legged house in Town that Hopper and Clara shared with Ham and Maybelle. They were deciding what to do with the 'bug' that had come out of the damp woodlands and crawled up the ladder into their house. They had found a black girl hiding in their house when they had come home from work tonight. To their eyes, she resembled a bug.

They at first thought that it was dangerous to hide a runaway slave. They knew that the black girl was not from Dragonard Hill. They suspected she had escaped from a neighbouring plantation and they knew that they could be whipped, branded, even hung for harbouring a fugitive.

The girl had been found cowering in the corner of the small house, a bush of black hair covering her pretty face. Clara and Maybelle both agreed that harbouring a runaway was one thing but that the girl was too big in the tits, they said, and too small in the waist to be sharing the house with their men. They did not want to keep her here even if they were not breaking a law.

She understood. The girl knew the women were jealous of her. But to assure them that they need not worry, she broke her frightened silence and whispered to the women, telling them why they need not worry about her. She beckoned them to the corner to share her secret.

Clara believed the story which the girl told her and nodded when she saw the proof of it on the girl's body. But it was Maybelle who called Ham – and then Hopper – to see what the girl had showed the women. The men must see it too. The men might get ideas about laying the girl but seeing this would stop them.

When the girl shied back, not wanting the men to see her, Maybelle grabbed her by the hair and forced her to pull up her smock for the men to look at her, too.

Slowly, the two curious males moved toward the girl in the corner.

The runaway girl sat with her back to the wall and held her ripped smock up to her pendulous breasts. Although her skin was ink black, and the hair on her head was as black as anybody's in the room, the thatch of hair growing around her vagina was pure white, almost silver in colouring, a phosporescent glow to the furry patch between her legs.

Then she repeated to the men why her pubic hair was not black like their wives. But she made them promise not to repeat why it was white down there and not black. And she begged them, too, not to tell their master that she had run away from Witcherley.

From the secret that the girl shared with them, the four slaves of Dragonard Hill knew that she was yet one more black person who had suffered from a white person. Her name was Rita but to Hopper and Clara, Ham and Maybelle, she looked like a bug, a shiny spider, but with silvery-white markings instead of red like a black widow. Or the curly blackness on a normal black woman.

Chapter Seven

THE SILVER FLEECE

Kate Breslin had few pieces of good news to tell Peter Abdee these days; their first chance to have luncheon at Greenleaf was a week after Barry came down with his cold – six days after Duncan Webb arrived at Dragonard Hill – and Kate did not press her cook to take special pains with the meal. Barry's condition was not serious but the cook busied herself making broths, lemon drinks, and mustard plasters to improve the young man's health. Kate knew that Peter would not complain over a simple but nourishing midday fare.

Peter returned again to Greenleaf the following week to visit Kate. His heavy mood had not lifted, as Duncan Webb was now into the second week of his visit and exerting a stronger presence in the household. There had not been a repeat performance of the whipping incident but Peter had released Royal from all table duties, permitting him to spend most of the day working in the study, concentrating his time on the details of ordering and shipping items for the new house.

Both the building and planting at Dragonard Hill had regained a normal pattern. The pestilence had disappeared and the carpenters were back into the house at full force, the labourers beginning at six o'clock in the morning on the field-work, hoeing and weeding a cotton crop which Peter foresaw as being a bumper harvest.

Kate also was pleased with the prospect of Greenleaf's crops, telling Peter that her overseer, Mister Mayhew, predicted a record yield this year. The cotton gin in Troy was already making preparations for a rich year from the entire neighbourhood.

Lunch was over now and Peter and Kate lay in her bedroom, discussing events in the neighbourhood, the pattern of their own lives, the prospects of the two plantations. Their love-making had been intense today, more so than last week's meeting as Barry had been ill and, also, Kate had been unable to send away the cook for the afternoon. They had made love quickly in the small summer house but, after today's return to a normal routine, they both confessed that more frequent meetings would be quite suitable, even necessary.

The only high points in their personal lives now seemed to come from each other's company. Barry had only risen from his sick bed yesterday, and gone to Troy today for the first time in weeks. He was due at Dragonard Hill this evening, a visit which Kate would not share because, since her last time there, she had felt a strong dislike for Peter's new son-in-law. She did not want to sit at a supper table again listening to Duncan Webb expound on Northern society and the short-comings he found in the South, the mistakes which Peter was making with the new house, a general dismal view of Dragonard Hill.

In Peter's company, now, Kate tried to be optimistic about events in both their lives. Her lively Irish blood would not let her dwell too long on the bad patches through which they were passing. She asked forgiveness for the unfair comparison she was about to make, and then proceeded to cite the life of Noreen Conway. She felt a deep pity for the woman, regretting how hard Mrs Conway had to work at the cotton gin, in the small shack, and — worst of all — the dog pens. Kate said that one look at the woman was all that was necessary to see that she was sickly and had an existence that was almost inhumane. She urged Peter to be thankful that his problems were not those of health.

Holding Kate's head against his bare shoulder, Peter smelled the verbena in her hair and smoothed the softness of her cheek with his fingers. He thrived on these close moments, when they lay naked and secure together after vigorous love-making. It created a sane balance for him, Kate becoming more and more of a balm for his soul.

147

Nonetheless, Peter did not want to burden her with his family's tribulations. He knew she realized that Webb was becoming more of a strain on him but he did not want to discuss his suspicions about the relationship he suspected that Vicky had with her husband. Peter left Duncan alone many nights at a late hour, the young man sitting in the parlour with a full bottle of brandy that would be empty by the morning. He did not think that his son-in-law was making love to his wife. Vicky's recent tenseness corroborated Peter's suspicions. He had forced himself to accept the fact that Vicky had married the man she loved, having failed to tell her father about it because she knew he would have a low opinion of her choice. Peter struggled to be that fair. But he still believed that now that a marriage existed, the husband should perform his manly duties. A life close to the earth gave Peter the mind to expect the basic behaviour of true consummation.

There were other troubles, too, that he wanted to vent from his soul, observations he had made about Imogen and Veronica. He saw reasons to worry about them, too. The problem of Imogen involved Kate's nephew but, as she did not know any more about Barry's intentions than Peter did, he did not pursue the matter. He told himself that he was guilty of looking for fault in all his daughters.

So, holding his peace on that subject, he agreed with Kate that, yes, he felt sorry for Noreen Conway. Then, he tried to make a joke of the matter and said that she obviously was neglected sexually by her husband. He did not know this for a fact, only pulling it from his imagination at the moment. He said that *that* was what put colour into a girl's cheek, and gave sparkle to her eyes. And reaching then for Kate's breasts, he began rubbing them with the wide palms of his hand.

In light-hearted agreement with his observation, Kate found her way to his penis and clasping the base of it with her hand, she touched the tip of her thumb with the tips of her fingers around it, slowly beginning to pull upwards, work which was assisted by Peter's own desires.

Soon, they lay side-by-side on the bed in the upstairs room,

148

lit only by a slant of daylight from the closed draperies, their bodies joining again for pleasures which were becoming more like food for them.

*   *   *

Master Peter was not at Dragonard Hill this afternoon. Maybelle knew this for a fact, as she had seen him ride the chestnut mare down the public road shortly before noon. She felt reassured that, in his absence today, that Jeb Conway was not coming to seek his pleasure here at Dragonard Hill. She had not heard of Conway coming here since the afternoon in the tool shed that she had to take his unwashed penis in her mouth and then suffer sharp jabs between her legs. But Conway was like a chicken hawk, Maybelle thought. She never knew when he was going to make his descent.

There was another white person she had seen circling around Dragonard Hill these days. Maybelle knew the lusty look which males got in their eyes, it was the same for black men or white men. And she knew that this particular white man was bad like Jeb Conway. He was not unkempt and physically dirty. He swaggered around the plantation in fine clothing, with a wide-brimmed straw hat and a riding crop in his hand, not looking at a black woman's face but studying their bodies, sizing their breasts, making his appraisals even after they had passed him.

This new white man was the Northerner whom Miss Vicky had married. His name was Master Webb and, although he lived in the old house with the Abdee family, he was spending more time lately in Town. He never worked. He only walked between the long-legged houses in the heat of the afternoon, when the black people were napping after their midday meal, before the next long shift began and lasted until sundown.

So far, Master Webb had not come to Town at night. Maybelle knew that he was frightened to be alone among black people after dark. But she knew that he would soon start his nocturnal visits because he had spoken to Maybelle, asking her where the black people strolled in the moon.

149

She understood what he meant. She knew what he wanted. And, being quick of mind and possessing a clever tongue, she played the fancy white man's game.

Maybelle had told him about one special part of the woodlands where black people strolled. It was close to the big house, on a path that led from the stables there. Maybelle embellished on her story, telling Master Webb that she also knew where a beautiful black girl lay alone at night on that path. She said that he would probably not be interested in such a piece of mumbo-jumbo nigger talk, but she continued to tell him that the black girl lay there naked in the moon because of an old African belief. She was an Ashanti princess.

Maybelle laughed to herself when she saw the white man believing her story, becoming excited about making love to such a special wench. So Maybelle made the story more erotic for him, describing this black girl's voluptuous body and the special coloration of the hairs which covered her vagina. She begged him not to tell what she had told him to Master Peter or the girl would not be allowed to continue lying naked in the moonlight. She said that if he wanted to see the girl with his own eyes she would probably be there on this very night.

Then, Maybelle hurried back to her long-legged house to tell the slave girl from Witcherley that the time had come for her to pay for hiding in their house.

*   *   *

Mabel and Ham, Clara and Hopper shared their supper of greens and possum tonight with the girl, Rita. She ate solemnly, her bushy head bent forward, trying not to listen as Maybelle excitedly explained to the others how she had met the Yankee, Master Webb, in Town today and arranged for him to lay an Ashanti priestess later tonight near the old house path.

The two men and Clara were laughing at the story when, suddenly, Nero's voice called to them from the road below.

Maybelle quickly shushed her audience, whispering for them

to hide Rita under a pile of blankets in the corner. She pointed at the earthen plate and the extra spoon near the brazier.

Then, parting the fly strings with her hands, Maybelle looked down the ladder at Nero, trying to erase all signs of anxiety from her face.

Still dusty from the fields, Nero called, 'Sorry to drag you from supper, Maybelle. But I was wondering if you could help me.' He moved to climb up the ladder.

Stepping forward, Maybelle sat down on the top rung of the ladder which led from the road to her door. She said, 'Knew you was coming by, Nero, I'd fixed more.'

'I got plenty at home, thanks.'

Settling her elbows on her knees, trying to sound as friendly as usual, she said, 'You need you a good woman, Nero.'

Dropping his head, Nero kicked at the bottom of the wooden ladder, saying, 'That's why I stopped by, Maybelle.'

She joked. 'You better not let my man here you say that. He'll forget you the big overseer here and clean knock your block off!' Then, putting her hands on her hips, she stuck out her pregnant stomach, saying, 'Don't know why, but a man gets mean when his gal gets big with his baby.'

Nero shook his closely-cropped head. 'I wouldn't cause Ham no trouble. No matter how pretty-looking his gal is. Mothering makes you prettier than ever, Maybelle.'

She laughed heartily at the compliment, but straining her ears for any commotion from Rita in the room behind her.

More serious now, Nero said, 'I thought I knew everybody around here, Maybelle. But a couple days back, I saw the cutest little wench crawling up this here ladder.' He held up both hands to his head, saying, 'She had the prettiest hair. All out to here. Just like a little West Indian gal I used to – ' He stopped and, lowering his head, he said, 'Well, she just reminded me of a gal I used to know some other place. And I was wondering if you could maybe tell me who she was.'

The thought that Nero had seen Rita chilled Maybelle. She thought not so much of the girl being returned to Witcherley but of herself, Ham, Clara, Hopper, all of them being whipped for harbouring a runaway slave. She knew Nero was an honest man, though, and if he expected that she was hiding someone in her house, he would come right out and accuse her. He was not trying to trap her now. His eyes showed that he was serious – even desperate.

She said, 'Don't tell me you thinking of getting you a woman, Nero?' She was trying to keep the talk happy.

Shyly hedging again, he answered, 'If you remember who that gal might be, I'd like to meet her, Maybelle.'

Pulling herself up on the ladder, Maybelle said, 'The one time I can help you and I can't! Man, you point to any other wench on this road and I'll bring her to you smelling so pretty you think I bring you some flowers. But a gal with – ' She held her own hands out by her head, saying, 'Nero, you must have got too much sun the day you think you seen a gal like that scooting up here.'

Shrugging, he said, 'Yeah, Maybelle. I thought so, too. But I didn't think it would hurt none to ask. You go back to your supper now. Tell your people I'm sorry to kept you jabbering. And tell Ham, too, I ain't got eyes for you. And don't let him work you too hard for him. You have to keep strength for mothering.'

He turned away from the ladder then.

And watching him walk down the road with his hands tucked into the top of his trousers, his head bent forward, Maybelle felt heartbreak for him. She realized that she could not hate Nero for working so closely with white people. Although she still did not dare tell him about Jeb Conway, she knew that Nero was a good man, just doing his job, an overseer who was kind to the people under him. And she thought now, 'Shit! The one black man on this place who needs a good woman and he can't have her. She's got to screw that white bastard!' Maybelle's head clouded with the irony of her plan and how the world played cruel tricks, too.

Parting the fly strings, she went back into the house to tell Rita to move very stealthily tonight when she went to meet Master Webb. But she did not tell Rita about Nero's genuine interest in her. Nero was no young buck but he had a fine body and would be a good man for any black wench. Maybelle did not want to make Rita's pain worse.

*   *   *

Imogen Abdee forced herself to concentrate on Barry Breslin tonight when he came to supper; she had become accustomed lately to thinking about the chores which lay ahead of her the next day whenever she had to be seated at the same supper table as Duncan Webb. Imogen noticed that her father and Veronica were also holding their eyes to their supper plates lately, thinking private thoughts, when Duncan talked nonsense about the building of the new house or reminisced about his childhood — tales of a pampered life among liveried servants, stories so pompously told that everyone took them as pure fabrications.

Tonight's meal was different, though. Duncan did not speak; he ate quietly and frequently checked the time on his pocket watch. He made no annoying observations nor quarrelled with Vicky, a supper pastime which had also become frequent since his arrival at Dragonard Hill.

Although Barry Breslin was the special guest at supper tonight, Duncan ignored Barry's presence on the other side of the table. Barry conversed freely with Peter Abdee about the conditions of the public roads, the arrival of a new attorney in Troy, the runaway slave girl whom the Witcherleys had come to accept as lost property. Barry appeared to be enjoying his inclusion at the supper table here for the first time, glad to be out of the doldrums of his sick room.

His only cause for embarrassment was when Vicky spoke to him; then, Barry would blush and look nervously at the finely-dressed Duncan Webb. He was frightened of a husband's jealousy, Imogen suspected, and thought that Duncan Webb looked like the kind of a 'gentleman' who would challenge him to a duel.

Imogen also was surprised at the attention which Barry

paid to her. Ordinarily, she would have been jealous at Vicky's flirtations with Barry but, again, tonight was different. Barry did not give Imogen a chance to be jealous. He acted far bolder than before, saying that he had heard about the good work that Imogen had done with the smudgepots and told her about an incident nearby at the Grouse farm, the smallholding run by a white woman, which had lost its entire small crop during the rains. Barry laughingly said that Mrs Grouse had probably been spending too much time in her slave quarters and had neglected the crops.

Across the table, Veronica coughed nervously into her handkerchief. It was known that Claudia Grouse carried on flagrant affairs with the black men whom she owned.

Peter did not rebuke Barry for introducing such an unsavoury subject at the supper table. He said quietly, 'We knew Mrs Grouse when she was married to Chad Tucker. He used to be the overseer here. But I believe that that woman has had her new name changed by deed poll. Isn't she and her new husband known now as "Goss" instead of "Grouse"?'

Barry nodded, smiling. He remembered that fact about her now. And then nothing more was said about the matter, the white female whose name – whatever it became – was synonymous with the popular Southern catchphrase, 'nigger lover'.

As Barry Breslin was enjoying himself so much tonight, he did not realize his *faux-pas*, nor did anyone at the table notice Veronica's sudden agitation over the mention of a white woman who was ostracized because of her relationship with black men.

The supper proceeded; Eulalia carried a towering strawberry blancmange from the kitchen and soon announced that coffee was waiting in the parlour. It was a simple evening but, with Duncan Webb's unusual silence tonight, and Barry Breslin's willingness to lead the conversation, it became one of the most enjoyable suppers at Dragonard Hill in weeks.

Then, Barry surpassed even his suppertime behaviour by asking Imogen if she cared to take an evening stroll.

Vicky seized the opportunity to push her way into the

invitation. She saw that Duncan was not going to walk with her and, so now, locking her arm through Barry's, she said, 'Imogen needs a chaperone! And there's nobody better for a chaperone than a little married woman!'

Imogen tensed for the first time this evening.

*   *   *

Only a few stars twinkled tonight in the dark sky and, as Barry led the two girls down the porch steps of the old house, he asked which way they wanted to walk.

Nodding toward the pole gates at the end of the drive, Imogen put her arm through Barry's and gruffly said 'That's good enough.'

Vicky pulled in the other directly, saying, 'I want to go . . . there!'

Imogen said flatly, 'It's too dark.'

'But the moon! We've got the wonderful moon to light our way!' She raised her hand to the heavens.

The moon was indeed bright tonight and, stiffly, Imogen followed on one side of Barry as Vicky led on the other side.

Originally, Imogen had planned to allow Barry to reach an orgasm with her again tonight. She wanted to keep him interested, even remind him of their possible marriage. But now Vicky had ruined her plans for that activity.

Vicky said now, 'My! Barry Breslin! Aren't you the most popular beau in these parts tonight. Look, two young ladies! One on each arm!'

'And one of them married,' Imogen icily reminded her.

'You need a chaperone, big sister.'

Imogen answered, 'Chaperones usually walk back one or two steps.'

'But that's when the chaperone's an old maid. But I'm married and even younger than you, dear Imogen!' She squeezed Barry's arm.

He looked nervously at her and then at the empty path behind them.

'You are so nervous with me, Barry Breslin. Now, you don't have to worry about my Duncan getting jealous. Why, excuse my indelicacy, but my Duncan's probably dead drunk right now. Inebriated in the parlour.'

Imogen said through tight lips, 'Try looking for him in Town.'

Vicky did not understand what Imogen meant. She said gaily, 'I think it's marvellous how infatuated Duncan is with plantation life.'

'Especially the wenches,' Imogen said.

Vicky was beginning to understand Imogen's snideness. But she would not let Imogen get the better of her. She tried to increase what she considered to be irresistible charm. She said, 'Northern gentlemen are always intrigued by the black wenches we have here.'

'But all wenches here aren't black, are they, Vicky?' Imogen said.

'Imogen!' Vicky said, looking at her across Barry's chest. 'I think you are jealous. Jealous of me cutting in on you and Barry Breslin like this. Me! A respectable married woman.'

Imogen said, 'The day I'm jealous of you . . .' But then she stopped. She would not squabble with Vicky like this.

Vicky knew that she was needling Imogen and she enjoyed it. She said, 'Aww, Imogen is disturbed with me, Barry Breslin. She wants you all to herself.'

Imogen stopped on the path. She saw that this stroll was not going to be what she had intended. She said, 'The fact is, I was just going to take a short walk and then say good-night to Barry.'

The announcement baffled him, as did the exchange just now between the two sisters. He had been having such a good time before they had come on the walk.

Imogen said, 'I'll leave you in expert hands, Barry.' She kissed him quickly on the cheek and then walked quickly on the path toward the old house.

Barry looked at Imogen disappearing and then looked anxiously at Vicky.

Squeezing his arm again, Vicky said, 'Let the old fuss budget go. Let's just you and me walk and get to know each other better.'

'Is that proper, Miss Vicky, Mam?'

'What would be improper about it? Unless you had ideas, Barry Breslin?'

'But I'm courting Imogen.'

'Go ahead and court her! I'm not trying to stop you.'

'But you're married.'

'Yes, I *am* married. And I confess that I'm often sorry about that when I think of me coming home and finding what a fine man you've grown into.' She nudged him playfully, 'Now, why didn't anybody write to me in Boston and tell me these things?'

Barry stammered. 'I better go now, Miss Vicky. It's late.'

She taunted, 'What's the matter? Are you scared of what Imogen will say?'

He shook his head. 'No. My aunt's expecting me home early tonight.'

Vicky sighed helplessly. 'A girl can never argue with a man once he's made up his mind.' Looking up into his soft brown eyes, she said, 'But don't you forget one thing, Barry Breslin.'

He waited.

She touched the tip of his nose with her forefinger, saying, 'I got my eye on you, Barry Breslin. On *all* of you. From here, down to – ' She ran her finger over his chin, down his chest, stopping just short of his waistband.

Then, laughing, Vicky turned away, leaving him standing alone on the patch, a lump forming in the crotch of his breeches He was imagining himself making love to her. Imogen had given him confidence but, now, he thought about trying her married sister. The idea made his penis even harder than when he thought about Imogen.

*   *   *

Looking around him in the night, Duncan Webb laughed

at his situation. What was he doing here? In the wilderness? Chasing up some cowpath after a nigger bitch? This was not how he had planned his life to take shape.

But he badly needed a woman tonight and he had met a slave wench in Town this afternoon who had told him where he could find someone, find a very special black wench near this spot. Duncan doubted if she would be as good as . . .

Duncan stopped. He saw a shape ahead of him on the moonlit path. Squinting his eyes, he saw that it was a female. He saw the inverted arc of her naked breasts and the roundness of her hips.

Then the girl turned to face him.

Duncan stood still and stared at her. He looked between her legs. There was no place else to look but there. The patch was so phosphorescent that Duncan thought that he was hallucinating.

He walked closer.

The girl held her eyes down to the ground but she was lifting one arm to Duncan. She was expecting him.

As Duncan cautiously approached her, his eyes studied the hair between her legs. He thought now of telling his friends in New Orleans about this rare female. This is surely what people meant when they referred to special negroes as 'Fancies'. But his friends would not believe this story.

Never before had Duncan seen a thicket – a fleece – coloured in such a way. It looked metallic.

The girl backed off the path, moving slowly through the ferns and the bushes where there was a blanket already spread in a small opening. She still did not look at Duncan. She sank gracefully to the blanket and, placing her bare feet on it, she planted her hands under her buttocks and spread open her legs for Duncan to see her – he saw how her fleece became lighter, more brilliant, as it grew closer to her vagina.

He dropped to his knees at her feet.

The girl did not behave like any female he had been with before. She did not look at him. She did not care about what he was bringing her. She ignored his penis, his body. She looked sideways now, tensing her neat stomach, breathing deeply so that her breasts rose and lowered, falling fully to the sides of her slim body, breasts that were plump with firm, dark-brown nipples that stood out in the moonlight like small mushrooms.

To Duncan, the black girl with the silver fleece looked like a strange goddess, exactly as the wench in Town had described her, a fertility idol. Quickly, he ripped off his clothes, his penis already bobbing without any need of foreplay, requiring no coaxing nor games to arouse him.

The girl lay back, keeping her legs spread but holding her arms up over her head and looking at her small hands in the moonlight, acting as if Duncan were not even there.

This disdainful treatment of him increased Duncan's desire for her and, unlike he had ever acted with a woman before, he plunged directly for the stark whiteness of her silver patch, driving deep into her without having, first, dragged himself over her legs or making a woman wet him with her mouth.

Duncan had never known a passage to be so tight, the tissues clinging to him as he entered, giving him a sensation that almost burnt. She planted her hands under her buttocks again to allow him a deeper entry and Duncan fell naked on top of her body now, grasping her breasts, licking them, nibbling her taut nipples, kissing her neck and cheeks and eyes.

Still, the black girl did not repay any of his attention, only working her muscles to clamp him tighter, deeper inside her silver-haired patch, contracting so hard on Duncan that he felt that she would never let him go, then expanding for him to sink deeper into the heat.

*   *   *

Vicky stood on the path, surprised at seeing Duncan making love to a black girl, looking at him and realizing that he was grovelling for the black girl. His naked shoulders, back, buttocks, and legs glistened with perspiration in the moonlight. Vicky had never seen him working so hard. And she had never

159

wanted to see him working so hard! She wanted him to be powerful, not crawling for some slave wench, not even to be subservient to herself!

Hatred for Duncan flared inside Vicky and, turning away from him and the black girl lying locked together on the blanket, she walked numbly down the path, the pathetic image of Duncan branded upon her mind.

The more that she thought about him laying the black girl with such abandonment, the faster that her footsteps became. She was almost running by the time that she reached the outer limits of Town, her eyes quickly surveying the tall-standing houses in the moonlight, her mind thinking only one thing: a man . . . a real man . . . a man to give me what I need.

Her mind's eye saw a black man, a black man with whom she could defy her husband, a negro to even the score between them, a strong negro to surpass her husband, to take complete control of her.

Stopping at the first house on the left side of the row, she angrily kicked the wooden ladder, causing it to shake on the threshold high above her. She wanted to scream up at the tall house but she still had some control of herself not to awaken the entire settlement.

A black man's face appeared between the strings hanging from the doorway. 'Go away, Friend,' he sleepily began, ready to complain about being disturbed at such a late hour. Sunrise and work were not far away.

But when he saw a white lady standing at the bottom of the ladder, his eyes widened and he asked, 'What's you wishing, Mistress Mam?'

Vicky called in a near-whisper, but with sharpness to her question. 'How many wenches you have up there?'

'Just one, Mistress Mam. But she do nothing wrong. She been here sleeping all night, Mistress Mam. She's just an old wench. She do nothing wrong.'

'How many bucks you got there?' Vicky asked next.

He answered, 'Me and three others, Mistress Mam. We getting one more to come live with us next spring. We waiting for next saplings coming down from The Shed. We ain't hogging this house, Mistress Mam. We waiting for next saplings.'

'How old are your other bucks?' Vicky asked, seeing that the man to whom she was speaking would serve her purpose if the others did not satisfy her.

'Same ages as me, Mistress Mam.'

'What's your name?'

'Rib-Eye, Mistress Mam.'

Vicky sharply said, 'Rib-Eye, you send that old woman down this ladder and you wake up those other bucks. I'm coming up there to inspect them.'

'You coming up to . . . inspect them?' Rib-Eye asked.

'That's right. And I don't have all night. So, you tell that old nigger woman to get her ass down here fast. And if I hear that she – or any of you bucks – blabs about me coming to this house, I'll . . . I'll . . . I'll sell you all to the meanest, most cruel slaver I can find. You understand me, Rib-Eye?'

The old negro woman was soon hobbling down the ladder with a blanket wrapped round her stooped shoulders. Vicky brushed quickly past the old woman before she had removed her bare foot from the bottom rung.

Lifting her skirt, Vicky quickly climbed up the ladder. She would not allow herself to think about the stupidity of this action, nor envision its possible consequences. She thought only of Duncan laying the black girl alongside the path.

The three black men were seated on the floor, all of them still naked, with only a blanket covering the lower halves of their bare bodies. But Rib-Eye was almost dressed, hurriedly cinching a rope around his breeches.

Studying the other three negroes, Vicky saw that Rib-Eye had not been lying. They were his same age, somewhere in their early-to-mid-twenties. She was not very good at telling the ages of black people.

Still single-minded about finding the right black man for herself, she ordered, 'Throw down that blanket.'

The men looked at Rib-Eye. He shrugged. They had no choice. She was a white woman.

Stepping closer, Vicky repeated, 'Throw down that blanket!'

The man next to the wall – the youngest of the trio – was the first to push away the length of worsted from his bare stomach. The others then followed, all exposing their dark clumps of genitalia.

Stepping sideways so the moonlight would shine through the small window and fall upon them, Vicky said, 'Now stand up!'

The three men slowly obeyed, moving to cover their crotches with their hands as they rose.

'Drop your arms!' Vicky snapped impatiently.

Their arms hesitantly lowered.

Beginning to study them, she called to Rib-Eye still standing by the door. She said, 'Don't think you're going anywhere, either. I want to see what you've got, too.'

The young man against the wall smiled at Rib-Eye. He was tall and slim, with shoulders too broad for his small waist. Even considering his height, his penis was disproportionately large, too.

Vicky caught his boyish grin and, looking down at the enormity of his penis, she said, 'Funny, is it? Well, good. I'm glad you like this. Because you're my first choice.'

The boy sobered, his forehead wrinkling, causing the straight line of his closely cropped hair to move.

Looking more closely at the penises on the other two men, noticing their long foreskins, she turned and quickly checked to see the condition of Rib-Eye's penis. It resembled the one she had already chosen, but not as elephantine.

Turning back to the line-up of the three naked negroes, she pushed her finger at the second and third man, saying, 'You and you, out! You both go down the ladder and wait with the old lady. But I want *you* to stay, too,' she said to Rib-Eye. 'I want you to stay by the door and make sure that these two niggers stay down there where they're told to stay. I might be needing them regardless of all that . . . flap.'

She looked back to the young man now, her first choice.

162

The vision of Duncan and the black girl was so strong in her mind that she did not even bother to start undressing herself yet. She stepped forward, reaching for the boy's penis and asking, 'What's your name?'

He answered, 'Billy . . . Mistress Mam.'

'Billy,' she repeated. 'Do you know how to keep a secret, Billy?'

He nodded his head.

'What else do you know how to do . . . Big Billy?' She played harder with his penis, squeezing its middle with her cupped hand. She still knew no fear of being alone here in Town. She was driven by anger and jealousy.

'I works in the cornfields, Mistress Mam.'

'I don't mean work, Billy. I mean play.' She was holding his penis with one hand and running the other up his flat stomach, feeling the hardness of his chest, pinching at his small paps.

He laughed uneasily. Her hand was beginning to excite him.

Dropping to her knees, Vicky began sucking the boy's hardening penis in her mouth, holding it there until it became too large. Then, when she could no longer accommodate its size inside her mouth, she began to pull at her skirt, lifting it up to her waist, trying to free herself from her drawers. Simultaneously, she rubbed her face against his now moistened penis and pulled him down to the floor beside her.

Quick to accommodate her, Billy pressed his erect penis between Vicky's bare legs, toying with her breasts as she thrust them up toward him, wanting him to hold them in his hands.

Still standing by the doorway, Rib-Eye begged, 'Mistress Mam, you sure knows what you wanting? Mistress Mam, we gets caught like this, we gets in big trouble.'

Vicky was too concerned with Billy's young body to listen to Rib-Eye's caution. She had never lusted after young men specifically, but Billy – his blackness, his enormity – made her completely forget about her husband. She was gaining a victory over him. And, shortly, she had stripped off her cloth-

163

ing, lying naked under Billy, holding him in her legs, letting him try to ease into her.

Billy knelt between her, beginning to drive the first inches of his penis into her with neat, deepening thrusts. And, as Vicky kept her eyes on the muscles gliding under the tight skin of his stomach, she motioned for Rib-Eye to come toward her.

Then, as Vicky lay taking more and more of Billy into her vagina, she began to work the second man's hesitant penis into hardness, too. It grew in front of her eyes and she began to talk to it, whispering, 'Black one, aren't you? A real black stranger!' Her lips now slicked against the moisture she had caused on Rib-Eye blood-tight penis.

Raising her head to kiss it, she continued whispering, 'No, I think we'll have to save those other two strangers till to-morrow night. I think you – ' She paused to kiss Rib-Eye's penis again, to enjoy this one stranger, to make him comfortable while the other one sank deeper in between her legs. ' – I think you and Big Billy are going to do me tonight. Do me just fine. Do me real fine if you – if you know how to be men. I need a real man. I don't want come. I don't want babies. I just want to . . . *feel* I'm with a man. To hear it. To know it.'

Billy and Rib-Eye no longer exchanged glances. They knew they were doing something wrong. They knew that this white female was one of Master Peters' daughters. They knew that they must keep this secret to themselves. The wrong was hers. And she did not have to tell them not to give her a baby. They would both stop before they burst inside her. They just wanted her to go away because, if word spread through Dragonard Hill that one of the Abdee girls had come to Town for pestering tonight, they were the ones who would have to pay.

Chapter Eight

DAUGHTERS OF DRAGONARD

Duncan went the next evening to find the black girl whom he had met on the path behind the old house but she did not appear. He searched out Maybelle the following day and she told him that, if the girl was not in the woods, she did not know where she would be. After repeating that she was a very special, often unpredictable wench, Maybelle begged Duncan not to mention her to any of the white people and expose her as an Ashanti moon goddess. Maybelle whispered that the girl would surely be punished for practising a taboo religion on Dragonard Hill.

No other black people in Town whom Duncan questioned had ever heard of such a priestess, a girl who lay naked in the moonlight. Duncan began to explain to them the extraordinary colouring of her pubic hairs but then stopped his description. He feared they would think he was mad and begin to talk about him. Word would spread through Town and the shops and all the black people would laugh about him, saying that there was a weak-minded Yankee in the old house who was looking for a girl with a silver fleece between her legs. Duncan Webb was too proud to have the black people mocking him.

But he knew that he was not going mad. He definitely remembered the girl. How could he possibly forget her? She had been the best woman he had ever enjoyed.

That week slowly passed, his frustrations growing, and no matter how cleverly he tried to question Peter Abdee about any extraordinary wenches on the plantation, asking him if there were any black people who practised voodoo or any other African religions, he still found no clue of the girl.

This obsessive search kept Duncan from noticing at first that Vicky was changing, too. She was always asleep in their bedroom when he came upstairs at late hours and, slowly, he realized that she had stopped trying to seduce him. She had stopped groping at his crotch, insinuating that she wanted him to treat her very roughly. Duncan hated Vicky's insinuations. He got as rough with her as he possibly could. Perhaps it was due to his mother's golden code – *Never strike a female* – but, whatever the reason, he could not bring himself to defile Vicky in any way other than innuendo, by harsh words and teasing.

Duncan became more of an insomniac, drinking late into the night and, after taking repeated exploratory walks in the night, he returned to the bedroom and began trying to force Vicky to release his tensions with her mouth. Mumbling into her pillow that she was too tired for him, she pulled another pillow over her head and ignored him.

Finally, by the end of the week, Duncan made a decision. He came down late to breakfast, his eyes dark from another sleepless night. But, unlike his previous mornings at Dragonard Hill, he was not dressed in his long maroon satin robe. He was dressed today in a frock coat, fresh linen, and a cravat.

Vicky was lingering over coffee at the table, thinking about problems of her own. She had developed a new private diversion for herself this past week, following her discovery of Rib-Eye and Billy. She had enjoyed the other bucks in their house, too, and was half-hoping to turn them into her fantasy lovers. They still were hesitant with her, though. And she also feared that word would spread; she knew how the black people loved to gossip and, often, talk from the slave quarters of one plantation carried quickly to the black people on a neighbouring plantation and they would pass it on to their white masters. Vicky was thinking this morning that, perhaps, she was doing the wrong thing, having carried her revenge against Duncan far enough and should content herself with him instead of her new black lovers. Of trying again to achieve bliss with Duncan. It would be safer.

Sitting down across the table from her now, Duncan announced, 'I'm leaving.'

Vicky looked blankly at him.

'I'm going back to New Orleans,' he said, staring into her eyes. 'I'm taking a job.'

Vicky knew that he had been acting strangely lately and, the first thought that came to her now was that he was running away with the black girl, the wench who had controlled him with such power.

Bracing herself, she waited for the details.

'I'm going on the stage,' he said, raising his chin.

'From Carterville?' she asked.

Realizing that she had misunderstood him, Duncan laughed at her, saying, 'You ignorant, provincial cow! The stage! I am going to be an actor.'

Her eyes widened.

He explained, 'Before I left New Orleans, someone offered me a job.'

'You never mentioned this to me, Duncan.'

'I wasn't considering it as a serious possibility. I thought things would be different here.' He could not tell her the truth, that Madam Naomi of *Petit Jour* had offered him a job in her bordello after he had run out of money in New Orleans, employing him – as he called it – to 'screw niggers' in a whorehouse arena. He had angrily turned down the offer, telling Naomi that he considered it an insult. That he was a gentleman.

But now he told Vicky half the truth. Not that he was slinking back to Naomi, saying that he had changed his mind. He told Vicky the news as if the idea had just come to him, as if it were yet another form of revenge against her – and, now, that vengeance was also aimed at her family, too.

He said, 'When your father asks you what I do for a living now, you can tell him I'm a stud on a whorehouse stage!'

She began to shake her head, bewildered.

Knowing that she was horrified, he increased her misery. It was the only enjoyment he had had for days now. He said, 'You know how you like me, Vicky. How *you* like me to treat you.'

She waited, her nostrils flaring. Should she laugh at him or strike him?

167

He continued, 'Well, I am going to do that in public. For money. With black women.'

Vicky thought of the girl on the blanket.

'I might even make my whores call themselves "Vicky". And I'll treat them the same way I treat you.'

She slowly rose from the chair.

Seeing her reaction made it easier now for Duncan to take the job; now that she hated it, he no longer considered it beneath him. It was a weapon.

As she walked from the table, he called after her, 'Aren't you going to wish me good luck?'

She kept walking.

'What? No goodbye kiss?'

She passed through the archway.

'Slut! Run to your daddy! See if I care!'

Stopping, facing him, Vicky had tears falling down her cheeks, her mouth quivered. She momentarily looked at Duncan as if she were going to run to him, fling her arms around him, begging for a reconciliation, asking him to stay at Dragonard Hill with her, saying that they would turn the new house into a home only for them, that they could both try to make themselves a good match.

But she did not; turning, she ran up the stairs.

*   *   *

Veronica carried a hamper of lunch to her father on the building site of the new house that noontime. She also brought him the news that Duncan Webb had left Dragonard Hill.

Peter's first question was about Vicky, asking if she and Duncan had quarrelled, wanting to know how she was reacting to his departure, had it been amiable or was Vicky left despondent and miserable?

Telling her father that Vicky had locked herself in her bedroom as soon as Boxo had taken Duncan to catch the coach in Carterville, Veronica tried to assure him that life would be easier now for everyone here.

Veronica then forced herself to tell him the truth about

Brownie; he would find out soon enough that she was pregnant, Vicky realized, and now that Duncan Webb had gone, she had no fears of her father confronting him, even a terrible fight ensuing. She knew how her father hated him and was firm about sexual liberties not to be taken with any of his black people.

Again, Peter asked about Vicky. He wanted to know if she had been involved in the scene that had taken place in Duncan Webb's Boston rooms.

Veronica told him the entire story, no longer able to protect her sister. She begged him to forgive her for lying about Brownie's bruises and the story that she had told him about Vicky going to New Orleans with a school friend.

Peter commended Veronica for protecting her sister, saying that he wished that more of the family had her sense of obligation.

At that moment, Veronica wanted to tell her father everything, confess to him how she felt about Royal, how their friendship was growing daily and that she was frightened by it. She wanted to ask her father's advice but something inside her stopped the urge. She knew that this was not the right moment. She could see that he had other matters that worried him. Apart from finishing the new house and preparing for the harvest, he had Vicky and her marriage to Duncan Webb to worry about, he had Imogen's curious relationship with Barry Breslin to consider, the possibility of their betrothal, and, now, he had to go to The Shed to talk to Lady Alice. Veronica had also heard the news that another yellow baby had been born on Dragonard Hill. She did not want to add to his worries nor his shame. She knew that he had so little pride left these days over the children he had raised, the three little girls he used to brag about, imagining their bright futures. They certainly had not grown into the perfect young ladies for which he had worked and sacrificed his own life.

*   *   *

The child was no more than a few days old. Its hair looked like black silky threads matted against skin that was neither black nor white. The child did not have a negro's dark eyes. They were green. And the child was born of Zena, a coal-black woman of Bantu stock. Her husband was Trill, another negro with dark pigmentation, a teamster who drove a wagon to the cotton gin.

This new-born child had come unquestionably from a white father and Peter was perplexed. He studied the sleeping infant, wondering who could be siring these yellow babies.

Again, the mother had refused to tell Lady Alice who was the father and Peter knew that he could not force the woman to speak.

Then, turning from the yellow baby asleep in its bark crib, Lady Alice asked Peter about snake weed, a nostrum which her predecessor at The Shed, Mama Gomorrah, had made as a cure for syphilis.

Peter sank to the straight-back chair beside the stone hearth in The Shed. His mind reeled. He did not need a problem like syphilis here now. He had enough worries.

Assuring him that she did not need the snake weed for one of their people, Lady Alice said that a Looming House wench named Maybelle had brought a foreign black girl to her. Her name was Rita. She had deserted Witcherley. And Lady Alice then explained that Rita had left there because she had caught the disease from one of the Witcherley nephews and that the nurse there had tried to peroxide it out of the girl's inside. The repeated applications of peroxide had bleached her thatch entirely white, giving her an almost exotic appearance when she was naked. But the bleach had done nothing for the syphilis, except to irritate it.

Peter asked where the girl was now.

Lady Alice told him that she had her in the cloth room at the back of The Shed. The girl was too frightened to come out and too scared to go back to Witcherley. The tissues of her vagina burnt as if they were on fire. But she was a strong girl and did not complain.

Remembering that he had heard the Witcherley's had given up the runaway slave as lost, Peter told Lady Alice not to add to the girl's misery, ordering her to forget about Mama Gomorrah's ancient remedy of snake weed. He said that after nightfall tonight, he would have Nero take the girl to Treetops. It was a workhouse for freed slaves, a place where the black people could learn a craft which they could apply to their own support. He had freed a slave girl and sent her there long ago; she was the mother of a son called Lloy.

But that was history. The important fact now was that there was a doctor at Treetops and Peter told Lady Alice that they would let him examine the contaminated girl and decide what was best for her future. He did not stop to consider the complications of aiding a black slave escape from her white master. He thought only of a human being unjustly made to suffer from a selfish act.

Before leaving The Shed, Peter stopped in the doorway and asked Lady Alice, 'This girl, Rita, she didn't have contact with any of our people, did she?'

Lady Alice shook her head. 'No, Master Peter. That Maybelle who brought her to me this week, she's a good wench. She promised me she guards that Rita girl like she was a real precious thing. Like that light coloured patch of hers was valuable as pure silver. No, Master Peter, none of our people got close to that Rita girl to pick up her awful disease. Maybelle, she took good care of that.'

Peter told Lady Alice to give Maybelle a bolt of bright calico from the cloth room to make curtains for her house in Town. It would be a reward for Maybelle's good work.

The black people were Peter Abdee's family, too. He was relieved they were safe from disease. And, now, that Duncan Webb had gone away, Peter Abdee would move into the new house with his other family. His true family. Imogen, Victoria, and Veronica.

Walking happily away from The Shed, Peter felt that life was going to get better now at Dragonard Hill.

Book Two

FLASHING SKIES

Chapter Nine

MOVING

Indian summer lingered in the Louisiana wilderness; the oaks turned red and the cottonwood formed golden borders along the creeks which veined the hilly countryside, whilst the flatlands whitened as the time approached for harvesting the cotton.

Thin curls of smoke could be seen from the public road, rising at dawn from the squat stone chimneys of small farmhouses set in the middle of fields, and from the taller chimneys of the plantation manor houses sprawling at the end of long driveways; like summer, though, the breakfast fires were left to die down by mid-morning and only reheaped for the cooking of dinner.

Local almanac readers found portents in this weather, interpreting the lingering warmness as Nature's perverse hint of a hard winter, also noting the late migration of geese and the deep coloration of the deer and the rabbits as warnings that this January could be even more severe than it had been in '16.

Halloween came and the balmy days continued; the black men wore no shirts as they picked cotton; the women brought the hem of their long skirts between their legs, tucking them into their sashes, making pantaloons which were cooler for their work, dragging hemp bags of cotton slowly down the rows in the fields.

Apart from the boosts that these days gave the harvesting, Dragonard Hill also welcomed the sunshine because the move was being made at last from the old house – through the edge of the woodlands, across the meadow, up the hill – to the new house. Neighbouring planters joked that Peter Abdee has spent his money in vain on the marble mantelpieces he had installed in his new home. They said he would not be using his fireplaces for a long time. The marble was white, coming from Italy, and those people who knew of Italy, said that the Mediterraean sun had come to Louisiana in the large wooden crates.

The plantation sewing houses spent many November hours completing the draperies, curtains, and cushions for the new house and the women then had to work late into the night to sew new clothing for the people of Town to wear in winter. Their added labour was rewarded with molasses and ginger by Peter Abdee.

Furniture was arriving by wagon from New Orleans; china, crystal and cutlery were shipped from New York and additional wagon caravans went to Carterville to bring them carefully back to Dragonard Hill, along with the carpets: Aubusson and Turkish for the parlours, large rolls of narrow rugging that had been loomed in Persia and would lay on the walnut floor of the staircases and mezzanine which hung over the main hallway.

Thanksgiving passed and, finally, the last touch was added to the new house. One day before the official housewarming which was to be given for the neighbours and friends of Dragonard Hill came Storky, wobbling her way up the hill from the old house.

She rode on a specially built litter that was carried on the shoulders of four fieldhands. Although she was dressed in her usual white uniform, with the starched kerchief tied around her head, she looked like the Queen of Sheba. The carpenters had used a lead engraving of that famous woman, hanging in the entrance to the new house, as a guide for building the conveyance to move the arthritic but most cherished slave on Dragonard Hill.

Walking in arrogant attendance beside her, Posey wore his long baggy white pants and apron, carrying a cut-glass crystal vase in his arms – the gift which Vicky had brought him from New Orleans.

The negro litter-bearers progressed slowly up the driveway,

now moving toward the Doric columns which lined the facade.

Storkey had not seen the new house before today but, instantly knowing that she was being taken to the wrong place, she thumped the wooden floor of the litter with her willow cane and shouted, 'Niggers! Where you taking me? To the back door! To the back door, niggers! The back door!'

Posey joined Storky in abuse against the fieldhands, knowing that, although they ranked the highest in the plantation's slave hierarchy, the front door was only used by white people – for Master Peter, his three daughters, and their friends who would be coming tomorrow for the open house at Dragonard Hill.

*   *   *

The old house now was empty except for Ta-Ta, placed in her high window, sitting tipped forward on the runners of her rocking chair, watching Storky disappear behind the trees of the new house, heading toward the kitchen attached to the house by a columned breezeway.

At last, there was no one left here to disturb Ta-Ta.

Peter had allowed her to remain behind, permitting her to continue living in the attic room with the reminders of her past. Food would be brought to Ta-Ta, her chamber pots emptied, the brandy jugs delivered on schedule. And those simple things were Ta-Ta's only wordly desires.

Everything else spread in fading colours on her four walls and slanted ceiling, memories which she could not leave behind.

Rocking back and forth now, Ta-Ta cradled a demijohn of rum between her legs, resuming her conversation with a woman named 'Madame Honore'.

Ta-Ta told Madame Honore that she would be pleased with the home that her son, Peter, had built for his family. The new house looked very much like Madame Honore's home had been in the West Indies, the house on the island of St Kitts which had been called *Petit Jour* by Ta-Ta's long-dead

French mistress, a white woman represented on Ta-Ta's wall by a primitive drawing of a stick lady with yellow hair and circles around her neck which were meant to represent an opal necklace.

* * *

The black people in Town were excited about the official opening of the new house. That is, those whom Storky and Posey had singled out for their skills and appearances and invited them to help at the party.

Maybelle was not among the honoured negresses who would be wearing new, long dresses, with yellow fichus tied around their necks, and helping at the new house. The unborn child was now big in her stomach and she could not even go to the Looming House these days to work.

She sat tonight on the top of the ladder which led to her house, watching woefully as other negresses her same age – women not as pretty as she was, and as clumsy as oxen when it came to serving – rushed from house to house, comparing their new white dresses.

The sight of them, and the sound of their proud voices depressed Maybelle. But there was no way she could disguise her bulkiness. And Lady Alice had told her to follow Master Peter's rule, to stay at home and wait for the baby to come. The only thing she could do lately was help Lady Alice in The Shed, tending the saplings when Lady Alice had other chores to do.

Although Maybelle knew that five other wenches on this road were near birthing time, and that the maid in the big house named Brownie was expecting a child, too, even sooner than she was herself, Maybelle felt like the only pregnant woman in the world.

Also, when she dreaded that the baby might also belong to Jeb Conway – wondering if Ham indeed had planted his seed in her before Conway had rammed in his carrot-shaped penis – she became more depressed and thought of throwing herself down the ladder and killing the child in her stomach. Even herself.

Maybelle's love for Ham kept her from doing that, though. Nor did she have an evil soul. She could not kill even a half-white baby.

The one fault to which Maybelle admitted – nosing into other people's business – was what brightened her mood now. Sitting in front of the fly strings hanging in her doorway, she saw the young man named Bub. He lived in the house next to hers and, as he was a good-looking boy who had no girl-friend in Town, Maybelle had privately assigned herself to find him one.

Bub rejected her many suggestions, though. And Maybelle was still kept in a mystery about what he did with his free time. She usually saw him leaving his house after supper and heard his bare feet climb the rungs when he returned again much later, when most people in Town were sleeping.

But tonight Bub was sitting on the top of the ladder of the house where he lived.

Maybelle called, 'You ain't been invited to help at no house-party neither!'

Bub shook his head, smiling at Maybelle. He had large teeth, wide lips, and a small, almost snubbed nose. Maybelle had noticed that he also had a lean, muscular body and was not what she called a 'big-show nigger'. He would be a good catch for some wench and she could tell by the size of his large black fingers that he was obviously hung big, which was a good extra to talk about when she described him to possible girl-friends in Town.

So, thinking now that she had nothing better to do than find someone for Bub, she called, 'Hear Cody and Pearl got them a pretty little gal moved in with them, Bub.'

Nodding his head, smiling, not being rude, Bub waved at Maybelle and abruptly rose on his ladder, disappearing into the house.

Why the shit he do that for? she thought. Does he hate wenches?

179

Then she wondered if her neighbour boy, Bub, was one of those fine-looking males who got seriously involved with that fieldhand called Ben and his nasty friends. She knew about them. They pestered bucks instead of wenches.

Quickly forgetting about her exclusion from the house-warming party now, Maybelle gave herself a job to do. It might be a long term task but she decided that she would think of some way to get black boys like Bub a taste of young wenches before they forgot about them completely and were trapped by men like Ben.

Ben was a big-show nigger, in her words. He was a big-show-screw nigger. Maybelle doubted if there was anything in the world that Ben did not poke, even a knot hole in a log full of ants. And she wanted to save Bub from being used like that. Bub or any other fine-looking black boy in Town.

*   *   *

The master bedroom in the new house, and the rooms for the three girls, opened onto the mezzanine above the main hallway. The walls were painted ivory and brass sconces hung on the walls at fixed intervals and fitted with beeswax candles. The yellow-red-and-blue Persian carpet lay on the walnut floor and, between each doorway, sat large Egyptian-style amphoras filled with greenery for the party tonight.

It was late in the afternoon now, a few hours before the first guests would be arriving. Imogen Abdee had just come into the house, having spent the afternoon at the blacksmith shop, trying to explain how to make the heavy iron needles she wanted forged for her. She did not say why she needed them, only that they were for a job on the plantation.

Still dressed in her lace-up boots, a drab brown skirt, thick leather belt and nankeen shirt – clothes which comprised her daily work uniform – Imogen stood in her bedroom and studied the dress that had been ordered from New Orleans to wear at the party. It hung on a hanger at the side of a tall mahogany wardrobe.

Slowly lifting the edge of the full skirt with the tips of her dirty fingers, Imogen studied the many yards of blue organza with which it had been made, suspiciously moving her eyes to the slim waist, the bell sleeves, the round neckline decorated with nosegays of white silk daisies.

From the dress, Imogen looked at her reflection in the full length mirror embedded in the thick door of the mahogany wardrobe. She saw her sunburnt face, the black hair piled haphazardly on top of her head, the dark V tanned onto her skin by the open collar of her work shirt, the darkness of her forearms and the blisters on her red hands.

Imogen saw a young woman in the wardrobe mirror who was not meant to wear such a feminine dress. She never had been that kind of girl. This dress was for someone frivolous like her sister, Vicky.

Thinking of Vicky, and how she would happily cinch her waist into a corset to fit this dress and spill her powdered bosoms over the low neck, Imogen ripped the dress from the hanger.

Dresses like this were made for women whom Imogen called 'pussies', flirtatious females who lusted after attention from males. And Imogen thought now how Barry Breslin had become totally infatuated with her pussy sister, Vicky, over the last few months, how he had hardly paid any attention to Imogen since Duncan Webb had left Dragonard Hill and Vicky had begun to flirt shamelessly with him. Imogen knew they were doing much more than flirting, too.

Imogen also knew that Vicky was not interested in Barry Breslin any more than she was. Vicky only wanted him for two reasons – to feed on his attentions when she was bored with the life at Dragonard Hill and to make Imogen miserable. And she felt that her own reason for wanting Barry Breslin was more justified than Vicky's.

Dragonard Hill.

Looking again at her weathered face in the mirror, Imogen then reappraised the dress and began to see it as a symbol for something despicable, a feminine way of life, a pussy's dress, equating it with Vicky.

Infuriated now that she had to suffer the humiliations caused by a flirtatious slut, wishing that she did not need a husband in her life, angry that she had not been born a male herself, and, like a son, could inherit Dragonard Hill as the eldest child, Imogen began to rip the blue organza dress, pulling at its sleeves, bodice, small waist, and yards of full skirting.

Long shanks of hair fell over her blue eyes as she continued ripping the dress with both her soiled hands, cursing her sister, damning her sex.

*   *   *

Victoria Abdee had learned to control – or, at least, disguise – her anxieties since her husband had abandoned her; she did not want to jeopardize the easy life she was finding at home but, at the same time, she had discovered discreet ways to eke revenge on Duncan Webb and the wild life she imagined him to be having in New Orleans.

There proved to be a small corps of black males on Dragonard Hill who were willing to satisfy Vicky surreptitiously and, bribing them with money to keep silent about their moments with her, Vicky used them as nourishment for her sexual appetites. But, even they did not give her the ultimate thrill. She threw herself deeper into promiscuity. Trying to forget that Duncan was working as a showman in a New Orleans bordello, treating black prostitutes the way he had treated her, perhaps even inflicting the pain on them that she herself wanted. Vicky had not heard from him since he had left her almost six months ago and the silence only kindled her imagination with illicit thoughts about what he was doing.

Gathering her own retinue of sexual mates on Dragonard Hill, Vicky discovered that black people quickly learned sexual ways that differed from their established practices of begetting children. She was thankful for the Southern slave system, and the many diverse ways it could be used for achieving one's selfish whims.

Apart from her black lovers, Vicky also had Barry Breslin. She had succeeded in her seductions and, making love to him represented revenge, too, but a revenge not directed toward her husband. Vicky enjoyed Barry Breslin because of the misery that their friendship caused in her older sister, Imogen.

There was one male at Dragonard Hill whom Vicky wanted but whose attention she had not been able to win. He was Royal. His conquest would be the most satisfying of all for Vicky. Not only was he handsome, powerfully built, and endowed in such a way that Vicky could never see him without looking at outlines of his penis and testicles spreading down his left thigh, but she also knew that her virtuous sister Veronica was fond of him, liking Royal in what appeared to be a non-sexual, rather spiritual way.

Yes, Vicky doubted if Veronica and Royal made love together, suspecting that Veronica was too frightened – and proud! – of actually becoming physical with a black person. But Vicky saw that Veronica was becoming increasingly more infatuated with the handsome houseboy, even more than Veronica probably suspected herself. And Vicky longed for the time when Veronica could know that she had been intimate with Royal. To seduce Royal was one more item to be ticked off Vicky's list of sexual ambitions, needs that were becoming increasingly more mental than physical.

The guests would be coming shortly for the house-warming party. Vicky did not care if she missed the early arrivals and, knowing that the first shift of fieldhands were to be stopping their work for the day soon, she realized that she must hurry if she was to meet her latest negro lover.

His name was Ben, a brawny black whose sexuality was far more sophisticated than any of the fieldhands whom she had met up to now. Not even Duncan had asked to penetrate her anus. Vicky had not allowed Ben yet to do it but she loved teasing him in the dim light of a hut, watching him become aroused as he looked at her twisting her body on the blanket, lying on her back and, first, toying with her vagina and, then, pulling her legs to one side, running her other hand towards her anus, fingering herself in both holes, still keeping him at bay while the juice began to stream from the hole from which he normally passed urine.

Standing in the library doorway, wanting to go quickly to join Ben, Vicky waited until she could carefully sneak out from the new house. But she could not move yet because she had just heard Veronica coming down the staircase.

Now, looking across the hallway, Vicky saw to her horror that Veronica was leading Brownie down the stairs, step-by-step, carefully guiding the pregnant girl by one arm whilst Royal was walking her on the other side.

Vicky dug her long fingernails into the palms of her hands with anger, realizing that Brownie at last was having her baby, a child that Vicky had watched her own husband seeding in Boston. The memory of that night filled Vicky with both anguish and hatred. Brownie's swollen body represented Duncan Webb to Vicky and his moments spent with women other than himself, and Veronica's thoughtful assistance to Brownie filled Vicky with repugnance. She hated Veronica's sense of charity, and seeing her and Royal now joined together to help Brownie, Vicky swore to bring about some hideous revenge against both of them, somehow, some way she had not yet devised.

Veronica and Royal had reached the front doorway with Brownie, carefully walking her from the new house to Lady Alice in The Shed.

Vicky momentarily forgot about her imminent meetings with Ben, straining her mind for a weapon against Veronica and Royal.

The solution came accidentally, less than an hour later when Vicky was standing unclothed in the vacant field hut with Ben. The late afternoon sun faded through the rag hanging over a small window and lighted Vicky's body as she pressed herself against Ben's glistening blackness. She stood with her back to him, snuggling against his perspiration-soaked skin, a smell she was beginning to enjoy as much as the sight of his rugged body.

Ben pulled back his hips, ramming the blunt head of his penis toward the squeezed roundness of Vicky's buttocks, saying that he was going to screw her ass yet, promising that she would probably even be a better, tighter screw than the houseboy Royal.

At the mention of Royal's name, Vicky quickly forgot about their own activities and she immediately began to question Ben about Royal.

Ben told her about his friends, the black men who gathered to bugger young black boys, a group of males about whom he had told Vicky before and whom she had been wanting to meet. They would be different! Her other negro studs lusted after females. But Ben's followers were brutal perverts!

Forgetting about that now, though, she asked Ben for details of Royal's past submissions to the group. Did Ben actually drive his penis — Vicky reached down and gripped it with both hands to emphasize the importance of her question — into Royal's anus? Ben shrugged, saying a few months had passed since they had had him here in the hut. Vicky persisted, demanding to know if Royal actually had held Ben between his legs, allowed him to come into him, even took the sperm into his body. Ben nodded. It was the truth.

Quickly grabbing her clothes, Vicky told Ben that she must hurry back to the house, that there was a party tonight and that she did not want to be late.

Chapter Ten

THE CHINESE UMBRELLAS

The red harvest sun was sinking behind the western slopes of Dragonard Hill, silhouetting the classic proportions of the new house as the guests began to arrive in buggies, carriages, work wagons, and on horseback, coming in a steady pace up the driveway which climbed between the avenue of young cypress trees.

Peter Abdee had invited everyone he knew and the people with whom he had done business. Cotton brokers and bankers from New Orleans. Shippers and livery men from Carterville. The tradesmen and professional people of Troy, including Jeb and Noreen Conway from the cotton gin, although he expected that Jeb Conway would not bring his wife. Peter even had sent an invitation to be left at Witcherley, inviting the family who lived on the land which adjoined Dragonard Hill on the west, but he also doubted if they would come. They did not.

Most of the guests arrived wearing travelling clothes for the dusty roads, changing into their finery when they reached Dragonard Hill.

A small country orchestra began to play in one corner of the front hallway at six o'clock, when the guests were still stopping in front of the four Doric columns at the end of the driveway. From the moment that Boxo and his three assistants for the occasion – all dressed in black-and-gold livery – took the horses and conveyances, the guests were engulfed in a warm welcome – ballads drifting across the bricked forecourt, the first glimpses of rich yellow walls, warm parquet flooring, long white damask curtains, and a fleet of house servants dressed in starched white, moving through the crowd with silver trays of champagne, whiskey, fruit punches, and plates of small sandwiches to refresh the guests from the journey and give them nourishment for their preparation for the party yet to come.

By eight o'clock, a cello had joined the musicians and a waltz drifted through the inter-communicating ground floor rooms, parlours now thronged with people. The double doors to the dining-room were open and a long table set under a crystal chandelier blazing with candles, platters, and bowls heaped with the extravagant food that Storky and Posey had prepared – or ordered to be prepared – for the dinner.

Storky and Posey had done their master justice with their skills. They offered honey-cured ham, roast turkeys and chickens, sliced beef and horseradish, salads of seasonal fruit and vegetables, parsley potatoes, candied yams, a variety of hot and cold beans, choices of nut, almond, lemon, or orange breads, apart from Storky's own loaves of pumpkin bread; the desserts stood alone on a long sideboard, an array of cakes, puddings, cookies, tarts, jellies, blancmanges, and jugs of rich cream, custard, and sauces. The china from which this feast was eaten was a new set of deceptively simple white dishes banded with gold, drawing gasps from those women who held up their plates and saw the bold stroke of 'Sevres' scrawled on the underside.

Peter Abdee glowed with his best boyish charm tonight, shrugging off the compliments for his achievement of both building and furnishing his new home with such thoroughness.

He wore a black frock coat, a jabot tumbling from his throat, spotless white breeches which hugged his hard thighs, and gleaming black boots that reached to his knees. His shiny black hair flowed back from his face, his skin bronzed from the long summer and his cornflower blue eyes glazed with contentment as he joked with his friends, many of whom he had not seen for a long time. And he occasionally caught Kate Breslin's eye and chanced a quick wink.

Kate Breslin wore an emerald green satin gown tonight; long white gloves and a diamond collar which showed off the creaminess of her skin, and a long rope of pearls was twisted through the tresses of her dark red hair, which had been arranged in soft plaits on her head, leaving just her earlobes to be seen, and a pair of long diamond and pearl pendants dangling to her bare shoulders.

Her escort to the house-warming was her nephew, Barry Breslin, who clung close to her, nervously eyeing Vicky across the room.

Vicky was not ignoring Barry but she gave him no more time than she did the many other men – both married and single – here tonight.

With her blonde hair parted down the middle of her head and twisted into loose rolls that completely covered both her ears, Vicky flitted through the crowd, knowing that her slim-skirted, high-waisted dress was the most fashionable of any gown worn here tonight. No one in the Louisiana wilderness had yet discovered the 'Empire' look.

Kate Breslin and Barry spoke to Vicky before she disappeared yet again, leaving Barry more agitated by her careless treatment of him. But Kate wondered where Vicky's sisters were; she had not seen Veronica all evening and, looking now for both her and Imogen, her face suddenly sobered.

Seeing Imogen slowly coming down the staircase, dressed like Kate had seen no woman ever dressed before, she murmured behind her fan, 'My God! How could she?'

Imogen Abdee now had short hair and wore the clothes of a man.

*   *   *

Conversation stopped in the wide hallway as, one by one, the guests looked to the staircase and saw Imogen Abdee coming to join the party. She was dressed in black breeches, a white blouse, a blue silk cravat that matched her eyes, black jacket, and her brown lace-up boots polished to a high sheen of blackness. Her hair was no longer pulled into a knot on top of her head but it had been cut and was now oiled and combed straight back from her forehead.

Telling Barry to stay exactly where he was, Kate moved through the crowd, meeting Imogen as she reached the foot of the staircase.

Holding both arms to her, Kate took Imogen's hand and said, 'Imogen! I thought you were missing!' How good to see you, my dear!' She held both her cheeks to Imogen.

Awkwardly, first looking at the faces staring at her, Imogen returned Kate's greeting.

Next, putting her arm through Imogen's, Kate walked her through the crowd, introducing her as they moved, not pausing long enough for anyone to question her or to show a reaction to her severe clothing.

An Irish fiddle cut through the air and, as word passed that a reel was about to begin, people hurried to the main parlour that had been cleared of all furniture.

Peter walked sober-faced toward Imogen and Kate.

Slowly extending his arm to Imogen, he said, 'Would you join me?'

Imogen hesitated. She showed her first taint of a blush in her cheeks.

Kate gaily said, 'What better?' She held Imogen's arm toward Peter.

Then, leading his eldest daughter toward the dancing in the large parlour, he said in a low voice, looking straight ahead, 'Nothing is going to ruin tonight for me, Imogen. You understand? Nothing?'

Imogen could only follow.

*   *   *

Peter Abdee had taken careful steps that the official opening of his new home would be a success and that his guests would be fed well and entertained; at ten o'clock, Nero came to stand in front of the orchestra as he had been instructed to do, and, as the music paused, he announced that a surprise awaited the guests if they all moved outside to the forecourt or took chairs on the upstairs gallery, which ran across the front columns.

No one knew what was in store for them now. People laughed and made guesses. A variety of men offered to escort Vicky to wherever she wanted to go, the forecourt or the gallery.

Choosing the forecourt, Vicky locked both her arms through the arms of two young men and, as they whisked her through the front door, she saw Veronica whispering into Royal's ear.

Telling her escorts to stop, Vicky called, 'Veronica! Why aren't you joining in the fun? Where have you been hiding?'

Veronica wore a pale green dress, with lace around its high collar and the cuffs of its full sleeves. She looked quickly at Vicky in her decolletage dress, then smiled at her escorts, and returned talking to Royal.

Vicky instantly knew what they were saying. Royal was happily grinning as Veronica talked to him in a low voice, both their faces beaming. Vicky guessed that Brownie had safely given birth to a child.

She called, 'Is it a boy or a girl?' She tried to sound gay.

Veronica stopped again and, unable to hide her displeasure with Vicky now, she announced in a clipped voice, 'It's a son, Vicky.'

Vicky's face sobered. A son. The thought flashed through her mind what its father, Duncan, would say about siring a son. And, to hide her annoyance, she said, 'Be sure to have Royal tell the good news to his boyfriend, Ben!' Then, nodding to her escorts, Vicky left Veronica and Royal standing alone by the front doorway, Royal staring at her with a shocked face. *Ben? How had Vicky found out about Ben?*

A loud popping suddenly sounded overhead and a series of brilliant white sparks flashed in the dark sky. The sudden explosion was immediately followed by a second one, a display of yellow sparks that shot higher into the sky, drifting down into the night like brilliant streamers.

The guests first gasped at Peter Abdee's surprise show of Chinese fireworks on the sloping front lawns of Dragonard Hill. But, immediately, a third rocket shot through the air and as it made a large umbrella of pink brightness overhead, its offshoots lit into a series of subsequent umbrellas of brightness which now illumined a long row of negro men and women at the bottom of the slope. When the fourth flare shot upwards, the negroes began to sing, their melodic voices heightening the gaiety of the night as the next – and the next – Chinese umbrella unfolded overhead, tapering down into yellows, blues, pinks.

*　　*　　*

The firework display streaked the sky surrounding the new house, even lighting the stone walkway along which Belladonna hurried now from the back door, hurrying now to the kitchen. This was one night that the house servants had to work harder than the fieldhands, the maids and attendants now preparing fresh pots of coffee and a new array of candies and nuts to have waiting for the guests when they returned to the parlours.

The popping noise of the fireworks was a bothersome sound, Belladonna thought as she carried a stoneware jug in her hand to refill with cream. She could not understand how people could stand so close to them. Even the black people were gawking out the front windows of the house. She wondered how Posey and Storky allowed the servants to ignore their work for such nonsense.

Suddenly, a figure stepped from the thick gardenia bushes growing along the covered walkway. At first, Belladonna did not recognize the man. He was dressed differently than she was used to seeing him.

She moved closer and soon recognized him as Jeb Conway. She wondered why he was not in front of the house with the rest of the guests. No one was back here now.

Grabbing for her, he sent the stoneware pitcher flying and pulled her toward the bushes. His breath reeked of whisky.

But Belladonna was not frightened of him. She knew that, despite the popping fireworks, she was still within screaming distance from the house.

Jeb Conway whispered, 'Don't you screech, Nigger Gal, or I'll slit your throat.' He flashed a penknife in front of her face.

Belladonna hissed, 'Get out of my way.'

Bringing the knife closer to her almond-shaped eyes, Conway said, 'You don't seem to understand, Nigger Gal.'

She remained rigid.

Conway's hand reached toward her blouse, rubbing her small breasts and then moving down her stomach toward her legs.

'Why ain't you scared?' he whispered.

She grunted.

His bloodshot eyes thinned as he held her forearm now with one hand and, closing his knife with a flick, he reached toward the crotch of his pants.

Belladonna said louder, 'Get out of my way.'

Shaking his head, Conway worked his hand hard on his crotch. Then, slowly, he began to undo the buttons of his fly.

She tried to pull back.

Tightening his grasp on her small arm, he threatened, 'Don't back away, nigger gal. I want you to suck me. Give me a quick suck. That's what I want.'

She looked at his trousers and, seeing his carrot-shaped penis cradled in his half-open fist, she smiled.

'You're scared, ain't you? Trying to act big and brave, but you're one scared nigger, ain't you?'

Belladonna's petite face remained hard.

This directness was not Jeb Conway's usual approach. There was no way he could seek revenge against Belladonna at the cotton gin. She had no husband, no boy-friend to maim. But he had been drinking heavily tonight. Few of the other guests had spoken to him. And, having seen Belladonna leave the house when everyone else went to watch the firework display, he followed her.

He whispered now, 'You're scared of my prick, ain't you? Scared of how my prick looks? Don't want to suck it.'

She repeated his word, but in a mocking tone. She said,

'Your prick! Ha! You ain't got no prick, Mister. You just got an old dried-up piece of dog turd there.'

Then, spitting in his face, Belladonna pulled away her hand and walked slowly back to the house, doubting if Jeb Conway had the courage to stab her from behind with his penknife.

Overhead, the fireworks still lit the sky from the front of the house and, through the continuous popping sound, the slave choir now sang their favourite song – *There Will Be A Green Hill Tomorrow.*

Chapter Eleven

VENDETTAS

Jeb Conway rose earlier than usual the next morning, dressing and leaving the cabin without a cup of coffee or his usual bowl of cornmeal mush.

Noreen called to him from her bed, asking where he was going. She had been asleep last night when he returned from Dragonard Hill. She wanted to hear some details about the fancy party there.

But Jeb was not in a talkative mood this morning. He pulled his hat down over his head, gruffly answering, 'Where do you think I'm going, you old fool?'

Noreen sat on the edge of her narrow bed in her linsey-woolsey nightgown. And, curling up her bare toes from the coldness of the plank floor, she called, 'Not the gin? Abdee's rig is booked into the gin this morning. Bernard's teamster on it. But he's just dumping one load. He doing that alone.'

'Woman, don't tell me my own business.' He opened the door.

She called, 'If you're going to see your dogs, why don't you take their pail of meat?'

'You just start boiling up some mush for me and shut your big mouth.' The door slammed.

The morning was crisp, lit by a faint sun rising beyond the low, eastern hills. Jeb saw the grey outline of the gin across the dirt yard and, as he listened, he heard the steady sound of a cotton bag being dragged. The wagon from Dragonard Hill was already here. The teamster, Bernard, was unloading the haul by himself. Everything was as Jeb had expected, had planned on his return from Dragonard Hill last night, after being humiliated by the serving wench, Belladonna.

Jeb Conway had no way to seek revenge on Belladonna

herself for insulting him. He had never heard of her having a man. But he had to seek revenge on somebody, on some negro from Dragonard Hill. He had to ease the pain which Belladonna had inflicted on his pride.

Bernard was a large-shouldered negro, powerfully built, and moved the bags of green seed cotton from the work wagon with the ease of two men. Dragonard Hill sent their cotton to the gin in field allotments, tonnage according to the fields from which it had been harvested. As the picking was finished in the south-westerly fields now, this morning's load was small, the last wagonful of cotton from one section, a pause of activity before the next wagons would start bringing in the harvest from the back fields.

A cotton gin, in practice, stripped the cotton clean and fed it through to the 'shovel men'. On slow days at Jeb Conway's gin, these 'shovel men' consisted only of his wife. But when Noreen Conway had men from the plantations to help her in that task, she stood by the machinery which cleaned the cotton for bulk packing. It was then sent from here in bundles to the markets in New Orleans.

The Conway gin looked similar to a lumber mill, a low roof covering the works : an unloading platform, a gangway surrounding the strippers, the bins at the far end where the packing was begun.

This morning, a draft horse stood hitched to the wagon parked at the unloading platform. Bernard worked in the bed of the wagon, pulling at a large hemp bag tied at both corners of one end. He did not see Jeb Conway slowly approaching the wagon.

Keeping his silence, Jeb looked around the yard for a large stick, a weapon that was long and thick. Finding a club of appropriate size, he carried it toward the front of the wagon, still walking stealthily so that Bernard would neither see nor hear him.

By now, Bernard had successfully dislodged the second to the last bag of cotton and was dragging it toward the end of the splintery, wooden bed of the wagon.

Jeb waited until Bernard reached the edge of the wagon and then, suddenly, he gripped the club with both hands and struck the flanks of the draft horse with all his might.

The surprised animal whinnied, reared on his hind legs, jolting the wagon, and then began to run, pulling the wagon behind him, sending Bernard in a fall to the ground.

Quickly running toward the platform, Conway raised his club again and brought it down hard against Bernard's head before he had time to lift himself from the ground.

There was a blunt sound of a thud. Bernard slumped forward on the ground. The bludgeon had split open his skull. Blood streamed forward, followed by a grey and yellow gush of brains and viscera.

Standing over Bernard's motionless body, Conway muttered, 'Dumb horse . . . can't even stand still to let a nigger do his work.'

This was Jeb Conway's excuse for the accident – that the horse had bolted whilst Bernard was unloading the last bags of cotton from the work wagon. Bernard had fallen from the wagon and cracked his skull on a rock. Jeb kicked the necessary rock into position and used the club to smear it with evidence. Using his foot again, he moved Bernard's battered head against the rock and then wiped his boot clean on the arm of Bernard's limp body.

Turning, Jeb threw his club into a nearby water trough and ambled back to the house for his breakfast, pleased that he had some revenge against the niggers of Dragonard Hill.

*   *   *

Imogen waited in a chinaberry grove, sitting astride her roan mare and watching the last carriage roll down the hill from the new house. She saw her father standing in the middle of the white columns on the forecourt, one arm around Veronica's shoulders as they both waved goodbye to the departing guests.

Midday was approaching; the house-warming was at last over but it had not been as gruelling as Imogen had anticipated. She gave full credit to her father because, apart from insisting that she join him in the reel last night, he subsequently had treated her with consideration and warmth, not chastising her for her clothing. She was indebted to him for that. Last night, Imogen had seen her father through new eyes. He thrived on the society of friends. He was willing to let his daughters live their lives as long as they did not spoil what he wanted. Imogen considered it a fair exchange.

Waiting now on a hill which overlooked the new house, Imogen thought of last night and decided that she was glad for what she had done, that she had made an important step forward. She had shucked-off the fripperies of a feminine role – long hair and clothes which she detested – and she had ultimately been accepted by her father's circle of friends and business acquaintances. She considered the incongruity of Kate Breslin's part in her acceptance, how such a ladylike female would be the one who first brought Imogen into the group of sceptical onlookers. She suspected that Kate had done it for her father's sake, wondering now if their friendship went further than a platonic relationship of mere neighbours.

But Imogen did not have the time nor desire to re-evaluate her father's and Kate Breslin's friendship. She had to concentrate on her own life. She had to make a positive move for Barry Breslin before Vicky had him totally enamoured with herself, to keep Barry from completely forgetting about herself.

Quickly standing in her stirrups, Imogen finally spotted the person whom she was waiting to see. Vicky strolled from the small pillars which arced from the rear of the main house to the summer quarters. Imogen could not miss seeing the figure dressed in a full-skirted white dress and carrying a wide-brimmed straw hat in one hand.

Squeezing her breeches-clad legs against the mare's belly, Imogen quickly rode down the incline, looking like a young boy with short dark hair as she raced toward the breezeway on the west side of the house.

Lifting a hand to her forehead to shade her eyes against the sun, Vicky watched Imogen's neat figure approaching her on horseback. She waited until Imogen dismounted before calling, 'I thought you were a farmer just now.' Vicky had not talked to Imogen last night at the party and, this morning, Imogen had left the house before the overnight guests, Peter, Veronica and Vicky had sat down to their breakfast.

Imogen ignored Vicky's flippant remark now, her face firmly set as she strode to the spot where Vicky was standing. She said soberly, 'I'd like a word with you.'

Vicky backed toward the pillars, protesting, 'Imogen! Must you let that horse stand so close? Look how his feet claw up the grass!'

'They aren't *feet*!' Imogen said, dropping the reins, annoyed that Vicky had been raised on a plantation yet had so little knowledge of animals.

Vicky fluttered her hat nervously. She saw that Imogen was angry.

Imogen said, 'I think it's time we have us a talk, little sister."

'I've been here all along,' Vicky said gaily.

'Don't try to brush me off. You know what I'm angry about.'

Vicky knew what Imogen hated. And she blinked her long lashes at her now, coyly shaking her head, trying to upset her.

Imogen said, 'I want to talk about Barry Breslin!'

Vicky's blue eyes glistened. The subject of men always intrigued her. She drawled, 'Barry Breslin?'

'I want you to stop throwing yourself at him.'

Laughing, Vicky said, 'Why, Imogen Abdee! I've never seen you quite so jealous.'

'You can't deny it,' Imogen said, trying to ignore Vicky's coquetry.

'I'm not "throwing" myself at anyone, Imogen. I don't have to. Barry Breslin's just hungry for good female companionship.' Vicky studied Imogen's clothing, the breeches, the nankeen shirt, the red bandana tied around her neck, and the lace-up boots. She continued wryly, 'You couldn't possibly think that Barry is interested in *you*!'

'You knew exactly how it was between Barry and me when you came home from school.'

Cocking her head, Vicky asked, 'How was it, Imogen? How was it between Barry and you? Was he courting you? Is that what you're fumbling to say? Was Barry Breslin courting my big tough . . . *sister*?'

Imogen's eyes remained cold, her small mouth tightening with anger.

Vicky maliciously continued, 'Courting you because you were the only female around for miles?'

Imogen's arms hung rigid at her side.

'. . . The only unmarried female who wasn't sixty-years-old? Or a *nigger*?'

Still trying to contain her temper, Imogen said, 'Barry and I were together.'

' "Were" is right, Imogen. But that's over. Finished. Why, just look at yourself! You look ridiculous. You look absolutely ridiculous, Imogen Abdee. As if you weren't plain enough. Ha! No, you had to do *this* to yourself! Hack off your hair! Wear those silly old breeches! And you made an absolute fool out of yourself last night at the party, Imogen. An absolute fool! I was so ashamed of you being my sister I could have . . .'

The backside of Imogen's hand slapped hard against Vicky's soft cheek.

As her own hand flew to her face, Vicky screamed, 'How dare you strike me, you miserable old maid!'

'You pussy,' Imogen sneered, swinging her other hand at Vicky.

But, seeing the next strike coming, Vicky pulled back and slapped her straw hat through the hair, catching Imogen's face.

Ripping the wide-brimmed hat from Vicky's hand, Imogen grabbed for both her arms and Vicky began kicking at her, the demure softness suddenly disappearing from her face, showing that she, too, was a fighter.

Seizing a firm hold on Vicky's long hair, Imogen pulled down her head by the hair while she slapped again at her face and returned some of Vicky's sharp kicks.

Vicky had long fingernails and she tore at Imogen's face like a cat, screaming profanities at her; both girls then tumbled to the flagstone walk, Vicky's feet kicking from beneath the cumbersome bulk of her skirt and Imogen holding her by the hair, jerking at the front of her dress.

From the far end of the columns, Nero rushed toward them, calling, 'Miss Vicky! Imogen! Stop this!'

They ignored him, rolling now onto the lawn, their fists flying at one another, their hands pulling hair and feet kicking.

Bending, Nero tried to separate them. But they tore at his clothes, too, and fingernails ripped at his skin. He was determined to stop them, though, and, thrusting himself between them, he pushed them apart.

Breathing deeply, Vicky pulled up her ripped bodice and pushed back her hair. She glared at Imogen and screamed, 'You bitch. You sad, miserable bitch.'

'Shut up, whore!'

'Don't call me a whore,' Vicky said, reaching to claw at her again.

Nero grabbed Vicky's arm and, as he rose to his feet, he pulled her up from the ground. He said, 'Miss Vicky, don't let your Daddy catch you like this!'

'You keep out of this, Nero,' Imogen said, rising now to her own feet, eyeing Vicky with hatred. She said, 'I'm going to make this pussy pay'

Vicky threw up her head. 'Go on! Call me names if it makes you feel better. But I'll see you suffer, Imogen Abdee. I'll see you suffer to your grave!'

Imogen lunged at her again.

Nero broke them apart, holding Vicky back with one hand and breaking Imogen's hold on her with another.

Vicky was screaming now. She said, 'Imogen, you're an old

maid and I'm married. I'm married and that's what makes you sick! But being married won't stop me from making life hell – hell! – for you, Imogen Abdee. It won't stop me from keeping you from marrying Barry Breslin. Over my dead body, will you marry him, Imogen. Over my dead body!'

Then gripping the soiled and ripped skirt of her dress, Vicky turned and walked down the columned breezeway toward the house.

Watching her leave, Nero said to Imogen, 'This scrap's going to hurt your Daddy, Miss Imogen. This scrap will hurt him more than you and your sister knows.'

'Piss on her,' Imogen said, turning away from Nero and walking toward her mare.

Angry that she had not been able to finish the fight, Imogen was relieved about one thing. She knew that Vicky's one concern was for men. Imogen realized that fact because, not once during Vicky's entire tirade against her, had she mentioned owning Dragonard Hill. She thought exactly like a pussy, only about men.

* * *

Piss on her.

Nero walked from the breezeway of the new house thinking about Imogen's crude words. And the fight between her and her sister. It disgusted him.

He did not mind Imogen's eagerness to play a man's role on the plantation, even admiring her for the long and hard hours she spent working. Dragonard Hill was large and Imogen actually helped him by being in the south fields, when he was in the northern or westerly quarters. He could not understand, though, why she had dressed like a man at the party last night. He saw it as an act of childish defiance and he respected the way in which Peter Abdee had coped with it, suspecting that he would let his eldest daughter continue dressing like a man, acting as if it were normal.

Nero could not decide if Peter Abdee was being too good to his family. In Nero's eyes, both Imogen and Vicky were renegades, easily capable of hurting their father. And he decided that, no, he would not tell Master Peter about the fight between the two girls. He only hoped that their sister, Veronica, would remain ladylike, the pride of her father.

Families were very dear to Nero. He had only sown one child of his own and that had been in the West Indies with the bushy-haired girl. Her name had been Pinkie. The child had been killed with her. It had been a boy. A son who had been called 'Bushy', in honour of his mother's crown of spun ebony.

Nero no longer hoped to replace her with another woman. His heart had been broken enough times and he still felt the last wound, the sight of seeing the bushy-haired girl last summer on Dragonard Hill crawling into Maybelle's house in Town. Peter Abdee had told Nero shortly afterwards that he wanted him to take a runaway slave girl to the work farm, Treetops. Always entrusting Nero with the truth, Peter had told him that the girl's body was full of syphilis and that she was badly in need of a doctor.

When Nero had seen who the diseased girl was, that she was the same bushy-haired girl whom he had seen earlier climbing up the ladder to Maybelle's house, his brain raced with a hundred plans. He would risk making love to her. He had a written pass to travel on the public road with her but, instead of going to Treetops, they would escape. They would live in the willow forests. Hide until they were caught. He would share the disease with her. They would be lovers. He might even find some cure for her. She would be his wife.

Now, on this balmy midday after the house-warming, Nero had ridden from the new house to Town. He sat on his horse at the end of a long row of long-legged houses. Looking at Maybelle's house, he remembered the first time that he had seen the runaway girl on the ladder there. She had probably gone there to hide from the Witcherleys. Her name was Rita.

She now was at Treetops. Nero had not escaped with her. He had not even ventured to put his arm around her slim shoulder on their long, bumpy ride over the public road. He respected her silence. She had her own agonies. And Nero was not a brash man. He could not crack another human being's world. He wondered if that was why he was a slave. If that was why the Lord had made him to be bought and sold and, because Nero still continued to live as best he could, was that why he had reached a position of authority on Dragonard Hill?

A position of authority. That included forgetting about his own anxieties and to tend to the obligations of his job. A man – the teamster named Bernard – had had an accident at the cotton gin and Nero now had to go and bring his body home.

*   *   *

Work continued all day in the new house, moving furniture back into position and putting away the plates, cups, glasses, and cutlery which had been washed throughout the night, many items which now would be stored until the next big festivity at Dragonard Hill.

Although entertaining guests meant more work for the house servants, and the extra people drafted from Town, the black people loved the excitement of a party, and, as they worked today, they talked about the clothes which people had worn last night and the lavish food prepared by the kitchen. They would take the remains back to Town, using the vast quantity of left-overs for a party of their own.

Storky drew energy for the extra work demanded by a party from the limitless authority she was given over the staff of extra servants. To her, bossing people was a tonic.

Posey became frantic with the excitement, the opposite reaction which the party had had on Belladonna, who worked sullenly the next day, and brooding over the pass which Jeb

Conway had made at her. She had thwarted Conway's advance and, still, she had told no one about it.

Royal was very tired by evening, more exhausted by the worries from Vicky's comment about his friendship with Ben than he was from the last few days of the preparations and the cleaning-up caused by the gala.

Veronica had been too excited by the birth of Brownie's baby boy to question Royal about Vicky's cryptic words. She had spent this following day with Brownie in The Shed and Royal was grateful for that. He could not explain Ben to her yet.

Also, Vicky had not approached him again. He had not seen her all day. But he had heard the gossip in the kitchen about a fight between her and Imogen.

If Vicky went on saying that he was Ben's boy-friend or not, though, Royal knew that he had to put an end to the stories once and for all. But he still could not understand how Vicky had learned about the sordid affairs of a fieldhand.

Tonight was the night that Ben met with his friends in their hut. Royal had escaped seeing them for more than three months now and, although he had hoped that they would soon forget about his existence on Dragonard Hill, finding other young men to use as the object of their perversions, he realized that that idea, too, had been a fool-hearted dream – as foolish as the friendship that he was building between Veronica and himself.

Knocking on the hut's rough door, Royal waited and then entered, seeing the black men squatting against the board walls. They smiled slyly as they studied Royal, some men making comments about his fine clothes, the white uniform of the big house being so much better than the rough tow pants of the fieldhands; other men whistled as he walked past him, clucking at the sight of his buttocks.

Ben sat at the far end of the hut, near the taper which flickered inside an earthen bowl of fat. A sober-faced black boy sat on the dirt floor beside Ben – a boy whom Royal had never seen before – and Ben beckoned Royal to come toward his other side, to have two young masculine men for his pleasure.

Hesitating, Royal saw that this was not going to be as easy as he had anticipated. He could feel the men's eyes already undressing him, remembering their words about Ben liking two boys at the same time. Royal had not seen that happen yet but he remembered Ben telling him once that he wanted to strap Royal to another boy with leather thongs.

Royal stopped in the middle of the dirt floor, his wide shoulders hunched forward in the low-ceilinged hut, his eyes straining in the faint light. He was surrounded by an open circle of leering, naked negroes. He could not see where the dull-black skin of one man stopped and the next began, their nakedness forming a bank of warm flesh.

Taking a deep breath, Royal began in a husky voice, 'Ben – '

Ben looked quizzically at him, cocking his head, waiting for Royal to speak.

'Ben, I've made a decision,' Royal said.

Ben smiled. 'Pretty boys don't make decisions. Pretty boys do like they told.'

Royal took another deep breath. He began again, 'Ben, I haven't been here for a long time. And I'm not coming here any more. I won't tell Master Peter about you. But I don't want you causing trouble for me, either.'

'You come here tonight to tell me that, Pretty Boy?'

Holding his jaw firm, Royal nodded his head.

'Maybe it's that white girl giving you these ideas. Your "Miss Veronica". She's putting these ideas in your pretty head? That you can screw her now? That you ain't my cunt?'

Royal ignored Ben's aspersion to his masculinity. His fist tightened at the mention of Veronica's name. But he fought the urge to throw himself at Ben, to pummel him until he was dead for suggesting that he was bedding Veronica like a wench.

Slowly rising from the dirt floor at the rear of the hut, Ben approached Royal. His black arms were gnarled with muscle and, holding one out to Royal, he called, 'Come here, Pretty Boy. Bring your cunt to your man.'

The memories of the past experience in this hut returned to Royal and, seeing Ben coming closer to him, and also seeing the other young man at the back of the hut – the boy lying on his stomach now, his head being held between a black man's thighs whilst two other men kneeded his buttocks – Royal felt sickness rising in his throat. And knowing that he could not stay here for one more moment, he quickly turned to the low door behind him.

The night was now cold and Royal saw his breath as he ran across the field. He did not look over his shoulder to see if the men were chasing him. The only noise he heard was his feet throwing clots of dirt as he ran, and the sound of his own breath. He saw the lights of the new house and kept running toward it.

He jumped over a mound of earth and, cutting through a copse of juniper trees, he still ran and did not look behind him.

Suddenly, he heard someone calling him.

'Royal!' It was a loud whisper.

He slowed. He knew it could not be Ben or his friends. The voice was too close to him in the trees.

It called again, and louder. 'Royal!'

He stopped and, seeing a figure he recognized, a woman wrapped in a shawl, he quickly ran towards her. It was Veronica.

Not knowing if he had been followed, nor if he and Veronica were being observed from the house, he threw his arms around her. She returned the embrace. This was the first time that they had touched one another. Their grip was strong, like a careless greeting of two people separated for a long time but – even if they were observed by the whole world – they held one another shamelessly because they were finally together.

*   *   *

It was an early hour in the morning in New Orleans and Duncan Webb had come back to his rented small room in the French Quarter, tired from participating in another orgy in the cellar at *Petit Jour*. The exhibitions there were beginning to bore, even disgust him. The novelty of these long sordid nights were losing all their appeal. But he was broke and needed the money. He had to continue them. He did not know what other work he could do. But apart from the prospect of having another party tomorrow night, Duncan Webb was frustrated now about having heard two men tonight discussing the brilliance of a party they had been to up-country at a plantation called Dragonard Hill. It had been a house-warming, a big party which the Southerners referred to as a 'crush', and Duncan had overheard the men describing the house, the orchestra, the firework display, the singing, the elaborate food and imported wines. He stood naked now in his bleak room, bending over a basin and washing the show grease from his penis. He was thinking about the words he had heard about Dragonard Hill and the Abdee family, realizing how he himself could have been there, too, but he had been too ashamed tonight to identify himself to the two men. He knew they would not believe him. Despising the low state to which he was sinking, Duncan's hand suddenly paused on his penis. He lowered his eyes and, washing away the soap suds, he studied a blister on the skin of his penis. Or was it a scab? Moving the candle next to the washbasin, he examined his penis more closely in the yellow light, finding another smear of redness on his skin and it, too, was hardening into a sore. What was it? Then he found another, farther down toward the root, a large blemish half-hidden by his black pubic hairs. What were they? His heart quickened, thinking of going to a doctor. A doctor might tell him he had contracted a hideous disease. Duncan Webb hated doctors. But what were these red marks? The hard scabs? The smears? He thought of a heat rash. Yes, he quickly told himself, it was a heat rash irritated by the grease he had to wear for the shows at *Petit Jour* to make his penis glisten in the light. He told himself that he must devise some other way to glorify his penis on those evenings in the cellar without using that oil.

Chapter Twelve

A PIONEER REMEDY

Kate Breslin's mind was divided during the days following the party at Dragonard Hill. She knew that she had to solve the problem of her nephew supposedly courting Imogen Abdee but paying more attention to her younger – married – sister, Vicky. It was part Peter's problem, too, and Kate desperately wanted to talk to him about it, but the person who had to make up his mind was Barry. She did not know whether to talk to him about it or to wait.

Following her Irish intuition, Kate did not broach the subject to Barry, sensing that if she kept quiet, he would eventually discuss it with her. Waiting, Kate thought, would give her better grounds in the argument that she knew would develop. She could not risk being a 'carping aunt', she had to maintain her position as someone in an advisory position; she wanted Barry to come to her with his problem and she would give him an answer.

Like a true pioneer, Kate Breslin saw that he would only perish if he continued in his infatuation with Vicky. She would virtually bleed him and then leave him to die like a tribe of vicious backwoods Indians left a captive in the swamps. Kate had to help him escape without actually telling him that he was in danger. Running away with Vicky might be the one bit of adventure he chose in his life, the first but one fatal choice.

Barry had been more listless than usual after the party. He had hardly eaten the next day and, on the day after that, Kate almost broke her promise and made him talk about Vicky. But, then, her better judgement took hold and she continued to wait for him to talk to her before she began to apply her remedy for his love-sick condition.

On the second day, Barry finally approached Kate in the sitting-room at Greenleaf. She was working on an embroidery for a cushion in Peter's new library at Dragonard Hill.

Standing in the archway, he asked, 'Aunt Kate, can we talk?'

'Of course, Barry,' she said, not looking up from her work, 'sit down.'

Seating himself across from her, nervously picking at his fingernails, Barry began in a low voice, 'Aunt Kate – '

She pretended as if nothing were the matter, that his conduct lately had been normal. 'Uh-huh?'

'I've got a problem, Aunt Kate.'

'Ummm.'

He continued, 'Aunt Kate – '

'Yes, Barry.' She stitched and pulled and knotted a blue thread.

'I'm in love, Aunt Kate.'

Snipping the thread, she said, 'My, aren't you lucky!'

'Aren't you surprised?'

Reaching for her sewing basket, she took out a skein of green cotton, saying, 'You *are* twenty-two years old, Barry.'

Sighing, he said, 'But I'm in love with a girl who's . . . married!'

Kate stopped. She raised her head and stared at him.

Lowering his head, fumbling with a button on his waistcoat, he said, 'I'm in love with Vicky.'

Kate did not say a word, keeping her eyes on him.

'What's the matter?' he asked. 'Why are you looking at me so funny?'

She said, 'Vicky? Imogen's sister?'

'I know it's awful but . . .'

'What about Imogen, Barry?'

He fidgeted, his cheeks becoming red.

Kate said, 'You've been courting Imogen, Barry.'

He shrugged.

Kate sat to the edge of her chair. 'But I always thought you were going to marry Imogen, Barry. Is that not what you led me to believe? And Imogen herself? And her father?'

He sighed. 'I guess. Half way. She wants to.'

Kate knew the awkwardness of Barry's and Imogen's relationship. But she also knew Barry's inability to make a decision. He would have difficulty finding a wife, she feared, and even a marriage of convenience would give him a better life than what faced him if he remained unattached and became shiftless. Kate Breslin was the first to admit that her nephew was a very lazy young man. She repeated his words now, 'You guess! You guess what? That you can drop a perfectly nice, innocent girl like Imogen? Just like that?' She snapped her fingers.

'Imogen's not so innocent,' he said, a sly smile covering his long face, a smile that Kate did not like.

She said, 'Innocent? Well, tell me who the hell is? By God, Barry Breslin, stop talking nonsense about "innocence" and tell me exactly what you are planning to do!'

'Now, Aunt Kate! Don't get your Irish up! I ain't planning nothing yet. Not till I talk to you.'

'I should bloody well hope you don't either, young man. Now, you sit there and tell me in plain words about you and Imogen's . . . married sister!'

He shrugged his big shoulders again, still picking at his fingernails. 'Nothing really.'

'Nothing? Then why are we wasting our breath talking? Why did you come to me and say you have a problem? Why have you been acting like a love-sick schoolboy lately? Do you think I am blind? Do you think I didn't see how you slobbered after Vicky at the party. And how she ignored you because she knew that she had you and flirted with everyone else there who wore *pants*!' Kate stopped. She wanted to bite her tongue for having mentioned 'pants'. But having said it now, she had to continue. She said firmly, 'I admire Imogen Abdee. It takes a lot of character to do what she did. What she believes in. And she believes in getting on with her life at Dragonard Hill. She's not some simpering, little trumped-up belle!'

Barry was not thinking about Imogen, though. His watery brown eyes drooped and he said, 'But I love Vicky!'

'Vicky! Young man, you are talking about a married woman!'

'Her husband left her, didn't he?'

Kate rose. 'And you mean to sit there and tell me, Barry Breslin, that you're going to court Victoria Abdee now that she and her husband are living apart?'

He sniffed. 'I could.'

'You're damned right you could! You could and not talk to me again, Barry Breslin! You could and move as far away from me as you could possibly travel on the face of this earth!'

He stared at her.

Kate was angry now, a temper that had been building inside her since she had first seen her nephew making a fool out of himself with Vicky, a frustration over his fecklessness which she had seen years ago when he had first come to live with her as a dull-witted orphan.

She said now, 'Barry Breslin, let me tell you something and let me make it very, very plain. You are my only nephew. I have no son. No daughter. You are my heir. I plan on leaving you Greenleaf. Any money I have accumulated in this world, both from my family and what your uncle left me. But if you think you can run away with a married woman, don't expect to count me as your aunt. If you think you can throw Imogen Abdee aside for her sister, I do not want to see you again. Do you understand that? I will not stand by dumbly and watch you ruin your life chasing women like Victoria Abdee, who now happens to be Mrs Webb!'

Barry was pale. He had never seen his aunt so furious, her face so red.

Throwing down her coloured cottons, Kate gathered her skirt and walked stiffly from the room, thinking that she had not overdone her act one bit. Now, all she had to do was to wait and, if her intuition proved correct, Barry would leave Greenleaf shortly and ride to see Vicky at Dragonard Hill.

*　　*　　*

Vicky was half-seething with anger, half-roaring with laughter.

The idea of Barry Breslin getting a job to support her was very funny. But the thought of his aunt threatening to disinherit him if he continued to see her made Vicky burn with outrage. How dare Kate Breslin interfere in her life! How dare she make moral judgements about her character! How dare she side with Imogen! And how dare – *how dare!* – Barry Breslin think that she would run away with a fool like him, anyway!

Yanking clothes from the tall wardrobe in her bedroom, Vicky threw them toward the one bag she had decided to take. She had already told Boxo to have the carriage ready in a half-hour to take her to Carterville where she would catch the coach to New Orleans. And she had warned him that, if he told anyone, even her father, that she was leaving, she would see that he was whipped.

Vicky had had enough of Dragonard Hill. She was getting out of this place where she had known nothing but misery and loneliness and boredom.

Having at last decided to go to New Orleans to join Duncan, she did not know where she would find him. But she had to get as far away from here as possible. She hated every member of her family and loathed all their neighbours. They were fools and meddling snoops. She would forget that her name had ever been Abdee, that her home was Dragonard Hill. To her, it was a pit in the wilderness, seething with vipers and rats!

Barry Breslin had repeated his aunt's strong words to Vicky when they were making love less than an hour ago on a mossy spot Vicky had found on a hill past the old overseer's cabin. Barry Breslin was a clumsy lover and even the fact that he only had one testicle failed to make Vicky find anything unique about him. She had tolerated his pawing hands and slobbering kisses only as a way to hurt Imogen. And after her fight with Imogen, Vicky had planned to intensify her attack on Barry. She was going to humiliate Imogen until she ran into the woodlands and hid there like a wounded animal.

But then Barry ruined everything.

The one rule which Vicky had insisted that Barry obey when they made love was that he did not talk to her during the act. He was too unimaginative to say erotic things, coaxing her like Duncan had done, talking to her in blunt sexual terms like the black men she had lain with on Dragonard Hill. Barry was a romantic. He wanted love. Vicky needed a man who treated her roughly, even as his inferior, feeding her mind with illicit thoughts as he tantalized her body. But the only perversion she enjoyed with Barry Breslin was the fact that she was keeping him from Imogen.

Lying between Vicky's legs this afternoon, Barry began to say into her ear, 'I don't care what they say. I don't care if they don't want me to do this. I will.'

Vicky tried to silence him.

But he persisted. 'I don't need her money. Hell! I can support you. I can get a job.' He had stopped his steady driving into Vicky, lying now motionless on top of her.

'What are you talking about?' Vicky asked, rising to one elbow to escape his dead weight.

'I love you,' he whispered, bringing his head down between her breasts, kissing the small but firm nipples.

She pulled his head up by the hair. 'You mentioned money. A job. What money?'

Snuggling into her bare, he said, 'I don't need her money. Let her cut me off. Who cares if I'm . . . disinherited!'

Pushing him up from her by the shoulders, she said, 'Disinherited? Why?'

Looking sorrowfully at her, he said, 'Because I come to see you. Not Imogen.'

'Your aunt said she'd disinherit you if you saw me instead of . . . Imogen?'

He nodded.

Pushing frantically at his naked shoulders, Vicky said, 'Get off! Get off me!'

Barry obediently pulled back, coming quickly and easily out of the hold of her vagina.

Reaching for her clothes, Vicky said, 'What am I? Some kind of plague? Does everybody hate me?'

'You're married.'

'Of course I'm married.'

Settling on his knees, Barry said, 'I don't care, Vicky. You can divorce him. Get a separation. I don't care what Aunt Kate says. We can run away together.'

'Run away? Have you support me?' She laughed.

Naked, Barry remained kneeling on the blanket, staring in confusion at Vicky.

Gathering her clothes from the ground, Vicky began to formulate what he had been saying to her, realizing what people *did* think of her here. She felt both angry and hurt, and to placate herself, she had to hurt someone else. Standing over Barry now, she said, 'Making love to you with your one ball has been bad enough, Barry Breslin. But don't think about running away! Not with me! I wouldn't go with you even if you had all the money in the world. And . . . *ten* balls!'

He stared at her, his mouth hanging open, shaking his head in bewilderment. Only a few minutes ago they had been making what he had thought was – love!

'Screwing with you has been bad enough. I don't need poverty, too. I can find poverty anywhere, Barry Breslin. And with men who are a lot more manly than you!

He was beginning to tremble.

Standing over him, she screamed, 'Do you know what? My best lovers have been black! Black men! Niggers, And they put you and your one ball to shame, Barry Breslin! You screw like a . . . toad!'

She turned and left him quaking on the blanket.

*   *   *

Kate Breslin was sitting on a chair in her parlour, twilight fading through the ecru-coloured curtains, when she heard the front doors open. Barry had ridden away from Greenleaf more than four hours ago, she supposed on his way to Dragonard Hill. She had not heard a horse gallop up the drive and she knew that the servants seldom used the front door. And, if they did, they always called 'Matty Kate!'

The house was silent, though; she only heard the clock ticking now in the hallway.

She called, 'Barry?'

A tall figure stood in the double doorway which led to the hallway. It walked slowly toward her and, before she had time to speak again – seeing that it was Barry, noticing even in this dim light that his cheeks were wet with tears – he sank to the floor beside her and buried his tousled head on her leg.

Kate could find no words to say to him, only stroking the back of his head, wondering if she was responsible for the hurt that now made his tears come in gulps.

She did not have to ask him if he had been to Dragonard Hill. She also trusted her instinct that he had seen Vicky and, most likely, had told her everything that his wicked, old aunt had said to him.

Guessing Vicky's reaction, Kate waited for Barry to stop crying, to quiet his sobs. When he eventually did, she continued to stroke his head, saying, 'The last thing in the world I want to do is hurt you, Barry. Neither do I want anybody else to hurt you. Maybe you're not as worldly wise as you think. Often we think we feel strongly about another person, know them very well. But then – '

She stopped, looking down at this fully grown man kneeling on the floor in front of her. She wanted to tell him precisely all the cruel facts she had learned about life, share the disappointments with him that she herself had suffered, to help him learn from her mistakes. List them for him in detail. Agony by agony. But that was not possible. People had to learn for themselves, collecting their own string of pain and disappointments.

She said in a hushed voice, 'Your uncle and I made a mistake about marriage, Barry. I've never told anyone this before but I think you're old enough now to understand what I mean. Your uncle and I were passionate. We thought we couldn't live without each other. But that feeling often goes very quickly. Nobody suspected that the last years of our marriage were insufferable. We created misery for each other. Physical love often turns against you like that. And, when your uncle died, I did not shed one tear. Not one, Barry. And the sad thing is that I am not ashamed to admit it to this day. Admit that it did not upset me in the least that he died, the person I couldn't live without when I married him. That's why I never re-married. I would marry for companionship. Common interest. Love can grow from that, Barry. But it is very rare for friendship to grow from a relationship built entirely on what you do in bed. People can be very cruel animals, I'm afraid, Barry. They can lead you into believing they love you. Need you. And, then, turn away and do and say the most cruel, awful things. But we must keep marrying. We must have families, work for self-respect, wring out some hope from our miseries. I often think of my poor Papa. He was nothing but a sawed-off Irish yobo who came with his bride to this country. A wilderness. They had their hopes. They knew hardships back home in County Donegal and did not have time to worry about love. They got married because Papa needed Mama's few shillings dowry and Mama had to get away from home because her mother – poor Granny Shine – kept having more babies. That was how my parents knew love, Barry. And they survived. They learned to love each other. Live with each other. They worked to build a home. A few acres into a farm. Then a plantation. They thought very little about bed. Except a place to lie down after a hard day's work. And it just shows us that sometimes life gives you your pattern. You really have very few choices. And when you do make your choices, you have to be prepared for the disappointments. You have to be ready to protect yourself from the people you'll meet, or how the people you know already might change. Nothing stays the same, I'm afraid, Barry. You can plan on nothing but disappointments. But you must be able to tackle them. That's what makes us people. We build on those disappointments and then we call them experience. And we try to share our experience with younger people, Barry. We try from the bottom of our hearts to help our beloved, our very beloved young ones.'

Kate was holding her head down against his, now patting his broad shoulders, tears in her eyes, too.

*   *   *

Veronica and Royal had gone no further last night than an embrace, tightly clutching one another in the copse behind the new house.

But their love became nervous today, almost non-existent as they tried to avoid one another in the house, not knowing how they would react when they met in daylight.

Then, tonight, as if by mutual design, they found one another at the same spot behind the new house. They walked slowly toward one another, not running, not smiling nor speaking. Royal's arms reached out for Veronica and she buried her head into his strong shoulder.

Royal held her closer than he had last night, now swelling in his pants until he ached for release. Veronica felt her breasts become alive as she pressed herself up against him, even the pressure of his stiff penis not making her pull away from him.

They did not pursue a physical love, though. Their daring tonight only advanced to the opening of mouths, moving of lips toward one another, kissing, a starved and long overdue kiss in which they plunged their tongues into one another, exploring each other's mouths, breathing the same breath. It was a kiss of sad desperation.

*   *   *

A small, green hand-lantern set on the board flooring in an attic room of the old house. It was late night. Ta-Ta was asleep in her room next door and Veronica knelt in front of a scarred chest, its bow-top thrown back as she slowly unfolded dresses and musty-smelling shawls.

These were clothes of her mother, belongings long ago packed away by the black servants after she had died.

'Mama . . .' Veronica whispered, holding up a faded blue and yellow sprigged cotton dress in the lamplight. '. . . oh, Mama!'

Veronica had never seen her mother. She had died giving birth to her and Vicky.

Vicky. She had seen Vicky rush angrily to her room late this afternoon. She had not seen her emerge. And thinking how often Vicky locked herself in her room lately, Veronica imagined what disappointments about life in the new house her father must be feeling. The house-warming had been grand but he had worked hard to build the house for his family!

What family?

Clutching the faded old dress in her arms, Veronica begged, 'Oh, Mama, what's happening to us?'

Then, pulling her legs under her, she leaned against the edge of the open trunk and gazed at the deep pile of dimities, laces, silk ribbons. They were all simple but feminine things. Just the possessions of a young country girl.

Taking a deep sigh, Veronica asked, 'Mama, am I doing wrong? Tell me. Please tell me if I'll hurt Father if I keep seeing . . .'

Resting her forehead on the edge of the trunk, she asked, 'Can you understand, Mama? I do feel love for him. I know I do.'

Silence.

'He's black. But is that bad, Mama? Really so wrong?'

No answer came.

Curling up against the old trunk, Veronica stared at the board flooring in the lamplight and, slowly, she raised the tips of her fingers to her mouth. Where Roy had kissed her. Her eyes remained dry. She still felt the glow from being so close to him. Was that feeling wrong, too? To be kissed by a black man? And feel so hungry for more? So much more?

Chapter Thirteen

PETIT JOUR

Veronica was surprised to see the new house fully lit when she later climbed the slope from the old house that night. Suspecting that something was the matter there, she quickly forgot about her own problems and rushed inside. Running up the stairs, she saw the door to Vicky's room open. Imogen was standing in the doorway. Then she saw that their father was inside the bedroom. And then she saw the state of the bedroom itself.

One look at Vicky's room told that she had packed only a few of her things, strewing the rest across the dressing-table, hanging from half-open drawers, her four-poster bed, backs of chairs. That she had left home hurriedly, secretly, hatefully.

Veronica stopped alongside Imogen in the doorway, watching her father soberly studying the aftermath of Vicky's departure.

Then, quickly moving forward, she put her arm through his, but not saying a word.

Imogen remained silently in the doorway, a half smirk on her face.

Looking at the mess of clothing, shoes, hairnets, scarves, Peter said, 'No reason for going. Not a goodbye to any of us. Nothing.'

Veronica tried to defend her. She said, 'Vicky's been upset, Father.'

Nodding his head, he said, 'She has. By him. And that's where she's gone. I bet any money she's gone to find *him* in New Orleans. And he hasn't written her a letter. Sent word. Nothing.'

Veronica began, 'If that's what she wants – '

Peter stepped forward and, picking up one yellow slipper, he looked at it and said, 'I must talk to her.'

From the doorway, Imogen called, 'To bring her back?'

'Home?' He shook his head. 'No, I won't force anybody to go some place they obviously hate.' He dropped the slipper and looked around the room again, the home he had built for his family. 'She's your sister, though. Your mother would've wanted me to go. But, then, if your mother had lived — ' Peter shook his head, refusing to start pursuing the idea of what would have happened if Melissa had not died. He said with finality, 'I'll go to New Orleans. I'll talk to the girl. I'll see what she plans to do.'

Putting his arm around Veronica, then, he said, 'Do you two girls think you can run things here for a few days?'

'Of course,' Veronica murmured.

Peter raised his voice. 'Imogen? Do you think you can take care of things while I'm gone?'

'Yes, Father.'

Veronica suggested brightly, 'What about me coming with you?' She hated to see him travel alone but, worse, she did not know what she would do alone in the house with Royal, an action she might later regret.

Squeezing her, Peter said, 'You just stay here and run the house. I know I don't have to worry about you, Ronny.'

She dipped her eyes to the carpet, nodding.

Imogen stood sternly in the open door of the bedroom, her eyes slits under her closely-cropped hair.

Peter then told both Veronica and Imogen to go to bed now. He left Vicky's empty bedroom, walking across the mezzanine to his own room and did not emerge until the next morning, when he went downstairs, leaving his saddlebag in the hallway and joined Imogen and Veronica for breakfast.

Both girls walked him to the house stables; the air was crisp and Veronica asked him if he had taken a slicker in case of rain.

Peter was fully prepared. He even had included a brace of pistols in his saddlebags, but was taking only one change of clothes for his journey to New Orleans. He did not intend to be away for long, he did not anticipate an occasion for which he would need any formal attire.

Then, after reminding his two daughters what to do in his absence, he kissed them each on both cheeks and, taking the reins from Boxo's hands, he galloped down the driveway, through the cypress trees, not turning to look back at the new house where Veronica and Imogen stood in front of the four white columns.

*   *   *

The Hotel LaSalle was the first hotel where Peter Abdee had stayed when he went to New Orleans as a child with Albert Selby. He rode directly to it when he reached town late this evening, now being well known there, his tired horse taken to the hotel stables and he himself being shown directly to a room on the first balcony.

Quickly bathing, changing into his clean clothes, he sent his travelling breeches and shirt downstairs with a black maid to be washed and pressed and, then, he ambled downstairs to the lobby to have a whiskey and look for familiar faces. New Orleans was now full of planters, the cotton crops being sold both locally and to agents from abroad at this time of year. Also, families came from the country to buy Christmas presents for their relatives and friends, as well as buying annual necessities – such as sturdy but inexpensive shoes for their slaves.

Peter Abdee was in no mood to be thinking about Christmas now and he had no plans to conduct business on this trip to New Orleans. Vicky's sudden departure from Dragonard Hill had puzzled him so much that he had formulated only a vague plan so far on how he would begin to trace her. He intended to start tomorrow at his bank to see if she had tried to draw any money on his name. He suspected that his son-in-law would be penniless and he doubted if either of them could live without luxuries.

Sitting now in a deep leather chair under a palm tree in the hotel lobby, he relaxed with the orchestra music which played behind him on a swagged dais. He half listened to the mumble of conversation coming from the dining-room which lay behind a wall of small panes of bevelled glass, the *maitre d'hotel* standing proudly in the tall open doors. Peter remembered eating in that sea of white-covered tables as a child, tasting iced Italian cream for the first time. He thought how he had never brought his wife, Melissa, to New Orleans. He wondered if he would ever travel here with Kate. He had so few people to share his life with now. Imogen disliked the city and even Veronica had grown distant from him in the recent months. He did not know if the gap between him and his daughters was his fault or theirs. But he felt a flaw in his life now, as if a great error had been made some place and he did not know how it had been, or when exactly it had occurred. He thought of the black people he depended upon – Storky, Nero, Lady Alice, even Boxo and Posey and countless other people he saw daily – but whose private lives were kept distant from his, almost as if he refused to recognize that they had personalities. He imagined sitting here in the Hotel LaSalle with Nero, knowing that they would have many interesting and variable subjects for conversation but, apart from the world in which he lived not allowing it, the idea of travelling with Nero as a friend would not normally occur to him. And that represented a terrible lack, Peter felt, a shortcoming in the way he was living. But how could he change that? How could he single-handedly restructure a world he had been raised to accept?

He also reflected, though, on how hypocritical it was of him to think of chastising selfishness in a younger generation – his daughters – when he kept other human lives bound to him like cattle.

Suddenly, he heard a man call his name and, looking across the lobby, he saw a planter from Natchez, a red-faced Scotsman called Frazer McDermott.

Inviting McDermott to join him for a whiskey, Peter lied,

saying that he was in New Orleans to see Bartlett and Keene, the cotton agents.

Frazer McDermott was a barrel-chested man, dressed flashily in a red and green plaid coat. He said, 'Cotton brings me here, too. But it don't keep me from having my good time.' Bending forward, he asked, 'Have you been to Octavia's yet, Abdee lad?'

'Octavia's?'

'The fancy house. Over on Bourbon Street. How about you coming there with me after supper?'

Peter slowly shook his head, saying that he was tired after a long, dusty ride and that he wanted to go to bed early.

'Hell, lad! You can sleep when you're in the country. You're in New Orleans now! Come with a friend! Open your eyes up at Octavia's place!'

Peter held firmly to his decision. He knew that the prostitutes were all fancy black slaves and he did not like to pleasure with women who could not refuse him. He did not need to kindle his melancholy tonight by taking an active part in the side of slavery that troubled him the most – the sexual liberties which white people took with negroes. He had laid with negresses in his younger days and was glad to be free at least from that guilt now.

Leaning closer, McDermott said, 'If you really want to see yourself a good show, how about *Petit Jour*?'

Peter's brow wrinkled. He asked, '*Petit Jour*?' It had been many years since he had heard that name. He thought that, surely, the place to which Frazer McDermott was referring had nothing to do with the *Petit Jour* he knew – the West Indian plantation that had belonged to his mother, the St Kitts' home which his father had renamed for his own perverse reasons as 'Dragonard', the name that had come to be the basis for Peter's home here in Louisiana, Dragonard Hill.

McDermott said, 'It's Friday night, too. There's always a big Friday night show at *Petit Jour*. They've got a new show stud, too. They call him "Dandy". But word's out he's a Yankee who's come south to poke all the black gals.' Patting

Abdee on the knee, he said, 'You think some of our niggers are hung, Lad, you wait till you see this Dandy at that *Petit Jour* whorehouse?'

Dandy? A Yankee? A Yankee stud at a whorehouse called *Petit Jour*? It was too much of a coincidence. A bad nightmare. Some kind of hideous revenge.

McDermot continued, 'He gives quite a show. It's worth seeing if you like that sort of thing or not.'

'*Petit Jour*?' Peter asked again.

'Ah ha! I see the lad weakening.'

'No,' Peter said firmly. 'Anyway, not tonight. But I might take you up on your invitation tomorrow night. But not now.'

Finishing his whiskey with a gulp, Peter rose and, after talking briefly about cotton prices with Frazer McDermott, he bade him farewell, turned, and walked toward the wide stairway which led to the three balconies which rose to the glass-domed ceiling.

But rather than going to his room, Peter waited to see McDermott disappear into the dining-room. Then, quickly, he went toward the hotel double doors, out to the front steps, and waited as the doorman hailed him a hire coach.

Stepping into the back of the open conveyance, he asked the black driver, 'Do you know a place called *Petit Jour*?' He felt strange even saying the name.

The black driver wore a tall silk hat decorated with a yellow and red cockade. He winked amiably at Peter, saying, 'I sure knows *Petit Jour*, sir. From the outside. But if you thinking of going in, you better have you a big roll of money.'

Peter tapped his chest pocket, forcing a smile for the jovial black driver, who now tipped his silk hat to Peter and cracked the whip over the head of the horse.

Sitting back on the shabby leather cushions of the open carriage, Peter looked at the tall houses lit with iron lanterns hanging by colourfully painted doors; he caught the sharp smells of Creole cooking interspersed with the odour of horse manure on the cobbled streets; he gazed blankly at the sidewalks full of people dressed in their evening finery – women in black lace shawls, blue-painted eyes, slippers with heels on them; men wearing tall pastel hats and slim white trousers with ribbons sewed down their legs. He showed little interest in the fashions of New Orleans, thinking instead about *Petit Jour,* what the name had always represented to him.

* * *

Standing in front of Naomi's desk, Jade, the burly negro guard with the shaved head, said, 'There's a white man asking to see you, Mistress Naomi.'

'What's this one complaining about?' A large ledger lay open in front of Naomi. She also had architect's plans for a gambling hall spread on the side of her desk.

Jade the guard answered, 'He's not complaining. Just asking to see somebody in charge here. Asking right polite, too.'

Naomi showed little interest, looking down a row of figures inked in the ledger, the black veil thrown back from her forehead, a fringe of white hair showing around the top of her burned face.

Jade continued, 'He's some planter. You can tell by his togs.'

'Send him to the rear parlour,' Naomi said irritably. 'Let him run credit to a thousand. No more. Then I'll see him.'

'I tried sending him to the parlour, Mistress Naomi. But he keeps insisting on seeing you. I asks him his name and he said . . .' Pausing, Jade strained to remember. ' "Aye-bee? Abney? Abernee?" '

Naomi slowly raised her head. She asked, 'Abdee?'

Jade pulled on his belt with both thumbs, thinking. 'Abdee? Yeah! That sounds like it. Abdee!'

Quickly rising, Naomi said, 'Where is he?'

Jade nodded to the carved office door which led to the hall-way. 'Outside.'

Walking to the door, Naomi looked through a small hole bored through the thick wood, asking with more interest, 'Who did he ask for?'

'To see somebody in charge. And about your Yankee stud.'

'Webb? He wants to see Duncan Webb?' Naomi asked, her eye still at the door.

'He didn't say he wanted to see Webb. Just asking if a Yankee worked here. He called him by that other name. "Mister Dandy"'

Standing back from the door, Naomi said, 'Tell him I'm busy for a while. Tell him I'll see him as soon as I can. Then get Webb. But don't let Webb see Mister Abdee. Bring Webb here through the back door. And, Jade. Be polite to that Mister Abdee. Be very polite to him. At least till we find out who the hell he really is.'

Naomi rushed to the mirror as Jade left the office through the carved door. Her heart was excitedly beating. She wanted to make certain that she looked her best for the caller. Even if he was not related to the Abdee whom she had known in the past, he might know something about him. Where Richard Abdee was now.

But it was only when Naomi looked at herself in the mirror that she remembered her face. In her excitement over meeting someone named Abdee – perhaps finding a clue to the whereabouts of the Englishman she had known on the island of St Kitts she had forgotten about her disfigurement. That her face was burned. That she was no longer young.

Then she heard a light knock on the back door. She knew it was Duncan Webb. She pulled down the black lace veil over her face and, reaching for the silver-headed cane she always kept near her when she was around people she did not know or trust, Naomi called for Webb to enter her office.

'How do you know somebody called Abdee?' Naomi asked as soon as Webb came out from under the tapestry of Diana the Huntress which concealed the back door.

Duncan Webb was dressed in only white breeches, boots, and a shirt. He had not yet put on his costume for the show. Although he still had a moustache and long sideburns, his face had lost its air of assurance, giving way now to a lean, arrogant look. He said, 'Abdee? How the hell did you find out about her?'

'What do you mean?' Naomi snapped, '*her*?'

'My wife. That's her name. Abdee. Victoria Abdee.'

'The girl who left you is an . . . Abdee?'

'I left her,' Duncan quickly corrected. 'But she came crawling after me. Vicky showed up here in New Orleans a few nights ago. But don't worry she won't interfere with my job here. If she does, I'll send her back home.'

'Where does she live?'

'With me. Here in the Quarter.'

'No!' Naomi said, becoming impatient with him. 'Where's she from. Her home?'

Slumping into a chair next to Naomi's desk, he pulled at his moustache and said, 'A place up-country. It's called Dragonard Hill.'

'Dragonard?' Naomi asked quickly.

'Dragonard Hill. They've got a new house there now but it wasn't much special when I was there.'

'Who are they? These Abdees? Where are they from?' Naomi was too tense to sit down now. She had even left her cane by the desk.

Duncan Webb shrugged. 'No place in particular. They just own a bunch of niggers in the middle of nowhere.'

'You're married to one of them, you idiot! You must know something about them!'

He hated Naomi's superior attitude with him. She was a black woman, a freed slave, and he considered her to be inferior to him, often thinking that he was doing her an honour by working here. But he knew that she was proud-headed, too, and that he could not become angry with her and say that he thought that she was nothing but a nigger whore. He could not afford to be without the money that she paid him. He said grandly, 'I try not to butt into my wife's affairs.'

'You said your wife's name. What was it?'

'Vicky. Victoria.'

'And her mother's?'

'She's dead. There's just Vicky. Her two sisters. And the father.'

'How old is he?'

'Not too old. He looks . . .' Duncan shrugged, then suggested, 'If you're so interested in them, why don't I have Vicky come here to see you. You might even see something about her you like. You might even – ' He waved his hands nonchalantly. 'She might even be able to work upstairs here.' He was thinking of the extra money that Vicky could bring home now that she no longer had any of her own.

Naomi snapped, 'I don't employ white girls.'

'You might make an exception about this one.'

'Leave now,' Naomi said, impatiently waving her gloved hand. 'I'll send for you later if I need you.'

Duncan rose, realizing he was being dismissed.

Naomi called to him as he walked toward the tapestry, 'And don't say anything about this talk we've had, understand? Not to your wife or anybody!'

He nodded.

She called again as he was just lifting up the edge of the tapestry, 'One more thing. I don't usually give compliments. But I like that black satin sock you're wearing around your prick. It looks good. Keep wearing it. But try putting some grease on the skin, your prick's head. With just that sticking out the end of the tight sock, with grease on it, people will like it even more than they do now.'

Duncan's chest swelled with the flattery from Naomi. It was rare. He knew that the black satin sheath he had fashioned for his penis looked good. Although he wore it to hide the scabs that were growing on him, he had fixed it in such a way as to add to the excitement for the audience. He cinched it tightly around both his scrotum and penis, letting it hug the penis when he was limp and contouring with it as he hardened, showing only the head of the penis. He did not pull the cord from the sheath to fall away until he was deep inside the girl's vagina. That action – theatrically executed – was always followed with raucous applause.

The only thing that bothered Duncan was that he could only get one orgasm a night now. That was all that was needed for the show at *Petit Jour* but he still wanted to drive into Vicky, making her take him as he was looking now. But they had not made consummating love since her return from Dragonard Hill.

*   *   *

Peter Abdee was shown into Naomi's office and he took the chair next to her desk. The silver-headed cane rested between them.

Naomi saw that he was not nervous of her. He was not agitated by talking to a woman who wore a black veil, not like so many men had been in the past.

He told her his story in sequence but first stating that he wanted to know if a Northerner by the name of Duncan Webb worked for her. He then explained that he had sent his two daughters North to school; one had married a young man from there – Duncan Webb, a man he did not approve of – and, after they spent time together at home, his son-in-law had left, followed shortly by his daughter. He suspected that they were both here in New Orleans.

Naomi appreciated his direct manner, how he told her his problems with frankness, not trying to hide family troubles. As she listened to him, though, her mind jumped ahead of his story – or moved years behind it – and she wanted to ask him her questions, establishing exactly who he was and if he had any connection to the Richard Abdee she had known on St Kitts.

She said now, 'What is the name of your plantation, Mister Abdee.'

'Dragonard Hill.'

She was glad that he could not see the anxiety which she was certain that showed now on her withered face. She said, 'Dragonard? That's a strange name.'

His face was immobile. He answered, 'No stranger than *Petit Jour.*'

She knew then that he suspected a link between them, too,

231

a bond other than Duncan Webb. She said, 'You've never been here before.'

'I've just heard about your *Petit Jour* tonight.'

'You know another *Petit Jour*, Mister Abdee?'

'Yes. But not like this one.'

Naomi matched his coolness. 'I know another Abdee, too. But not like you.'

She watched his bright blue eyes quickly glaze. She continued then, '*Petit Jour*. It's a name I took from the West Indies.'

'St Kitts,' he said.

Her voice remained soft. 'The name Dragonard is from St Kitts, too.'

He said, 'But they don't use it any more, I understand.'

His words were too confident now and they bewildered her. She asked, 'What are you saying, Mister Abdee?'

He explained, 'Dragonard. It was the public whipmaster there. A term used by the British for a mercenary.'

She took a deep breath. 'It was also the name of a plantation on St Kitts.'

'A plantation,' he continued, 'owned by a man who had once been the whipmaster for the British. A mercenary who whipped the black slaves.'

She did not speak for a moment. She felt both excitement and weakness. His calmness unsettled her. Talk about Dragonard and St Kitts came difficult to her. She had tried so long to forget it all, only concentrating on the man – Richard Abdee.

'Dragonard was a very great plantation,' she said, her voice catching.

'You're Naomi.'

She said quickly, 'They told you my name outside.' She nodded to the carved office door.

Peter shook his head. 'No. A black man called Nero first told me about you, Naomi.'

The name stunned her. She said, 'Nero!' She realized for the first time that this stranger was ahead of her, that he knew more about her than she did about him. She asked, 'Nero? How did . . . Nero escape?'

'He didn't exactly escape. They took him away from the island in shackles.'

'But he's alive!'

'Nero is my overseer. He's been with me on Dragonard Hill for more than fifteen years.'

Naomi took a deep breath, talking as if to herself, 'I've been here for twelve.'

Then, raising her head to him again, she asked, 'What did Nero say about your father? Where is your father?'

'Richard Abdee?' Peter asked.

She pleaded, 'Is he alive? God-damn-you, tell me?'

Keeping his eyes on Naomi's veiled face, Peter said, 'I have come here to find a daughter. I do not want to talk about a man I have never even met.' His voice was rising, showing its first sign of emotion. 'I do not want to dig into a past I've learned to hate. A man I despise!'

Naomi's white gloved hands gripped the arms of her chair as she screamed, 'Is he alive, damn you?'

Peter sank – but not cowered – back from her. He answered, 'As far as I know or care, the man named Richard Abdee is dead.' He looked from the top of her veiled head down to her slim shoulders, her full breasts, the black skirt covering her legs. He said, 'But then I thought you were dead, too.'

'You knew we were lovers!'

'Nero told me all he could,' Peter said.

Holding her head again, Naomi repeated the name. 'Nero.'

'He loved you, Naomi. He was devoted to you and he was devoted to my father, too, as much as anybody could be devoted to a man like that.'

'I loved your father,' Naomi said, as if threatening him.

'You were probably a good match.'

She moved to jump from her chair to strike him but then she fell back. She tried to relax. She nodded her head and finally said, 'Yes, we were. A very good match.'

233

'Better for him than my mother. He ran out of uses for her, didn't he?'

Throwing back her head, Naomi's voice mellowed. '*Petit Jour*! That was your mother's name for the house on St Kitts. That's why I named this place, this den – ' She flourished her hand, '*Petit Jour*. I thought your father would hear about it. He would wonder. He might come here. It is like a signal I'm sending out to him, wherever he is.'

'But instead you have me.'

She straightened her head. 'The name? That was your clue? *Petit Jour?*'

Peter said firmly, 'You're forgetting again. I did not come to you because of the past. That has nothing to do with me. I am looking for one of my children. I want you to understand that. I'm convinced only about *my* family!'

Naomi's lace veil moved as she nodded her head. She was studying him closely. She said, 'Stubborn. Selfish. Single-minded. But very handsome. Very sexual. Oh, your father has blond hair. You have dark. That's your French blood. From your mother. But his eyes are bright blue like yours, too. Your chin. Your body. Your – ' She lowered her eyes to his breeches and then stopped.

'Go ahead. Don't be discreet now. I know how you size men. I know you called him your only "white nigger".'

She laughed for the first time. 'He is! And you, too. Look at you! Bulging down there like a horse!' She laughed louder, a shrill laugh she had not used for years.

Remaining sober, Peter said, 'But there is only one thing that baffles me.'

'What's that?'

'How you talk as if he's still alive.'

She became sharp now. 'He is alive! Richard Abdee is alive some place. They thought I was dead. But you see I'm still alive, too.' Quickly rising, she rubbed her gloved hands together nervously, insisting, 'I know he's down there someplace. On some island with the English or the French and the grimy Spaniards. He can survive any place. I know he's alive!'

234

'In hell!' Peter said, jumping to his feet.

Naomi turned to face him, saying, 'Your mother's name was Honore, wasnt' it? Honore Jubiot. Before she married him. Then she left St Kitts to go back to France. To have you. Tell me, why did you come to America?'

'My mother never got to France. I was born on a ship set off course by the French revolution. My mother died in East Floria and I was kept alive by a poor frightened black woman. My mother's maid called Ta-Ta. A black, uneducated, frightened woman who was suddenly responsible for the lives of two children, one was myself, the other was a yellow boy called Monkey. Monk. A bastard son sired by my father. All three of us – Ta-Ta, Monk and myself – were bought at a slave house here in this very city. Paid for in cash by an old man called Albert Selby. He discovered I was white and I grew up to marry his daughter. While Monk grew up to be a slave! A nigger! A yellow bastard son of my father. My half-brother who Ta-Ta shot dead when he tried to kill me. That's Dragonard, Naomi. That's the curse you still hope is alive!'

Peter and Naomi stood now in front of one another, only a short distance apart. And, as she looked up at him, her hands hesitated but, then, she suddenly reached to her face and threw off the lace veiling, showing him her wounds, her stretched eyes, her spoiled nose, she screamed,

'Do you think *this* is easy to live with? Do you think he'd still want me now? Don't you think I have pain, too, you selfish son-of-a-bitch?'

Then, she threw herself onto his chest, begging, 'Hold me. Just hold me. Let me have something of him close to me. Just something.'

Slowly, hesitantly, Peter raised his arms to comfort Naomi's small quivering body.

*   *   *

The memory of the uprising on St Kitts still brought misery to Naomi. Richard Abdee had lost his plantation – Dragonard

– on that night. And it was the last time that Naomi had seen him.

Another windmill had been set afire that night, its straw flaps slowly revolving – burning – against the streaked Caribbean sunset. And, again, Richard Abdee tried to persuade Naomi to leave the plantation while there was still time for her life to be saved. The drums told that the troubles were close. That the freed slave Calabar had done his evilness here.

But Naomi would not desert him. She said that she could not leave him alone with the black people.

Richard Abdee was not frightened of the blacks. He treated them well and he did not think they would hurt him nor allow him to be hurt. But he repeated to Naomi how the Dragonard slaves hated her, were jealous of her position both as a rich free negress and his mistress.

Naomi laughed at him, but her laughter was low, almost a growl, unlike its usual high pitch; it was nervous, showing that she was at last frightened. Her long black hair was brushed back from her prune-coloured face, her eyes painted with blue cosmetics, her fingernails freshly lacquered red. She told Richard Abdee that she knew black people better than he did. They would see her coming in her fine red dress and they would bow to kiss the feathers on her hem. She tried to laugh again, hoping to convince him of her bravery.

It was then they heard the shouting from downstairs; both going to the top of the steps, they saw the black girl, Seena, overpowering the black cook, Sugar Loaf, sitting on her breasts and slicing her brown neck as if she were a big animal, the blood flowing onto her white dress and spurting up to the stiff folds of her flower-like turban.

Rushing down the stairs, Naomi screamed at Seena, waving a sabre, threatening to kill her for bringing death into the house. It was then that she saw Calabar appear in the doorway to the centre garden. He was holding a pitch torch. Naomi remembered Abdee running down the stairs past her. He had snatched his whip from the table, the tip splayed like a dragon's tongue.

Naomi pursued Calabar. He had worked for her in a bordello in Basseterre before she had come to live here at Dragonard and she knew him and she thought she could stop him from spreading fire with the torch.

Seena shouted to Calabar that she wanted to get Richard Abdee, that he had cast her off as a lover and that she wanted to kill him. She left Sugar Loaf lying in a blood-drenched heap on the floor and stalked Abdee with the knife in her hand.

Naomi heard Abdee's dragon-tipped whip lash behind her, she heard Seena laughing, and then she saw the blaze on the ceiling and the walls of the centre-garden. She rushed from the hallway and found Calabar dashing around the room, spreading more fire with his torch. She held her sabre to go for him when she heard the first strips of tenting rip from the ceiling. She did not know what was happening to Richard Abdee and the black girl, Seena, only hearing a cry from behind her, not knowing if it was from a male or female. The last thing that Naomi saw was Calabar's ugly black face lit by flames, his mouth open, his pointed white teeth flaring like the white centres of flames, and then the tenting fell from the ceiling and the walls, enveloping Naomi as if she were being rushed into hell.

Book Three

THE LAST OF NIGHT

Chapter Fourteen

THE IRON NEEDLES

The iron needles were two feet long, being wider at top than the tip, like a sewing needle, having a hole at the top through which a length of rope could be tied. Most Southern planters – or their overseers – held a black slave in control for whipping by binding him to a post, or stringing him up by the feet from a barn rafter. But Imogen Abdee had discovered that pegging a man spreadeagled down to the ground was the best position, considering her stature – the length of her arms, how far she could flail a bullwhip – and she had devised the iron needles to replace the wooden pegs she had originally used on Dragonard Hill.

Today, Imogen used the iron needles for the first time. She had ordered four needles to be driven into the ground at a slant, leaving only the hole visible and, then, the negro was brought forward and pressed down to his face, both wrists and ankles bound with the ropes which, in turn, would be tied to the needle holes. This prevented him from twisting and moving, for the wooden pegs often gave under stress, but the iron needles were thick and long and held strongly. And to insure that the negro would not try to twist, ruining her aim, Imogen had ordered not four but six needles from the plantation blacksmith, the remaining two being driven into the ground today at both sides of the negro's waist after he was tied into place: a rope 'belt' was strung between the waist needles, cinching him into position, the rope burning his skin raw if he pulled upwards or squirmed from side to side.

This was the fifth day that Peter Abdee had been away from Dragonard Hill and the negro whom Imogen was punishing this noontime was the fieldhand named Ben. The reason for whipping Ben was that he had been found sneaking around the new house late this afternoon, peering in the parlour windows.

Imogen did not know Ben by name but, recognizing his tow clothing as those of a field labourer, she knew that the house was off bounds to him and did not listen when he pleaded that he had not come there to steal. Imogen called Boxo and his helper, Willy, to tie Ben's arm behind his back and take him down the hill to the blacksmith yard near the old house. The iron needles were still kept there, unused.

The late day sun had a December chill to it but was warm enough to bring beads of perspiration to Ben's black skin now as he lay face-down on the dirt, the rope cinching his waist into position, his arms and legs spread wide apart and attached to the needles.

Imogen stood a short distance to the right of Ben's spread-eagled body, aiming again at his back. It was already marked with eight lashes, his skin cut and bleeding, and his tow pants soiled from the terror.

The whip lashed through the air, landing between his shoulder blades with a crack. Then drawing it back, Imogen started to walk quickly around him, dragging the blood-moistened whip in the dirt, to choose another angle for her next aim. She was learning, testing, gauging the most advantageous position. And, also, she was becoming increasingly exhilarated by this position of new power.

Quickly, she swung the bullwhip with all her strength, listening to it sing through the air, landing on Ben's naked body with a loud snap. Again, she scrambled like an excited dog to find the next position from which she would strike.

Word had spread quickly in the household that a fieldhand had been found lurking there but more controversial now was the fact that Miss Imogen was whipping him in the blacksmith's yard.

Veronica and Royal stood side-by-side, Veronica calling for Imogen to stop.

But Imogen heard no one. She saw nothing but Ben and thought how she was going to make an example out of him, not wanting to have the new house crawling with slaves who did not belong there.

Lady Alice now came running to the yard, too, and standing alongside Boxo, she looked anxiously from Imogen to Veronica and back to the manlike figure of Imogen again, hoping that Veronica would stop her older sister. She remembered how Imogen had mercilessly punished Hopper the last time.

Stopping after the fifteenth stroke, though, Imogen dropped the whip to her side and breathlessly wiped the perspiration from her face. She nodded for Boxo and Willy to untie Ben from the needles, then she turned to Veronica and Royal.

Sauntering toward them in her dusty boots, she said in a winded voice, 'You told me you know why that nigger came sneaking around. Let's go up to the house and talk about it.' The five-day absence of her father had given Imogen the authority of a true mistress, even over her own sister when they were outside the house.

Veronica quaked with anger, shouting at Imogen, 'It's a little late now to talk, isn't it?' She pointed at Ben's unconscious body being untied from the ropes.

'Suit yourself,' Imogen called, trudging past her up the hill.

Royal stepped forward to follow Imogen but Veronica reached for his arm. She shook her head. The damage had been done. There was no need now to tell Imogen that Ben had come to the house looking for him.

Veronica knew now about Royal's history with Ben, having forced him to tell her why he had been frightened by the mention of Ben's name. Veronica's mind did not comprehend sexual perversions and she saw Ben's appetite for Royal more like a larger animal preying on a younger and more refined one. And she saw no reason now to explain any of this to Imogen. For the next few days, Ben would be troubling no one on Dragonard Hill.

*   *   *

243

Imogen Abdee's last chore before nightfall was to drive to Troy and talk to Jeb Conway about the cotton tonnage. He had not submitted his rendering to Dragonard Hill for the first half of the harvest and Imogen wanted to clear the matter before her father returned home from New Orleans.

Peter Abdee had left the plantation at the worst time, or, to Imogen's way of thinking, at the best. The long autumn had ripened a fine crop and, although the picking had passed its zenith by the time that Vicky had run away from home, the bag men still worked the rows. Nero rode the field each day, checking the drivers responsible for each picking gang, but another person was needed to synchronize the dumping and the hauling of the harvest itself. Peter often had allowed Imogen to work in the past as the link between the fields and the wagons but now her authority extended from the plantation to the gin, bearing the burden of her old job and the duties of her father.

She had made two work trips to Troy already today. But going back there again at this fading hour, she saw the picking shift walk wearily toward Town for their supper. Their work was done. She bounced on the hard seat of the wagon, leaving a cloud of dust behind her as she rattled along the public road. Her body felt sore now; she was glad that she had kept the lashing down to only fifteen good strokes. But the lingering vision of a male spread on the ground in front her still thrilled Imogen. She had enjoyed the position of absolute power and she thought now as she held a tight rein on the horse team that the colour of a man's skin did not matter to her. She could just as easily discipline a white man as a negro. She doubted if she could strip the flesh off a woman, though. And, as the wagon rattled on toward Troy, she contemplated how far her taste for flagellation could go.

Reining the team in front of the Conway's shack, Imogen climbed down from the wagon and looked for some sign of Conway's wagon. But she saw no sign of it in the garbage-strewn yard. She raised both hands to her mouth and shouted, 'Conway!'

244

She waited, then shouted again.

A loud din rose from the rear of the shack and she remembered that the Conways kept a pack of dogs in a pen back there. She walked in the direction of the noise which, made by such a large quantity of dogs, simultaneously barking at the same high and rapid pitch, sounded almost like a coop of gobbling turkeys.

Noreen Conway came around the corner of the shack then, wearing a long, ragged apron, her grey hair pulled back from her wrinkled, drawn face. She had the vanquished look of a once-comely woman now abandoned in the wilderness. Her manners were unguarded – woebegone – rather than just rough.

Imogen called, 'Afternoon, Mrs Conway.' She had always harboured a sympathy for the prematurely ageing female.

Having seen Imogen only a few hours before, Noreen Conway instantly recognized her. She said, 'I thought you'd gone back home by now, Miss Abdee.'

Imogen said, 'I come back to see if Jeb's home yet. He hasn't given us the account for the first half.'

Noreen Conway lowered her head, shaking it in wide turns. She apologized, 'That's my darned fault, Miss Abdee. I do his book-keeping and I just ain't found a minute to get you your tonnage.'

'I saw you this noon in the gin, Mrs Conway. I see you there most every day. How come you work books, too?'

'Work books? Ha! That ain't the half of it. I work books. Slave in the gin. Keep house. Then there's the animals to slop.' She thumbed her hand toward the rear of the shack. 'Those dogs are the worst!' She shrugged helplessly.

Imogen commiserated with Noreen Conway's heavy work burden with a few shakes of her head. Then, brightening, she asked, 'Mind if I look at those dogs?'

'Nothing but dumb dogs. Nothing special. But Jeb loves them. Come on,' She beckoned Imogen to follow her, disappearing around the side again.

The animals were large with sleek black flanks. They had

square faces, their mouths all open now and their short ears lying back as they barked inside the wire pen. A pail of raw meat set outside the pen, which was constructed with a square wooden frame covered with mesh wires. The barking dogs tore at the pen, crowding each other to get to the meat waiting to be fed to them.

'I was just fixing to feed them when I heard your shout. That's why they're yapping so loud now. They're hungry. Damned noisy dogs.' Noreen Conway sluffed across the dirt toward the pail of raw meat.

'You get in there to feed them?' Imogen asked, looking at the strongest of the black dogs climbing over the backs of others, the sharpness of their white teeth bared in open red mouths.

'It ain't too dangerous. Not as long as you got some hunks of meat ready to throw at them. Tames them down first, it does. Gets them away from the gate. Keeps them from tearing the flesh on your own bones.' She was reaching to turn the wooden latch on the gate.

Imogen called above the barking, 'How often you feed them, Mrs Conway?'

'Jeb tells me to hold it down to two times a day. He says that keeps them fit. Suspect they'd eat five times a day if a person would let them.'

'And if you missed a day feeding them?'

'Ha! They'd probably chew up the pen. Gnaw down the wood, wire and all.'

'Ever hire them out for tracking down niggers?' Imogen asked, watching Noreen Conway reach into the pail for a hunk of meat. The gate was still open.

'No. Jeb don't like them tracking niggers. The Witcherleys offered Jeb twenty-five dollars. Twenty-five dollars! They wanted him to track a nigger gal that ran off from their place a while back. But Jeb refused. Turned them down flat. A damned fool he was, too, I said.' She shrugged, then quickly pulled open the gate and threw in the first meat. Slamming the gate, she and Imogen watched the dogs turn from the wire,

246

scrambling over one another for the food. Noreen Conway quickly threw in two more pieces.

The dogs were all away from the gate now, fighting amongst themselves for the few pieces of meat, growling and snapping at one another.

Opening the gate again to empty the meat inside, Noreen Conway called to Imogen, 'My apologies for doing this, Miss Abdee, not fixing you some coffee.'

Imogen answered, 'You forget about me, Mam. You got enough work to do here without thinking about company. I'll just stand here and watch, if it's no bother to you. '

'No bother at all. I don't get much company,' she said, taking a stick from the outside wall of the pen and, poking it into the pieces of meat, she flung them to various parts of the dirt floor.

Watching Noreen Conway feeding the dogs, Imogen could not help from feeling sorry for her. She looked like a lonely woman and Imogen wondered what she had in life except work. Imogen bleakly wondered if she could end up this way, too, doing nothing but work. She wanted to reach out to her and say that she understood, inviting her to be a friend, two women who found themselves in a man's world but had no one in it with whom they could share anything they were doing or wanted to do.

*   *   *

Pain racked Ben's body late that night. His back was raw. His kidneys ached from the rope that had cinched him to the ground. He found it difficult to speak but he made himself understood to the men clustered around his pallet. They must wait and, then, when Ben gave the word, they would go get that Pretty Boy. Get that Pretty Boy Royal from the kitchen in the new house and make him pay for the whipping that Ben had suffered from that . . . bitch! Imogen Abdee was hated. But Royal would pay.

Good as a slave, bad as a person. And since Royal had allowed his feelings for Veronica to control his life, he was not even a good house-servant. Not even that.

Privileges. Royal walked the length of the kitchen breeze-way tonight, his hands clasped behind the back of his white jacket, his head lowered, and tried to make sense of the values that had been driven into his head since he had been born on this land.

It was a privilege to work in the big house. It was honour-able to wait on white masters and mistresses. A negro worked for esteem. He did not cause troubles and, if he did, punish-ment would follow. The worst punishment was to be sold from Dragonard Hill.

But Dragonard Hill did not sell its slaves. Before Miss Imogen began to exert her authority here, the negroes were not even whipped. Master Peter and Nero had somehow allowed the slave quarters to evolve like a small township of citizens. Black people working, living with self-respect, only going to 'jail' if they broke rules.

Stealing and murder. They were unknown on Dragonard Hill. The worst altercations ended in fisticuffs in Town. But that was soon stopped by a pail of water thrown from a long-legged house by some negress whose peace had been dis-turbed. Crimes of lust were not uncommon. Black people forcing other black people to commit sexual acts with them. Like Ben. And stopping on the breezeway, Royal asked him-self, Am I no better than that son-of-a-bitch, Ben? Am I . . . lusting after Veronica?

Pacing again, he realized that that was not true. He knew how she felt about him.

Then, shaking his head, Royal reclasped his hands behind his tapering back and turned at the far end of the breezeway to begin another length.

He knew that he was acting like a very old man, like some

ancient friar in a faraway monastery that he had read about in a book borrowed from the study. Such old men tried to solve great mysteries, problems of philosophy and the universe.

Stopping again, Royal cocked his head, his black hair hugging his skull like a tight cap. The whites of his eyes glazed as he thought now. *My reading. Being allowed to write. To learn mathematics. Accounting. These privileges. Is that why I can't do a thing lately? Do none of my work well? Have I been given so many privileges on Dragonard Hill that, suddenly, I'm overwhelmed? I've become so absorbed with the white people's world that I think I can actually enter into it? Even . . . love one of them? Am I forgetting that I was raised in The Shed as a piccaninnie? A sapling? That I don't even know who my own mother is. My father. Am I being a fool, not remembering I'm just a nigger?*

The brown skin wrinkled on Royal's forehead as he thought about this turmoil of identity. He did not know any answer except that, deep down inside him, he had this feeling for a woman. She happened to be a white girl who had been raised in a world entirely separate from his own. He had not even seen her as a small child on Dragonard Hill. He remembered her only as some precious object when Lady Alice had first brought him to the big house. Veronica Abdee and her sisters were like exotic princesses to young Royal when he was first allowed to study with their tutor in the big house. But now he, Veronica were . . . *Are we really in love? Is that possible? Me and 'Miss' Ronny?*

Standing in the darkness of the kitchen breezeway, Royal no longer felt like a religious person in some remote abbey. The small columns of the breezeway were bars on a prison. He could see no way to escape. He felt the hopelessness of his position as a black person of Dragonard Hill.

Chapter Fifteen

A PROPOSAL

N o one from Dragonard Hill had stopped at Greenleaf since
Peter Abdee had gone to New Orleans. Kate Breslin had
only received word of his departure from her overseer, Tom
Mayhew, who had seen Imogen in Troy. And Kate's maid,
Chloe, had told her the gossip that Vicky had run away from
home.

Kate Breslin was more amazed by black people's inter-
communication between the plantations than she was about
Vicky's disappearance. She had suspected all along that Vicky
would follow her husband. But Chloe had not left Greenleaf
for two weeks and, somehow, she knew more about what was
happening in the neighbourhood than Kate. Since Barry had
come home upset last week, Kate could not depend on him
even for news. He listlessly wandered around the grounds,
staying away from the work, disappearing into the trees and,
Kate presumed, licked his wounds on the mossy banks of the
swimming pond there.

Kate had seen Imogen driving her wagon on the public
road since Peter had gone. Yesterday, she had seen Imogen
make three trips, two during the day and one in the early
evening. But Imogen never stopped at Greenleaf. She did not
bring Kate any word of Peter or dropped in to see Barry.

But Kate asked herself, 'Why should Imogen Abdee come
here? If I were cast aside for my sister, would *I* drop by the
house where my ex-suitor lived? Certainly not!'

Knowing that Barry was in no mood to go visiting Imogen
(another fact with which she could sympathize), Kate decided
that it was her place to make the next move.

So, on the sixth day after Peter Abdee had gone to New
Orleans, Kate Breslin drove her buggy along the public road

to gather pine cones and boughs for making Christmas wreaths. But she knew that she would end up by dropping in at Dragonard Hill.

* * *

Belladonna answered the door of the new house.

The sight of a kitchen girl receiving guests stunned Kate. She certainly did not consider herself a snob, but, seeing Belladonna at the door, she knew that no one was supervising the household. Imogen was too busy with man's work. But she had expected to find Veronica acting as mistress of Dragonard Hill.

Following Belladonna into the parlour, Kate received her second surprise. Belladonna politely asked her if she would like a cup of tea and, having not expected that kind of attention from a kitchen girl, she thought that she might have been rash in reacting so strongly about her answering the door. She knew that it was a great fault of slave-owners not to recognize the abilities of their blacks and she felt that she also was guilty of that, too, even in such a petty incident as this.

Accepting the offer of tea, Kate said, 'I really would like to see Miss Imogen. Or is Miss Veronica here?'

'Miss Imogen's gone to Troy,' Belladonna answered.

Kate had not seen the wagon on the road this morning and she had hoped to find Imogen at home. She wanted to test her feelings about Barry, to see if there was any hope of them becoming, at least, friends again.

Also, Kate thought that she might get more news about Vicky's departure from Imogen than she would from Veronica. Imogen was often close-lipped but Kate felt that Veronica was more discreet than her older sister. She could refrain from telling Kate incidents about Vicky, stories which Imogen might readily impart. Kate had thought, *Hell hath no fury like a woman scorned* . . .

The sound of hoofbeats suddenly sounded on the front driveway.

Belladonna forgot about Kate's tea and moved to the window to see who was coming up to the house, saying, 'That can't be Miss Imogen, can it? She took the wagon.'

After looking out the French window Belladonna dropped back the curtain and said, 'Master Peter's come home.' She moved toward the archway, saying, 'I'll bring you your tea, Miss Breslin, Mam.'

'No, no! Forget about the tea. We'll see what Mister Abdee wants to drink!' Kate said, quickly tucking at her hair. The thoughts about Imogen and Barry and Vicky and Veronica were suddenly gone from her head. She even forgot about her Christmas greenery withering outside in her buggy.

*   *   *

Kate instantly saw that Peter was tired and drawn, and even though he kissed her on both cheeks, saying that he was glad to find her here, she knew that his mood was low.

Now, he propped himself up by one arm on a parlour settee as Kate sat in a chair opposite from him. She offered, 'Let me ring for some lemon tea. And you have yours with a big shot of whiskey. Excuse me for saying so, Peter, but you don't look at all well.'

He shook his head. 'I'm okay. Just a little tired.' He threw back his head and, running one hand through his dusty hair, he said, 'I'm tired and dirty and – ' He shook his head.

'Maybe you should have a pot of good strong coffee. Or, the other extreme. How about some camomile tea and go upstairs to get some sleep, poor dear.'

Waving his hand at her he said, 'No, I'll be okay. In fact, I don't even want whiskey.'

'It'll do you some good.' Kate wanted to do something for him.

Looking at the high, cream-coloured ceilings above him, Peter asked, 'This is a nice house, isn't it?'

The question surprised her. 'You know how nice it is!'

'From the road, even how tired and depressed I felt, I still was proud when I saw it.' He shrugged. 'That means some-thing, I guess.'

'You should be proud, Peter Abdee,' she insisted, trying to hide her concern over his unnatural mood. She had never seen him with such damp spirits.

He continued, 'But it's brought us nothing but trouble. It's not how I planned things at all. Not at all.' He shook his head.

Kate sat silent now, seeing that Peter had not finished, that he had something more important to say.

Closing his eyes, squeezing the bridge of his nose with the tips of his tumb and middle finger, he said, 'I didn't bring Vicky home.'

'I see that.'

Peter continued, 'I sent word around to where she lives with . . . him. I told her that I was at the hotel. How long I would be there.' He shook his head. 'She never came.'

Kate asked with concern, 'Did you have difficulty finding her?'

'I'll tell you the whole story some day, Kate. Excuse me now but – no, I just can't think about it now. I want to forget about New Orleans. Everything that happened there.' Lying flat down on the settee, his boots hanging over one end, he said, 'I shouldn't have gone there.'

She murmured, 'I understand why you did.'

Suddenly raising himself to his elbows, he looked around the room, saying, 'We should have a piano here. It was nice having music at the house-warming, wasn't it?'

'Your party was wonderful!'

'Don't you think a piano would be nice here.'

She nodded enthusiastically. And feeling now that she could be slightly gay herself, she said, 'Before we drop the subject of your family, though, Peter, and start talking about musicales and lessons in pianoforte, would you like me to go now? Would you like to be alone? Or talk to Imogen and Veronica? I can always come back tomorrow. As much as I loathed – '

'Stay,' he said firmly.

Nodding again, she laughed and said, 'Lovely! We were talking about pianos!'

Looking at the parlour, the French doors, the Italian marble fireplace, the ivory wainscoting, he said, 'It's a nice house. A big house. But I'll not find the kind of life here I expected.'

'You must give it time, Peter.'

He sighed. 'Time . . . He shook his head. Then, raising himself to a sitting position on the settee, he faced Kate and said, 'I've been thinking about Imogen and Barry. And the trouble that Vicky made for them.'

She was relieved that he had brought up the subject. She had waited so long to hear his solution.

Rising to his feet, Peter said, 'In the last six days I've had plenty of time to think. And I've decided that we – you and I – have been worrying about them too much. Your nephew. My daughters. The time has come for us to think about ourselves, Kate. You,' he said, pointing at her, and then he thumbed his chest, saying, 'and me! We are the only ones who can give us the kind of life we want. Nobody else.'

Standing over Kate now, Peter held both hands to her and said, 'Kate, can't we stop this silly business of meeting in secret? Living for other people? Grabbing a kiss and a cuddle and then running back to our little separate lives?'

He did not wait for her to answer. He asked, 'Will you marry me?' He moved his hands for her to take them, to let him pull her to her feet, to rise.

But Kate could not stand. She could not believe her ears. She was stunned.

He said, 'You must forgive my crude proposal. I'm tired. My mind's not up to much formality.'

Smiling, she took his hands in hers and, holding them together, she said, 'Of course I'll marry you, you poor sleepy thing!'

Bending forward, he kissed her gently on her dark red hair and said, 'Good. Now I can go upstairs and have a nice, good rest.'

He then turned, leaving her sitting alone in the parlour,

laughing to herself. But passing into the hallway, he called back, 'Think where you want a piano.'

Kate sat with her hands across her breasts, her head thrown back, still laughing with happiness.

*   *   *

Kate Breslin had first made love to Peter Abdee without him being in bed with her. It happened eight years ago when her husband was still alive. They had returned late at night to Greenleaf from a supper party at Dragonard Hill.

Still mellow from the claret which Peter had served his eight supper guests, Kate could not get the thought of him out of her mind. She had known Peter Abdee since she had come to live at Greenleaf, moving into her sickly father-in-law's home and hearing stories about the handsome young widower who lived down the public road at Dragonard Hill.

These were the first years of Kate's marriage to Charles Breslin, though, and she was still trying to make their marriage survive. She knew that Charles slept with black women on Greenleaf. This was not uncommon in Louisiana. But Kate still wished that he would make love to her. Or, at least, try to have a family, to give her a child.

Kate became bold with Charles on the night they returned from the supper party at Dragonard Hill. She told him outright that she wanted him to lay with her. The good French wine had obviously worked the same urges in him, too, because he obliged her, although not partaking in any form of foreplay.

His coldness did not bother Kate. Her mind was still consumed with the tall, dark image of Peter Abdee – the man whom she had looked closely at for the first time tonight, being struck not only by his undeniable good looks but his calm, gentle manner and the boyish mischief shining in his cornflower blue eyes.

Kate had a strong mind, now cutting out her husband's rough treatment of her – as if he were getting pleasure from a slave girl in the barn – and she imagined that it was Peter Abdee she was feeling inside her. She even grasped for his face in the darkness, kissing him, thinking it was Peter, and then she forgot about Charles completely, abandoning herself to the one man she realized tonight that she really wanted to be holding between her legs.

When they finished, Charles said, 'You've never done that before.'

Lying limp beside him, she murmured, 'What?'

'Scream like that?'

'Scream?' She did not understand.

He explained, 'When you were . . . coming.'

Kate raised herself on the mattress, asking, 'I screamed?'

He nodded. 'Like a banshee. I just hope no servants heard you.'

Falling back down on the bed, she said, 'Probably because it's been so long, Charles.'

She did not say the words to him as a reproach for his lack of attention to her lately. She had meant that it had been a long time since she had felt any passion. Passion which exploded.

Kate Breslin had felt passion that night when she first made love by proxy with Peter Abdee. And passion on every occasion she met with him in person – after her husband was killed, her father-in-law died – and they had become lovers.

It was only Peter Abdee who made her scream out, the man who was now going to be her new husband.

Peter enjoyed her screams and now she would not have to send the servants away from the house on the days he came to Greenleaf. They would be living together on Dragonard Hill, where the doors and walls were very thick.

Chapter Sixteen

MATTY KATE

The marriage between Kate Breslin and Peter Abdee took place a week before Christmas in the new house at Dragonard Hill. Garlands of dogwood and pine cone wreaths decorated the mezzanine in the main hallway. Posey had arranged sheaves of wheat and corn stalks in the Egyptian-style amphoras and they set on the steps which led from the hallway, where Judge Pontifract now stood to perform the wedding ceremony. The autumnal-coloured setting looked not like a marriage feast, nor a pre-Christmas celebration, but more like a harvest festival, an earth ritual over which a king and queen had been chosen to reign.

Kate Breslin wore an isabella-coloured gown with a high neck, tufted bodice, and long trumpet sleeves. A thin crown of dried straw flowers rested on her head, its colours matching her dark-red hair and the yellow of her dress. Peter Abdee's only decoration on his cream-coloured suit was a cornflower pinned to his buttonhole, repeating the blue of his eyes.

Veronica Abdee acted as maid-of-honour and the best man was Barry Breslin. Today was his first visit to Dragonard Hill since he had asked Vicky to abandon her husband for him.

Keeping the occasion true to an earth celebration, the guests were only those people who had participated some way in the harvesting – apart from Imogen Abdee, the overseer from Greenleaf and his wife, Mr and Mrs Mayhew were there, Jeb Conway, Kate's house servants from Greenleaf, and the irreplaceable negroes of Dragonard Hill – Storky, Posey, Belladonna, Boxo, Lady Alice, and, of course, Royal.

Nero stood at the base of the four columns in front of the house, leading the black people from Town in hymns. They stood in rows facing the house and their voices filled the hallway, acting as the choir for this wedding ceremony that was both simple and curiously elaborate – like the riches of this land.

Presents were not brought to the bride and groom. Instead, they themselves gave gifts to the workers after the wedding guests adjourned to the upstairs gallery.

Peter and Kate stood side-by-side in front of two long tables draped in white cloths and placed in the shade of the columns. The slaves formed a long line down the sloping driveway, slowly filing past the columns to meet their new mistress.

First, Peter handed each person a brown-paper parcel containing a new pair of shoes and a length of calico, telling them that he was giving them their Christmas presents a week early this year. Then, he added a silver dollar to mark today's special event and introduced them to his new wife.

Another mountain of uniformly wrapped gifts rested on the table behind Kate, small bundles made up of almond cookies, a date loaf, and an earthen pot of honey all tied into Paisley-printed cloths. The maid from Greenleaf, Chloe, handed Kate each gift and, bestowing them one by one to the people of Dragonard Hill, she said that she was known as 'Matty Kate', remembering to call each of them by the name by which they had been introduced to her. The gift-giving was a long, tiring ordeal but Kate remained gracious throughout, a new and valuable asset to Dragonard Hill.

*   *   *

Nero joined the house servants, the other devoted black people of Dragonard Hill, and the small number of white guests now drinking fruit punch on the gallery overlooking the front lawns. Most of the house servants' attention was focused on the long line of Town slaves still coming to meet their new mistress. But Storky sat regally by the white railings, looking down at the slaves as if they were lining up to pay homage to her.

Tom Mayhew talked about the future of Greenleaf and

Dragonard Hill, repeating to Nero the plans which Kate had told him, that both plantations would be kept running on a separate basis. Veronica spoke with Mrs Mayhew and Judge Pontifract about the simple beauty of today's ceremony, only occasionally letting her eyes drift to where Royal stood behind Tom Mayhew and Nero – he tried to show interest in their words. Veronica fought her desire to go over to Royal and insist that he be more comfortable. She was learning how difficult it was for a black person to be at ease in the company of white masters and this education was painful for her.

Like Veronica, Imogen also was talking about one thing but letting her attention wander to another. She could not avoid speaking to Barry Breslin in this small group and, as they half-heartedly discussed the warm weather last fall and early winter, debating whether January would bring the coldness which the farmers were predicting, Imogen kept noticing Belladonna. Storky had assigned the kitchen girl to ladle punch from a large cut-glass bowl but Imogen saw that Belladonna kept spilling the punch over the sides of the small cups as she glared hatefully at Jeb Conway.

As usual, Conway was ill at ease in a gathering. He had not brought his wife with him to the wedding and Imogen wondered why he had come himself, always appearing to be so tense at any social occasion.

Jeb Conway was more nervous than usual today. He was not merely suffering from being excluded from the few conversational groups of white people but he nervously kept avoiding Belladonna's blatant disapproval of his presence here.

Asking Barry Breslin now for his opinion about his aunt's marriage to her father, Imogen listened to half of his answer and then glanced at Belladonna again. She had just walked past Jeb Conway with a silver tray, pointedly avoiding him when she was distributing fresh cups of punch. Disliking Conway, too, Imogen could not help smiling at the black girl's impudence. She had never before realized that Belladonna had such spunk to her and she made a note to confront the sylph-like girl later today about her brave conduct. She would not reprimand the girl; if anything, she wanted to congratulate her.

Barry repeated his words.

Looking at his drooping brown eyes, Imogen apologized for having been distracted.

He lowered his head and, staring into the small red pool of his punch cup, he said, 'I think I owe you an apology, Miss Imogen.'

She waved her hand, saying, 'Why bring that up? We're still both alive, aren't we?' Imogen was in a rare mood today, readily forgiving Barry Breslin for having jilted her for Vicky. She was more interested now in the apparently fiery-tempered Belladonna – a female to admire, and a far prettier female than Noreen Conway.

*   *   *

Belladonna moved silently from the door under the staircase, emerging from the passage which linked the front hallway with a serving-pantry. She was making the last rounds in the house tonight for plates, glasses, or cups left behind from the reception. Everyone else had gone to bed or retired to some far corner of the house. Peter and Kate were now upstairs in their bedroom and Veronica and Royal were working in the dining-room.

Coming down the stairs, Imogen called to Belladonna when she saw her. 'Girl! You there!'

Belladonna jumped at the sound of Imogen's voice.

Continuing to the bottom of the steps, Imogen said, 'I was watching you on the gallery this afternoon. You were being very rude to Jeb Conway. Why?'

Belladonna lowered her head, asking, 'Master Conway from the gin, Miss Imogen, Mam?'

'Call him "Mister",' Imogen corrected her. 'He's got no authority around here to be called "Master".'

Still keeping her head low, Belladonna confessed, 'I'm glad for that, Miss Imogen, Mam.'

'Why? Has he done something to you?'

Belladonna glanced around her in the hallway, her almond-shaped eyes looking for someone who might overhear her.

Seeing her caution, Imogen beckoned her to the parlour to the left of the staircase which served as Peter Abdee's private study. Shutting the tall doors, she said, 'What did Jeb Conway do to you, girl, that makes you hate him?'

'Conway is a bad man, Miss Imogen,' Belladonna said, standing nervously by the closed doors.

'You're not answering my question.'

Belladonna began twisting her hands now, suddenly ill at ease in Imogen's presence, completely unlike the assured way she had conducted herself this afternoon in front of Jeb Conway.

Imogen said, 'He felt you up, didn't he? Or did he try to do more?' She moved closer to Belladonna, asking, 'Did he do more?'

Belladonna was beginning to quiver. 'He tried to, Miss Imogen.'

'So why didn't he?'

Belladonna raised her head with a jerk and, knitting her thin eyebrows, she asked sharply, '*Him*?'

A smile broke Imogen's face. She asked with amusement, 'You mean to tell me he tried to do more? But – ' she laughed, ' – you didn't let him?'

'Let him? I spit on him!'

'You spit on . . . Jeb Conway?'

'Course I spit on him, Miss Imogen,' Belladonna said. 'He's a bad man. He sows all these yellow babies around here. He's the one those black wenches are scared of. It's Jeb Conway!'

Imogen was suddenly serious. She asked, 'You know that for certain?'

Belladonna realized that she might have gone too far, repeating stories from the slave quarter. She lowered her head.

'Girl, look at me!' Imogen ordered.

Slowly, Belladonna raised her head.

Imogen repeated, 'You know that for certain about Jeb

Conway? That he's the one knocking-up our wenches?'

She nodded.

'Can you get those wenches to talk?'

Belladonna shook her head. She said, 'They're too scared of Master . . . Mister Conway. They won't tell Master Peter or Nero or Lady Alice. They're too scared.'

'Will they tell me?'

Belladonna studied Imogen closely. 'Lots of niggers more scared of you than him, Miss Imogen, Mam.'

Their eyes met and held. Imogen asked, 'Why?'

Belladonna said, 'They're scared you whips them.'

'You aren't scared of me, though.'

Again, Belladonna shook her head, saying, 'Those niggers you whipped had it coming.'

'What if you'd get whipped for being disrespectful to Jeb Conway?' She put her hand on Belladonna's shoulder, asking, 'Be whipped for spitting on him?'

'If he tries to pester me, Miss Imogen, I'd spit on him again!'

Laughing, Imogen pulled Belladonna toward her and, hugging the small girl to her breasts, she soon felt Belladonna's slim arms surround her waist. Imogen did not know how it happened but, soon, they were kissing one another on the mouth.

*   *   *

Imogen discovered then that her own body was an object of beauty, a thing to adore, and she learned this by watching Belladonna's eyes and feeling the touch of her hands and the warmth of her mouth.

It began with Belladonna undressing Imogen. They were alone in her bedroom. Only a few minutes had passed. Belladonna was nervous at first by being upstairs, out of her territory in the big house.

And being out of bounds was more unnatural to Belladonna than the awe which she showed for her idol – Miss Imogen.

She slowly undid the buttons of Imogen's blouse, falling

silently to the floor to unlace her boots, then tracing the legs of Imogen's breeches until she reached the waist.

Imogen remained standing, completely naked now, feeling a sanctity for this moment that matched Belladonna's. She continued to watch her in silence as, next, the girl pulled the shift from over her own head and, wearing nothing underneath, she stood naked in front of Imogen, moving to stand passively in front of her again, her arms hanging limp at her sides.

Reaching, Imogen pulled the girl toward her and, as their mouths met, she reached to fondle Belladonna's small brown breasts. Imogen then slowly raised her bare knee and rubbed it on the rough patch of Belladonna's vagina, working her leg back and forth as they continued kissing, beginning to stimulate the girl.

Soon, Belladonna was overcome with excitement and began to kiss Imogen on the breasts and her body, falling to her knees and kissing the hair between her legs – but still keeping her eyes staring up, holding Imogen's sober gaze.

There was no doubt of roles between the two naked women. Imogen was the male; but, having no penis with which to take the virginity of her woman, she lay her on the bed and, spreading open Belladonna's brown legs, Imogen knelt between them, rubbing their furry patches together as she reached with moistened fingers to begin probing the slit.

Running her hands through her hair, Belladonna lay on the bed, thrusting her groin at Imogen, giving herself to be prodded deeper, tensing with the sudden shock of pain and, then, gasping, falling back onto the bed, prodding her own breasts, watching Imogen proceed to perform acts with her that she had never imagined were possible between two women. That they could fondle, kiss, make desperate love.

Love-making was new to Belladonna. She had never been with a man but she knew that the feeling building inside her must be the first stages of the climax about which she had heard Storky speak. Belladonna saw a look of power, of growing accomplishment on Imogen's small face as she fingered her vagina with more intensity, knowing that she was bringing Belladonna closer to a crest.

But Belladonna's instincts told her that Imogen, too, must share this excitement. Imogen had no penis to erupt seed in a flood of pleasure and, with instant consideration, Belladonna squirmed on the bed until her open mouth was between Imogen's naked legs, a position in which she could tongue Imogen's slit, probing her tongue deeply inside Imogen to give her satisfaction, too. She wanted them both to share this feeling to its completion.

Imogen lifted one leg higher on the bed, giving Belladonna's tongue deeper entry, and as her moistened finger continued rhythmically in and out, scooping and squeezing Belladonna's tight vagina, she began to respond to the black girl's fervent oral workings.

They gauged one another's readiness by the tone of their gasping and, simultaneously, both females began to tighten, then to expand again, to shake with this new excitement. Their slim bodies – one light, one dark; one dominant, the other passive like a wife – heaved then in the last stages of their first union.

Finally, they lay together on the large bed, spent, their arms wrapped around one another's naked legs, unashamed that they had found a consummation for a love which was natural to both of them.

*   *   *

Posey's place to sleep in the new house was on a pallet beside the white-washed brick hearth in the kitchen. He had first considered this location a demotion in rank as he was not sleeping under the same roof as his masters now. But realizing that Storky had slept in a small cabin away from the old house, and a similar accommodation having been built for her here, he soon accepted his place in the low-roofed annex that was attached to the main house by the breeze-way of small white columns.

Tonight Posey had not fallen asleep as Belladonna had not

yet come back to the kitchen and gone into the adjoining larder where she slept on the floor. Posey knew that Belladonna was not the kind of wench who went off at night to pester with bucks and, although he showed little respect to her during the work day, he privately admired her celibacy. The act of mating, to Posey, was disgusting and represented uncleanliness. And knowing about Storky's flings in her younger days with the blacksmith, Samson, Posey considered himself to be superior to her in that respect. He was pure and totally virginal.

Now, when the kitchen door slowly opened, letting a bright shaft of moonlight stream onto the bricked floor, Posey sat up on his pallet to watch Belladonna creep back into the kitchen. He wore one of Storky's cast-off nightgowns and, as he did every night, his head was tied in a kerchief similarly to the way in which Storky covered her head in the day.

But Posey saw then that it was not Belladonna coming into the kitchen at this late hour. He saw two half-naked black men walking quietly in through the door and, crouching, they looked around at the dark room.

Reaching for the meat cleaver which he kept on the floor beside his pallet at night, Posey slowly rose against the hearth, the whiteness of his night gown camouflaging him into the background. He raised the meat cleaver above his head with both hands and suddenly screamed into the darkness, 'Don't move! I'll slice you both up for breakfast!'

The two men stared at him, their eyes widening in horror. They backed away from Posey as he walked toward them, the cleaver ready to descend.

Posey shrieked, 'What you dirty niggers doing in my kitchen?'

One man pleaded, 'We didn't mean no harm, Missy.' He had mistaken Posey as a female.

'I'm Posey! And you trash niggers better talk to me by my proper name or I'll slice off your necks!'

The second man begged, 'We ain't meaning no trouble, Miss Posey!'

'No, Miss Posey!' said the other negro, knowing that high-ranking blacks in the big house were often addressed as if they were white people and, to him, too, Posey looked decidedly female in the long nightgown and a kerchief tied around his head.

Posey did not correct them. He immediately liked the important ring which the title 'Miss Posey' had to it. But it only increased his authority over the two intruding fieldhands.

He threatened, 'You tell me what you doing here or I'll have you whipped, you sneaking black trash!'

At that moment, Veronica appeared in the kitchen doorway and, seeing the two fieldhands being held at bay by Posey with a meat cleaver, she knew why they had come here. Since Imogen had caught Ben lurking around the big house and had whipped him for it, Veronica had been constantly waiting for the next black men to come for Royal, either to force him to return to their sinister group or to seek revenge on him for their leader being whipped. She had not mentioned her suspicions to Royal and she was glad now that he was still waiting for her in the dining-room, that she had come herself to the kitchen to prepare them some late night refreshments.

Fury overtaking her rather than fear, Veronica rushed into the moonlight kitchen and said to the fieldhands, 'How dare you come here! How dare you come to the house!'

'Get back, Miss Ronny,' Posey warned, moving closer. 'I get them fixed.'

Veronica was not going to trust Posey to drive them away and, looking quickly to the hearth, she snatched a long iron poker. Waving it at them, she said, 'Ben sent you here, didn't he?'

The two men backed away from Veronica, looking from the iron poker in her hand to the sharp cleaver which Posey was brandishing.

Circling them, Veronica said, 'Ben sent you here! And I know why! But you tell him, you tell that Ben man of yours, that Miss Veronica will whip him herself this time! You tell him that! I'll whip him and any man who steps a foot near this house!' The threat of punishing a black person came easily to her now. She was protecting someone she loved.

Backing toward the open door, the two men shook their heads as Veronica spoke to them, glancing nervously from her to Posey.

Then, reaching the door, they turned and ran toward the rhododendron bushes bordering the white columns, and disappeared across the back lawns into the night.

Posey was perplexed by Veronica's fierce words to the husky men, her uncharacteristic show of strength, and the mention of Ben's name. He asked, 'Miss Ronny, what's this all mean? Should we get Master Peter, Miss Ronny? Tell him about this?'

Setting down the poker, she said, 'No. Definitely not. Don't tell anyone. Go back to sleep, Posey, and forget this ever happened.' She turned to the door.

'Where are you going now, Miss Ronny?'

'I came here to get some milk and ginger cookies. I was working in the dining-room with Royal. But – '

She stopped. She was thinking now about Royal's safety in the big house. She could not risk him staying near the kitchen any more. She could certainly not keep him in her room at night. And then she thought of the one place where she could hide him where he would be safe. She would take Royal to the old house and hide him in the attic with Ta-Ta. She rushed out the door now to get Royal, forgetting even how she would later explain her action to her father. The most important thing to her was Royal.

*   *   *

Royal did not mind the discomfort of sleeping on this bundle of rags in the attic. Physical comforts, or the lack of them, never impressed him. It was the thought that Veronica had to jeopardize herself to hide him here in the old house that troubled Royal.

He had seen the anger in her eyes a few hours ago when she

267

had told him about Ben's men coming to the kitchen to drag him away in the night. He had recognized her desperation when she told him to hide here next to Ta-Ta's room. Royal had agreed, if for no other reason, to calm Veronica. He had no fear of Ben now. But he did not like the new look in Veronica's eyes.

Love was changing Veronica. She was becoming stronger. And this was not for her own good. She was fighting, threatening to whip and kill people. This is not how she's supposed to be, Royal thought. Veronica's a gentle human being. And he felt responsible for this change.

Alone now in the candle-lit room, Royal hung his pants and shirt from a peg driven into an exposed rafter beam. And neatly folding his small clothes, setting them on a stool, he then bent down to sniff the rags which would serve as his bed for the next few days. They were musty but clean. He saw no spiders. Tomorrow he would shake out the dust and re-arrange them into a more comfortable manner. But he was too tired to do that tonight, barely able to hold open his eyes.

Although stuffy, the air was warm in the attic space and Royal stretched out naked on his temporary bed. As the small tallow stub still flickered in a tin cup beside him on the floor, he thought again about Veronica.

She had not answered when he asked her what she was going to tell her father about hiding him here next to Ta-Ta's room. Veronica had even spoken brusquely to Ta-Ta when she had told her that she had a temporary neighbour. She even refused to discuss the implications of fieldhands being found lurking at night in the kitchen.

Lying stretched out now, Royal thought about what a strong person Veronica could be. And then thinking about her other side, her sweet femininity, Royal felt his naked penis begin to harden.

Taking a deep breath, he quickly tried to change his thoughts. As he and Veronica had not made love to one another yet, neither had he masturbated, thinking about her, clenching his fist around his penis, holding her only in his imagination.

He did not think that that was fair to her or to himself.

His changed thoughts, though, included the consequences of eventually making love to Veronica. Royal was not what people called 'cock proud' and he never dwelt on his size of testicles. But he did not want to be castrated, to be held down by a mob of angry white men and feel a cold blade slit open his bag, cutting out his balls, even severing the cords of the penis itself.

But the other thought came back to him, the dream of feeling Veronicas' soft body under him, a hope that made the blood rush to the head of his penis.

His mind flashed again, though. First, seeing Veronica and him coupled together, he then saw the mob again, white people gathered around him holding pitch-torches, Ben and his men standing amongst them, all shouting to nut the God-damned pretty nigger boy. And he felt the ragged-edged knife beginning to tear at the skin of his scrotum.

He blew out the sputtering tallow flame.

*   *   *

The long navy-blue velvet draperies were drawn tonight on the windows in the master bedroom at the front of the new house. A brass-and-ebony French clock ticked on the white Italian marble mantelpiece. The smell of Kate's possessions – richly scented with lavender, verbena, clove pomanders – filled the room. The flame from a single candle in a silver stick danced through a crystal decanter of port. And at the base of the tall and elaborately-scrolled headboard of the bed, Peter Abdee lay with his new wife's head on his naked shoulder, their legs intertwined and they talked in low voices about food, future trips they would take together, things they wanted to do to their home.

Kissing Kate now on the ear, Peter finally brought up an old subject. He said, 'They've been funny, haven't they? The girls. Barry. Not guessing that we've done anything all these years except be neighbours. But no real surprise about us suddenly getting married.'

Snuggling into him, Kate murmured, 'They've got their lives to occupy them.'

'Yes. But you would've thought . . . I mean, doesn't it seem kind of selfish? Like they're thinking only about themselves? No concern for you. How I – '

Then stopping, giving Kate a playful jolt with his arm, he said, 'Listen to me! We get married to stop worrying about what people say and here we are, finally in our own bedroom. And I'm *still* worrying!'

Kate smiled sleepily. 'You're just a good father.'

'I suddenly feel as if my life has been given back to me again, Katie.'

'It's not easy being a single parent.'

After a pause, he asked, 'Do you think we'll ever have a child? Us?'

'I bet we try,' she said, lying her head on his bare chest, gently kissing the warm skin.

Chapter Seventeen

THE POISON PODS

The following morning, Imogen and Belladonna sat side-by-side in the work wagon on their way to Troy. Peter and Kate had stayed in their room to eat breakfast so Imogen did not have to give her father an excuse for taking a kitchen girl with her to the cotton gin.

Earlier, Posey had been in the dining-room inspecting the covered breakfast dishes set on the sideboard when Belladonna entered alongside Imogen. He began to berate her for not having been in the kitchen this morning to stoke the fire.

Imogen said curtly to Posey that Belladonna had been working for her. She did not elaborate and, when Posey continued to nag at Belladonna, Imogen told him to shut up, to stop acting like an old woman.

Pulling back his head indignantly, he said, looking wide-eyed at Imogen, 'There's nothing wrong with old women, Miss Imogen! Miss Storky's old! But Miss Storky's been the pillar to this family for many long years now. She's worked hard and long enough even to to be called "Miss"!' Sputtering, still blinking his round eyes at Imogen, he said, 'And last night, helping Miss Veronica in trouble, I was made "Miss" Posey! Maybe I'm getting more important now, too!' He did not tell Imogen who had given him the verbal badge of authority. Nor how Veronica had been in what he called 'trouble'. He was only glad to have an opportunity to tell someone about himself being mistaken for the head cook, not caring if it demeaned his masculinity. Turning abruptly, his feet kicked against his long apron as he left Belladonna and Imogen alone in the dining-room.

Smiling at his eccentricity, Imogen decided that she would

grant him his wish, calling him hereafter Miss Posey. She laughed about it now with Belladonna.

The night before, the two women had crossed the boundaries of sex themselves and they were not troubled this morning by forms of address. Posey could aspire to be the matriarch of the kitchen. Imogen and Belladonna were now lovers.

*　　*　　*

They reached Troy shortly before midday. The sky was overcast and, as it was only four days before Christmas, there was no one at the gin. Hearing the dogs barking, Imogan drove the wagon around the side of the shack.

The black mastiffs lined the inside of the pens, standing on their hind legs and their large red mouths opening and closing rapidly as they barked for their food.

A voice suddenly called behind Imogen, 'Morning, Miss Abdee.'

Turning in her seat, Imogen saw Noreen Conway holding a pail in one hand. She answered, 'Morning, Mrs Conway. You just coming to feed these hungry animals?'

Noreen Conway wiped the sweat from her brow with her forearm, saying, 'Believe it or not, they've eaten! I'm busy now swilling the pigs.'

'Is your husband about?'

Noreen Conway wearily shook her head.

Tying the reins to the wagon, Imogen hopped down to the ground and gave Belladonna a hand to follow her. She said to Noreen Conway, 'This is Belladonna. She's my girl from home.'

Noreen Conway nodded suspiciously at the slim black girl. She did not have house servants here and did not like the superior attitude of those who worked for other people.

Walking toward her, Imogen said, 'I've come to talk to you about your husband, Mrs Conway.'

Noreen Conway set down the slop pail on the ground and reached for her long apron to wipe her hands.

Imogen began, 'Mrs Conway, you don't have children, do you?'

'Jeb's not able,' she answered directly, her eyes narrowing as she studied Imogen and then looked again at Belladonna.

'You know that for a fact?' Imogen asked.

Folding her arms now across her sagging breasts, Noreen Conway said, 'Miss Abdee, you've been right civil to me in the past. Now, if you've got something on your mind, I wish you'd come right out and tell me.'

'I don't want to hurt you, Mam.'

'It's about Jeb, ain't it?'

Imogen nodded.

Looking at Belladonna again, she asked, 'Jeb and a wench?'

'Yes, Mrs Conway.'

Taking a deep breath, then puckering her mouth, she said, 'Jeb's hurt me a lot, Miss Abdee.'

Imogen asked, 'Do you love your husband, Mrs Conway?'

'Love?' She laughed bitterly. 'What's that mean? Jeb's always too pooped for love. That's why he married me in the first place. To give him some rest.'

'He ain't too tired for black women, Mrs Conway.'

Noreen looked again at Belladonna.

Imogen continued, 'We've been having mysterious birthings at home, Mrs Conway. Black women married to black men, couples having half-caste babies.'

Noreen waited.

Imogen repeated the stories which Belladonna had told her, points that even her father had overlooked.

'All those wenches had men working at the gin.'

'What you saying, Miss Abdee?'

'I'm saying your husband threatens black men who drive here. Threatens them that they'll have an accident if their women back home don't pleasure him. That's what he's been doing with our wenches, Mrs Conway. Knocking them up when he comes to Dragonard Hill. Probably doing the same at other places, too.'

'Jeb? Doing that?'

273

'When he came to our house-warming last month, though, he got drunk on whiskey. He made a pass at this girl here.'

Noreen looked at Belladonna. 'Jeb? My man? He tried pestering with this little nigger gal here?'

Imogen and Belladonna both nodded slowly.

Then Imogen continued, 'But she ran away. He had no way to strike back at her 'cause she doesn't have a man who comes to work here. He finally made a mistake, Mrs Conway, and I brought her along with me today. I didn't want you thinking I was a liar.'

'I'd never call a nice person like you no liar, Miss Abdee.'

'Maybe not. But I want you to know the truth, Mrs Conway. And hear the facts from this girl here.'

Belladonna repeated what she had told Imogen last night, speaking now with no further prompting, 'Your husband, Mrs Conway, Mam, he's skinny and pointed like an old carrot.'

'You're describing Jeb's pecker, aren't you?'

Nodding, Belladonna said, 'It looks like an old frost-bitten carrot.'

'Then you ain't lying, Miss Abdee. Not that I thought you were. But looking like an old carrot . . .' She nodded her head. 'I ain't seen his pecker in a coon's age. Not close. But that's it she's talking about. No woman could make up that story.'

'That's why I bought her with me, Mrs Conway.'

Holding her head at an angle, Noreen Conway asked, 'So why you telling me this, Miss Abdee? Why you taking up your time to make sure I know all this?'

'Two reasons, Mrs Conway. Jeb is making trouble on our land and, secondly, I don't like seeing hardworking women being cheated, Mrs Conway. In my eyes, you work almost too hard. So, can you understand why I'd want you to know this?'

Noreen Conway had stopped listening to Imogen. She was thinking about a recent incident at the cotton gin. Eyeing Belladonna again, she asked, 'You ain't the wench of some nigger buck called Bernard, is you? He was killed here about a month back. Fell off the back of a wagon. Cracked his skull

274

too hard for just a fall, I thought. Even to land on a rock.'

Imogen spoke. I remember Bernard's accident. It happened the night after our house-warming. The same night that – '

Noreen finished the sentence. 'The night Jeb left me here alone and went off to your fancy party. Went off to pester this poor wench.' She now understood the entire pattern of her husband's past. Bitterness and anger swelled in her. She muttered, 'The bastard. The dirty sneak bastard. I knew he was doing something sneaky. He was always a sneaky one, that Jeb Conway. It comes from that trash mountain blood in him.'

Imogen said, 'I knew you'd want to know.'

'Know? I knew all along. But I didn't just know what I knew. Not the truth.'

'You're the only person I told about this, Mrs Conway. I ain't even told my father. I don't plan on it, neither.'

'That I appreciate, Miss Abdee.'

'I thought you'd want to deal with it in your own way.'

Noreen Conway was suddenly perplexed. Lost and bewildered. She asked, 'What can I do? How can I get back at him? I remember nigger bucks being hurt here. Accidents that didn't make no sense to me. I remember arms being cut off. Legs going. That Bernard's skull cracked open. And, oooh, do I remember him going off and leaving me alone here hours on end.'

Imogen nodded. 'I'm sure you've got years of hate, Mrs Conway.'

'Hate? What's that compared to shame? Shame I ain't willing to talk about, especially to someone as quality as you, Miss Abdee.' Looking down at the slop pail on the ground, she said, 'He deserves the worst suffering to happen to him.'

'I thought you'd want to know, Mrs Conway.'

She mumbled, 'I knew. I knew all along. I just didn't know what I knew. Not the truth. Now, all I want to know is – what in heck do I do?'

Imogen offered, 'The other day when I was visiting you, Mam, you were feeding the dogs.'

275

Noreen Conway jerked her head up in sudden anger. 'Dogs? His dogs. His dogs to pet and fawn over. But mine to swill and water and clean up their stinking darn shit!'

Imogen kept her voice calm. 'I remember you telling me how hungry those dogs get. And how you have to be careful when you start feeding them. They get very hungry.'

Noreen Conway did not immediately grasp what Imogen was trying to communicate to her. She complained, 'Feed them? He won't even trust me giving them the right portions of grub! He cuts up the meat beforehand. He dumps it in the pail and then I has to drag it out to them. Day after day, I drag out their food.'

'Your husband gives you the meat to feed them?' This was one point that Imogen had not known.

Noreen Conway nodded.

Thinking, Imogen asked, 'What if you buried their food for a day or so? Take their meat from him? But not give it to the dogs? Bury it.'

'Them dogs would go crazy! Damn near eat up their pen.'

'It could appear they were sickly, too. Look like they were sick to someone who didn't know they weren't eating.'

'Like Jeb,' she said, beginning to understand. 'He'd think they was sick.'

Imogen nodded. 'Like Jeb. You take the food from him. But bury the meat instead of giving it to the dogs. The dogs would yap louder and Jeb would think they was sick. Have a case of worms. Then on the second or, say, the third day, you could tell him that he should look at his dogs.' Imogen lowered her voice, saying, 'You'd tell Jeb to go look good and close.'

Nodding her head, Noreen picked up the idea, saying, 'The dogs would be hungry. But he'd think they was sickly. He'd go to the pen. Open the gate . . .' She stopped.

Imogen said, 'It all depends how much he's hurt you, Mrs Conway. How much hurt you've had from him.'

'Hurt? It ain't so much the hurt as it's the shame.'

Imogen bade Noreen Conway goodbye, saying that she

276

hoped to see her again soon. She and Belladonna climbed back into the wagon and rattled toward the road as Noreen Conway stood in the dirt yard, staring at the ground, watching, squinting, as if waiting for a poison tree to sprout suddenly from where pods had been planted, from holes fertilized by raw meat.

*　　*　　*

Veronica took Ta-Ta her covered tray of dinner this noontime. Then, she and Royal left the old house together, where he had safely stayed the night, and they went to see Nero in the chapel situated at the intersection of the two roads in Town.

Nero did not have to ride the fields today as harvesting was over and the field workers spent Christmas week making repairs on their tall house, or hunting and fishing in the woodlands.

The chapel's louvred windows lay tight in their frames, the only light slanting through their slats, the voices of the people outside sounding like the hum from busy insects.

Nero sat behind the scrubbed pine table, his hands folded, facing Veronica and Royal seated side-by-side on the front bench. He had listened to their story and now began to speak himself.

In a sober voice, he said, 'Miss Veronica, your Daddy's the owner of this plantation. He's the master here. You and your sisters are expected to follow him.'

Veronica waited.

'But Royal here, he's your daddy's property. He belongs to your family. Royal belongs to you like your animal. Some livestock.'

Veronica shook her head in disagreement but she did not speak.

Looking at Royal, Nero said, 'You know what I'm saying, Boy.'

Royal answered respectfully, 'I keep reminding myself I'm

an Abdee slave. But since Veronica's come back home and we've been friends, I just can't – ' He shrugged helplessly. 'I love Veronica.'

Nero said, 'I'm going to ask you both a question now. I'm going to ask if you've been sampling this love you're talking about?'

Royal lowered his head. 'That's one reason we've come to you now. No, we haven't made love, that kind of love, Nero. But – '

'We want you to say nuptials over us, Nero,' Veronica said boldly.

'Those are slave nuptials, Miss Veronica.'

She asked, 'Would Judge Pontifract marry us?' She shook her head.

Nero remained calm. He turned back to Royal. 'You know what would happen to you, Boy, if folks thought, even thought you had eyes for Miss Veronica here? The torture they'd put you to? And do you know what they'd say about her?'

Veronica spoke again, 'I know what the reaction would be, Nero. I know what would happen if they even suspected. They'd say worse things about me than they say about Mrs Goss.'

Nero said, 'You're a white lady, Miss Veronica. Folks would say bad things about you but they wouldn't say things like they say about that Goss woman. She's trash.'

Sitting to the edge of her seat, Veronica said, 'Nero, do you know what you're admitting? You're a black man! Royal is black! If somebody loves you – loves Royal – loves any black person, does that make them trash?'

'Miss Veronica, you think different from lots of white folks. You got lots of your daddy's ways to you. But not everybody here thinks like that.'

'Not here. But what about in the North?' Veronica asked.

'You think your daddy would be willing to let you go North with Royal, Miss Veronica? Do you think your daddy would let a nigger marry his daughter?' Nero shook his head, adding sadly, 'Your Royal ain't even a free man, Miss Veronica. He may be smart. He may be kind. He may be pretty and sweet to you. But your Royal, he's a nigger and he's a slave. That's asking a lot for your daddy to understand, Miss Veronica.'

She pleaded, 'At least you could talk to him, Nero!'

'Your daddy has a mind different from most planters hereabouts. But stretching it this far – ' Nero shook his head again, ' – I don't think so, Miss Veronica.'

She insisted, 'Just tell him we don't want to sneak behind his back. That we don't want to hide in the shadows. Tell him we came to you. Here in your chapel! We even placed ourselves in front of God! That can't mean we're being bad, Nero. We aren't trying to hide anything.'

Nero sat on the other side of the pine table, his hands still folded. He said, 'Yes, you two did right to come to me. You did right not telling your daddy about Ben, neither. You did right, Miss Veronica, to hide Royal in the old house, trying to let those troubles pass away by themselves. You did everything right except one thing.'

'We fell in love,' she said flatly.

Nero nodded.

Veronica bitterly continued, 'We did wrong by not "pestering" like most people. Me, a white woman. He, the black buck. We did wrong by expecting you, my father, and God, Nero, *God* to give us a blessing.'

Looking from Veronica to Royal, Nero said, 'Black Boy, I hope you know the troubles you're setting yourself up for?'

Royal reached for Veronica's hand and, holding it in his, he said, 'I just don't want her getting hurt.'

Taking a deep breath, Nero rose from behind the table and, lifting his hands, he raised his eyes to the pine rafters and said, 'Lord, I hope you don't strike me dead for asking You to bless this young couple. I don't think You will, somehows. They don't mean no harm. They plan to do You justice as good as any matched white folks or a black couple. They just made a mistake by finding each other, Lord. They don't want to sin. They're young. Their bodies are ripe. And before it can be decided that a proper white preacher should join Miss

Veronica Abdee here to this fine young boy, Royal of Dragonard Hill . . .'

Stopping, Nero said, looking at Veronica and Royal now
kneeling in front of the table, 'The Lord has just stops me.
He says, "Nero, before you say one more word, make sure that
this boy Royal knows how to keep from giving Miss Veronica
a baby. We can't chance no babies yet, Nero", the Lord says.
Not when the daddy don't even have him a proper last name
to pass down the line".'

Royal nodded, Veronica squeezing his hand.

*　　　*　　　*

Veronica wanted her first sacred moments with Royal to
be spent on a proper bed but Royal said that he would not
submit her to sneaking him into the new house, nor would he
search Town until he found an empty slave hut for them to
use, nor lay on rags in an attic.

So, they chose a far spot on a hill beyond the meadow,
using the earth as the bed for the consummation of their
natural marriage blessed by Nero.

Their kisses were gentle now as their hands explored one
another's bodies. They kept their eyes open, advancing openly
and calmly, not being voracious in their first steps. They
appreciated each movement and grew warm with every new
touch and embrace.

Royal's confidence was total, holding Veronica's head on
his arm, feeling her breasts through the fabric of her dress and
then unbuttoning the bodice to reach in to her breasts. He was
her husband.

As a wife, Veronica kissed Royal's hands, putting them
more firmly against her breasts, exploring the hardness of his
chest, rubbing his copper-coloured paps, forgetting the
propriety that she had learned to be fitting for young white
ladies. She had a natural marriage to this man and, having
waited patiently for it, she wanted to enjoy every feeling and

appreciate the excitement which her husband had built for her.

The touch of their skin together brought their fondlings closer to love-making, their nakedness now being as thrilling as their first kisses had been, enjoying even the sight of creamy white skin pressed against and locked together with the tobacco-brown firmness of the other body. This naked coupling represented an achievement to both of them, a battle won by endurance and love. The differences of the bodies were more than being male and female; they varied in colour, but, now, it became natural and beautiful and equal.

Royal longed to enter Veronica and she fought her body's pull to him. But when they moved forward, they pulled away again, looking at each other, not believing that at last they were this close to each other, his hard penis pointing its swollen head at the mound of chestnut-coloured fur which glistened between the thrust V of her thighs.

Stroking Veronica's white breasts, Royal leaned forward and kissed each pink nipple, sucking them, relishing each with his tongue as his brown hand moved down her stomach and found the warm patch that she was offering him.

Veronica lay back, heaving as she felt his darting tongue progress down her body. He flicked his tongue in the brown hairs of her vagina, prodding the slit to moisten her with his mouth, spreading it with his fingers to reach deeper. When the excitement grew too great, she reached to hold onto his strong shoulders, pulling him up to her again to repeat that she loved him, and they gazed again into each other's eyes.

Slithering from his grasp, Veronica began to cover him with kisses, too, progressing from his head, down his chin, crossing his chest, taking each finger on both hands in her mouth. And, then, crouching between his spread knees, she pressed his hard penis gently in her hands and, following its arced strength with her tongue, she worked toward the head, which she moistened with saliva, taking as much of it as she could in her mouth, and then worked back down the arc to lick his soft brown bag of testicles.

Raising, kissing him on the mouth again, sharing the taste of their bodies on their tongues, she whispered to him to be gentle with her, to be very patient because she was – she smiled – frightened that he might hurt her.

Holding her tightly to his chest, Royal answered that he never wanted her to be hurt; he would not hurt her nor let anyone else hurt her. He also reassured her that he would follow Nero's advice. He would be cautious that he would not give her a child. They would wait to leave his seed inside her. But, gently pressing against her now, lubricated by both their excitement, he made the first move to inch himself into her, showing her that his size could be easily absorbed by her tightness if he moved with love, careful when he broke her virginity, cautious when he sank deeper to give her the first womanly feeling.

Veronica held him between her open legs, thrusting up toward him, mesmerized by the magic of this phenomenon of nature that permitted a female and a male in love to become one body, and in such a beautiful, natural way.

*   *   *

Petit Jour was the only place in New Orleans where Vicky knew to find Duncan Webb.

She feared that he had disappeared completely this time. He had not returned to the small rented room in the Quarter for three days now. It was a horrible place to live, stained wall-paper and mould growing in the corners, but they did not have money to afford anything better.

Vicky cursed herself for not having taken valuables from home. She could have pawned them and got much more than what she had received for her wedding ring – the flimsy thing had not even been gold! Only a yellow vermeil!

In reflection, she also had been a fool not to have gone to the Hotel LaSalle and seen her father when he had come to New Orleans to take her home. Pride had kept her from even

282

answering his note. Pride which now had placed her in poverty!

Her sex life with Duncan had disappeared faster than their money. He acted at home as he did at the whorehouse, teasing Vicky with his penis wrapped in its black satin sheath but never going far enough with his debasements. She had come to hate the sight of the wrapped penis, but she still gazed at it, even when he said that he had nothing left for her, that he had spent himself at *Petit Jour*. She was taunted by Duncan's cruel words, kneeling on the floor in front of him, masturbating herself with her finger, swearing afterwards that she would never do it again. But she did, and the same empty feeling always returned to her. She had lost all hopes of turning Duncan into her idea of a perfect lover.

But now came her worst misery, a debasement from which she could reach no sexual pleasure or diversion. She suddenly had a bleak, humdrum life. It was only two days before Christmas. Duncan had deserted her again. She only had a few pennies left in her purse. She was hungry and had no choice but to go to a woman called Naomi at the whorehouse, *Petit Jour*.

Vicky entered the office at *Petit Jour* and saw Naomi wearing a black lace veil over her face and standing beside her desk, both white-gloved hands resting on the silver knob of her cane.

Not offering Vicky a chair, Naomi said, 'So your husband left you?'

The blunt words stunned Vicky. She said, 'Hasn't he come here?'

'If he did, I'd kill him,' Naomi said, slicing her cane through the air. 'I hope you've had yourself examined by a doctor.'

'Examined? For what?'

'The pox!' Naomi shrilled.

Vicky did not understand.

'Syphilis,' Naomi explained. 'That's why he's been wearing that stupid black pouch, obviously. Hiding the sores. But two

283

of my girls caught it last week. And if it weren't for bribing the law here, I'd have to close this God-damned place down.'

Vicky began to feel anger, thinking that Naomi was the most coarse woman she had ever met. She said, 'How dare you complain and blame Duncan! If he has a . . . disease, your whores probably gave it to him!'

'He brought it here! And you have it, too, probably.' Settling her hands on the cane again, she said, 'I should thank God that he was such a big show-off. That he mostly wanted to strut himself and tease!'

Quickly, Vicky remembered her recent encounters with Duncan and, no, he had not allowed her to touch him once. Not even letting her put her mouth around him.

Nodding at the chair beside her desk, Naomi said, 'You wanted to talk to me. Sit. Tell me why a pretty girl like you ever married a bastard like him in the first place?'

'I don't have to answer that,' Vicky said haughtily. She was glad that at least her clothes gave her an appearance of having money.

'Ah! I see. You're a feisty little brat, are you?'

'Madam, please!'

'Don't "madam" me, girlie. If you married a man like Duncan Webb, I know exactly what kind of slut you are. So don't put on airs with me.'

'I came here to find my husband. Not to listen to your abuse.'

'You came here to find a job!' Naomi shrieked at her. 'You came here because you're broke!'

'Are you saying I want to be a whore? For you?' Vicky pulled back with disgust.

'A whore does it because she has to! It's her business. You are a cock-happy slut and I don't employ your type here. They're too selfish!'

Although angry, Vicky was not intimidated by Naomi's strong, foul words. She shouted back, 'If you think for one minute I'd screw and suck cock in your place, Madam, and give you a profit, you're badly mistaken!'

'So! A real fine Southern lady, are we?' Naomi laughed at her. 'Go on. Sit down. Tell me what your name was before you married that tramp.'

'I don't see it's any of your business.'

'It was Abdee, wasn't it?' Naomi asked.

'How dare Duncan discuss my personal life with the likes of you!'

'You don't have a personal life, slut. No dog ever does!'

Raising herself, Vicky said, 'I don't know why you're hiding your face, but, to me, you sound very much like a nigger. Do you wear the veil because you're ashamed you're not white?'

'I'd only be ashamed if I was a white . . . like you! White sluts like you are the worst. You crave any coloured peckers you can get but, when you're through with them, you think you're all pure and refined!'

'I refuse to discuss my personal life with you, you who are more than likely a freed slave. But, as a woman, a female, I'm quite confident I could satisfy any man – black one or white – better than you! Look at your body, you're nothing but old and funny-looking!'

Naomi laughed at Vicky's youthful arrogance, even delighted by the spark of her cheap tongue. She said, 'I don't want to waste my day squabbling with slutty children. Why don't you go back to your father. Let him straighten out your life.'

Vicky paused. 'How much did Duncan tell you?'

'Forget about him. He's not interested in you. He left town with a man. A fat pink male admirer called Hiram Hayward. Your husband thinks he allergic to cunts now! Thinks that's why he has the scabs!' She laughed at the ridiculousness of the idea. 'But we'll see how allergic Hiram Hayward gets when your husband can't get that cock dressed in a dollys' dress up his ass!'

'You lie! Duncan would never run away with a man! He'd never do that!'

'Why should I waste my time lying to you? And why

should you waste your time worrying about him? Go back to Dragonard Hill before it's too late. If you need cock, I'm sure there's plenty available there. But don't waste your life on Duncan Webb. And don't disappoint your father too much.'

Listening to Naomi talk about her home, Vicky narrowed her eyes and now asked, 'How much do you know about me?'

'More than you know yourself. And enough to know you can sink to the lowest pits of hell. You have a pretty good start already by the sounds of your tongue. But stop it. You've got strong blood in your veins. You can make something out of yourself or you can rot in the street like a pile of . . . horseshit!'

'Is that advice coming from a woman who runs whores?'

'That's advice from a woman who knows your family.'

'I find that hard to believe. None of us would ever dream of stepping foot in this – 'Vicky waved her slim hand in the air – 'wicked place.'

Naomi was smiling behind her lace veil. She said, 'You've just invited yourself to leave, *Miss* Abdee! And, please, do me the favour of never coming back.'

'Don't think that I will, you wretched old hag,' Vicky said, turning, walking angrily from the office, leaving the carved door open, followed only by the sound of Naomi's shrill laughter – the same laughter she had used against Vicky's grandfather, Richard Abdee, when he had been equally arrogant and profane with her years ago on St Kitts. She knew that Vicky would survive, too.

*   *   *

Vicky fumed. Naomi's harsh words rang in her ears. She had never been spoken to so rudely in her whole life, treated like such a tramp by a woman – a strange female. From a man it might have been erotic. But from a woman it was awful. Especially from the woman who was her husband's . . . boss!

Duncan. The bastard, she thought as she walked quickly

286

down the narrow sidewalk, stepping over rot in the way, but sailing directly across a vendor's hemp mat of pistachios rolled into paper cones.

Vicky hated to walk. Only having the few coins left in her purse, though, she did not want to waste it on a carriage. But she knew where she was going to spend it. She knew how she was going to seek revenge on Duncan Webb for abandoning her this time. He's left the city for good, has he?

She thought of his disease and laughed. She thought that it was typical of him to blame it on women, that he had run away with the fat man who had given him that silly grey cat, Jezebel. She hoped a black family would eat it for their supper!

Now, entering a pair of louvred doors from the street, Vicky conditioned her eyes, trying to focus in the smoky darkness of this club called Octavia's. She had never been here before but knew its reputation from what Duncan had told her about it.

She soon saw a faint light filtering through a green glass window in the ceiling. She saw a long bar to her left. Men and women stood together in front of it. It was afternoon and most of the round tables were empty now.

Moving forward, Vicky suddenly bumped a person sitting in a chair. Looking closely at the person, she excused herself and saw a man wearing a wide-brimmed Panama hat and had a thin moustache which raised now as he smiled at Vicky. He was not handsome, but swarthy with piercing black eyes.

He said, 'Would Mademoiselle care for a drink?' He raised a glass filled with a foggy white liquid.

The man's mature looks and deep voice – tinged with an accent – excited Vicky but she decided not to accept an offer from the first person she met. She shook her head and moved forward.

But this time her foot caught on an unseen blanket wrapped around the man's legs. Stopping to hand the blanket back to him, Vicky began to apologize profusely for disturbing him again. Then she saw that he was not sitting in an ordinary chair. He was seated on a wooden-straw wheelchair. The man's legs were crippled.

He repeated his invitation. 'Would Mademoiselle like a drink?'

Vicky raised her eyes from his legs to the rest of his body. She saw a thick gold chain draped across his red and green brocade waistcoat. Diamond and emerald rings glistened on his dark, hairy fingers. The lapels of his jacket were edged with silk braiding. All were very costly.

She suddenly became demure. 'I am looking for a . . . friend of mine.'

'The gentleman is probably late,' he answered. 'Please sit with me. Let me buy you a drink.'

Vicky recognized his accent as Spanish. Also, she suspected that the crippled man was very rich. She already knew her decision. But, not wanting to appear too anxious, she said, 'Perhaps I should wait outside . . . in my carriage. If my driver has not gone.' She twisted her hands in mock frustration.

'Ah!' the swarthy man protested. 'Outside is hot. Even in a carriage. Here it is cool. Sit down. Please. Let me protect you until your gentleman arrives.'

Protect. That was exactly what Vicky desperately felt that she needed at this moment. Protection from a rich man. Without further hesitation, she sank to the chair next to him.

'My name is Juan Carlos.'

Vicky nodded.

'I come from Havana,' he said, his eyes studying her body across the round table. He continued slowly, 'Havana is on the island of Cuba. I have a plantation there. I grow tobacco.'

Vicky let the shawl slowly slide from her shoulders, as she sat higher in her chair, dabbing genteelly at her forehead with a face square, allowing the man a better view of her body. She remembered her father talking about the riches of Cuban planters. And she thanked her good luck because this was exactly the kind of stranger she had wanted to meet at

Octavia's. Rich, swarthy, and having the unexpected bonus of being confined to a wheelchair; she had never welcomed a stranger like him before. The newness already excited her. And the sudden promise of money and . . . authority.

Chapter Eighteen

BREAKTHROUGH

Nero went to the new house on the day after Veronica and Royal had come to see him at the chapel. He used the back entrance, a low-ceilinged hallway lined with brass coat hooks and a rag rug covering its plank flooring. Seeing the maid, Eulalia, coming from the pantry, he asked her if she would tell Master Peter that he would like to talk to him.

Eulalia returned a few minutes later and, beckoning Nero to follow her, she led him to the doorway which opened under the staircase of the main hallway and pointed to the parlour on the left side of the staircase which served as Peter's study. One of the tall, double white doors was slightly ajar.

Crooking his forefinger, Nero rapped on the door and then pushed it open. He saw Peter seated at a long table in front of the windows, documents piled around him and cardboard boxes covered with marbled paper stacked at one end.

Peter waved Nero into the room, turning a sheet on a document which he was reading.

Closing the door, Nero walked toward the chair at the side of the table. He was glad that Peter's new wife, Matty Kate, was not here at this moment. He knew they had many affairs to settle so soon after their marriage but he wanted to talk to Peter in private.

Folding the document, Peter laid it down on the leather-topped table and said, 'I'm glad you stopped around, Nero. With all the fuss of the wedding, we're keeping Christmas quiet here this year. No tree. No presents. Just a family dinner. Kate and I would like you to eat with us.'

Nero looked at his folded hands, 'Thank you, Master Peter.'

'What's the matter, Nero?' Peter asked.

'You're good to me.'

Peter knew by Nero's tone that something serious had happened. He had been debating whether or not to tell him that he had met Naomi in New Orleans, thinking that Nero might like to know that the black woman who had once owned him was still alive. But he also wondered if it would be wiser to leave the whole matter of Naomi untouched. Nero might want to forget about that part of his life.

Nero began, 'White planters here sometimes worry about you spoiling your niggers, Master Peter. They say niggers will either resent it. Or start thinking they're good as a white man.'

'For God's sake, Nero, stop beating around the bush. Tell me what's the matter.'

'It's Miss Veronica.'

'Ronny? Peter had suspected that if Nero were going to complain about anyone it would be about Imogen. Since his return from New Orleans, and during the hectic days of the wedding, and all its legal aftermath, Peter had allowed Imogen to continue doing both her and his work on Dragonard Hill. He had been waiting for some complaint about her, that she had been too strict or acting like a red-neck farmer again. He was surprised now when Nero mentioned his other daughter.

Nero explained, 'Miss Veronica's fallen in love with a black man, Master Peter.'

'In love . . . with a . . . black man?'

Nodding, Nero said, 'With your boy, Royal. They came to me yesterday. I was sitting in the chapel and they come together like, what? Two lambs? Gentle and harmless. Royal scared, too, I could tell, knowing it was wrong. Miss Veronica thinking it was wrong, too, in most people's eyes. But both of them asking me what they thought was rightful to ask, Master Peter. They ain't been doing nothing bad, they said. They been holding themselves in check. But they gone about as long as they could. Miss Veronica said she was too scared to come to tell you. And they asked me to say nigger nuptials over, them, Master Peter. They don't want to hurt God and you both.'

Peter stared at Nero, his face drained of blood, his eyes blank.

Nero continued, 'I warned them both, Master Peter. I told Royal what could happen if folks suspects he's even friendly with Miss Veronica. I told him about lynchings. How they burn niggers alive on bonfires for bothering a white lady. I told them what folks do sometimes to white ladies who take a shine to a nigger buck. But they know that. They know that some trashy white women are tarred and featherd for loving a nigger. They explained they weren't being trashy. They mostly worried about hurting you, Master Peter. And not causing no sin against the Lord. That's why they come to me, to bless them. Then asking me to tell you.'

Silence.

'Master Peter, I think they want to go away. I think Miss Veronica wants to leave Dragonard Hill. I think she and Royal are wanting to go North. Live some place where love like that is easier than here.'

Peter was holding his head in his hands now, staring blankly down onto the desk, at the documents involving his marriage to Kate Breslin.

Nero said, 'I got to speak plain to you, Master Peter. You ain't told me about Miss Vicky running away but you know I hears about it. I know about Miss Imogen, too. She's having a hard time finding a place here that suits what she wants and lives up to what you wants for her, Master Peter. I know how lots of your hopes are pinned on Miss Veronica. So, I know how this pains you down deep. It ain't easy for me to be the man who tells you, neither. It's hard telling you, Master Peter, because your goodness – ' He nodded his head, continuing, ' – your goodness to folks here, that's may be what makes this problem for you now. Royal's no dumb nigger. You give him a chance to learn reading when he was no bigger than a grasshopper. Do figures like some professor, he does. You almost turned him into as good as you. And look at me. You made me your overseer. Heck, Master Peter, there's lots of niggers living in Town who's not dumb niggers and I know if you had the time, you'd probably find out what they good at doing, too. You probably will, when you get more and more time. You're trying to give rights to black folks, Master Peter. Liberties that most white people don't want us to have. You're doing it all by yourself. Planters ain't calling you no Abolitionist yet, Master Peter, but they sure could start. Yet it's you, the man who's doing all the good that's the same man being hurt. You never bought nor sold one nigger in your whole life. Not except me in the parcel when you was a kid. And that was just to find out what one word meant. Dragonard. I tells you finally and cause pain for you. But you grew out of that hurt because you learned from it. Now – '

Peter's jaw was firmly set now. His eyes cast toward the table.

Nero had not seen him like this in a long time. He seemed to be in a coma. A trance. He said, 'Did I say too much, Master Peter?'

Peter did not respond. His blue eyes were glazed. His hands lay limp on the desk.

Reaching to put his hand on Peter's shoulder, Nero said, 'Miss Ronny loves you . . .'

Before Nero had finished his words, though, Peter sprang from the chair and, pulling back his right fist, he drove it into Nero's face.

The chair clattered onto the floor. Nero fell onto his back. Blood gushed from his nose.

Peter stood above him, his fists still clenched at his side, his eyes wide now with madness and hate.

Pulling himself up on to his elbows, Nero wiped his bloody nose with one hand and stared at Peter. Taking deep gulps of air, he asked, 'You do that cause I'm the nearest nigger? You taking hate out on *me*? You think *I'm* Royal?'

Peter nodded his head one time. His eyes were still glazed. He had not emerged from his trance.

Sniffing now, struggling to raise himself to his feet, still panting, Nero said, 'That's good. That's good then. You must be – here, help me,' He held his hand up to Peter.

Still dazed, Peter stepped forward. He extended one arm.

Grabbing Peter's hand, Nero sprung to his feet and hit him in the stomach with his clenched fist. And, then, pulling back his other hand, he drove it toward Peter's jaw. But instead of hitting him again, he stopped the drive, he grabbed Peter's chin tightly with his strong black fingers, and he said, 'Friend, I got hate, too, God-damn-it! I got hate but I don't take it out on you, do I?'

Nero was holding Peter's jaw too tight for him to speak. He just shook his head. He stared into Nero's angry eyes, his own eyes still blank.

Dropping his hands, Nero said, 'Niggers human as you say, I guess you won't lynch me for that.'

Staring at the floor, Peter still did not speak.

'I'll leave you alone now,' Nero said, adding, 'Master Peter.'

The voice was faint. 'Nero?'

Nero turned from the door. 'Yes?' He was dabbing at his face with his shirt, mopping away the blood from his nose.

'She . . . loves him?'

'Yes, Master Peter.'

'She wants to leave here? Veronica . . . too?'

'She's not wanting to hurt you, Master Peter.'

'Go North?'

'That's up to you, Master Peter,' Nero said. Then he opened the door and left the study, not having felt this close to Peter Abdee since he had told him about his father and the plantation on St Kitts. How his mother had been driven away from there with Peter still unborn in her stomach. Yes, Nero felt that he had a bond with Peter Abdee that no slug in the gut – or bloody nose – could break. Only strengthen.

*　　*　　*

Juan Carlos was the oldest man with whom Vicky had ever been and she was still with him this next day. She enjoyed talking to him, and he to her; amongst the things

294

which Vicky learned was that his family were grandees from Spain, a titled line with large holdings in Cuba.

But Juan Carlos mostly enjoyed Vicky's young body. She did not consider his advanced age until it was time to undress him and, then, she saw the loose skin sag from his chest, forming the pouch of his stomach covered with black hairs.

The idea of his age stayed with Vicky as she next undressed herself, obediently following his words – instructions which Juan Carlos delivered to Vicky in his low, richly accented voice, completely clearing her mind of Duncan Webb.

Juan Carlos had an authority, too, which told Vicky that her search for the right man might be over.

The paralysis of his legs did not affect the Cuban's stout, dark-skinned penis. Vicky knelt in front of his chair and now began to work her mouth on it as he sat in a patriarchal position above her.

Because of his physical infliction, it was difficult for Juan Carlos to drive himself into Vicky's vagina. He did not want to satisfy himself always by exploding into her mouth. Or relieving himself with one hand as he swatted her bare buttocks with a length of cane. He wanted to penetrate her anus and, today, Vicky stood obediently in front of him, grasping her ankles, moving her buttocks back and forth on his firm penis covered by her own saliva for a smoother entry.

To keep his penis firm, Juan Carlos laid a thinly folded bandana under his penis at its roots and, pulling each end of the bandana in opposite directions, he locked the blood inside it that way, also keeping it positioned to sink into the target, lubricated now with more of Vicky's saliva.

Holding back his head, Juan Carlos studied Vick's skilful movements onto him with calculated eyes, his knuckles becoming red as he tightly gripped the ends of the bandana.

He spoke to her as she worked herself on him. His voice was confident. 'You are a good girl today. You do not need the cane. But tomorrow . . .'

Pausing, his breath catching with excitement, he threatened, '. . . tomorrow, your bottom will be red . . . bright red from a spanking . . . and I will do this again . . . harder . . . with none of your . . . spit . . .'

After Juan Carlos reached his orgasm inside Vicky this way, he relaxed his hold on the banadana and ordered her to turn around. To kneel back down on the floor in front of him. To finger herself. To wash his soiled penis.

Obediently doing this, too, Vicky's mind still kept working. She was not disappointed with how their friendship was progressing. She had originally gone with this swarthy stranger for his uniqueness — and his offer to protect her.

In the darkness of Octavia's she had not noticed his age. But now even that did not matter to her.

And as she obediently knelt back down in front of his wooden and grass-sided chair, she was overwhelmed by the degradation this mature man was inflicting on her. It was the thought of such self-effacement that thrilled her. And the threat of being punished by him tomorrow. He knew how to tantalize her.

Suddenly, another thought occurred in her mind. She began to understand herself better than ever before. Although Juan Carlos was corpulent, hirsute, the most perverse person she had ever met — and crippled — she felt a draw to him. She was a girl. He was her father . . . !

Yes! That was the name of the stranger she had been wanting to welcome all these years! It was not the phallus brought to her by frivolous young Duncan Webb. It was Peter Abdee. A mature man who had authority over her.

Thus, having accomplished her oral ablutions on Juan Carlos, she wrapped her arms around his crippled legs, whispering her eternal subservience, obedience, devotion to him.

He patted her head like a father, too, saying they must go now to buy her some pretty frocks. Although he had not spoken to her yet of marriage, he already called her his 'Little Marquessa' in moments of tenderness after their love-making. They both knew they had a future to share. Perhaps it was waiting in Havana.

Chapter Nineteen

CHRISTMAS DAY, 1829

The decision to ignore the Christmas festivities this year at Dragonard Hill had an adverse effect in the kitchen. Without the wrapping of gifts, making decorations for the tree and dressing it, the household servants spent their energy on the preparations for the Christmas dinner.

Kate, now known as 'Matty Kate' to everyone in the house, discussed the menu with Storky, a consideration which not only flattered Storky but reminded her of the glorious days when Melissa Selby had been alive. This act won Storky's instant devotion to Matty Kate and, as Posey had not before seen a white lady working so closely – and efficiently – with black people, he was agog at Matty Kate's obvious show of interest in their world and listened excitedly as she explained that she wanted wild turkeys, chestnut stuffing, cranberry jelly, candied yams, being careful to ask both Storky and Posey for their own suggestions on the preparations of these holiday foods. Kate had not brought her cook from Greenleaf but she was tempted to bring Chloe to Dragonard Hill when she saw the sudden change in Belladonna during Christmas week. When Belladonna was not with Imogen, she stood at the window, like a prisoner in a cell, waiting for Imogen to come free her forever.

There was another problem in the kitchen this week, too. Posey insisted on being addressed as 'Miss Posey' by all the black people. Despite Storky's intense mockery of Posey, sharply reminding him that he was a male and threatening to snip off his minute-sized penis with the pair of kitchen shears if he so desperately wanted to be known as a woman, Posey still clung to his new title. He even wore his nightcap during the day now, the kerchief tied around his head like

Storky's protruding over the nape of his long brown neck like a bird's beak.

But Kate turned a deaf ear to their bickering and, although she could address the slaves in any way she wished, she always took care to call Posey 'dear', which shot Matty Kate up even higher in his estimation.

Like the servants, Kate also was relieved for the work necessary to prepare Christmas dinner. Peter had told her about Veronica and Royal and she understood Peter's dejection about the affair. But she could not stifle the selfish feeling inside her that her first days of marriage were being clouded by Peter's renewed gloom. Their wedding had eradicated all the misery with which Peter had returned from New Orleans; he told her about meeting Naomi at the bordello called *Petit Jour*, and at last became lucid about his past. He shared bits of information with Kate which even he had not known, curious snippets which Naomi had told him – such as his father's favourite breed of African slaves had been black people from the Fanti tribe, some of their tribesmen being cannibals. Another fact she had told him was that his paternal grandfather had been the 8th Earl of Wycliffe in England but his father had sold the titular rights for a ware-house of rum in the West Indies.

Reminding herself that she must be patient until Peter arrived at some solution for Veronica and Royal, Kate did not indicate to Veronica that she knew anything about the matter. Veronica seldom came to the kitchen in the new house these days. But she had approached Kate to ask Peter if she could eat her Christmas dinner with Ta-Ta in the old house. Praising Veronica for her generosity with Ta-Ta, Kate made a mental note to include enough turkey and stuffing and yams for three people in the food baskets that would be carried to the old house on that day. She knew that Royal was still secretly living there.

Dragonard Hill was changing. Peter Abdee was losing his family, as if it were an ancient ruin, falling away bit-by-bit. But Kate reminded herself that she was married to him now and they were living in a new house. A home of which she was the first mistress. And, although Christmas would not be marked here with yuletide decorations, nor a Christmas tree towering over brightly wrapped gifts, Kate worked hard to bring a contentment to the house in the preparation of food. She did not care if the meal never reached the table. She hoped that the stirring of glacé fruit into batters, the bubbling of syrups in brass pans, the sweet aroma from baking, and the rich smells of roasting turkeys would dispel any odour of gloom from Dragonard Hill.

*　　*　　*

Noreen Conway did not mark Christmas Day with a specially cooked fowl or holiday pudding. She remembered it instead because it was the only day she knew for certain that her husband stayed at home. The surrounding plantations were alive with festivities on Christmas, the slave quarters busy with their own celebrations, and Jeb Conway had no place to wander.

Two tin plates sat on the rough table in the Conway shack on Christmas Day and Jeb Conway had just finished eating the fried pork, soaking the last of the watery gravy now with a hunk of cornbread.

Noreen Conway had barely touched her meal. She and her husband had not talked during it, the only noise being the wind blowing through the chinks in the wall and the sound of the dogs barking in their pen.

The dogs had barked all night and, even after Noreen had taken the pail of meat which Jeb had cut for the dogs and gone out with it to the pens, they barked even louder, a noise that was not like their usual howling and bays.

Noreen Conway now broke the silence of the Christmas meal. Setting down her tin cup of chicory coffee, she said, 'That Abdee girl seems a nice enough person. That Imogen one.'

Jeb stuffed the last of the corn bread into his mouth, smacking his purple lips. The noise from the dogs had kept him awake most of the night and he was in an irritable mood today.

Noreen continued, 'She don't seem uppity like most of them girls. When she talks, she makes sense.'

Jeb was not listening – not to his wife.

The dogs barking was now beginning to weary him.

Noreen said, 'She's right about your dogs, too, I reckon.'

Jeb showed his first sign of life. 'Dogs?'

Noreen picked at her cornbread. 'Imogen Abdee had herself a look at them the other day when she came for the tonnage. She said they sure looked sickly to her.'

Jeb grunted, 'What she know about animals?'

Noreen then began her own fabrication. 'She said she has a cousin with a whole penful of dogs. Just like yours. She said it was sad when they caught it, too.'

'Caught what?'

'That sickness,' Noreen said, stirring her plate with a wooden spoon. 'You can tell by examining their poor bellies.'

'Bellies?' he shouted at her. 'What are you talking about, woman?'

Noreen controlled her temper. 'The bellies show the first signs. The dogs eat good enough. But you see by the patches on their bellies that they got it. That dog sickness.'

'What kind of patches?'

'Patches on their hide. Something to do with worms. You can't see the patches just looking at the dogs. You got to get close.'

He asked, 'Have you had a look?'

'At your dogs? Them let *me* that near them? Pshaw? Those dogs take food from me, Jeb Conway. But no more. They're your critters. Trust nobody but you. Loyal. Mighty loyal dogs you've got out there in that pen, Jeb Conway.'

He sniffed his nose, wiping it on the cuff of his flannel shirt, thinking about what she had told him.

The dogs' barking grew louder, their noises began to sound hoarse, as if their throats were sore from barking.

Noreen quietly continued, 'Don't know if their yapping

means what she says, though. Maybe her cousin's dogs died of some other disease. Not those patches.'

Jeb Conway took a deep breath and, pushing his chair back from the table, he rose to his feet.

Grabbing his greasy hat from a peg by the door, he opened the door and stepped outside into the wind.

The dogs lined the inside of the pen, crowded on their hind legs along the mesh wire, saliva dripping from their red, barking mouths.

Noreen now stood a few yards behind her husband, her fists clenched in the two pockets of the long, ragged apron as the wind blew at its hem.

Approaching the pen, Jeb called to the animals, holding out his hand, trying to soothe them.

Noreen shouted, 'You've got to look close, Jeb.'

He answered, 'Hell, woman! They act like they've ain't been fed!'

Noreen quickly looked to where she had buried their raw meat in the dirt yard. There was no sign of her spade work. She called back, 'They've been eating real good. Fact is, they're eating more than ever. But the worms are getting it!' She walked closer to the pen. 'Your critters are sick, Jeb Conway. Just see how happy they are just to *see* you.'

Reluctantly, Jeb reached toward the wire meshing. The dogs snapped at him and he quickly pulled away his hand.

Noreen looked quickly behind her to see if she was being observed. Then she moved toward the pen, letting the dogs see her. She knew they would recognize her as the one who brought them their food. Jeb was a stranger to them.

But she lied, saying, 'See that! See how they're changing already seeing you, Jeb.' She cautiously unlatched the gate but did not open it. She turned to him standing a few inches away from her and she said, 'Course, if you're scared of inspecting your dogs for sickness, I can always ask Miss Abdee to come back here. She's just a woman but – '

Jeb pushed in front of her and pulled open the wooden-frame gate.

Noreen quickly stepped back and, before the hungry dogs had time to flood out from the pen, she pushed Jeb through the gate. Then, slamming the gate behind him, she shrieked, 'Screw nigger wenches, will you, Jeb Conway? Screw nigger wenches and leave me with a dog chewing my cunt, will you?'

Jeb spun around in fury. He had fallen for his wife's trick!

Noreen brought her face close to the wire meshing. She was inches away from her husband's contorted face. She hissed, 'And what about those bucks you killed? What about Bernard? What about the rest?' She spit at his face. *'Die!'*

Panic now replaced Jeb's anger. The barking dogs were surrounding him, jumping onto him. He clung to the pen, his bloodshot eyes wide with terror. The dogs now leapt on his back, their paws scraping against the wire meshing. Jeb screamed, 'Open this gate, God-damnit! Open this gate!'

Noreen backed farther away, her eyes still on her trapped husband, her lips twisted with anger. She shook her head in refusal to free him.

Clinging to the meshing with one hand, Jeb began to strike at the black dogs with his free arm, becoming more hysterical as he begged his wife to save him.

Noreen watched only until Jeb fell to the dirt floor of the pen. She saw the hungry dogs flood like a black, surging wave over him.

Turning, she rushed toward the shack, ripping at her own clothes, trying to make herself appear as if she had tried to save her husband from his pet mastiffs – their growls and snarlings now growing louder behind her in the pen as they ravenously fought for his flesh.

Noreen Conway had to go for help, to drive furiously to Dragonard Hill to tell Peter Abdee about the terrible accident that had happened to Jeb while he was feeding his dogs just after they had eaten their Christmas dinner. Tell the story her way.

*   *   *

The words came easy to Noreen Conway when she reached Dragonard Hill.

They began – exploded – when Eulalia answered the front door of the new house and, rushing hysterically past her, paying no heed to the fact that Peter Abdee and his family were eating Christmas dinner, Noreen looked frantically around the hallway. She disregarded the vastness of the space, intent on only telling her story, her mind now churning like a big wave in her head, building to a crest.

She screamed in the hallway. She pounded on closed doors. She ran from one pair of doors to another, calling for help. Peter Abdee soon appeared from the dining-room. She threw herself at him, talking incoherently about dogs. Dogs killing Jeb. The pens. Christmas dinner. Her husband. How good Mister Abdee was. She flung her arms around his chest, begging him to help her, to save her, saying that he was the best man in the country, crying that Jeb had no right to die in such a horrible way.

There was no way to calm her down.

Her husband was dead.

Kate next appeared in the hallway. And Noreen beseeched her for help, too, pulling at Kate's hands, then tugging at her own ripped and soiled clothes, saying that she was the shame of Christmas Day. Then she tried to talk coherently, to repeat the garbled story about the dogs. Her husband. Jeb had no right to die in such a shameful way.

Glancing back to the doorway where Kate stood, she then saw Imogen. She rushed forward, calling her 'Miss Imogen', asking her for pity, saying that the cotton gin would probably be sold. Burnt. Destroyed, too. The dogs had gone wild. Jeb was dead. Eaten alive!

Throwing herself on the next person, Nero, she asked him if he understood how a poor white woman like her could be so miserable. That she had no place to go for help. Her husband was dead. Jeb! Killed by his dogs! And, again, she fell to the floor, shrieking, grabbing at her ragged clothes.

When Kate offered to take Noreen into the parlour and

give her a cup of hot tea, she protested – no, no – she could not drink tea. The Sheriff. That's what she wanted. The Sheriff. She had to go to Carterville and get Sheriff Burns. He would know what to do. The dogs. They went wild. Went wild and crazy. And Jeb, he was just playing with them. The two of them – she and Jeb – had just finished eating their meagre little Christmas dinner . . .

Peter Abdee quickly offered that he and Nero could ride to Carterville to fetch the Sheriff themselves.

Noreen no longer protested. She lay on the floor of the hallway, babbling about her husband being attacked by the dogs, about seeing his head and arms and legs being chewed from his body, and about her inability to do anything to help him . . . *to help him!*

Imogen moved forward to lift Noreen from the floor, to take the upset woman into the parlour whilst Kate rushed for tea and Peter and Nero left to inform the Sheriff in Carterville. And, regardless that this was Christmas day, somebody would have to retrieve Jeb's body – whatever remained of it – from the pens.

It was plain for Peter and Kate to see that Noreen could not do anything. And Imogen supported the upset woman toward the parlour, fighting to suppress a victorious look as she gently closed the door.

Chapter Twenty

FOUR SEASONS

The farmers were wrong; the winter of '29–'30 did not prove to be as severe as '16, the new year beginning with sunshine which grew warmer as the long month of January passed more rapidly than it ever had done before. The announcement that Veronica Abdee would leave at the end of the month to return to Boston accounted for the quick passage of time; everyone loved her and hated to see the day arrive when Boxo would drive her to Carterville to catch the coach for Singer's Landing, and, then, the paddle-wheeler steaming north.

Peter Abdee chose not to disclose the reason for Veronica's departure nor to mention the work for it which he was conducting in the law offices of Groggin and Harworth in Troy. Word spread through Town that Miss Veronica was taking two servants with her to Boston this time, the black people repeating the story which the house servants had spread: now that Veronica's maid, Brownie, had Abraham – the name bestowed on Duncan Webb's child – and that the Northerners frowned upon unwed mothers, Miss Veronica was taking Royal with her to Boston, too. He would pose as Brownie's husband. Even Storky believed this fact because Peter Abdee trusted her and Posey least of all to keep the secret that he was giving Royal his freedom, that Brownie would pose as his wife only until they reached Ohio and then Veronica would marry the handsome young black boy.

Apart from arranging manumission papers for Royal at the lawyers, Peter also was giving him a surname. Royal would be known as 'Selby' and, when he and Veronica were married properly in the North, she would bear the name of the man who had bought Peter at a slave house in New

305

Orleans and made him the heir to this land. Peter's consideration for Royal included an arrangement for his son-in-law to be taken on as a trainee clerk in the Boston-New Brunswick Bank. Royal could advance in a commercial world according to his own skills and ingenuity.

Brownie would receive her freedom once she reached Massachussets, too. But Peter had carefully explained to both Veronica and Royal that he felt they should keep Brownie in their household, paying her a wage to work for them, allowing her child, Abraham, to grow up in a comfortable surrounding. Veronica's dowry included money for them to live on during Royal's training period at the bank, and a respectable home in which they could start their new life, a house big enough for a family.

Although Peter Abdee sent his daughter away far from disgraced, he did not promise to visit her and Royal once they were settled in Boston. He was thankful for the legal work that had been necessary to help Royal because it had helped Peter, too, keeping him from thinking about what he was doing. He still did not completely comprehend his actions, nor did he want to contemplate how his daughter's marriage to a freed negro slave would evolve in the future.

His last words to Veronica and Royal were not a blessing but a request for Dragonard Hill. Peter asked them to pray for everyone here and not to forget that he was their father and that this land was their home, even if they never saw it again in his lifetime.

*   *   *

The last months of winter were dampened by heavy rains and the sadness caused by the sudden death of Lady Alice. She was buried from the chapel in Town and carried in a pine coffin to the slaves' cemetery beyond the meadows, draped in a blanket woven from the first flowers of spring.

And Kate, true to her optimistic nature, soon found a way to remedy this loss for Dragonard Hill. She remembered a black woman who worked in the Looming House but occasionally had helped Lady Alice with the children in The Shed. Her name was Maybelle and, although she was married, being a much younger negress than Lady Alice, Kate saw no reason not to break some rules and put Maybelle in charge of the black children born on Dragonard Hill. There was no viable way to do away with the birthing schedule, nor to avoid taking infants away from their mothers at birth. But both Kate and Peter agreed that it could be beneficial for the black community to have a woman with an active sexual life – and a healthy young black child of her own – to help other mothers in their pregnancy and prepare the children for an adult life.

Maybelle remained living with her husband, Ham, in their long-legged house in Town and other equally young black women took shifts staying at night with the children in The Shed, thereby completely crumbling a tradition established long ago when this plantation had been called The Star.

Living arrangements also saw changes this springtime for members of the Abdee family.

Imogen and Barry unexpectedly announced their betrothal in March, at which time Imogen moved from the new house to make preparations for a married life, to make a home again of the old house.

Kate tried to dissuade Imogen from doing this as she was giving Barry the deed to Greenleaf as his wedding present. She had thought that Imogen and Barry would live there. But Imogen insisted on remaining at Dragonard Hill, to live in the old house, taking Belladonna with her for companionship.

Imogen and Barry were married in Troy at the end of the first week of June. But, because Greenleaf now belonged to Barry, he showed a sudden interest in helping his overseer, Tom Mayhew, with the planting, and continued to live there whilst his new wife, Imogen, spent her nights in the old house at Dragonard Hill with her lover, Belladonna.

Imogen's recent industry on the plantation included working with handicrafts in her spare hours and, during this springtime, she concentrated on deerskin. She soaked and stretched the pliable hide over a short bone, wrapping layer upon layer of skin around it until she had fashioned herself an instrument which was firm and resembled an erect penis. When she and Belladonna went naked to bed at night, Imogen now could kneel between Belladonna's spread legs and watch her loved one accepting the deep plunges of the greased phallus, being passive like a grateful wife to the aggressions of a hearty and well-endowed husband.

*   *   *

Barry Breslin's new interests in Greenleaf took him frequently to Troy, making his own arrangements at the cotton gin with Noreen Conway.

By summertime, Noreen Conway had hired three men to work for her at the gin and had built a small office in which she dealt with her paper work. There was word in the neighbourhood that, not only had her health recovered, but that she would soon shed her black mourning clothes and marry the preacher of The Blood Of The Lamb Baptist Church in Troy.

The Louisiana summer was hot and, as work was mounting for this year's crop at Greenleaf, Barry went less and less to Dragonard Hill to visit his wife. His few trips there were to visit his Aunt Kate, who was now heavily pregnant with Peter Abdee's child.

Barry also went to Dragonard Hill in August to attend the burial of Ta-Ta. That funeral was an important event in the neighbourhood. Apart from being esteemed by Peter Abdee, Ta-Ta was the first black person to be buried in a white family's cemetery. At Dragonard Hill, this cemetery was located across the public road from the pole gate posts which led to the old house.

Ta-Ta's death had been as visionary as the life she had lived on Dragonard Hill. Her mind had still been in the West Indies.

The fatality had happened in the first week of August when Belladonna had carried up a midday meal to Ta-Ta's attic room. Ta-Ta ignored the girl holding the tray of food and kept talking excitedly to two imaginary people. One of them was a woman. Ta-Ta addressed her as 'Madame Honore'.

Ta-Ta believed that the imaginary woman was having a violent argument with a man. The man began to chase the woman across Ta-Ta's room, and Ta-Ta was trying to keep him from whipping the woman – her mistress, Madame Honore.

Ta-Ta rushed around and around the small room, following them, screaming, 'No dragon whip! No dragon whip!'

And, still trying to help her mistress, Ta-Ta followed the imaginary couple out through the French windows of the big house in the West Indies . . . falling to her death from the attic room in the old house on Dragonard Hill.

*   *   *

There's no way a man can trust Nature, Nero thought as he hurried along the path which led from Town to the new house. It was September and the path was already strewn with crisp red and yellow leaves. Instead of late, autumn was coming early this year.

The fields were crawling with the black workmen and women and, normally, Nero should be riding down the rows, checking with the leaders of each work gang. But today was a very special day on Dragonard Hill. Also, lately, Miss Imogen was virtually the overseer on this land. She was taking over now and Nero did not mind. It gave him more time to prepare his sermons for Sunday chapel in Town. And to be free to take advantage of special occasions like today's.

Matty Kate had given birth to a child. Peter Abdee had a son. And today was the day that Nero would see the baby boy for the first time.

The blue draperies were pulled back on the tall windows in the bedroom at the front of the new house. A fan arrangement of straw flowers sat on the white Italian mantelpiece. The smell of crushed cloves sweetened the room.

By the time that Nero was shown into the bedroom by Eulalia, Storky and Maybelle were already seated on each side of the crib, an elaborate white wrought-iron crib with a yellow half-canopy and lace-trimmed swagging and skirting.

Storky sat erect in an armchair, one withered brown hand resting on the head of her willow cane as she looked proudly at her 'Matty Kate' – lying across the room from Storky, propped up by pillows on the elaborately-carved bed, her red hair pulled back from her face and bundled in a black net snood.

Kate, in turn, was smiling at Maybelle, who was the temporary nurse for the new heir to the plantation until a regular nurse was found for him in Town.

Peter Abdee sat on the bed, holding Kate's hand in his, watching now as Posey proceeded from him and approached Nero with a silver tray left with four small crystal glasses. Like his and Kate's, they each contained peach brandy made from Storky's ancient recipe.

Nero took a small glass from the tray, nodding his head, murmuring, 'Thank you . . . *Miss* Posey.'

Primly nodding his kerchief-covered head, Posey glided across the bedroom to serve Storky and Maybelle.

When everyone in the room held a glass, Peter nodded across the foot of the bed to Nero. He said, 'What do you say about *you* leading the toast, Nero?'

Lowering his head, the black curls of his closely-cropped hair looking greyer these days, more like peppercorns than ever, Nero looked bashfully down at the pair of black leather shoes he saved for special events.

Peter insisted, 'Come on, friend! You've seen – what? Three generations of Abdees? I think you're the only one of us today with any right to speak. Now that we have David here – Lord willing – you might even see a new batch!'

Clasping Peter's hand, Kate joined him in insisting that Nero speak, to lead the toast for their son, David Abdee.

Nero's face was sober when he raised it, an expression that was even more serious than he wore in Sunday chapel.

Holding the small glass by his waist, he looked blankly at a spot above the tall headboard in front of him and began, 'I've got nothing but thanks for you, Master Peter. Thanks to your family. Oh, some of you Abdees done mighty bad things. Wicked, evil things that chill men to the bones. They hurt some bad. But you've got goodness in your blood, also. The best of it being shown on this rich land here. Dragonard Hill. And no matter where you all be this noontime. Here. Far-away some place. Dead. Maybe not even yet born. Not like little Master David here who's kicking away already. I wishes the best luck to all you Abdees every place. To – '

Nero slowly raised his small glass of plantation-made liqueur, toasting 'Dragonard Blood!'